HIGH PRAISE

THE PANTHER & THE PYRAMID

"As searing an adventure boasts of emotion underlying a roller-coaster treasure hunt. Vanak is moving into the ranks of the finest romantic adventure writers with this thrilling read."

—*RT BOOKreviews*

"The fourth book in Bonnie Vanak's Egyptian series, *The Panther & the Pyramid*, is every bit as tantalizing and entertaining as the previous novels. Well written with dynamic characters, [it] has adventure, pathos, humor, and a growing romance."

—*Romance Reviews Today*

"This story captured my attention from the start and held it to the very last page."

—A Romance Review

THE COBRA & THE CONCUBINE

"When a heroine haunted by her brutal past finds new hope and love with a hero torn between two cultures, their passion for each other proves to be as scorchingly hot as the desert sands in the latest of Vanak's vivid, lushly sensual historical romances set in colorful nineteenth-century Egypt."

—*Booklist*

"Vanak's latest novel recalls the big, exciting historical romances of the past—ones with lots of adventure [and] exotic locales."

—*RT BOOKreviews*

"Ms. Vanak sweeps the reader away with a fast-paced tale of adventure, intrigue, betrayal and the healing power of love. With love scenes that are hotter than the sun-scorched sand of the desert that surrounds the lovers, this is a book you won't want to put down until the final page."

—*Fresh Fiction*

MORE PRAISE FOR BONNIE VANAK!

THE TIGER & THE TOMB

"A rollicking, romantic adventure with an intelligent, feisty heroine and an alpha hero every woman will want to take home."

—*New York Times* Bestselling Author Bertrice Small

"Bonnie Vanak…create[s] a highly entertaining, exciting, romantic read…. You can't go wrong when you read anything by Bonnie Vanak!"

—Romance & Friends

"Vanak has written a totally sensually satisfying and action-packed romantic adventure."

—Historical Romance Writers

THE FALCON & THE DOVE

"Bonnie Vanak touches upon a fascinating period of history with charm and panache. A wonderful first novel."

—Bestselling Author Heather Graham

"Bonnie Vanak writes with humor and passion. She masterfully weaves a stunning vista of people, place and time. I truly enjoyed this unique and compelling love story."

—*Old Book Barn Gazette*

"A fast-paced tale that hooks the audience…a riveting novel."

—Harriet Klausner

PASSION UNSHEATHED

"Poor Fatima," he rumbled in his deep, teasing voice. "So ignorant of the ways between a man and a woman. The fragile flower witnesses passion. Does she want the same?"

Shocked he'd read her so easily, Fatima could only stand motionless. Tarik stroked the white blossom across her cheek. Its delicate aroma teased her nostrils, mingling with his scent. Her gaze collided with his. Something sparked there, dark, forbidding and mysterious. The hand holding the flower clenched, turning his knuckles white. Then the same mocking smugness entered his eyes.

"Run along now, before you see something else to strip you of your innocence, little Fatima. Before someone plucks the tender flower and enjoys its sweetness."

The Sword & the Sheath

BONNIE VANAK

LEISURE BOOKS NEW YORK CITY

A LEISURE BOOK®

March 2007

Published by

Dorchester Publishing Co., Inc.
200 Madison Avenue
New York, NY 10016

ISBN 0-8439-5756-5

Visit us on the web at www.dorchesterpub.com.

For my brother and sister-in-law,
Drew & Glenna Fischer, who know the meaning of
true love; my wonderful hero Frank, who is always there
for me; and the rebs: Pamela Clare, Norah Wilson,
Jan Zimlich, Alice Duncan, Alice Brilmayer, and
Mimi Riser. You guys rock, always.

Chapter One

Eastern Desert, Egypt, 1903

He could not make her cry. Not her. Fatima refused to weep before the mighty heir to the Khamsin's desert throne. Not from his taunts or from his arrogance.

"You can't be sheikh and that is final," Tarik stated.

"I can too be sheikh," the ten-year-old Fatima blurted. She glanced at her twin brother, signaling for help.

Asad's large, expressive green eyes—the same color as hers—blinked. He shrugged. "Let her, Tarik."

"Never. A girl cannot be sheikh. That's my final word."

At eleven, the only son of Jabari bin Tarik Hassid radiated confidence. His mother, Elizabeth, said he could "charm the wool off a sheep." Bold and intrepid, Tarik always thought of the best places to hide, the most daring adventures to have. Unlike Fatima's shyer, more timid twin, he never hesitated to climb the rocky crags surrounding their home and jump, pretending to be a falcon. Or, what Fatima liked best: sneaking into the warrior exercise grounds to spy on the men training for

1

battle. Fatima adored Tarik's daring. She hated his stubbornness.

"Let me be sheikh. It's my turn," she put in.

Tarik shook his shoulder-length blond hair. "Girls can never be sheikh—nor even Khamsin warriors of the wind."

"I can too be a warrior."

Tarik let loose an adult-sounding snort of derision. "Women cook and weave and have babies. Not fight."

The twins and Tarik played amidst the flat, grayish sand of Egypt's imposing Arabian Desert. The Khamsin camp sprawled across a sandy plateau, row upon row of black goat hair tents. Tall date palms and sprawling acacia trees provided slim shade; towering mountains of rock sheltered the valley on either side.

Fatima couldn't imagine a better place to live. Not even her grandfather's mansion in England compared to this wide desert that she adored. Who wanted the stuffy protection of a big house when you could have crackling bonfires at night, and her father's stories to share by them? Often she'd ride her mare, turn her head up to burning yellow sun and just gaze. At a bird soaring across the piercing blue sky. At how sunsets cast the towering cliffs in brilliant shades of sienna. At all the desert's beauty.

Fatima loved exploring hiding places in the rocks with her brother Asad and his best friend, Tarik, and Tarik's closest cousin, Muhammad. But on his eleventh birthday, Tarik began evading her. He'd told Asad she was too slow. Destined to become Tarik's Guardian of the Ages—his bodyguard—Asad had sided with his friend, not Fatima.

Such rejection stung. In all Fatima's ten years, Asad had never left her side. But now he did. Ignoring her, Tarik, Asad and Muhammad often scampered off, leaving Fatima behind. Sometimes they'd split up, using

Muhammad as a decoy while Tarik and Asad sped off in a different direction.

But determination loaned her stealth and speed, and she chased them relentlessly. Today, after hearing Muhammad was sick, she'd easily caught up with them and decided to change tactics. She'd suggested a new game: slave girl.

Tarik liked the attention she gave him, pretending to serve him grapes, bowing in admiration. He did make a handsome sheikh, she reluctantly admitted. He had his father's eyes, as fierce and intensely black as the sheikh's. And he had his father's regal bearing and dignified carriage that echoed his clan symbol, the proud falcon.

Other children teased Tarik about what he inherited from his American-born mother, Elizabeth. They called him "The White Falcon" because of his lighter skin and wheat-colored hair.

But Fatima privately admired his unusual looks, and she publicly defended Tarik. When the name-calling first started, she had dramatically spread her arms and announced in a solemn voice that the spirit of his namesake, the great Tarik the Warrior Sheikh, would send snakes into their beds in retaliation. The Khamsin children had nervously peeped under their covers and stopped calling Tarik names. She, Asad and Tarik had howled for hours.

Fatima liked Tarik. That was, when he wasn't being as stubborn as a donkey about what mattered most to her.

"All right. You be sheikh. Instead of a slave girl, let me be a warrior and defend you," she offered.

Tarik's thin chest heaved with laughter. "Defend me?" His ebony eyes sparkled with good humor. "Don't be so silly." Fingers rapping on his chin, he considered: "You serve me well enough. Perhaps I will allow you to be my wife. I would even let you kiss me."

Such a generous offer! Fatima pursed her lips as if he offered her a lemon to suck. The sheikh's son sprang forward. Two warm lips brushed hers, like a butterfly landing gently on her mouth. Fatima hovered a minute, enchanted, then recoiled.

"Eeeeww! What'd you do that for?" She scrubbed her mouth with an angry fist.

"You looked like you wanted a kiss," Tarik protested.

Fatima started to object when her vision blurred. Oh God, please, not again! Dizziness gripped her. Tarik and Asad became fuzzy images in white skullcaps, indigo trousers, cream-colored kamis shirts and short indigo jubbes. Pressing her hands to her spinning head, she surrendered to the Sight.

She lay on silken sheets beside Tarik, a man grown. He was longer and broader than the skinny boy. Bare chested, sheet tugged up to his lean waist, he stared at Fatima with an intense look she'd seen her father give her mother. In the dream, Tarik took her into his arms and kissed her. Then he said in a deep voice, "Mine. You are now mine, Fatima. Forever."

Fatima's eyes flew open. Her mouth wobbled. As always after a vision, she felt disoriented and drained.

They looked at her; Asad with alarm, Tarik with concern. The sheikh's son placed steadying hands on her shoulders. He led her to a boulder, helped her sit. Asad joined them, sliding a comforting arm about her waist.

A gift, her mother called it.

A nightmare, she had replied.

"Tima, did you have another vision? Was it very bad this time?" Tarik asked, holding her hand.

His gentle concern only made it worse. She suppressed a shiver. He must never know. Ever.

"Yes," she snagged, pushing aside his hand and springing to her feet. "I had a nightmare of what your poor wife will have to suffer, kissing your she-camel lips."

Shock then anger filled his dark eyes. Tarik stood up, scowling. "I do not have she-camel lips!"

Jumping off the rock, Asad peered at his friend's mouth. "Well, Tarik, your bottom lip is large like a she-camel's."

Tarik silenced him with a scathing look. His slight shoulders drew back with pride. "It is an honor being the sheikh's wife and having the privilege of kissing me."

She glared. "I'd rather kiss a stinky goat. I want to be a warrior. I could even be your Guardian of the Ages."

"But Tima, *I'm* supposed to be his Guardian of the Ages," Asad protested.

"Well, two Guardians are better than one. You can watch his left side and I'll watch his right," she reasoned. She raced to a nearby thorn tree to pick up a dead branch as a sword. She waved it in the air.

An odd prickling raised gooseflesh on her arms. She heard herself say in a faraway voice, "You need me as your Guardian, son of Jabari bin Tarik Hassid. You must not die as your mother's babies did."

Blinking, she focused on their shocked faces. Anger twisted Asad's features. Tarik looked wounded. Even though her Sight prompted the words, she felt guilty mentioning the grievous topic. Tarik's mother had lost five babies after his birth, and before his sister Nadia was born four years ago. His parents still mourned their deaths.

"That was mean, Tima," Asad lectured.

Flustered, she started to apologize then stopped. Words had power. So did her Sight. Destiny called her to a greater purpose than simply being a girl. If this were a gift, why couldn't she use it to become Tarik's Guardian? Who better to protect him? Respectful of her Sight, Tarik would relent.

In a slightly pleading voice, she stated her case. Tarik and Asad exchanged glances. Her heart sank.

"My Guardian of the Ages is my loyal defender who would give his life for me," Tarik stated quietly. "He is the tribe's fiercest fighter. True, you have the gift of visions, Tima. But you could never be my Guardian because you are a girl. *Girls don't fight.*" His voice held a deeper timbre, as if he had just taken a step into manhood.

Fatima drew away from the hard resolve in his dark eyes, then remembered. She was the daughter of Ramses bin Asad Sharif, the fiercest of all the Khamsin warriors. And like her father, she didn't fly from a challenge.

"I can protect you better than Asad. I'm a better warrior."

"You will never be a warrior of the wind," Tarik replied.

The truth stung so grievously, he became a red haze in her vision. "I could, too! And I'll prove it!"

Fatima grabbed hold of Tarik's silky golden curls and yanked. As he reached up with a balled fist to swing, Fatima ducked and dove to the sand with feline grace. She rolled, her left foot shot out and hooked around Tarik's ankle and pulled. He tumbled. She'd seen her father perform the move while spying on him practicing.

He lay on the sand and she jumped on his stomach. Tarik grunted with surprise.

"Give in," she panted, capturing his arms with her hands and pressing them against the ground. He scowled and struggled, but her weight pinned him. Like her brother, Fatima was taller and heavier than Tarik.

"Fatima, stop it," Asad snapped. Fatima ignored her twin and dug her heels into Tarik's sides.

"Surrender, infidel. Admit defeat," she ordered.

"Fatima!"

The horrified shock in her father's voice gave her pause. With a guilty start she glanced up to see Ramses approach, accompanied by a tall, handsome man clad in an indigo binish. Oh no. The sheikh, Jabari, Tarik's father! Fatima turned her gaze back to her prisoner, but caught the gleam in his eyes too late. The blow came sharply, stinging as it landed squarely on her lower lip.

Fatima fell away, sprawling on the ground. Pain filled her mouth. She touched her bottom lip, drew away scarlet fingertips. To her horror, tears spilled down her cheeks. Tarik struggled to his feet with a look of intense satisfaction.

"Tarik!" The shock in the Khamsin sheikh's voice was greater than her father's.

"She jumped on me like a caracal. Fatima should learn the consequences of attacking a Khamsin warrior," Tarik snarled.

"And you are not a Khamsin warrior yet. You need to treat her with the respect a Khamsin maiden is due. Do you forget yourself?" his father asked. His quiet voice was laced with command.

Tarik gulped. Fatima knew Tarik worshiped his father and feared him a little, as most Khamsin children did. Everyone but her. Jabari had a soft spot for her, as Fatima had been the only girl among the two close-knit families for the longest time.

She felt a warm hand squeeze her palm, and looked up at her father's somber face as he pulled her upright.

"Tarik, apologize now to Fatima," Jabari ordered.

Tarik shuffled his feet and muttered, "I'm sorry." Mutiny glittered in his dark eyes. He was not sorry. Not one little bit.

"Now go get the camel crop," the sheikh added sternly.

Tarik's tanned face blanched. He swallowed hard, large black eyes widening. Suddenly he went from swaggering braggart to little boy; his brows furrowed into a pleading look. Jabari's stony expression gave no quarter. Resolutely, Tarik marched off in the direction of his tent.

Fatima felt alarmed. The sheikh had never been so angry. She tugged at his indigo binish. "Please, sire—please do not punish him. It was my fault. I started it. I did."

Jabari's black-bearded mouth softened into a smile. He squatted down. "My dear Fatima, it does not matter. Tarik needs to learn that it is not permissible to hit women. Khamsin women should be protected, loved and respected. As long as I am sheikh, and Tarik after me, such abuse will not be tolerated." Anger tightened his face as his gaze settled on her cut lip. She drew back. Jabari smiled, opening his arms.

"Stop crying. Come give your uncle Jabari a big hug. How long has it been since you hugged me?"

Relieved that he was not angry, she stepped into his embrace. Jabari hugged her. She inhaled the clean, spicy, masculine scent of him, so much like her own father's. He released her and stood.

"She is very much your daughter, Ramses," he said, chuckling, and she was glad to see his good humor restored.

But her father did not smile. He merely looked at her sternly. "Too much," he muttered.

Tarik returned, carrying the long camel crop. He walked straight and tall. Without flinching, he handed the stick to his father with a solemn look. Fatima felt a sudden, unexpected spurt of pride.

"I am ready for my punishment, Father," he said quietly. "What I did was wrong. I should never have hit Fatima." Approval shone in the sheikh's dark gaze, but Tarik stole a sly glance at Fatima. "You were correct, Father. Khamsin women should never be hit. They should be protected and cherished, for they are the weaker sex. They can't fight, ride into battle or become warriors of the wind."

Choked laughter rumbled from Asad. Fatima glared at her twin. Tarik had had the final word, after all.

"Come, Tarik," Jabari said firmly, but the hand he laid upon his son's shoulder seemed steady, not steely.

As the sheikh hauled his son toward the warrior training ground, Fatima muttered, "I hope he beats your bottom raw."

Asad scowled. "Oh, our sheikh will. Tarik's never gotten a beating before. And it's all your fault. You should have left instead of fighting him."

Deeply upset, Fatima drew back. Her twin had never directly sided against her. Never.

"Quiet, Asad," her father said sternly. "Tarik should not have hit her. It is against the Khamsin code of honor."

"Papa, are you going to punish me like Uncle Jabari is doing to Tarik?" Fatima asked.

Her father hunkered down. He touched her cut lip. Fatima winced, although his touch was absolutely gentle. "Sweetheart, I think you have been punished enough."

"Just because you're a girl," Asad muttered.

That remark, made under his breath, rankled her pride. "I can take it. I'm as tough as any boy," she declared. She looked hopefully into her father's frowning face. "Should I get the camel crop?"

Her father scratched his short-trimmed beard. "No, Fatima. I wish to talk with you. Asad, return to the tent."

She watched her brother stride off, his hair glistening blue-black in the sun. Grief pinched her chest. Once Asad had been her best friend. No longer. Tarik had taken her place.

She headed for a large, flat-surfaced boulder and plunked herself down on it. Her lower lip trembled as she struggled to contain tears of betrayal. She looked up into her father's wise amber eyes. He touched her hand.

"Asad doesn't like me anymore, Papa. Why?" she whispered.

"That is not so, sweetheart. He is merely growing up. Do not begrudge Tarik his company—he needs his friend right now. It is a sore thing to his pride when a son receives punishment from his father."

Swallowing past a lump clogging her throat, Fatima looked away. "Asad is always with Tarik. He never wants to be with me."

"It is only natural. Asad is my firstborn son," he reminded her gently. "He is destined to be Tarik's Guardian of the Ages, just as I am Guardian to his father. When Asad turns thirteen . . ."

Fatima waved a hand. "I know, I know. He will receive the initiation of manhood and take the Guardian oath to guard Tarik with his life and be tattooed with the falcon, the mark of Tarik's house, upon his right arm. Asad talks of nothing else all day. I'm so tired of it!"

"Fatima, you must accept it, just as you must accept the fact that Tarik will become our sheikh. What you did to Tarik was wrong. You shamed him."

"But, Papa, I can beat him! Tarik teased me. He said I am weak just because I am a girl. And I have to marry and learn to cook and have babies and I can never be a warrior."

Ramses sighed deeply. "Fatima, he is correct. There is no place for a woman warrior in our tribe. It is everything against our laws, our way of life."

"But you taught me how to fight!"

"I should not have," he muttered. "It is my fault."

A pout puckered her mouth. "It's not fair. I hate being left out just because I'm a girl."

"You are growing up quickly, my beloved daughter. I talked with your mother. You need to start spending more time with girls. I forbid you to follow after Tarik and Asad."

Stung, Fatima stared. If he had beaten her with the camel crop, he could not have hurt her more. "Please,

10

Papa, I *am* sorry. I will not hit Tarik ever again. I promise. I promise."

Usually her pleas softened her father. This time, his face was set in rock. His look frightened her with its intensity. He would not give in.

"It isn't fair," she whispered. "Why can't I be a warrior of the wind like you? I want to be like you, Papa."

Her father's handsome face softened. He reached over and cupped her chin, raising her eyes to meet his gaze.

"Please, sweetheart, please understand. This is for your own good, because when you get older you will only be disappointed. You cannot be a warrior of the wind. Or a Guardian. I know it is not fair, but you are a girl and it simply is not done."

Her father gave a jovial smile again. "You enjoy Alhena's company. She's only a year younger than you, and has a new china tea set your grandfather sent from England. Alhena is a treasure, helping out with her new baby brother."

Fatima fumed. Alhena was such a goody-goody. She had a sweet, giving nature. Fatima liked her cousin, but . . . babies? Ugh. They smelled of sticky spit-up and made stinky messes in their napkins. She would rather swing a make-believe scimitar or jump on her horse's back, riding across the desert, pretending to fight unseen enemies.

Yet a small part of her knew she had to conceal these thoughts from her father. "Yes, Papa," she muttered.

He jumped off the rock, turned and opened his arms wide. "Well, Fatima?"

Her spirits soared at the invitation. Fatima raced to him, holding her arms up, begging. "Twirl me, Papa!"

Clutching her wrists, her father spun around. Sailing like a spinning top, Fatima shrieked with joy, secure in Ramses' grip.

Slowing down, he laughed, then set her on solid

ground again. "You are getting too heavy," he teased, hugging her. She watched with shining eyes as he strode to his mare, grabbed her mane, swung into the saddle. She adored watching him mount this way. Indeed, she had even learned it herself. Ramses winked at her, clucked to Fayla and galloped off. Clouds of dust rose in the air from his mare's pounding hooves.

Fatima watched, plans forming. There were chores to perform . . . and other means of escape. She would learn. She *would* be a warrior and learn to fight. Nothing would get in her way.

As Fatima watched her father ride off, she touched her fingers to her heart and then her mouth in the traditional Khamsin gesture of honor before battle. A soft ululating cry, the Khamsin war call, purred between her lips.

Chapter Two

They'd locked the gate.

Fatima scrutinized the thick wood barring her from the schoolhouse in Haggi Quandil. Three hours from the Khamsin camp, once it housed the sheikh's concubines, but the sheikh's strong-willed wife had changed that.

Tarik and Asad were inside—doing some mischief they wanted to keep quiet. Rumors fluttered in the camp like doves. Tarik had had a surprise from America delivered to the schoolhouse. But determined to see the twin she'd been parted from for eight long years, Fatima would not wait.

Her mare made an excellent footstool. Fatima led Sheba close to the high stone wall. Mounting and then standing on the horse's back, Fatima balanced herself. Fingers more accustomed lately to dainty sewing clutched the wall's edge. Hoisting herself up, she swung atop it, then jumped to the ground.

Inside, pink desert roses flowered in the lush gardens

13

of the U-shaped courtyard. Beneath a shady tree, Tarik's white mare and Asad's black stood patiently. Fatima tugged down her rose silk scarf. Secrets lingered here, like ancient dust.

Where were her brother and Tarik?

Approaching the schoolhouse entrance, she jiggled the doorknob. Locked. Curiosity rose. Fatima searched the courtyard for Asad, anticipating the surprise on his face when he saw her. But . . . no Asad or Tarik. She'd just have to break in.

In silence, Fatima stalked the perimeter. Shaped like a large, square horseshoe, the schoolhouse had latticed windows and some rooms open to a cool oasis of roses, palms and flowers. Peasants in this village relied upon the Khamsin for protection, for providing the resources to sell their crops and educating their children. In turn, the tribe took a percentage of the crops cultivated. It had been a beneficial arrangement for all, until the English taxes began bleeding away too much money from both parties. Fatima detested the English for running her country, and treating her people as if they were children.

Sounds drifted out a window. A high-pitched girlish giggle and a man's deep chuckle. Fatima recognized Tarik's laugh.

She crept under the window and listened. Low moans and sighs. A furious blush ignited her cheeks. Such sounds she'd heard before in the night. Quiet rustles, low moans and the rubbing of flesh against flesh. The schoolhouse had bedrooms to house visiting students from the Khamsin's southern tribe. Apparently Tarik was making good use of one.

Curiosity won over caution. Fatima had never seen a man and woman making love. Spotting a wooden crate holding oranges, she quietly dumped the fruit on the ground. She carried the empty crate to the wall and stood on it. An excellent vantage point for eavesdropping.

As she peered through the latticework, Fatima stifled a shocked gasp. Tarik lay naked between a woman's legs on the narrow bed, his back to the window. His golden head blocked the woman's face, but the woman's curved legs were hooked around his waist. Moans rippled from her lips as her fingers curled around his broad shoulders. Braced on his hands, he moved slowly against her, breathing in ragged pants. Muscles in his back rippled under bronzed skin.

A queer burning rose in Fatima's loins as she stared at those firm, pumping buttocks. Unrestrained jealousy filled her. What would it feel like to lie beneath Tarik, her hands gliding along his hard body, her legs clutching his waist, Tarik's kisses on her trembling lips? What did it feel like to make love?

Kisses, well, she'd been kissed. Wet, sloppy kisses by tall, gangly men who waltzed with her during formal balls at her grandfather's mansion in London. They'd take advantage of quiet, dark corners, would whisper how pretty she was, how exotic. How they wanted to take her for rides in their new motor cars.

Cynical Fatima would whisper back how poor she was. How Lord Smithfield wasn't truly her grandfather.

"I'm just the under maid. The poor dear is lonely. He likes passing me off as his granddaughter." Then she'd silently laugh as they slunk away to seek out another rich heiress.

Tarik's kisses would not be sloppy, she decided, staring at his naked bottom thrusting frantically. His lips would be warm, firm, and taste slightly of the oranges he loved. His kisses would make her dizzy, would set her blood on fire. Then he would lower his mouth to her breast and do the things she'd heard of whispered by women in the black tents. The secret of a hundred kisses.

Her blood quickened. The queer feeling in her loins intensified. Her breasts felt heavy, full, their nipples aching.

Tarik for a lover? Never!

Scowling, Fatima shook herself out of the daydream. She eased down from the crate, angry and resentful. Tarik using the schoolhouse for sex? She had a good mind to . . .

Glancing around, she spotted her weapon on the ground: a smooth round stone, just the right size. Fatima hefted it in her hand. She shouldn't. Long ago she promised her father never to hit Tarik again. But she would.

Remounting the crate, she eased the latticework window open. Now she had a clear view of her target. Tarik's breathing increased and he was moaning. Judging from the sound, and the frantic pumping of his buttocks, she guessed he neared his release. Warmed by the sun, the stone felt hot in her palm. Drawing it back, she took aim . . . fired just as Tarik lifted his head and let out a loud groan.

With a loud thwack, the stone hit bare flesh—dead on Tarik's bare left cheek. His groan of pleasure turned into a howl of pain. Fatima closed the window and scrambled down, racing into the garden. Leaning against an olive tree, she couldn't stop sobs of laughter. Tears rolled down her cheeks. With the edge of her scarf, she wiped her streaming face.

Fatima imagined the look of shocked pain on Tarik's face as the stone hit him, and she laughed harder.

"So, you have finally returned to us, Fatima. And living among the titled gentry of England has failed to mold you into the lady your father desperately hoped," a deep male voice rumbled.

Fatima looked up at the imposing, majestic figure of

16

Tarik bin Jabari Hassid. Clad only in his indigo trousers, the unsmiling, bare-chested son of their sheikh faced her, hands on his lean hips. Burnished wheat-colored curls flowed down past his shoulders. Darker hair covered his chest, taut, concave stomach and dipped into the waistband of his trousers. Fatima wondered what the fabric hid, and the very thought threatened a blush. She gulped, unable to prevent staring. Tarik had grown from boy to man in her absence.

He had his father's height. Once she'd towered over him; now she barely cleared his chin. A short-trimmed sandy beard covered that same square chin and taut jawline. Broad, sculpted shoulders rippled with muscle. Even half-naked, he maintained the commanding presence generations of aristocratic ancestors had bred into his blood. Quiet control trumped the fury in those hard black eyes.

"So, did you enjoy spying on me?" he asked. His deep voice, smoky from spent passion, scraped across her jumbled nerves.

Fatima arranged her face into an innocent mask. "Tarik, so nice to see you," she burbled. "I have no idea what you're talking about. Why, I am just here in the garden, enjoying the fragrance of the jasmine."

He strode over to the bush, picked a blossom. Fatima's senses rekindled as she watched his graceful stride, as languid yet dangerous as a stalking cat.

He was sleek and golden, slick with the sweat from newly spent desire. Perspiration beaded his temples, as if he had run miles through the desert. She shook her head at the transformation, at the hard muscle replacing the skinny boy's sinew. He had widened as well as lengthened. His hair, the color of cloudy sunshine, swung free as he strode over to her. She had never seen a man's bare chest before, despite having seven broth-

17

ers, for they all were extremely conservative. The sight fascinated her.

Tarik closed the distance between them until she could count the dark lashes feathering those smoldering eyes. "Poor Fatima," he rumbled in his deep, teasing voice. "So ignorant of the ways between a man and a woman. The fragile flower witnesses passion. Does she want the same?"

Shocked he'd read her so easily, Fatima could only stand motionless. He stroked the white blossom across her cheek. Its delicate aroma teased her nostrils, mingling with Tarik's scent of spices and maleness. A pulse throbbed in his throat. She could see his lips, swollen and reddened, part slightly.

Her breath hitched at his nearness. She felt confused, aching, filled with a need she didn't understand. Fatima stared at the brown circles of his nipples. Tiny beads of sweat glistened in the crisp hair covering his chest. What would it feel like to run her hand over the knobby ends of his collarbone, press her mouth against his shoulder and taste him?

Her gaze collided with his. Something sparked there, dark, forbidding and mysterious. The hand holding the flower clenched, turning his knuckles white. Then the same mocking smugness entered his eyes.

"Run along now, before you see something else to strip you of your innocence. Before someone plucks the tender flower and enjoys its sweetness. Go home, little Fatima, like a good girl." Then Tarik laughed. At her. At her innocence.

Pique blossomed into outraged fury. She seized his hand, tore the flower from his grip. Fatima ripped the tender blossom into ragged strips. Triumph surged through her as he lost his condescending expression.

"Flower, Tarik? I ceased being one long ago. I'm

twenty-five and a woman of the world. You showed me nothing I haven't seen or done myself. England offered me the opportunity."

Piercing black eyes turned from teasing to thunderous rage. She could almost swear he looked . . . jealous?

Alarm swept through her as he advanced, dark gold brows drawing together. "Who was it?" he thundered.

Caught, she spilled out the first name her frenzied brain seized upon. "Michael. The Duke of Caldwell's heir."

They had kissed, nothing more. Though she enjoyed his company, she felt no desire for him and had ended the brief liaison.

"Fatima!" He blew out a breath in a violent hiss. "Have you no shame?"

"Haven't you?" she shot back.

"A Khamsin woman is supposed to remain a maid until she marries. Only your husband has the right to take such a precious gift from you," he said in a low, threatening tone.

"Such a gift is mine to bestow on whom I choose. I can shoot a gun better than most men, defend myself like a man and I'm as smart as most men. So why should I expect to keep my virginity when men don't? You, Tarik, with your insistence on warming the mattresses of the school, certainly haven't!"

For a moment they locked gazes like ancient enemies. Tarik's ebony eyes, as penetrating as his father's, held hers. He circled her like a jungle cat stalking its prey. A finger of fear stroked her skin, raising gooseflesh. She had deeply offended him with her fib, for Khamsin warriors highly valued the purity of their women. What if he told her father? Fatima shuddered, thinking of the hurt her father would feel.

Tarik stopped circling. A large warm hand descended

on her shoulder and he turned her toward him. A wicked smile curved his firm lips.

"I have not done so with all the mattresses. Perhaps you and I should test them, since you boast of being so accomplished."

His thumb slid along the underside of her jaw, brushing her overly sensitive skin. Blood roared in her head. Her body raged with yearning, primitive need. Fatima cursed her lie and recoiled from the raw sensuality of his touch.

"I didn't come here for the same purpose as you, Tarik. I want to see my brother. I think you've had enough mattress romps today to satisfy your needs."

His nostrils flared, but Tarik's thumb lingered on her skin. The dark promise in his smile frightened her a little.

"I'm eager to see what you learned. I'm certain there's many things I can teach you, despite your, ah, experience."

Oh the arrogance of the man! Fatima seethed with rage. She wished she had thrown a bigger stone at him. Come to think of it, a boulder wouldn't have been sufficient.

Fatima's skin beneath his thumb felt silky, stirring Tarik's senses. A warm breeze teased her billowing scarf, stroked her waist-length curls the way his hungry hand wanted to run through the glossy mass. Green, catlike eyes, the color of Nile river grass, narrowed in hostility.

Fatima, his caracal, the wild desert cat. Small and graceful, she never surrendered her fierce independence. She was here, at last. The girl haunting his dreams, the lovely face he saw while bedding others, now glared at him with fearless audacity. After gaggles of fawning women too timid to voice even half-hearted criticisms, his jaded sexuality roared to new life. Fatima, always Fatima. Each time he thrust into his current mistress, it was Fatima's silky thighs wrapped around his waist he imagined. Fatima's whimpering moans in his ears. Her yielding body pressed beneath his. Ironic amusement lashed him. *Imagination is not reality.*

Tarik decided instantly to break off his current affair, which had been risky enough anyway. Those lips coaxing hot desire from his sex as she sank naked on her knees before him, thwarting his refusal, no longer held any appeal. There was only Fatima.

Ah, I'd die a thousand deaths of pleasure for your sweet kiss and nothing more, little caracal, he thought.

Tarik sucked in a deep breath, summoned his control. Little remained of the chubby girl he had teased in childhood; only svelte curves and delectable roundness here. He throbbed with want as he dragged his gaze away from her. Fatima. A rebellious spirit striving to be a man in a woman's sumptuous body. His flesh ached at fantasies of the carnal delight of taming her sexually, of coaxing sweet cries of surrender from that slender throat.

Seven years passed since he had studied her this close, when she had visited Oxford while he and Asad were attending university there. She was just a gangly, coltish teenager he'd tried to ignore, Asad's twin who thought she was so tough. She was not awkward now. Fatima was a few inches shorter than her brother. Both twins had large, luminous green eyes, tipped with long, sooty lashes, but specks of tawny amber darkened Asad's irises while Fatima's resembled green river grass growing in the Nile. The twins' midnight black hair curled in waves, Fatima's spilling to her waist, while Asad's barely touched his shoulder blades. All similarity ended there.

Her silk scarf draped around the graceful curve of her long throat. She had her mother's pert nose, high, aristocratic cheekbones, heart-shaped face and full, pouting lips. Asad more resembled their father, with his laughing mouth, piercing brow, sharp nose and strong, square chin.

Instead of the usual indigo kuftan most Khamsin women wore, Fatima wore a silk gown of yellow and rose. The gown's billowing folds clung with naughty possessiveness to her curves. Tarik glanced at her full breasts and reluctantly dragged his gaze away. When had she blossomed into a woman? And such a woman!

Seeing her like this flooded his body with warmth. He tensed against the rising lust to take her hand, to lead her back to the bedroom he just evacuated, to tumble her on the bed, strip her naked and kiss her satin flesh. He would not, despite his veiled promises or her lack of virginity: He honored her father too much to bed Ramses' only daughter.

Jealous rage filled him. No longer a virgin? He wanted to twist his powerful hands around Michael's neck. Michael, Graham's nephew—the insolent debaucher who had deflowered her. Bile rose in his throat as he envisioned the pale-skinned duke's heir pawing Fatima, being the first to sample her sweetness.

She should have been mine. Mine! The thought howled through him like a desert wind, blazing with possessive intensity.

"Shall we retire to the bedroom now, Fatima? You may demonstrate for me what exactly you learned in England," he goaded.

"I'll never lie beneath you, Tarik. That I can promise." Her voice, tinged with an English accent, rubbed over him like a cat's silken fur.

"Promises can be broken."

Tarik relished the roses of anger blossoming in her soft cheeks. Tempted to see them bloom, he started to provoke her more when Asad marched around the corner. His Guardian of the Ages gave a guilty look, then spotted his sister. The black-bearded lips cracked into a wide smile. Ignoring Tarik, he released a loud whoop and bounded past him.

"Tima," he yelled, holding out his arms.

Fatima lost her sullen pout. Her lovely face was lit by an expression of pure joy. "Asad!"

The twins tumbled into each other, hugging. Tarik felt a stab of loneliness. What would it feel like to experience such closeness? A six-year age difference separated him from Nadia, his oldest sister. Tarik loved his sisters, but he'd never known the special intimacy the twins shared. They had a unique bond that shut others out. He knew. How many times in his childhood had he been shut out by it?

Asad released his sister and stepped back. "You look different."

"Since you last saw me, before the war?" she asked with a laugh. "Good thing Uncle Jabari decided to send you and Tarik to Oxford, otherwise I would never have seen you."

Asad squeezed her shoulders. "Tima, it's been too long. Never again. Never! An eternity since I've seen you."

Moisture filled her green eyes. "I've missed you all so much. I hated this war. I died a little inside each day I knew I couldn't return home. I was so jealous . . . When you and Tarik graduated and they whisked you home, right before the war started . . . And I was stuck there in England, with grandfather and Nana. No one could come and visit. I felt so alone." Never one to hide emotions, Fatima hugged her twin again. Asad squeezed his eyes shut. Two tears slipped down his cheeks.

Tarik watched, emotion clogging his own throat. The war had caused them all great pain. But only Fatima had lacked her close-knit family to see her through it.

Asad wiped away his sister's tears with his thumbs. "You're crying, Tima. Don't cry."

"I won't if you won't," she choked out.

Bending their heads, the two laughed together in the silent communion of twins. Asad wiped his own face.

Struggling to conceal his emotions, Tarik nodded. "It's good to see both of you together again, finally."

Asad glanced at Tarik, and he frowned. "Tarik? Why are you half-dressed?"

Tarik scowled as Fatima snickered. "Where were you? You were supposed to be watching my back," he grated out.

"Instead, I did it for him," Fatima teased, her face scrunched up with merriment. "You see, I can be your Guardian. I was watching your back. Who was she, Tarik?"

Tarik silenced her with a murderous look.

But Asad wasn't easily browbeaten. "Your mother had textbooks delivered for me from Cairo. It's the first chance I've had to indulge. I thought you would be longer."

Chagrined that he'd been so preoccupied he'd ignored his Guardian's own needs, Tarik resolved to give Asad more time to read; it was not fair he had denied his best friend so much. Tarik glanced again at Fatima's lovely face. He dragged in a deep breath. It was not fair, either, that he desired the man's sister as well. She'd succeeded in spoiling his plans. He couldn't risk exposing his flaw now in front of her. Soon, he promised. Very soon.

Fatima slipped away from her brother. She cocked her head. Mischief sparked her green eyes. Instantly, his guard rose.

"Tarik, Asad, why are your horses tethered outside? Why not put them in the stable, with plenty of fresh hay? Does this have to do with the surprise from America?"

Guilt showed on Asad's face. Tarik crossed his arms over his chest. "It's none of your business, Tima."

"Perhaps I'll go see for myself. And *tell* everyone your tremendous secret."

He seized her arm, halting her. Beneath his fingers, her bare skin felt smooth, tempting. Tarik resisted the urge to stroke her silky flesh. To run his fingers up her arm, caress the smooth curve of her graceful neck.

Scowling, he dropped her arm, chose to block her path instead. "No, Tima."

"And how will you stop me, Tarik?"

"I'll sling you over my shoulder, march into the schoolhouse and lock you in the bedroom without your clothes," he said levelly.

The unspoken challenge hovered between them. Asad watched the two of them with interest, as if observing a duel.

"I doubt you'd have the nerve to try," she shot back.

"You think not?" he mocked softly. "Don't tempt me."

Two bright patches of crimson rose again in her cheeks. Fatima scowled. "When are you telling them? You can't keep it a secret for long. Not here."

"I'm waiting for the council meeting for the official unveiling. I don't want anyone—*anyone*—to know before that. Is that clear, Tima?"

Fatima silently fumed, resenting Tarik's attitude. She felt ready to push past to the stables, just to goad him. But he stood a foot taller, and she didn't want to test the strength in those thickly muscled arms.

She didn't want his body next to hers, either, her breasts pressed against the firmness of his back. To feel him dump her onto the bed where he had just made love, and reach for her dress to tear it from her body . . .

Dryness rose in her throat. The same odd feeling tingled in her lower region. Fatima swallowed, staring at Tarik, who refused to drop his gaze. Its burning intensity licked her skin. She put both hands to her flaming face.

Fortunately, Asad broke the tension.

"Tima, how did you get in? We locked the gate. The

only ones with keys are Elizabeth, Tarik and myself . . ." Mischief filled her twin's eyes. "And whatever woman Tarik gives a key to that day. Like Hula. Or was her name Farah? No, that was last week. Or yesterday? Ah yes, yesterday was Leila. So many women, so many bedrooms, so little time for the mighty staff of Ra, as the women call it. The golden sun god, and mighty Ra's enormous pleasure rod!" Asad lifted his eyes upward in a worshipful air. "Homage to thee, mighty Ra, who rises tall and strong on the horizon and the bedroom, making women swoon with anticipation."

Fatima watched Tarik's mouth flatten as Asad chuckled. His reaction should have pleased her, but she was too distracted by the jealousy raking her with sharp talons. The sheikh's son paraded women in and out of the schoolhouse as regularly as Khamsin women milked camels.

"I climbed the wall and jumped. Unlike Tarik's many women," she snapped.

"You would," Asad muttered.

"Another little tactic you learned in fancy English ballrooms?" Tarik taunted. "Besides throwing rocks?"

"Throwing rocks?" A frown creased her twin's handsome face.

"Never mind," Fatima said hastily. "I want to ride back now. I've missed everyone so much."

Asad kissed her cheek. "As they missed you."

"Father will prepare a feast for you tonight," Tarik said, thawing. "Houbara bustard, your favorite."

Instantly she cheered. "Houbara bustard? Oh, I've missed homemade cooking! I don't care if he serves old mutton, as long as it isn't English tea and crumpets."

"Or blood pudding," her twin added, shuddering. "English food tastes worse than donkey dung."

The trio burst out laughing. Tarik sobered. "Tima, how did you stand it, being gone all these years?"

Her lower lip wobbled. "I didn't. Even college didn't help. Some days I didn't think I could remain another day."

"You always could," he said softly. "You're a strong person."

She smiled in gratitude. Tarik flashed a sudden grin that spoke of their old friendship. It evaporated, as if he remembered their adversarial relationship.

"So Tima, what will you do now? A degree in English literature, knowledge in ballroom dancing—you're so accomplished. What we can offer you besides doing laundry and marriage to a warrior?" Asad asked in his gentle, teasing tone.

A sword. I will become a Khamsin warrior of the wind. But she only smiled, and patted Asad's arm. No one must know her secret plans.

Tarik put hands on his lean hips. "I think your sister has her own agenda besides washing clothing and marrying, Asad."

Fatima's stomach lurched at the knowing look he shot her. "Aren't you planning on dressing, Tarik? Or will you return to camp looking like you lost your clothing?" she asked archly.

He shrugged, vanished into the schoolhouse. Minutes later he returned, dressed in a binish and turban. A curved dagger and scimitar dangled from his belt. Asad opened the gate, led the group and their mares outside and relocked it. Tarik mounted, flinched and uttered a low curse, rubbing his left buttock. Bemusement flashed on her twin's face and Fatima snickered.

Tarik tugged the trailing end of his turban over his face. Over the top of his veil, his gaze burned into her. Fatima shivered. Her laughter died. The sheikh's powerful son did not forget such injuries easily.

Tarik didn't wait for the twins. Galloping away, he rode off through the narrow streets. Dust became a cloud beneath his mare's pounding footsteps, and he stood in his stirrups. Shutters banged open as peasant women stared, smiling in admiration. He loosed a wild, ululating yell. The Khamsin war call.

Fatima was home at last.

Chapter Three

Jabari prepared a mighty feast to celebrate Fatima's return. Outside the sheikh's spacious tent, her entire family and Jabari's sat on luxurious red carpets. Fatima felt a burst of emotion, then anxiety as she studied the crowd sitting on the ground before rounded tables.

Asad. Her six brothers. Her parents. Aunts, uncles, cousins. The sheikh and his wife, their four daughters, including Nadia and her betrothed, Salah. Tarik, sitting next to his cousin Muhammad, stopped talking and coolly stared at her.

Kareem and Jamal watched. Both on leave from Giza University to celebrate her homecoming, they dressed in woolen suits instead of the indigo binish and trousers worn by Khamsin warriors. Red tarbooshes covered their close-cropped hair. Khamsin warriors had long hair. Her brothers looked as she felt. Different.

"What's wrong, Tima?" Kareem teased. "Forget how to sit properly after all those years in England?"

Sandwiched between Tarik and Asad, her cousin Alhena waved. Gold bracelets jingled on the girl's slim wrist. "Fatima, come sit by me. It's been forever since I've seen you!"

Fatima smiled at her closest female friend. Men fell over themselves courting Alhena, but the pretty twenty-four-year-old had refused all offers thus far.

She sat beside her cousin, admiring Alhena's rose and violet kuftan. Her hair was combed to a glossy sheen, topped with an emerald-studded clasp that fastened a blue silk scarf to her hair. Her cousin's triangular face, hazel sloe eyes and rosy cheeks resembled her own. Similarities ended there. Delicate, petite Alhena moved with a feminine grace Fatima could never duplicate.

Delicious, spicy aromas she hadn't smelled in years teased Fatima's nostrils. Platters of rice and the birds her brothers and the sheikh had hunted lay in an appealing display.

Muhammad, Tarik's cousin, stole a shy glance at her. A respected warrior of twenty-five, he kept quiet counsel. "You look lovely, Fatima. It's good to see you back with us again. I'm glad the English didn't change you."

Warmed by his praise, she thanked him, relaxing a little. This was family. Home. She belonged nowhere else.

Fatima quickly caught up on news. Jamal, twenty-one, and Kareem, twenty-three, were excelling in their studies at university. Her youngest brother, Radi, fifteen, had spent time at a dig at Luxor.

Alhena questioned Fatima about Western fashions. Patiently, she responded. Women cut their hair short. Dresses were hemmed to the ankle. Her supply of fashion knowledge depleted, she fell silent. Talk focused on Nadia, Tarik's eldest sister, who soon would marry Salah. Fatima hid a grimace. Though strikingly beautiful with blue eyes and silky black hair, Nadia, twenty, was a spoiled braggart, adored by doting parents. She spent time gazing at herself in the mirror and boasting of her many suitors.

"Our little princess is getting married, Elizabeth," Jabari said, glancing at Nadia fondly. "It seems like just yesterday when we were blessed by her birth."

The proud parents clutched hands, smiling.

"Nadia, you are so lucky to marry an honorable Khamsin warrior." Alhena sighed. "I adore weddings."

Nadia tossed her raven curls and flashed them a scornful look. "Salah is the lucky one. Out of all the Khamsin warriors courting me, I picked him. Maybe one day you'll find someone willing to marry you, Alhena. I could give you advice . . ."

Fatima coolly interrupted, hating Nadia's smug hauteur. "I'm sure you have many suitors, Alhena. Every bachelor in our tribe adores you and would be honored to marry you."

Alhena dimpled. "I'm waiting for the right man. Besides, why settle for one camel when you can have a herd chasing you?"

Fatima obliged with the expected laugh, but it sounded hollow to her ears. In England, men had only wanted to marry her for her grandfather's money.

Tarik drank, rubbed the back of his hand over his mouth. The expressionless mask he wore shifted into a worried frown. Leaning forward, he spoke in a low tone. "Fatima, what did you hear in England about Egyptians protesting British rule? Are the English concerned?"

She glanced at Alhena, who was enraptured by Nadia's description of her wedding dress. "Switch places," she said. When her cousin obliged, Fatima told her twin and Tarik about the English nobility's concerns about Egyptians desiring to break free. "But what I heard in England wasn't as important as what I heard in Cairo. More talk in coffee shops and cafés leans toward protest. The people are primed for a revolution, now that the war is over," she whispered.

Tarik nodded, glanced around and began talking in a loud voice about their horse breeding business. Fatima fell into easy chatter with him, asking about the latest Arabians they'd sold to wealthy Europeans. Then Salah commanded her attention by mentioning an enemy tribe he'd spotted while on a scouting expedition with her brothers. How Fatima wished to ride with them!

"Enemy Bedouin tribes?" Jamal dusted off his hands. "The real enemy is much greater, and more difficult to fight. Until Egypt frees herself of British rule, we are all enslaved."

"Uh-oh, here we go again," Asad said softly.

Kareem nodded. "Britain's puppet in Egypt, Sir Reginald, talks out of both sides of his mouth, wanting to keep us oppressed and under control while pretending to sympathize. Her Majesty's government refused Saad Zaghlul permission to represent our people at the Peace Conference."

Salah, a young man with large, mournful brown eyes like those of a lost puppy, glanced at his future father-in-law. "It's horrible to think of the situation with the British. Enslaved? I never considered myself so. But I will fight, if a fight is necessary."

Salah sounded like a sad warrior resigned to war, but Nadia looked smug and proud. Fatima saw the troubled look Jabari exchanged with her father.

"Britain was preoccupied with negotiating to end the war," Jabari put in. "We must wait and see the outcome. Separation from the British will not come easily."

"We have no armies, not enough weapons to fight the British," Ramses added. He shifted his weight, winced slightly.

Fatima bristled. Her father had fought for the British in the war, represented the Khamsin tribe and protected his children and the sheikh's from serving. A Turkish bullet had pierced his thigh. He still limped.

"The British need to see we are serious about being free. A demonstration is in order. When I was in Cairo, I heard Saad Zaghlul is not content to wait. I agree. I would gladly follow him in the cause for freedom," Fatima said evenly.

Shocked silence followed. Kareem and Jamal looked at her with approval, the others with censure. Tarik showed no emotion.

"We'll have no more talk of a revolt against the British," Ramses said tightly. "Is that understood, Fatima? Your grandfather may have allowed such talk. I will not permit it."

Fatima studied her plate, ashamed she had upset him.

"Yes, the British are revolting everyone—and since everyone knows it, why spoil the meal?" Tarik jested.

The whole group laughed. But Fatima did not. She kept looking at her two brothers.

After they had eaten, Jabari stood. The fond look he bestowed on her erased his earlier censure. "We give thanks to Allah for delivering Fatima safely home and keeping her safe while she was away," he said.

All bowed their heads in prayer, then the families let loose a wild, ululating cheer. A proud flush filled Fatima's cheeks. It was the Khamsin war call, used only for special occasions such as battle, weddings or the birth of a child.

After dinner, they all sat outside around a roaring campfire, clustered near her father who told his famous tall tales about ancient Egypt. Asad threw Fatima a slow wink. Ramses was famous for embellishing the truth.

Sitting furthest from the fire, Tarik watched her with a guarded look. She squirmed under his exacting scrutiny. Angling her body toward her father, she concentrated on his tale, willing the intimacy of the fire and the spell of his words to melt her stiffness. But she couldn't relax. Instead, anxiety flowered, making her body as rigid as the rocks ringing the blazing fire. It was as if she expected Osiris, the Egyptian god of the underworld, to jump out from the shadows.

Her trepidation mounted every minute. Danger lurked nearby. Every nerve in her body burned. Her pupils widened in the darkness. Then she felt it. Fatima knew. She just *knew*. Her gaze shot over to Jasmine, Tarik's youngest sister. The little girl was walking away from the circle, near Tarik. She craned her neck, staring up at the beauty of the glistening stars in the ebony sky.

Fatima stood. She pulled up her trouser leg and swiftly unsheathed the straight blade strapped to her calf. Out of the corner of her eye she saw Tarik pivot toward her.

"Fatima, what are you doing with a dagger?"

His voice became a distant buzz. Everything inside her concentrated on his sister. Fatima held the blade. Letting loose a loud cry, she flung it directly toward Jasmine's feet. It speared the ground a few inches from the ten-year-old's left toe.

Jasmine released a startled shriek and ran toward Tarik. He swooped her into his arms, hugging her tight. Others directed several shocked gasps at Fatima. Nadia leapt to her feet, blue eyes glinting with rage.

"Fatima, are you mad? How dare you scare Jasmine! And why are you carrying a weapon? My father will have your—"

"Quiet, Nadia. Stop it right now," Tarik snapped, cutting off her tirade. Salah gripped her shoulders.

"Tarik is right. Do not be so upset. Let us determine what happened first, Nadia," he advised quietly.

"A dagger, Fatima? Why were you carrying one?" Even Alhena sounded perplexed, her eyes wary.

All Fatima's energy drained. Her shoulders slumped. She sagged downward as if her limbs had turned to camel's milk.

Jabari and Ramses approached. Fatima looked up into their stern faces. The sheikh's dark brows beetled with a deep frown. She cringed, expecting him to yell. Instead, he bent and plucked the dagger from the pebbled sand. As he brought it over to the dancing firelight, more shocked gasps sounded.

Fatima craned her neck to see her dagger. Its point had speared a small scorpion.

"A white one," Ramses said in awe. "They are rare, but their poison is . . ."

"Lethal," Jabari finished. "Very peculiar it should happen to crawl near our fire." He flicked the scorpion into the fire with a look of disgust, wiped the blade with a crimson silk cloth hanging from his belt.

Nadia gasped. "Jasmine could have been killed! Fatima, you should have said something! You have no more sense than a donkey. Using a dagger? You have no right."

"Quiet, princess," her father admonished.

"Where did you learn to throw a dagger?" her twin asked.

Grandpa taught me. Offering a weak smile, she shrugged.

The sheikh handed her dagger back to Fatima. She palmed the blade, watching him warily. It was against their laws for women to carry weapons.

"This is yours. Keep it hidden, Fatima. What happened tonight stays among us, and only us. You saved my daughter's life," he said quietly. "I cannot thank you enough."

"How did you know?" Ramses demanded, a mixture of pride and bewilderment on his face.

Cradling Jasmine in his arms, Tarik approached. The little girl snuffled into his broad chest. He hushed her with a soothing stroke of her hair.

"You've all forgotten. Fatima has the gift of the Sight." Tarik's gaze flicked to Nadia. "She would never hurt Jasmine. Only protect her. So stop your caterwauling, and apologize for calling her a donkey and insulting her."

Nadia's mouth closed and opened like a gasping fish. The effect would have been quite comical had Fatima not been close to tears. "I apologize," she said sullenly. •

"Oh, those queer episodes you had long ago. I thought you stopped them in England, Fatima." Alhena wrinkled her pert nose.

"Fatima, what other tricks can you do?" Muhammad stared at her with interest as if expecting her to turn handsprings.

Her wide blue eyes distressed, the sheikh's wife, Elizabeth, put a hand on Nadia's shoulder. Her other two daughters gathered close. "Fatima has a special gift. All of you should thank her for using it to save your sister."

But the three girls merely gawked.

"Since my sisters seem struck mute, accept my thanks from all of us, Tima," Tarik said somberly. He handed Jasmine over to Jabari, who cradled the crying girl. No emotion showed on his face. But his eyes—oh how they blazed with something deep, unbidden and challenging as they studied her. It tossed all Fatima's senses into a sand tornado.

Murmurs started, riding the desert breeze. Whispers slid over her skin, burrowed into her ears, roared in her head. Familiar, dear eyes stared. Mouths gaped open in slack-jawed shock. Family and friends turned to fearful, repulsed spectators. The same expressions she'd seen her English friends display: the stares. The mistrusting looks.

When would the snubbing start?

The dagger spilled from her open palm into the sand. "Stop looking at me!"

Fatima fled the warm campfire and the shocked stares. Scalding tears blurred her vision. Always so different. Always these queer visions, warnings of danger. Why was she so cursed? Finally she crumpled to the ground, burying her head in her hands.

Scraping noises sounded behind her. Her mother sat, held out her arms. Fatima nestled against her and began sobbing. Her mother unwrapped the scarf from her head and dried her tears.

"Fatima, it's not easy, this burden you bear. You were blessed with a rare gift, the Second Sight. I knew it at your birth when your grandmother removed the caul from your face."

"Stop calling it that! It's a curse. A curse!"

Katherine kissed her temple. "A blessing," she insisted. "Learn to accept it. You can see the future and sense when others are in danger, honey. It isn't easy being different. How I wish I could remove this pain for you. But unless you accept, and live with it, you'll never find happiness."

Her mother took Fatima's hand, guided it to her left cheek. Fatima touched the rough, deep scar her mother bore.

"How did you ever learn?" she asked brokenly.

"For so many years, I was afraid to show the world my face, hating the stares, the whispers, the looks of disgust. I was an earl's daughter, and all I wanted was the safety of my room to hide away. My fears almost cost me your father's love. Only your father could see past my mark. His love healed the bitterness in my heart, for he loved me just as I was, scar and all."

"Papa is an extraordinary man," she murmured, stroking her mother's cheek, aching at her pain.

"He is. But Fatima, don't be like I was, wasting years of your life, hating what you cannot change." She squeezed her daughter's hand, the grasp comforting and strong. "Learn to harness this power, to embrace it and use it for good. You're different."

"I don't want to be different—not like this," Fatima whispered. "I hate it when they stare. Look at Nadia. Screaming and squealing as if I were a witch."

"Nadia enjoys finding reasons to scream and squeal. I pity her poor husband on the wedding night. Perhaps your brothers should make him earplugs."

Fatima burst into laughter.

Her mother joined her then sobered. "Fatima, there's no cure for a white scorpion's sting. Jasmine would have died. Isn't that worth a few stares?"

Gulping down air, she considered. "You don't know what it was like in England. Ever since I warned a girl against riding her horse. She rode and fell and broke her leg. I knew it would happen. The other girls, they looked at me strangely. And in college, it continued."

"I know," her mother murmured. "Your grandfather told me you were unhappy. When the war ended, I wanted to bring you home, but your father and I discussed it and we decided your best chances for marriage . . ."

Katherine's voice trailed off. Stomach clenching, Fatima sat up. "You kept me in England, away from all of you, to find a proper English husband? Mother! How could you? The English girls looked down on me because I am Egyptian, just as the English treat Egyptians in our own country as if we are children! I needed to come home." She jumped to her feet, hugging herself. "Why did you allow me home now—because I'm officially considered a spinster?"

"It was time, Fatima," Katherine said quietly. "Don't blame your father. I pushed him into it. You're the granddaughter of an English earl and will inherit a great fortune. I wanted you to find happiness among the English *ton,* as I never did. Because no Englishman wanted me."

A painful note in her mother's voice gave Fatima pause. "But you had Papa!"

"We fell in love. But our marriage was still arranged."

Fatima sniffed. "Who would want a fussy, pale Englishman when you can marry a Khamsin warrior of the wind?"

Katherine laughed. "Still your father's daughter! Egyptian to the core. But there's more to life than being a warrior."

"I wouldn't know," she muttered.

Her mother sighed deeply. "Fatima, you and Asad are the new era. The war, it changed us. Flying machines! They wanted to pinpoint locations of Bedouin tribes. Your father and Jabari sent our livestock south. Tarik saved us. He painted our tents brown to match the mountains. He organized us so when lookouts spotted approaching German airplanes, the women and children hid in the sacred caves. I wanted to give you the chance to live a western life, in a mansion, with electricity, a telephone, motor cars, enormous wealth." Katherine's voice quavered. "I wanted you to fall in love on your own, honey. To choose your own husband."

Fatima scrubbed tears away with a fierce fist. "I don't want money. Or telephones, electricity or to dance with foppish English boys. My home is here, in the desert. I'm Egyptian. I suppose you wished different, that I would never return."

"Don't say that," Katherine burst out. She enveloped her daughter in a crushing hug. "I wanted you back more than the world. But I wanted your happiness more."

"And I can only be happy here, with all of you," Fatima whispered into her mother's fragrant kuftan.

They broke apart. Fatima wiped her face again. She

would cry no more. "All of you . . . well, except for Tarik. And Nadia. Her whining hurts my ears."

Katherine burst into laughter. Fatima adored the sound; it reminded her of light, tinkling bells.

"Why Tarik, honey?"

The innocent tone of her mother's voice raised her suspicions. Fatima shrugged. "He's arrogant and insolent."

"And handsome and charming. All the girls think so."

Her heart lurched. She tried not to let her feelings show. "I'm sure of it. Tarik always did have herds of women following him like sheep." *Tripping into his arms. Into his bed.*

"Which you of course never would do. Seeing as you despise him so much." A hint of amusement tinged her mother's voice.

"Only if I were ordered to do so." Gooseflesh pricked her arms. Fatima rubbed them again.

"Come, honey. Let's go back."

Fatima hung back. "I don't know if I can face them."

Katherine's gentle hand cupped her cheek. "You must, daughter. Now, for in the morning it will be too difficult."

Dread filled her as they returned to the group clustered near the dying fire. Silence draped the air as they entered the circle of light. Several pairs of eyes focused on her. Tarik's sisters bent their heads, murmured to each other.

Oh God. The whispers. She hated them.

Fisting her hands so tightly that pain speared her palms, Fatima pasted on a frozen smile. Her frantic gaze swung over to her twin. To Tarik. Tarik gave her a long, thoughtful look.

Jabari stood, turning toward Fatima. Panic flared. Oh God. Now he was going to question her. More attention.

"Fatima, I wish to ask you about this gift of yours."

Tarik swiftly interrupted. "Father, I have something important to share. I wanted to wait until the council meeting, but it's best to break the news now. It's about the surprise I've imported from America." Squeals of delight came from his sisters. Asad merely stared. Jabari gave his son a thoughtful look. He gestured for them to sit again.

They gathered around the dying campfire. Flames crackled as her brothers added fuel, casting long shadows on the grayish sands. Chin propped on his fists, Tarik faced them all. But he directed his gaze at his father.

"The surprise concerns the money you gave me to invest after college, Father. The money I received from selling some of the tribe's treasure to the British Museum. The result of my investment is hidden at the schoolhouse."

Jabari and Ramses exchanged glances.

"And what did you purchase, son? Did you consult with your Aunt Jillian about American stocks? Or did you buy good horseflesh to increase our breeding stock?"

"I bought a motor car."

Shocked gasps flittered about the campfire. Fatima hid her own surprise. Tarik's face remained smooth as he studied his father. "It is a Model T, the latest rage in America."

"Rage?" the sheikh roared.

He nodded, ignoring his father's own anger. "I partnered with a college friend who lives in America. He needed money. I needed opportunity. It was perfect."

"You spent our tribe's money on a . . . a . . . motor car?"

"A stable of them," Tarik said cheerfully. "It's called a dealership. It's an investment in prime breeding stock."

"Motor cars do not multiply, Tarik."

"Money does. The Ford company started mass producing a few years ago. My friend wanted to buy his uncle's dealership. Brian told me we'd double our money and then purchase more. Motor cars are just like horses, except you fuel them with gas, not hay or grass. They're the horses of the future for our people."

"Horses eat grass. Hay. Motor cars eat gas." Ramses slapped a hand against his head. "I am not believing this conversation.

"Tarik, I gave you that money as a test. I told you to invest it, to make a profit. And you squandered it on horseless carriages. How can you expect—"

"Is ninety thousand American dollars enough of a profit for you?"

Astonished shock flashed across the sheikh's face. "Ninety?" He turned to Ramses, whose jaw had dropped. "Did Nadia's caterwauling ruin my hearing, or did my son just say . . ."

"Ninety thousand dollars," Tarik finished.

The sheikh looked dumbstruck. Never had Fatima seen him lose his composure. Jabari turned to his wife.

"Elizabeth, our son is breeding horseless carriages. And, it appears, making us quite rich."

Tarik's mother offered a serene smile. "Would you expect anything less from your only son and heir, my love?"

"No." The sheikh gave Tarik a long, thoughtful look. "No, I would not. You have done well, Tarik."

Tarik accepted his father's praise with a slight nod. Only Fatima guessed it meant more. All his life, Tarik had struggled for independent recognition.

"The council will be pleased with the money I've earned," he said, locking gazes with his father.

Fatima looked with interest at the sheikh's suddenly tight expression. "You are too concerned about their opinions, Tarik."

"And you are too little concerned, Father. They carry

a great deal of influence among our people. You advocate advancement, but such advancement cannot come without convincing the Majli to embrace it. What future do we have if our own council opposes its leader?"

Jabari gave his son a level look. "We will not discuss this now, Tarik. It is Fatima's homecoming, remember?"

Tarik sat back, mutiny briefly flashing in his eyes before one of his sisters asked him about the marvelous Model T. Talk continued for a few minutes, with everyone begging for chances to see the marvelous Model T. Finally the women shooed everyone away, herding them all to bed. Tarik remained behind.

Lingering, Fatima shuffled her slippers in the sand. Finally she raised her gaze to his. A sliver of pale moonlight glossed the gold hair spilling from beneath his indigo turban. She said, "You did that on purpose. You didn't want them to know, not now. Why did you tell them?"

Tarik's broad shoulders lifted in a shrug. "Does it matter? Father would find out sooner or later."

"Why?" she insisted.

He tilted his head back to stare at the round moon, exposing his throat muscles. "You've just returned, Tima. I know how your visions upset you. How silly Nadia can be. I knew they'd be excited about the motor car."

Fatima melted. He'd purposely diverted attention away from her? Such a considerate gesture healed old wounds, reminded her of the friendship they'd shared. She stretched on tiptoes, leaning up against his strength. The scent of clean male skin and sandalwood soap teased her nose as she kissed his warm cheek.

Tarik flinched perceptibly, drew away. "What are you doing?" he asked roughly.

"That was for saving me from their stares. Thank you."

His expression shuttered. Troubled by his response, Fatima turned to leave.

"Tima?"

She whirled, forcing herself to smile.

"The next time you want to see my naked bottom, please, let me know. I'll be most happy to oblige you."

Fatima made a strangled sound. Tarik laughed softly and walked away, vanishing into the shadows like a desert wind.

Chapter Four

Though overjoyed at being back in Egypt among her people, Fatima found it difficult to adjust to the traditional role for women in the Khamsin tribe. Women were honored among her people, but still not treated as equals. She wanted more: As much respect as Khamsin warriors were respected.

Fatima attended Nadia's wedding with her family, hiding a smirk as the nervous groom stammered through the sacred vows. The following morning her twin laughed as he revealed how, according to tradition, the men hung outside the wedding tent to make ribald remarks about the warrior's prowess with his bride. "Nadia squealed like a sheep being shorn."

Weddings hadn't changed, but there were other remarkable changes in the desert. Windmills pumped water from the sacred caverns through underground tubing to basins throughout the camp. The sheikh's wife had built a school and trained several teachers.

There were other changes, too. Worrisome ones. The war had divided the council of elders. Ibrahim, the council elder who assumed power after Jabari's grandfather died, clung to the old ways. He scowled at modern appliances and conveniences and wanted the women veiled.

Ramses quietly informed his daughter the war might be over, but Jabari faced a far greater battle. "Our people are divided, my beloved daughter. The war has left them embittered and insular. They despise change. I am afraid for our Sheikh, and even more so, for what awaits Tarik when he assumes command."

Now, as she scrubbed her face in the women's bathing facilities, Fatima mused over her father's words. Very troubling, for if anyone discovered what she had brought back with her from England, the council might punish her. Severely.

Fatima glanced in the mirror. In the hot bath, surrounded by her friends, Nadia held court like an ancient Egyptian queen, bragging of her wedding night. Fatima was reminded of her time in England, her alienation as the other girls gossiped about their beaus. They acted so normal. She herself was not.

I am so much not like them it scares me. But it scares them more, she mused. Look at her, bragging so desperately!

"Yes, I was frightened," Nadia said. "I lay on my back, my knees open as my husband instructed. He came to me. His snake was large and stiff, like a giant cobra rearing its head."

"Tell us everything!" one girl begged.

"He put a white sheet beneath my hips. Salah said he would present it to my father to prove I was a virgin and the marriage had been consummated. Salah told me what was to happen would please him. I felt his snake pressing against my thigh. It was hard, and I trembled. Then his body covered mine. He pushed into me. It hurt so much I wanted to cry, because he was so large! Then he broke the barrier that made me a maid. I couldn't help a scream. He moved some and then collapsed."

Fatima swallowed a distressed laugh. Surely it could not be that awful. Nadia made it sound like torture. A woman's first time should be tender, special—like her first kiss. And the idea of a man's male part compared to a snake . . . She suppressed a faint shudder. Snakes terrified her.

She said, "I heard some snakes aren't as large. So it wouldn't hurt as much." She brushed her hair, glancing at Nadia in the mirror.

Tarik's sister sniffed. "All warriors have large snakes."

"I heard Tarik has a large snake," one woman confided. "The staff of Ra. It creates sunshine in a woman's secret tunnel."

Giggles accompanied the remark. Fatima felt a telltale blush burn her cheeks. Her gaze shot to Nadia; a large purplish mark on her shoulder stood out in stark relief.

Her gaze met Nadia's in the mirror. "Nadia, did you hurt yourself? That's a nasty bruise."

The blushing bride glanced away. "It's a love bite."

Salah must have very big teeth. Fatima dried her face, murmured congratulations, and fled before anyone else made ribald remarks about Tarik's sexual prowess. As she neared the ceremonial tent, she noticed the flaps were up.

The council. But they weren't to meet until later. The Majli, the council of elders, met with the sheikh on matters such as warfare or the breaking of tribal rules. Slowing to a shuffle, Fatima strained to hear. She caught the words, "Jauzi," and "scouting party." Her blood chilled. The Riders of the Jauzi. They lived in the Western Desert and crossed the Nile to raid other desert tribes.

Jabari spotted her and beckoned. Fatima stepped out of her sandals, entered, bowed before him and the Magli.

"Fatima, have you seen my son?"

Remembering her twin riding off with Tarik and

Muhammad earlier, Fatima thought of Tarik's bedroom activities. She stammered some excuse about seeing him heading toward Amarna. Jabari's gaze remained steady. "Fetch them for me immediately. Tarik needs to be here, not dallying in the sands."

Fatima bowed and left, silently cursing the sheikh's son. Burdened with chores, she only wanted to finish and race off to practice. For Fatima had a secret: In England, she hadn't merely attended balls. Her grandfather knew such activities bored her. She'd done many other things, things that would never be allowed for a Khamsin maiden.

Storming off to where the horses grazed, she saddled her mare and rode off. Fatima tracked hoofprints as her father had taught. Irritated, she realized they led toward the village. Was Tarik heading back there for another tryst?

Cradled by intricate artwork in the enormous hall of Ay's tomb, Tarik sat cross-legged on the ground. Lamplight cast flickering shadows over the ancient walls. His hands cradled the sketchbook as his Guardian turned the pages of a medical textbook. Nearby, Muhammad made notes as he studied an ancient Egyptian text. Unlike most warriors, who learned to read hieroglyphics from an early age, his cousin struggled with the language of the old ones. Tarik recently had begun tutoring him.

This abandoned tomb in the towering cliffs of Amarna felt cool and comforting as a stone womb. Tarik sought refuge here when he needed to escape, and to think.

My sister could have died last night!

Tarik's fingers tightened into white-knuckled fists. Beneath the pressure, his pencil threatened to snap. He drew in a deep breath. In a minute, his normal aplomb returned. Silence but for the scratching of his pencil settled over him in a comfortable calm. Tarik released his inner turmoil in long sweeping strokes.

No one would discover this secret. Childhood taunts echoed cruelly in his memory. Tarik, Tarik the gold-haired sheikh! Always so different. His blond hair made him stand out like a towering palm on a sand dune. Other children mocked and whispered about his hair, that he was not as dark as they.

He hid his feelings as he hid his art, silenced the whispers from other boys by toughening his outer shell. Walk with pride, his father told him. *You are my son.* Oh, he walked with pride, but pride did not soften the longing to be like everyone else. Only three of his playmates never treated him differently: Asad, his tough, boyish sister, and Muhammad.

Tarik stopped drawing, moved by the memory. He glanced at his Guardian and cousin. "Asad, Muhammad—thank you."

They glanced up. Asad looked bemused. "For what?"

"For being my friends."

His Guardian grinned. "Your father pays me well."

Muhammad bent his dark head over the text. "If you teach me how to read this papyrus, cousin, I'll stay your friend."

Picking up his pencil again, Tarik resumed work. And contemplation. In his youth, a new attention finally came Tarik's way. Girls. At twelve, they'd begun noticing him. Gaggles of girls flocked around him. Offers to fetch him water and curry his mare shouldered aside the stinging insults. What caused contempt among men caused admiration among women. His golden locks attracted them. Tarik had set out to prove himself.

He'd lost his virginity at thirteen.

He'd killed his first enemy at fifteen.

As he'd begun proving his valor, respect flowed. Hard-earned respect, it did not flow as freely as camel's milk, but came sluggish, a thick stream of honey. Grudgingly given.

At Oxford, he'd become a celebrity. Tarik had told fascinated classmates he was a wealthy prince of Egypt, Asad his loyal cousin. He'd dressed English. Spoke fluent English. Girls whipped their heads around to stare when he passed. Their generous offers to share his bed were graciously accepted.

Now, finally, he commanded respect. His prodigious height made other warriors look puny. His scimitar was lethal. And with only the flick of a finger, Tarik commanded the attention of a legion of comely Khamsin maids eager to do his bidding. The men at last deferred to him as they did his father.

But they would no longer if they saw this. He glanced down at his sketching. The taunts would begin anew. Tarik the artist sheikh! Men did not draw. Certainly his father did not. Khamsin sheikhs were rugged. Artists were soft. Womanly.

Womanly as Fatima was womanly. Tarik sketched, calming himself as he remembered Fatima's laughter. She tormented him, this dream vision, this girl turned woman, this woman wanting to be a man. He burned for her as he'd done for no other.

One gentle press of her lips to his cheek last night had ignited long-tamped fires. Tarik clenched his jaw. His pencil raced over the textured paper, capturing the wistful look in her eyes, the wind hooking her hair in its tight fist as she sat like an ancient queen upon her mare.

Thundering hoofbeats cautioned him to stop drawing. Abandoning his pad, he ran to the tomb's entrance, squinting at the brilliant sunlight. Fatima was bent over her mare, midnight locks flowing behind her, riding toward them. Tarik barked a warning to his friends. Grabbing his drawings, he ran between the columns to the tomb's corner and the steps leading down to the unfinished burial chamber. He buried his artwork beneath a loose rock on the stone steps.

Muhammad extinguished the lamp. The men left the tomb just as footfalls sounded on the rough ground outside. Tarik gave a cool, amused smile as Fatima approached.

"Spying on me again, Fatima?" he drawled.

Her sparkling green gaze, as refreshing as river water, traveled the length of him. "I have better things to do. What are you doing all the way out here? Your father called a meeting of the council and he needs you right away."

She glanced at her twin, who shifted the heavy book beneath his arm. "Asad, are you reading medical textbooks again? You want to be a doctor. Why didn't you remain in England and study? You have a real talent for healing. It should be used."

"A talent my destiny doesn't call me to use. Tima, we've had this discussion before. Stop bringing it up. Understood?"

Her quivering lower lip slid out. Ah, Fatima. She wore her emotions on her face as some women wore henna.

She caught Tarik studying her.

"Will you stop staring at me, Tarik?"

They descended the cliff to their waiting horses. Fatima swung up using the pommel, a graceful move that hid a man's strength behind that slender womanly body. He admired the curved arch of her spine, her chin's proud thrust. Slender thighs hugged the horse. Heat bellowed into his groin as he imagined those lovely legs, naked and squeezed against his waist.

51

Giving him an exasperated look, she settled her feet into the stirrups. "Now what? Ready to criticize the way I ride?"

He gave her a slow, suggestive smile. Her brother and Muhammad were out of earshot. "It's not as skilled as how I do it."

"My experience with horses equals your own."

"I am not talking about horses, Tima. I am referring to a different kind of mount." Deliberately he let his voice trail off, allowing her imagination to fill in the rest. Judging from the sudden rose staining her cheeks, she did.

"I could demonstrate, if you like," he offered, enjoying the wildfire flaming across her face.

"Save the bragging, Tarik. It will never happen. I will never lie beneath you."

Both fell silent as Asad and Muhammad led the horses over.

Oh, I would mount you in a minute, my sweet, and make those green eyes of yours spark with passion, not anger. Tarik flexed his shoulders, eyeing his mare.

"Watch this, Tima." He grabbed a fistful of mane and leapt upon his mare. "The trick to mounting is all control. I am firm yet gentle. My mount recognizes her master's hand and will yield to my expert touch," he said, patting Alya's whithers.

Thunder clouded Fatima's lovely brow. Tarik chuckled, knowing she wouldn't dare blast him before her twin.

"Yes, you definitely have a masterful touch. Wouldn't you agree, Tima?" Asad asked, clueless to the byplay between them. Tarik roared with laughter as Fatima sputtered, spun her horse around and galloped back toward camp.

Her pique over Tarik's teasing soon faded. When Asad and her father stopped by for a lunch of fresh milk, dates and yogurt, Fatima seized her chance. She pulled Asad outside.

"Asad, what happened with Tarik's announcement?"

Mirth filled her brother's eyes. "It was a rare moment, Tima! You should have seen old Ibrahim when Tarik told them about the Model T. He looked ready to explode. Tarik spent a long time questioning Ibrahim, asking about his concerns. When the old man finally stopped talking, Tarik told him how much money he'd made the tribe, and how many more weapons we can purchase now." Asad gave the sheikh's tent a rueful glance. "Tarik is clever. He wormed out of him the old man's biggest worry and swapped out a reason to accept the motor car. Money for weapons! The council is worried we lack sufficient rifles."

Weapons. "What enemies do we fear?" Fatima asked her twin.

Assuring himself their father still remained in the tent, Asad dropped his voice. "Our men reported fifteen Riders of the Jauzi are crossing the Nile into the Eastern Desert. Jabari wants a scouting party to pinpoint their location."

"Who will be in the scouting party?"

"Thirty of us, including Father and Tarik. Jabari wants us to leave this afternoon, for the Riders are swift."

A frown creased her brother's smooth brow. Fatima squeezed his arm. "Asad, do you think they'll mount a direct attack?"

"Jabari says such a small band will not risk it. They are probably searching for our horse-breeding grounds to steal stock. And I have a more pressing matter. One of our best ewes is in labor, and I promised to help with the birth. She could die." Excitement flashed over his face. "I have ether and a scalpel that a medical student gave me. It's my one chance to perform a Cesarean sec-

tion. I've wanted to do it since seeing the operation performed in England."

Fatima frowned. "Asad, what if there is a battle?"

Distress shadowed his face. Asad clearly wrestled with
his decision. "Tima, can I trust you with a secret?" Seeing
her nod, he continued. "I want to be a healer, not a warrior. I mentioned it once to Father, who only replied it's
my duty as first-born son to be Tarik's Guardian."

A sudden idea blossomed. "Trade places with me,
Asad. I'll ride out and fight the Riders."

Her brother's hand clamped over her mouth. Asad
looked about frantically. "Are you mad?" he hissed.
"Saying such things will bring down the council's wrath
on you! It's against our code of honor for a woman to
even carry weapons."

Fatima removed her twin's hand. "An archaic code,
and Jabari knows it."

"A code he cannot seem to change. Not now." Asad
rubbed his forehead. "I think he's hoping Tarik will.
Jabari seems to be tired lately. Tired of fighting those
old she-goats, tired of what the war did to all of us. It was
difficult, Tima."

If she didn't take this chance, another might not
arise. All her hopes stood to vanish like desert rain.

"Asad, trade places with me. I've been practicing—
with Grandpa's approval. I'm an excellent shot as well."

"The council—"

"Those whining old she-goats will never find out. I
promise, I will resume becoming a meek Khamsin
maiden once I have had one chance to be a warrior."

Asad wrinkled his brow. "Why do you so want to
fight?"

She drew in a breath, hesitant at sharing the answer
because it had been kept hidden for so long in her
heart. It wasn't that she enjoyed fighting. But ever since

she was little, she had dreamt of becoming a Khamsin warrior and an equal to the men. She had known she was capable, and skilled. And the lowest warrior commanded more respect than a woman.

Fatima dragged in a deep breath and locked gazes with her twin. "Because I need to prove that I can do it." He glanced over his shoulder again, then signaled with his gaze. Fatima made an innocent remark about picking fresh mint for mutton stew as their father approached.

"Talk of dinner so soon after lunch?" Ramses rested a hand on his son's shoulder. "Come, Asad, they are expecting us."

"Burnt mutton. You know I can't cook," Fatima muttered, resentfully watching them walk toward the ceremonial tent. Men's problems. Men's roles. While she was to fuss over washing laundry and burning dinner.

Fatima stared after them, dreams of becoming a warrior turning to ash. She slogged back to her tent, smiled a hello to her mother, and ducked into her room.

There she fell on her knees on the bright orange-and-red carpet before a large cedar trunk. Opening it, she dug past clothing and books. The silver scimitar lay next to her dagger in its metal sheath. Her grandfather had given it to her while in England. It had belonged to her grandmother's Egyptian father.

The blade slid from its decorative silver sheath with a sigh. Fatima caressed the hilt, admiring the intricate Islamic runes. She stood, twirling the scimitar, imagining snarling enemy faces rushing forward. Thrusting and slashing, she heard their echoing cries of wounded defeat. Fatima warbled her own silent war cry, whipping the sword around her head.

How unfair! Asad itched to practice his medical skills, while she itched to practice her swordsmanship. The idea of switching places filled her with excitement and fear. If the deception were discovered, the council would punish her. Her father would be livid. Yet the risks were small compared to the adventure of a lifetime.

Fatima sheathed her scimitar and laid it carefully back in the trunk. She dug farther down and removed her other prized possession: a gift from a British colonel enamored with her. His ardor had faded after discovering she was a better shot.

Fatima examined the Colt pistol. She pointed it at the tent wall, pretending an enemy Rider stood before her.

"Bam," she said softly.

Asad returned as she later churned milk into butter in a goatskin bag. Her twin clearly struggled with a decision. "We're riding out soon. I came to say good-bye."

Fatima remained quiet. She knew her twin.

"Tima, I don't want to leave. That ewe will die. She's suffering. I know we will have to shoot her if I do not stay."

"Then I must take your place," Fatima said simply.

"No," he stated, but he sounded unconvinced.

"Only you can save the ewe. I'll be riding with twenty-nine other men. What could happen? It's probably just a simple ride into the desert. I'll go in your place."

Her twin fingered the long, black curls tumbling past his shoulders. "Tima, it will never work. Your face! Your hair is too long. And your voice. And your . . ." Scowling, he looked at her breasts.

She frowned, twisting her long hair up into a bun. "We'll ride veiled into the desert. I can bind my chest, arrange my hair so it is about the same length as yours, loop it up under the turban like so." Fatima demonstrated. "And I'll keep my mouth shut."

"The last would be a miracle," Asad replied, grinning.

"My skill with the scimitar is good, and my riding . . ."

"Is better than mine. As is your swordsmanship." He

sighed and rubbed his black beard. "But you've never been tested in battle. What will happen if someone finds out?"

"Who would find out? And this isn't a battle, just a scouting trip. Besides, I have a secret weapon." Pulling him into her room, she went to the trunk, lifted her Colt from its hiding place. "See? And I'm an expert shot."

Asad examined the handgun and whistled. "Damn. Where'd you get this? The few pistols we have are Webleys."

"The Colt is better. More accurate and easy to handle."

He handed it back. "My sister, the weapons expert," he muttered. "Instead of collecting shoes and jewelry, she collects guns."

"Don't you want to save your poor, suffering sheep?"

The last remark did it. Asad heaved a deep sigh, indicating defeat. "I'll fetch you spare clothing."

He ducked out and into his room as she removed her indigo kuftan, her yellow trousers and the yellow kamis shirt. Naked, she bound her ample breasts with strips of white sheet. The curtain jerked back slightly as her brother tossed her the uniform of the Khamsin warriors of the wind. The indigo binish, trousers, stockings and shirt were slightly large. Fatima padded her slender shoulders and dressed.

A moment later she was ready. She whispered that it was so, and he came back inside bearing a roll of indigo cloth. Fatima looped up her hair. Asad wrapped the turban around her head, leaving one end trailing down.

"Now tuck the veil across your face," he ordered.

Fatima did, and Asad followed suit. He steered her over to a mirror hanging from her tent pole. The twins stared at their reflections. With the veils concealing their lower faces, they were nearly identical—but for a slight difference in their eyes. Fatima's emerald ones sparkled with excitement. Doubt clouded Asad's green and amber gaze.

They tugged off their veils.

"I can stuff your boots with fabric and I'll be as tall," Fatima mused. She was breathless, could hardly believe her longtime dream of acting the warrior was coming true.

She did as she'd suggested, then put the scimitar and dagger into her belt. She loaded her Colt and shoved it there as well. "Do you carry a Webley? I don't want anyone noticing the Colt."

"I doubt anyone will notice it's a different pistol." Asad took up a rifle and several cartridges. "Remember, guns are the very last resort. Khamsin warriors are men of honor who fight with swords to see each others' eyes. Now, Tima . . . I need to see you handle the sword."

She gave a quick demonstration and felt a proud satisfaction at seeing her twin's eyes widen. "Amazing," he murmured.

He gave her some advice: "Don't speak. Grunt a lot. It's good that I'm known for being quiet while riding into battle. If you do engage the enemy, watch Tarik carefully. He tends to charge recklessly into the fray. Let Father set the pace. If Tarik attempts to take control, all you need to do is this." And to her embarrassed shock, her twin reached down, clapped a hand over his crotch and grunted. He grinned. "It's an old trick of mine. It tells Tarik he's trying too hard to assert his manhood and is being ruled by his . . . never mind."

"You want me to grab myself?" She asked, incredulous.

"You must. Otherwise Tarik will suspect. Try it."

Fatima felt a flush steal up her neck. She reached down awkwardly and clutched her groin with a squeak. Asad sighed. "That sounded more like a sheep's fart. Deeper in your throat."

She glared. "Perhaps if I stuffed my trousers with fabric and had something to grab I'd sound more like a man!"

Trying again, she felt despair. Asad looked uneasy. "Well, maybe Tarik will behave this time."

Asad removed the gun from his shoulder and handed it over. "Tima, I don't know about this. . . ."

"I do. Go save that sheep." She gave her twin a quick kiss and tucked the veil across her face, then left the tent.

Fatima sat on a nervous Barirah, digging her knees expertly into the horse's side to keep the beast from dancing. Leading the group, Ramses rode his own lovely black mare, Maysa. On Fatima's left, Tarik sat astride Alya. She had the sinking feeling he could see past her linen bindings to her breasts. Yet he said nothing.

As they set out across the desert, Fatima concentrated on controlling her mount. Blue and yellow tassels swayed with the animal's impatient dancing. Wind slapped her binish, teasing the veil draped across her lower face.

They rode south in silence, each warrior concentrating on the task ahead. Tarik rode beside his cousin Muhammad, the two talking quietly.

Jagged mountains rose on either side as they traversed the plateau between the Arabian mountains. Steep cliffs of granite, volcanic and metamorphic rocks nestled in mountain ranges to their west. Fatima loved this land. Some called it harsh. Inhospitable. Barren. But those people failed to see the open desert's stark beauty, the solitary ruggedness that was her tribe's proud heritage. They did not see, as she did now, the life flourishing in the desert. A snake slithered along toward a rock and vanished. Overhead a bird cried.

The few friends she'd made in England couldn't appreciate the majestic beauty of the mountains dominating this arid landscape, nor understand how the dry river beds, the wadis, were givers of life. Wadis snaked through the Eastern Desert from the Nile Valley to the

Red Sea. In ancient times they served as trade routes, leading the way to the Red Sea.

Her few friends had laughed in disbelief when Fatima mentioned flash floods in the desert. During infrequent storms, torrents capable of drowning a sleeper gushed through the wadis. Water effervesced into the pebbled sand, creating rich veins of vegetation. The Khamsin tapped into these underground pools.

Her friends had never experienced the sheer beauty of an Egyptian night sky, and the dazzling array of stars that her ancestors thought were transformed souls of the dead. Fatima herself found comfort in that ancient thought. When she lifted a tent wall to peer at the night sky, it reassured her to think her ancestors were looking down and protecting her.

Her father broke into her thoughts as he talked about the Riders of the Jauzi. Cloaked all in dark brown, they had reputations as fierce fighters. They had rifles, but like the Khamsin, fought primarily with swords. Fatima glanced down at the rifle stored securely in her saddle, within easy reach.

Finishing his speech, her father began singing, a habit on long rides in the desert. Fatima listened with admiration. Confidence filled her. She could pull this off. Just then, her two youngest brothers appeared on her right.

"So, Asad, any more stories you wish to tell us of living in England?" Radi asked.

"Yes, tell us again how pretty the English women are," Fakhir, sixteen, said eagerly.

Tarik looked over at them. He seemed kingly, sitting upon his mare as if he ruled the sands. Fatima's breath hitched. How could she fool him?

He spoke. "Pale-skinned English women can never compare to the beauty of our Egyptian women, with their grace, style and sweetness. Our women are like rare pearls, and should be cherished as such," he stated. "Do you not agree, Asad?"

Fatima nodded, surprised by Tarik's praise.

He stared at her. "How interesting. Only last week you told me English women easily rivaled Egyptian women, what with their creamy complexions. And you kept reminding me how your mother is half English, and how I insulted her with that comment."

Blood drained from Fatima's face. Tarik regarded her with cool, calm black eyes. She gave an indifferent shrug.

"Then again, Asad, maybe you're right. English women are beautiful, with their pale skin and rosy cheeks. I've enjoyed sharing their beds."

Oh, the arrogant ass! Fatima wished for another stone to fling at him.

"English women are more demure, gracious and well mannered. Unlike your wayward, rebellious sister. They mind their place and have no grandiose aspirations . . . aspirations of becoming warriors."

Fatima's heart dropped into her stomach. She swallowed hard, glad for the veil hiding her distraught expression.

"What do you think, Asad?"

A deep grunt was her only response.

Tarik leaned forward in his saddle. "You sound odd today, my friend. Are you well?" Amusement danced in his gleaming black gaze.

Fatima shrugged again, while silently begging him to stop chattering. Could he possibly know they had switched places? Fatima raised her gaze to the brilliant blue skies and burning yellow sun. *Let him be struck temporarily mute. Please.*

"Tarik, tell us more of the Model T. Will you teach us to drive?" Radi asked.

Diverted, Tarik patiently answered Fatima's brother's questions. She exhaled slowly, her shoulders losing their rigid tension.

Ramses led the two columns of riders. Tarik nudged his own horse into a trot, pulling up to his side. Just as Asad predicted, he was endangering himself.

Fatima urged her mare forward, next to the sheikh's son. Giving a loud grunt, she clapped a hand on her crotch. Men! Tarik's eyes widened, then crinkled as he grinned beneath his veil. But he dropped back into place, letting Ramses lead.

This crotch-grabbing business worked! Cheered, Fatima concentrated on scanning the jagged mountains surrounding them.

Within an hour, they approached the twists and turns of a deep wadi. Ramses held up his hand to halt. Every hair on Fatima's nape saluted the air. She glanced at the outcropping of boulders, sensing what her father knew as well: The enemy was near.

Ramses lifted a pair of binoculars. Fatima knew he looked in the wrong direction. The Riders would not gallop across the open plain; they were foxy, cunning, and were known to surprise an enemy by hiding in the . . .

Rocks to the east. Kicking her mount, she galloped to her father's side, grabbed his arm and pointed at the narrow canyon. He lowered his binoculars. She lowered her voice to what she hoped would pass for Asad's. "They are hiding deep in the wadi."

Her father flashed her a quizzical look. "What is wrong with your voice? You sound hoarse. Are you sick?"

Fatima nodded.

Ramses shifted in his saddle and studied the rocks. He tucked his binoculars back into his saddlebag with a nod.

"Yes, I see them, hiding there. I know this wadi. It dead ends a few yards from the entrance. They're trapped. Dismount!" he called.

The men did so. They unsheathed their scimitars, touching their hearts and then their lips in the Khamsin gesture summoning honor before battle. From here, they would proceed on foot.

Unease filled Fatima. The towering limestone walls squeezed them tight. A perfect place for an ambush. Every sense went on alert. Adrenaline surged through her veins.

Gripping her scimitar in a sweaty hand, she recalled all she'd learned from spying on her father and her twin. Show no emotions in battle. Let calmness rule you. Keep alert. Watch for your enemy's weak spots and exploit them. She ran all these through her mind just as her father released a blood-curdling war cry, and a band of brown-cloaked men charged.

Fatima's jaw dropped. Their scouts had reported a small band of fifteen. A wall of perhaps fifty warriors rushed toward them. Her palms went clammy.

Ramses raced forward, his war party charging behind him. Fatima sprinted next to Tarik, desperately trying to keep pace with his long-legged stride. Breath wheezed in and out of her lungs in huge spurts. She had forgotten his swiftness.

The two parties clashed.

A Rider appeared on her left and swung. She ducked and retaliated clumsily. Her sword clanked against her opponent's. His lean brown face sported a grin, showed yellowed teeth. She knew what he thought of her: a boy, unfit for battle. He was half right.

How foolish to think she could be a warrior! She was a mere woman. Everything she'd taught herself vanished. This was real battle. Men died.

Her frantic gaze whipped around to find her father.

Ramses was snarling with righteous fury, attacking two Riders with one blade. Admiration and love for him restored Fatima's confidence. *I am the daughter of Ramses bin Asad Sharif, Guardian of the Ages, second in command, and the fiercest fighter of our tribe!*

She gave a roar—admittedly kittenish—in imitation of her father. Then Fatima drove her scimitar point forward just as her opponent lifted his scimitar for his killing blow. It speared him between the ribs, and she released a high-pitched Khamsin war call. The Rider groaned and toppled, clutching his stomach. Blood stained her sword. The heavy coppery odor filled her nostrils and Fatima struggled for air. Nausea knotted her insides. She dragged in a calming breath. No emotions. Kill or be killed.

Sand kicked up, creating dust clouds as the warriors clashed. Chaotic cries echoed through the rocky canyon. Men were screaming, groaning, dying. Steel clanking against steel. Sweat rolled down Fatima's temples, stinging her eyes. She raised her blade. Droplets fell like scarlet tears staining the sand.

No fear. I am my father's daughter.

Charging forward with every last ounce of courage, she engaged another warrior, feinted, slashed. He fell. The man's agonized scream rang in her ears as he writhed on the sand.

She searched frantically for Tarik. He was magnificent, fighting with ferocity equal to her father's, dispatching men like sheep. But shockingly, she saw that his back was unprotected. A Rider charged forward, drawing back his blade. Fatima sprinted up and stabbed him in the thigh. The Rider toppled with a groan.

Tarik fell. He recovered in a graceful roll and sprang back to his feet. But as he clashed with a new opponent, a thick cluster of Riders shifted position, all aiming for Tarik. Like a curtain lifting, their thoughts blazed across Fatima's mind.

The White Falcon. He is ours. Kill the sheikh's son.

A surge of power flowed through her, along with absolute calm and absolute knowledge. The Riders had lured them here to kill Tarik. This was no random ambush, but a trap.

Dust swirled everywhere as she raced toward Tarik. Fatima screamed out in warning. "Get your rifles. Protect Tarik!"

"We are men of honor," her father yelled.

"Then you will lose the sheikh's son, for he is their true target!"

Eight brown-cloaked Riders had charged Tarik, already backed against a rocky canyon wall. He raised his weapon as the enemy rushed forward.

Fatima screeched and, mindless of danger, raced forward, pulling out her Colt. Never had her mind been so clear, her body so sure and strong. No head shots. Those were too difficult; she would attempt crippling shots. Whirling, she emptied her cartridge into the group rushing the sheikh's son. Five fell. Screams of pain sounded as they fell writhing to the sand.

The three remaining Riders fell upon Tarik, vultures on carrion. His sword swirled, parrying the rain of descending scimitars. One grazed his arm. Blood flowed. Two more Riders appeared on his left. Fatima dumped her empty gun, sprang in front of Tarik. Scimitar lowered, dagger in her left hand, she charged, singing out the Khamsin war cry. She fell to the ground, rolled and sprang, intending to engage both.

But as she raised her weapons, gunfire crackled. Blood sprayed her as bullets riddled both men. Relief flashed through her. She had not killed. Not yet.

More shots rang out. Blue smoke filled the air, the thud of falling bodies. A shrill Jauzi cry echoed through the canyon. *Die with honor!*

Amid thunderous hoofbeats, piercing screams

echoed everywhere as the Riders retreated, galloping away. Eyes watering, Fatima squinted, gazing around anxiously for the sheikh's son.

Tarik stood, bloodied sword raised, gazing at the dead men at his feet, felled by Ramses' gun. He lifted his gaze to her. For a moment fear flickered there. Then that vanished, replaced by his usual aplomb. Crimson stained his binish sleeve, showing a deep gash where one Rider's blade had bit.

Her sword and dagger falling to the rocky ground with a clatter, Fatima rushed to his side, clucking anxiously at his wound. Taking the silk sash from her belt, she tied it around Tarik's arm. Over the top of his veil, his dark eyes regarded her silently. Her fingers rested, trembling, on his arm. The bastards had hurt him! And they wanted him dead. Why?

Tarik wiped his blade and sheathed it. He picked up her abandoned sword, dagger and Colt. His eyes narrowed as he handed them over.

"You dropped your weapons, Asad. Have you forgotten our rules of honor? A Khamsin warrior never lowers his guard, nor drops his weapons, leaving himself defenseless. Ever."

Cold dread filled her. Her hand trembled as she wiped both blades and sheathed them.

Suddenly the air cleared. The others approached. Her father ran to the Riders on the ground.

"They are all dead," he said softly. "By their own hand."

They'd killed themselves? Deeply disturbed, Fatima stared. Die with honor, rather than be taken prisoner: Was this a code of the Riders? Or had they been sworn to silence?

Slowly her tribesmen encircled her. Like a lamb surrounded by wolves, she felt very alone, and very small.

"You saved Tarik's life. And that was brilliant double

blade execution," Radi said slowly. "I don't understand, Asad. How did you learn it? You can't usually use your left hand."

Oh God. Asad never could perform the double-blade move. Her gaze shot to her father, who tugged off his veil, staring.

Tarik tugged off his own veil. "Yes, Asad. How miraculous you have equal use of your left hand. Just like your sister." Intent glittered in his black eyes. "We should remove our veils now. As we always do after victory."

Fatima felt her heart drop to her knees. Asad had never mentioned this. Remove her veil? Her trembling hand shot protectively to the cloth shielding her identity.

The men all removed their veils, crowding around her. Suddenly they were no longer the same warm, friendly faces of her tribesmen. Cornered, she shot Tarik a pleading look. No bargaining. She must escape. If they found out her identity . . .

She backed off, whirled. Before she could flee, Tarik pounced. He pulled at her shoulder, spinning her around and then yanking off her veil and turban. The long black mass of her raven hair spilled in a tangle of curls to her waist.

Shocked gasps filled the air. Her father's jaw dropped. Her gaze wildly shot to Tarik, who held her indigo turban in his hand. He flashed a satisfied smile, as if he'd known all along.

"Fatima."

Chapter Five

Fear clouded her green gaze, but he'd known it was she all along. The way she rode: Asad sat in the saddle stiffly; Fatima had a natural grace. The skittish way the mare acted and the immediate calming: It always took Asad several minutes to control his horse before setting out. Those guttural grunts: Well, she'd almost fooled him with the crotch-grabbing gesture.

And her eyes: In the harsh sunlight, they sparkled with challenge. Green river grass tossed by the Nile. Of course the final clue, the double blade execution, had erased all doubt.

Satisfaction at unveiling her turned into cold fury. How dare she ride into danger! Anger and protective instinct surged through him. What if a Rider's blade had pierced her breast?

I would die, he thought frantically. I would die.

Tormented by the image of her life blood staining the thirsty sands, he drew in a ragged breath.

"I should turn you over my knee and rap your bottom for attempting such a stunt," he grated out.

Despite looking shaken, she courageously lifted her chin. "I doubt you'd have the audacity to try."

"Don't tempt me," he said.

Ramses was too stunned to react. His mouth kept opening and closing as if he could not force words between his lips. Finally he croaked out the same word Tarik had. "Fatima?"

She gave a weak smile. "Yes, Papa?" Her trembling voice did not erase the fury darkening the man's face. Muscles in his chiseled jaw tightened.

"Fatima, ride back with your brothers. Immediately. You will go to our tent and wait for my return. Is that understood?"

Fatima blanched. "Yes, Papa," she whispered.

Ramses turned to nineteen-year-old Kamal, standing straight and quiet. "Kamal, find Asad and take him to our tent immediately."

Surrounded by her four brothers, Fatima was marched off. Tarik watched them all ride away.

Troubled, he silently regarded Ramses. His father's Guardian was not one to trifle with. Ramses was powerfully built, with a broad chest and thickly muscled arms the size of palm tree trunks. His father's best warrior could intimidate the most ruthless enemy with one menacing look. Ramses had an intense protective streak, and was ferocious in his duty to guard those under his care. He expected Asad to be the same. Fatima had violated everything Ramses honored.

Why would she risk it?

Even more troubling was Fatima's instinct of the attack on him. Her Sight had saved his life. But why would this ragged band of fierce but poor Bedouins attack him? They gained nothing by killing him. Unless . . . Tarik gripped his scimitar hilt, his jaw tightening.

Shock twisted all the men's faces. Finally, gray-bearded Musab spoke. "A woman fighting as a warrior.

She must be possessed by a jinn. She has violated our honor and must be punished." He made a sign against the Evil Eye.

Ramses' amber eyes blazed. He took a threatening step toward the older warrior. "She is my daughter, Musab. I alone will deal with her. No one else. Do not insult her again or you will face my wrath."

Haydar, Ibrahim's grandson and an opinionated warrior of twenty-one, chimed in. "I agree with Musab. What woman would don a warrior's garb and fight? We swear oaths to protect women. What if other females wish to take up the sword as well?" He turned to the others. "Do we wish all Khamsin maidens to fight? I for one, do not. Whom will I choose for a wife, then, if our women all become warriors?"

Approving murmurs greeted his words, and turmoil flashed in Ramses' amber gaze. Bristling, Tarik fisted his hands. "Quiet, Haydar."

Haydar's large brown eyes narrowed. "I honor the laws guiding our men and women. Fatima does not. She has broken our sacred code."

Tarik narrowed his gaze. "This is not a matter for us to dispute. And have you forgotten? She did save my life. I'd be dead if not for Fatima."

"Allah forbid. I would hire a legion of women for that not to happen," Ramses said quietly.

"I as well," Muhammad echoed. He shot Haydar a level look. "Don't insult my cousin, Haydar, or the only daughter of Ramses, our greatest warrior. Fatima has a gift we must not ignore."

Haydar muttered a sullen apology and stared at the sand. The lovestruck man had asked for Nadia's hand in marriage, but Tarik's sister had rejected him for Salah. Since then, a bitter Haydar had acted cold toward all of Tarik's family. Tarik resolved to watch the young man more closely.

Ramses cast a worried glance at Tarik. Carefully, he unwrapped the makeshift bandage Fatima had secured. "The bleeding has slowed," he said. "It is not very deep. Still, consult with Katherine. She has a salve that heals wounds." Then, straightening his shoulders, the older warrior looked Tarik squarely in the eye. "I am deeply sorry for my daughter serving as your Guardian, Tarik. I do not know what caused her to act this way. She has never been so defiant."

Tarik merely nodded. Ramses probably felt as confused as he did. Had it been Asad, there would be much congratulations offered. Pride, not anger, would shine on Ramses's face.

Yet Asad lacked the Sight, which had clearly saved his bottom, Tarik realized ruefully. But what did that make Tima? A warrior? A woman? Where did she fit?

No women were more honored or loved than Khamsin women. Warriors took one wife and recited vows of love and fidelity they took as seriously as their oaths to serve the tribe. They protected their women with the same ferocity extended in battle.

Women were expected to love their husbands with equal intensity, bear them children, care for the family and obey their husbands just as daughters obeyed their fathers. Women did not carry weapons. They certainly did not dress as warriors and kill men. Fatima had upset a carefully managed balance that had sustained the tribe for more than three thousand years. She'd firmly broke the tradition. Ramses's only daughter!

Focusing on Fatima pushed aside his earlier fear. When the riders had charged him as one, cold terror filled him. They'd planned to kill him. Only him. What had made him the target? Did they hate Jabari so much as to murder his heir? Tarik doubted it. The Riders were known to raid for livestock, food and rifles. They coveted money, not power.

Money. Of course. He swore beneath his breath.

Ramses glanced at the bodies of the dead Jauzi littering the sand, then gave him an admiring glance. "Fierce fighting, Tarik. Your father will be proud."

Shrugging to hide his feelings, Tarik placed his hands on his hips. "If not for Tima's warning . . ." He tensed against the shudder snaking through him. "Your shots were accurate, as usual, my father's Guardian. As were your daughter's."

"Anyone can shoot. It takes a skilled warrior to fight with the sword."

I couldn't have done it. Not like Fatima. Not that you'll ever see me shoot a pistol. Tarik gave a stiff nod to hide his humiliation. Defended by a woman!

Yet what a woman, he mused.

Fatima's father grinned and slapped his unhurt shoulder. "You have your father's fighting skills—and you are as reckless and rush headfirst into danger much like Jabari. How many times have I had to be at his side, warning him not to take on all the enemy and leave none for us!"

Tarik laughed as Ramses grinned. "I fear Asad has the same challenge." His voice trailed off at the grief twisting the man's features. "We should return," he suggested gently.

His anger against Fatima intensified. How could she disgrace her father like this? Yet, he secretly admired her. How fierce she was in battle! It whetted his desire. Would she display the same passion in bed?

As he mounted his mare, Tarik wondered what fate awaited his childhood friend. Whatever it was, he didn't envy her.

The camp waited quietly for the rest of the scouting party to return. Fatima sat on a Persian carpet with her brothers.

Maybe I should have let the Jauzi kill me. Since they didn't, my father will.

People passed, glancing inside at the four grim-faced brothers and their sister. By now word must have spread. Automatically her brothers sat in front, shielding her from view. Although she suspected they did so as a matter of family honor, it filled her with gratitude. No inquisitive stares reached her.

At last Ramses arrived, hand securely on his sword hilt. Sweat soaked the edge of his turban, streaked down his brow. He barked an order to roll the flaps down. Fatima gulped. Oh dear. She was in for it now.

Her dust-ridden, blood-streaked younger brothers, looking upset, obeyed his order. They shuffled off to the side, out of the line of fire. Thanks, she told them silently. Last time I ever stick up for you.

Then Kamal entered, followed by her twin.

Asad, clad in a kamis shirt, hip-length indigo jubbe and cream trousers, stood before Ramses. Blood stained his shirt.

Ramses crossed his massive arms on his chest and leveled a piercing look at his son. To Fatima's growing dismay, she realized it would all be taken out on her twin. Not her.

"We have just returned from engaging the Riders of the Jauzi in battle. *Battle.* You were not there. Now, Asad," Ramses growled. "Explain the reason for your absence."

"I was helping to birth a sheep."

Fatima winced, seeing her father's incredulity.

"You neglected your duties for a *sheep?*"

"Both the lamb and the sheep were in danger of dying. I performed a cesarean section," Asad said quietly. "It was one of our best ewes and—."

The sharp crack of her father's open palm on his mouth cut off his words. Asad reeled back, staggering.

A phantom pain stung Fatima's own lips. Shame filled her. He'd hit her twin. Ramses never hit any of them. Never.

Except once, when Asad was seventeen. And again, it had been her fault.

She knew how hard that camel crop had felt on Asad. Fatima felt every strike in her heart. And after that, they'd sent her to England. *Women do not become warriors.*

"Have you taken leave of your senses? You let your sister take your place while you delivered a sheep? Do you realize what would have happened if she were injured or killed? She is not a Khamsin warrior. And what of your oath to protect Tarik?"

Her father's normally mild voice was a roar. Her younger brothers—even Kamal, who prided himself on his bravery—drew back.

But Asad remained stoic. Blood dripped from his torn lip. "Fatima wanted to prove she could be a warrior. Just as I always wanted to perform an operation. Father, I've told you before that I have a gift for medicine, yet I'm denied practicing it because I'm first-born and obligated to be Tarik's Guardian. Fatima and I both had the chance to fulfill a dream and we took it. I would never have agreed if I didn't think she could do it. I'd never place her in danger. I'd die first myself."

"She is a woman," Ramses growled. But he sounded uncertain.

"A mere technicality, Father."

Ramses's mouth became a tight slash. "The council will call a meeting. Never before has such a thing happened."

Cold fear squeezed Fatima's spine. "Papa, what do you think they'll do to me?" she whispered. Asad went to her, draped a comforting arm around her shoulder.

"Nothing, if I can help it," he said.

Ramses gave her a reassuring look. "Jabari will call a meeting of the Majli and ask our shaman's advice. Ahmed is wise, and discerning. We shall have to wait and see. But do not fear, sweetheart. I can assure you, you will not be punished." Her father pronounced this in a protective rumble, then glanced at her twin. "How is the lamb?" he asked in a milder tone.

Asad shrugged. "Alive. She will make it. The ewe is strong and in good health. I believe she can be bred again in time."

"Good. I am still upset with you, Asad, but it is no small thing you did today in using your talents. We will talk. Later. Right now I want time alone with your sister."

He gave a meaningful glance at all the brothers, who scampered to leave. Asad gave Fatima's shoulder a comforting squeeze.

Her heart's normal cadence began a double-time beat as her father motioned for her to sit on the carpet. Fatima lowered herself in a graceful move, sitting on her haunches. Her father sat cross-legged, palms on knees.

"Fatima . . ." Ramses sighed, rubbed his beard, bewilderment crossing his handsome face. She felt encouraged by his evaporating anger. "Why did you do it?"

"Asad needed to save that lamb. We are almost of equal height, and . . ."

"No." Her father made an abrupt cutting motion. She fell silent. "I want to know why you *chose* to do it. Life gives us all choices. You chose."

She summoned courage. "I knew I could succeed," Fatima said simply. "I had no doubts I could fight, if necessary."

"Knowing how to fight and actually fighting in a battle are two different matters. What if you had been injured? What if Tarik had died? Asad is Tarik's Guardian, and he has pledged his life in defense of him. It is a sacred oath, a matter of honor. Do not forget Tarik. He is our sheikh's son, and honor in battle is all he strives for. You shamed him. A woman saving his life!"

"Papa, I knew I could do this well."

His golden gaze, as fierce as a tiger's, softened. "You did save his life, my darling daughter. Had you not shouted at us to grab the rifles, Tarik would be dead."

A strangely oppressive air hovered in the room as she pondered his words. Her father sighed. "You have always been so different. Even as a little girl, you had an . . . aggressiveness. I blame myself for training you. I thought England would suppress these tendencies. I see I was wrong. And yet, how can I not be grateful for what you did today? Perhaps your powers are not being used correctly. Others should know this."

Panic filled her. It was one thing to be a warrior for a day, another to be displayed like a freak.

"Please, Papa. Don't make me stand before the whole tribe like some circus sideshow. It was bad enough in England at school, the girls always pointing and staring. I can't help my visions, and I hate how they already stare at me. Please, don't punish me for what I did. And I couldn't stand it if you noted me."

Ramses's face was creased by a tender smile. "Hate you? My beloved daughter, I love you. I always knew you would be different, from the moment your grandmother placed you in my arms. You looked up at me and my heart melted. I knew you had a difficult road ahead, Fatima. I tried to protect you, but destiny calls in a different direction. I only wish I could shoulder the pain that comes with this new direction you head. I do not want to see you get hurt."

He paused, and worry shadowed his eyes. "You must understand this, Fatima. Khamsin warriors are trained to protect our women with our very last breath. Your actions today challenged our ideals. Even if destiny calls you for a greater purpose, you have many obstacles to overcome. Many men will oppose you and say you should be a wife, not a warrior."

She dragged in a deep breath. "And you, Papa? How do you see me? As a warrior or a wife?"

His troubled gaze searched hers. "I will always see you as my little girl. Warrior or wife, my duty tells me that your powers call you for a higher purpose. But in my heart, I do not wish to see you get hurt, and as a warrior, you will."

Her lower lip trembled violently. "Oh, Papa . . ."

"You are a woman now, Fatima. If the council orders you to marry, you must accept it with grace and strength. But know this. I will stand by you, no matter what. You will always be my little girl," he said softly.

"Papa, I love you. But I'm scared. What will they do?"

"I do not know, Fatima," he said thickly. "I do not know."

As predicted, Jabari called a meeting of the Majli, the council of elders. Fatima and Asad were ordered to appear as well. Fatima dressed in an aqua and flame pink kuftan and tied a pink scarf around her head. Dressed once as a warrior, she now intended to show the old goats she was every inch a woman.

Stealing a last look in the gilded mirror, she studied her appearance. A round face filled with worry stared back at her. Fatima tried smiling. It came across as a cockeyed grin.

Ramses raised his eyebrows as she entered the tent's main room. "You think to fool Jabari with your dress, but his eyes are sharp. He sees beneath the outer layers and knows what counts is the heart." He took her hand as they walked outside. His grip was comforting.

Inside the black ceremonial tent, her stomach

pitched. Elderly men of great stature sat on rich Persian carpets. The air was balmy with pride, power and masculine force. Fatima bowed before the men, glanced at her father. Ramses motioned for her to sit before the horseshoe-shaped circle. She did so, squaring her shoulders.

Jabari sat, unsmiling, Tarik at his left side at the center of the horseshoe, Ahmed the shaman next to Tarik. The sheikh did not seem pleased.

A hand rested gently on Fatima's right shoulder. She looked up. Ramses had had not assumed his usual place at Jabari's right side. A tremendous rush of love and gratitude filled her. Then she felt another hand on her left shoulder and knew it was her twin. The two most important men in her life had abandoned their Guardian roles to shelter her. Her spirits soared.

I can do this. Confidence filled her.

Jabari rubbed his graying beard as he regarded her. "Our laws are clear. The Khamsin code of honor states that a woman cannot wield a weapon. And you know, Fatima, when these laws are broken, there must be punishment. If we do not uphold the law, we violate every principle that rules us." He paused, glancing at her father. "The punishment for violating that rule is public flogging. Ten lashes."

Fear coagulated in her stomach. Her father gave her shoulder a gentle squeeze.

"However, these circumstances are different. The law was formed long ago to instill in our warriors a responsibility to protect our women. And to prevent disorderly wives from hacking up their husbands in the middle of the night."

Jabari stopped talking. Why, he actually winked at her! Fear fled. All tension eased from her shoulders.

"The law is not absolute, for there is a clause that

states if a woman raises a scimitar to save a life, or to defend herself, the sheikh will decide the outcome. Because you saved the life of my son, I am dismissing this charge against you."

So great was her relief, her shoulders sagged and her body slumped. "Thank you," she whispered to Jabari.

"Tarik is my only son, the fruit of my loins. I am grateful to you, daughter of Ramses, for defending him in battle against those who would harm him."

The fruit of the sheikh's loins himself propped his chin upon one fist. "Yes, Fatima. I forgot to thank you. What a unique little warrior you make. Perhaps if you removed your shirt and showed the Riders your breasts, that also would have stopped them in their tracks," he drawled.

Asad snorted. "It would have stopped you faster."

"Asad," Ramses warned.

"I've seen how you look at her," Asad continued, ignoring his father. "I think if Fatima bared her breasts, you'd have risked the wrath of Osiris to cover her so no other man would gaze upon her. Only you."

Astonished, Fatima whipped her head around to regard her twin. A calm, knowing smile touched his mouth.

Tarik, on the other hand, looked murderous. His gaze burned into hers, as if he did envision her stripped. Heat stole over her body. Fatima resisted the urge to put hands to her burning face. Why did he cause such a reaction in her?

"Stop talking about me as if I weren't here," she grated out. "I would never do such a thing."

"Of course not," Tarik shot back. "You were too busy grabbing yourself, pretending to be a man."

"And I fooled everyone, did I not?" she taunted.

"Only because Asad trained you. I knew, Tima. And there was nothing down there for you to grab."

"Wouldn't you like to see for yourself?"

Tarik gave a thin smile. "I warn you. Don't tempt me."

The elders murmured among themselves. Definite chuckles sounded. But Ibrahim, the chief elder, looked exasperated. "Enough! Your quarreling hurts my ears. You two sound like a married couple squabbling," he barked.

Silent, Fatima glowered at Tarik. He folded his arms, offering a satisfied smile. He'd had the last word again, damn it!

Jabari gave them both a long, speculative look. Fatima's father squeezed her shoulder gently but firmly in warning.

I saved your life, you sorry jackass, she fumed, glaring at Tarik, whose bronzed face lacked expression. Fatima wished she could display such quiet control. Deep down, she knew he winced. Defended by a woman! How that must hurt. After all, Tarik had an image to uphold. Son of the powerful sheikh! Braver than brave! Women wrote poetry about his warrior prowess, his mighty strength.

Yes, it must be humiliating, having a woman save his life, she decided.

"Tarik, I am sorry if I upset you by saving your life," she offered, giving him a singularly innocent smile. "I know having a woman defend you in battle must be intimidating. Me, a mere woman with a large sword."

"Fatima!" her father muttered.

Tarik's eyes glittered. "No, Tima. I'm not in the least intimidated. My own sword is quite larger and it causes women to quake in their sandals when I wave it before them. Then, of course, they surrender quite graciously. And their contented cries assure me my sword has done its job."

The men around her chuckled. Crimson flushed her cheeks.

"Enough," Jabari said, rubbing his chin. "I want to address the other matter concerning Fatima." He looked at the shaman, who had sat quietly throughout the whole exchange. "In this I defer to you, Ahmed. Fatima saved Tarik through her Sight. What say you?"

Thin as a river reed, the shaman held a position of honor equaling Jabari's. His salt-and-pepper beard was longer than the other men's, and instead of a binish and trousers, he wore the traditional thobe most desert nomads preferred.

"I have meditated long and hard upon this. Fatima is gifted with the Sight. Such a gift goes to waste in a woman, since women are not warriors. But Fatima has her father's skills. She would serve our people well as Tarik's Guardian. She will serve us well. Asad will guard Tarik's left side and Fatima Tarik's right. This is the vision I have seen."

His words permeated her brain. Fatima's jaw dropped. Tarik's dropped even lower.

"Fatima, my Guardian? Are you mad?"

"No," Ahmed replied serenely. "But when I become so, I will politely inform the council so they may find a replacement."

Tarik's Guardian? Never could she have imagined such an honor. Her mouth was dryer than cotton.

Tarik's firm, sensual mouth flattened. Yet as his eyes darkened with anger, he did not move. Jabari looked unsurprised.

"A woman warrior? A woman as a Guardian of the Ages?" Ibrahim went gray with shock. His face screwed up in fury as he turned to Ramses. "What say you to this, Ramses bin Asad Sharif? She is your daughter."

"If the council and my sheikh wish it, I will bend to their desires." Her father's flat voice filled her with guilt. The words were forced from his lips as if each syllable pained him.

"A woman cannot handle a scimitar as a man! Our

women are not permitted to handle weapons. Such actions are punishable by law," Ibrahim said, his thick gray brows drawing together.

"Our sheikh has already pardoned Fatima for using them once. Demonstrate for us, daughter of Ramses, your skills now. The Majli wish to see for themselves," Ahmed ordered.

Sensing a trap ahead, Fatima bit her lip. Showing them her skill with the scimitar risked them gathering evidence against her. Fatima looked at her sheikh.

"Why should I display such prowess, if any exists? If my skills are proven worthy of those of a warrior of the wind, yet you do not approve, I'm condemning myself. As the noble elder points out, women are forbidden to use weapons. Why should I incriminate myself?"

Admiration shone in Jabari's eyes. Ibrahim frowned. "Your daughter, Ramses, speaks not with the tongue of most women."

"Thank you," she inserted serenely.

"Fatima," her father warned, "mind your tongue and be respectful of these quarters."

"Yes, sir. I apologize and mean no disrespect."

Jabari's tone was mild. "You have my word that whatever you show us today will not be used against you."

Fatima was her father's daughter and had her mother's heart. She stood, accepting the scimitar Ahmed handed her. Jabari nodded, resting his palms on his knees.

Filled with confidence, Fatima demonstrated. Steel twirled, sang and arced through the air. She performed a flawless rendition of the "sword dance," the dangerous move only the most skilled swordsman tried. But her moves were graceful and lithesome, compared to the bulky power of men. Murmurs of approval sounded from her father, brother and Jabari. The elders frowned. Tarik yawned.

Incensed, she glared. "Afraid I'll prove you wrong, Tarik?"

He leaned back on an elbow. "Easy enough to demonstrate pretty moves with a blade. But an enemy doesn't stand still; he strikes swiftly. How will your pretty moves slay an enemy?"

Fatima bristled, but as a rustling sounded behind her, instinct kicked in and she whirled, blocked an attack and parried effortlessly. Then she did her father's famous roll, hooking her foot around her assailant's ankle. He fell in a similar graceful roll. Not waiting, she sprang upon him, lithe as a cat, placing one foot upon his chest. The tip of her blade stopped an inch from her assailant's throat, and her shocked gaze locked with the calm one of her attacker.

Her father.

Ramses nodded, a rueful smile on his lips. "Sire, honored members of the council—my daughter has swiftness and grace with a blade," Ramses said quietly, sheathing his sword as he stood. "I had to see for myself her expertise, and she has proven it well. It is enough for me."

"Asad, Fatima, leave us," Jabari ordered. "We will make our decision and send for you, Fatima. Ramses, remain here. I need your counsel."

Fatima bowed before the council. She didn't look at Tarik.

Outside, she drew in a ragged breath as she donned her sandals. Her twin put a finger to his lips. Nodding, she followed him out of earshot of eavesdroppers.

"Asad, will they make me Tarik's Guardian? And what if they do? I don't know if I can handle guarding that insolent ass!"

"Tima, what scares you more—guarding Tarik or guarding your heart?"

"I'm more afraid I'll kill him myself," she shot back.

Asad laughed then sobered. "The council . . . well, you saw those old she-goats. Some will fight this with all they have, including Ibrahim. But I saw the way Jabari watched your moves with the sword. He is a wise one, and he loves his son more than life itself. He wants the best for him, and you are the best."

He hugged her. "Chin up, Tima. The first mark of a warrior of the wind is to bravely face whatever destiny calls him, or her, to fulfill."

"I'm not a warrior of the wind," she protested.

He winked. "Not yet."

Uncertainty filled her as she watched Asad stroll off. Being Tarik's Guardian brought complications. Worst of all would be the close proximity she'd share with the sheikh's son. Not a good idea. She shivered.

Chapter Six

"She'll get hurt. I will not see Fatima hurt. Is that understood?"

Tarik kept his voice calm. His prodigious control, inherited from his father, served him well. He needed it now, as he wanted to roar with outrage, yell with fury. Fatima as his Guardian? Tarik could see his grandfather—his proud, warlike namesake—rise up in his grave and groan.

Warriors protected women. Not the opposite!

"She will serve you well as your Guardian of the Ages, son of Jabari," Ahmed said in that indifferent manner of his, as if they discussed Fatima cooking Tarik's dinner, not guarding his life.

"The best way for a woman to serve a man is flat on her back, knees bent, legs spread," Tarik shot back. The other men in the tent chuckled in agreement.

But Tarik's father shot him a warning glance. "Son, I know this is unusual and against our code of honor, but Fatima possesses an extraordinary power. If Asad has meditated upon it, I trust his advice."

"And exactly who is supposed to defend and protect whom?" He locked gazes with his father. "I am a Khamsin warrior, first and foremost. My oath of loyalty and duty is to protect our women. Should I become my Guardian's Guardian?"

Sly chuckles greeted his words. If only they knew what was at stake, the men would not laugh. At all costs, Fatima must not risk herself in protecting him. Not even her twin, his current Guardian, knew the danger. No one must know, not until Tarik gathered enough information. Because the minute Jabari found out, he'd raise the alarm. Tarik's fists clenched until his nails bit into his hands. Damn it, he needed more time.

Ibrahim scowled. Tufts of iron gray hair hung below his indigo turban. Tarik silently detested the man for his conservative, closed-minded views, even though they happened to be on the same side this time.

Given an opening, Ibrahim began to expound. Women were meant to be wives, to serve men and bear children, not to become warriors! On and on he went, waving his arms dramatically. Respect grew on the faces of the honored elders. Jabari, Ramses and Ahmed remained expressionless.

Tarik held his tongue. Siding with this old goat would open a further rift between his father and the elders. He disagreed with his father about the council's importance, but he would not become a political pawn.

As Ibrahim droned on, Tarik picked up an orange from the woven basket near his feet and tossed it into the air. Then he took another. Then three. With calm confidence, he juggled the fruit.

Ibrahim spluttered. His rheumy brown eyes regarded Tarik in narrow disbelief. "Son of Jabari, do you mock me by this disrespect? Have you not listened to a word I said?"

"I am weighing your words as I weigh this fruit. Both require careful concentration," he replied, studying the oranges as he wove them through the air.

Certain he held the council's full attention, Tarik let two oranges drop. In a swift move, he whipped out the dagger at his belt. As the third orange descended, he speared it. The blade impaled the fruit neatly.

"I understand your concerns, honored Ibrahim. My objections are different. Can a woman spear an enemy with the swiftness I just did, or will Fatima's soft heart cause her to falter at a crucial moment? Yes, the daughter of our greatest warrior, Ramses, is intelligent and possesses a power our people should respect. Yet she is still a woman. The last battle she fought didn't truly test her. She did not kill."

"This is true," Ramses admitted. He looked thoughtful.

Tarik lifted his dagger, stared at the orange. Slowly he withdrew his blade. Juice spurted. He let the liquid dribble over his fingers, held them out before the council.

"Unlike this juice, the blood of an enemy is not easily washed away," he said slowly. "I remember well the day I first killed. I made my mark as a warrior. I remember also the man's screams echoing in my darkest nightmares. Those haunted me for days, until my honored father assured me all men of integrity—even warriors—feel such regret. I would not wish such remorse on any woman—especially not Fatima with her sensitive heart."

Murmurs of agreement flitted through the tent like windblown silk. Ramses gave him an approving look.

Jabari rubbed his chin. "Tarik, I respect your concerns, but we must trust Ahmed's vision. Fatima saved your life. She is no ordinary woman. Her powers cannot be ignored. Ahmed says her destiny lies in using her Sight to protect you."

"I respect her powers. But that doesn't make her a Guardian. She wasn't even trained to become a warrior of the wind."

"She was," Ramses said quietly.

"Ramses?" Jabari shot his best friend a startled look. "Fatima has the training?"

"When I began training Asad, taking him into the desert for long days and nights, she pined for her twin. She could not bear to be parted from him. I brought her along."

"You trained your only daughter as a warrior?" Tarik felt his breath leave his lungs.

"Not intentionally," Ramses admitted. "But she watched. She learned. Very quickly. Quicker than Asad." He dropped his head, studying his hands. "I stopped it when she turned ten."

"The day she sprang on me, tripping me with that move," Tarik said, marveling. "You taught that to her!"

The older man raised his head. Fierce pride radiated in his amber gaze. "I did not. She picked it up on her own."

"Skills she learned merely by imitation," Jabari murmured.

"That failed to stop Fatima, however," Ramses continued. "She begged her twin to teach her. Asad assented."

His best friend had taught warrior skills to Fatima? Tarik felt deeply betrayed. "Asad should be thrashed," he muttered.

"He was," Ramses said calmly. "I did so myself when I found out. And then Katherine and I discussed it, and we decided it was best to send Fatima to England."

That was the real reason for Fatima's sudden disappearance: not finishing school, but a banishment to that cold, foreign land. Tarik thought about how painful his own punishment at his father's hand had been. And Asad's own beating must have been agony. Yet he'd never breathed a word.

Anger dissolved into respect. Ramses had sent his daughter away to follow the code of the tribe. Tarik realized how painful that must have been, for the man loved Fatima dearly.

"And in England, she learned to shoot." Jabari smiled. "Fatima is like the desert. One cannot control her. She will ride the winds of change wherever they blow, for her nature is that of one of the ancients who led our people—a free spirit who will not easily be twisted to conventions or rules."

"How much easier my sleep would be if she were less so," Ramses sighed.

Mine, too, Tarik thought. But he kept his own counsel, waited.

"It is not a simple matter of Fatima being able to act as my son's Guardian. She must sacrifice much. She can never marry." Jabari paused, glancing at his best friend who was sitting so still. "It must be a condition of her acceptance of this duty. If Fatima were to marry, it would create many problems. She must not bear children, for her first duty will be to guard my son, and a mother's first duty is to protect her children. Our warriors swear an oath of protection toward their brides. If Fatima were to marry, her husband would be obligated to prevent her from carrying out her oath to my son, for doing so would constantly place her in danger."

Tarik closed his eyes, deeply grieved. His heart sank. Lovely Fatima—to grow old, no man at her side, with no love?

I would be her husband, gladly, in a heartbeat.

His eyes flew open. The sudden thought had startled him. He mused over it. Fatima, his wife? Tarik pondered the idea. His blood quickened at the image: Fatima in his bed each night, her wild, irrepressible spirit his to tame and enjoy.

Jabari's gaze swept over the council. "We shall vote." He stood, unsheathing the dagger at his waist. With assured steps he walked five paces to the front, faced his men, raised the blade. "I, Jabari bin Tarik Hassid, sheikh of the great Khamsin warriors of the wind, cast my vote now before the honored council. I approve of Fatima bint Ramses Sharif as Guardian of the Ages for my son and heir, Tarik." With a firm thrust, he stuck the dagger into the carpet, then resumed his seat.

Elderly Ibrahim walked a pace or two forward and faced the men. "I, Ibrahim bin Siraj Nusayr, chief elder of the Majli, cast my vote now before my honored sheikh. I disapprove of Fatima bint Ali Ramses Sharif as Guardian of the Ages for our sheikh's only son and heir, Tarik." He stabbed his knife into the carpet a distance from Jabari's.

Other council members rose, cast their votes. Tarik watched with guarded hope as the votes became six for Fatima, seven against. His father regarded Ahmed with a steady look.

"Ahmed, it is your turn. You must vote, as this is a matter of gravest importance."

The shaman stood in his usual, dignified way, his long thobe billowing around his ankles as he walked over to Jabari's dagger. He gave Tarik a thoughtful look, removed his dagger, and added it to the pile for Fatima.

An even tie. Tarik's heart thundered. The sheikh looked at his second in command, his best friend, his blood brother.

"Ramses, as is our custom, you must cast the deciding vote. His voice was low, respectful of the impact of his friend's decision.

Stricken, Tarik studied the man. His father's best friend stared at the daggers on the carpet. He could almost read Ramses' thoughts. Why me? Why my daughter? His only daughter. His little girl.

Ramses withdrew his silver-hilted dagger, testing its weight, gazing at the blade. He smiled. "This is the dagger I used to cut the birth cord tying her to her mother," he mused aloud. "I remember my joy. Blessed with both a son and a daughter! My first-born son, a Guardian to follow after me. And a little girl, to spoil and love."

He raised his troubled gaze to Tarik. "As a Guardian of the Ages, my duty is to protect my sheikh and assure that my progeny do the same. I am obligated to give the best I have to offer. I swore an oath to give my life willingly for our sheikh—as my son did for you, Tarik. Both our lives are yours and your father's."

"But your daughter—she was all yours and Katherine's," Tarik said gently.

Ramses' gaze grew distant. "I tried to squelch her warlike spirit. I did everything. And yet, Fatima's true nature has proved itself. I dreamed of her future as a wife, a mother. I saw my grandchild—a little girl with laughing green eyes, dark hair and a fierce spirit, just like her mother." The Guardian held up his dagger, studying his weary reflection in the blade. "This is not a dagger. It is my daughter's life I hold in my hands, just as I held it in my hands twenty-five years ago at her birth . . . And now, just as it was then, it is time to cut the cord."

Ramses walked over to his the dagger piles, faced the men. "I, Ramses bin Asad Sharif, Guardian of the Ages to our honored Sheikh, second in command of the great Khamsin warriors of the wind, cast my vote. I approve of my daughter, Fatima, as Guardian for our sheikh's only son." As his blade struck the carpet, he gave a barely perceptible shudder.

The men honored the choice with silence—a silence

in which Tarik heard the cries of Ramses's phantom grandchildren forever vanished. With enormous dignity, Ramses straightened his shoulders and walked with pride back to his seat. He was still a fit man, hearty and hale. But he suddenly looked terribly old, as if suddenly bearing a great burden.

Tarik stared at his father's best friend, this man who'd taught him to play the darrabukka, who'd always praised him. As he sat, Ramses murmured, "I just lost my little girl."

Tarik's father looked at him with an air of heavy expectation. Tarik had the right to refuse this protection. With one sentence, he could banish Fatima from his side as his Guardian. He could restore Asad. Things would be as they were meant, tradition flowing on like before, like the eternal wind blew across the sands. But he knew exactly how much this vote had cost Ramses. He could not dishonor the man he loved as his second father.

Tarik glanced at Ibrahim. The chief elder waited, arms folded across his thin chest. The air was heavy with anticipation. More than Fatima's destiny swung in the balance here; his own father's command was at risk. Should Tarik vote against Fatima, he voted against his father. Dissension. Exactly the ammunition Ibrahim needed to stir up the other elders. Jabari's own son voted against him? Should we continue to listen to a sheikh whose own son disrespects him? The chief elder might even use Tarik's dissension to seize control and vote Jabari out as sheikh. Despite his disagreements with his father, Tarik would never want that.

Anger bubbled up inside him. *I will not become your political pawn, old man. The Hassid clan has held power in this tribe for thousands of years. I will not dishonor my sacred ancestors who shed their blood for our people.*

Tarik stood and removed his own dagger. Though his

vote was not required, only words, he wanted to display his commitment before the council. So there would be no whispers or doubts.

"I, Tarik bin Jabari Hassid, only son of the great sheikh of the honored Khamsin warriors of the wind, vote for Fatima bint Ramses Sharif as my Guardian of the Ages." He stabbed the dagger into the carpet next to his father's.

Mutters of both approval and disdain greeted his statement. Ramses offered a slight smile of gratitude from his seat. His father reached over, squeezed Tarik's right shoulder. It was a rare public gesture that signified, *I am proud of you.*

Tarik felt no pride, only hard resolve. He glanced at Ramses, who was still silent, his face creased with worry.

There was a way out. There always was.

"The decision now rests with Fatima. There will be adjustments, of course," Jabari began.

Having expected this, Tarik studied his father. "What are these?"

"She will be tested as a warrior and become initiated, for only a warrior may become a Guardian. Asad will remain a Guardian but step aside for now. He will resume his duties in special situations, such as . . ." Jabari glanced at the silent Ramses. "Her time of the month."

Fatima would become his Guardian, but she was still a woman. Oh yes. This might prove the escape Tarik needed.

He studied the scowling Ibrahim. Though the council had voted, the elder still carried great influence among the people. He could make life difficult for Jabari. Indeed, he already had. The chief elder would keep watch on Tarik. Act too quickly to remove Fatima, and Ibrahim would tout it as mutiny. Tarik must tread cautiously. Diplomatically.

"It's a shame Fatima will never marry. She'd make a wonderful wife," he mused aloud. His gaze flicked to his father. "Though she will be a warrior, she is also a Khamsin maiden. I worry about her surrounded by our men. Though they are warriors of honor, they are still men. Men who might seduce her."

Ramses scowled. "I dare any of them to try."

Tarik rapped his fingers on his chin. "What would happen, wise Ahmed, should such a dreadful thing happen?"

"She would be stripped of her Guardian duties and expected to marry her seducer, as is the case for any Khamsin maiden," Ahmed replied.

Jabari gave the shaman a long, thoughtful look, then glanced over at Ramses, whose lips gave a barely perceptible twitch. His head dipped, ever so slightly. So slightly one would not notice, unless one looked hard. All the confirmation Tarik needed.

"Why do you smile, son of our sheikh?" Ibrahim demanded. "Having a woman Guardian is no laughing matter."

"I am not laughing, honored elder," Tarik replied softly, tossing another orange into the air. *Not at all.* Not when Fatima would become his Guardian.

He'd publicly accepted this to avoid disgracing her father. Resting his hand upon Ramses' shoulder, he regarded the man with the greatest respect and thought, *you don't know what you want, but do not fear, great warrior, honored Guardian. I shall see Fatima falter. She will be removed as my Guardian. You will get your daughter back. This I solemnly vow.*

Rising, he dusted off his binish. "Excuse me, honored ones," he murmured. "I'll break the news to my new Guardian."

Bright sunshine stabbed his eyes as he ducked out of the tent and tugged on his soft leather boots. Nearby, Fatima paced back and forth, kicking up a tiny sand-

94

storm. Seeing him, she whirled. Uncertainty played on her face.

"Congratulations," he said dryly. "You are now my new Guardian of the Ages."

Fatima had worn a path in the sand while waiting, agonizing over the possible decision. Tarik possessed the power to reject her. The sheikh's proud son would never allow a woman—especially her—to be his protector. But now joy raced through her. Fatima beamed.

"Thank you, Tarik. I will be the best Guardian I can, and will protect you with my life."

The smile he offered looked dangerous. Feral. He resembled a cat about to pounce on a small bird.

"We shall see. I agreed for you to become my Guardian, but you won't last. This won't be a matter of you protecting me; it's war. And I will win. I always do. Yes, you'll surrender to me, Tima, because I have another position in mind for you. Beneath me, in my bed."

Incredulous disbelief rushed through her, followed by anger. Fatima gave a humorless laugh. "I will be your Guardian—the best damn Guardian you can ever have. But we'll never share a bed. Never. Understood?"

His hungry gaze traveled slowly over her body, as if he already stripped her nude. "Oh you're so wrong, my little caracal. We *will* be lovers. Rest assured, you will be mine."

And he walked off, leaving her staring in utter shock.

Chapter Seven

She was Tarik's Guardian. Eight days after the news, Fatima still harbored disbelief. Today she started initiation as the first ever female warrior of the wind.

Silently she laughed, her woman's secret successfully concealed. Her monthly courses were just ending. Her lower belly had cramped so hard she wanted to lie in bed and curl up tight. If Ibrahiam knew, he'd stall her initiation or perhaps postpone it forever. Fatima hid the pain.

"I can't believe you are going through with this. Fatima, women aren't supposed to be warriors!"

Her cousin Alhena sat on Fatima's bed, one slippered foot swinging to and fro. Fatima placed a white skullcap atop her head. Her kamis shirt, short indigo jubbe and indigo trousers looked odd, and the air inside the tent felt heavy and dense despite the breeze filtering through the partly-opened flaps.

"You look like a boy," Alhena sniffed.

"That's the idea," Fatima replied.

"And you can never marry. How can you bear it?"

Her elation twined with a chilling sorrow, yet loss of marriage presented no great obstacle. No warrior wanted her, an aberration, as a bride. Not the woman who went into strange trances and predicted the future. She scared men too much.

"It's worth sacrificing marriage for this chance to achieve what I've dreamed of all these years," Fatima countered.

Hazel eyes wide, Alhena jumped off the bed. "Guarding Tarik? Is that your dream?"

"No, that's more like a nightmare," she replied.

Alhena giggled. "He can be rather severe, can he not? I don't envy you having to guard him, Fatima. I wish you luck."

I'll need it, she thought grimly.

They had given her a chance to back out: seven days, while Tarik traveled to Cairo with her twin. Fatima suspected Tarik wanted to enjoy the beauties in the brothels there. The thought stabbed her. It shouldn't. Why should she care?

Alhena hugged her good-bye, leaving to give Fatima private time with her family. Bristling with excitement, Fatima went into the tent's main room where her mother and brothers awaited. Her father and Asad also entered. Fatima looked at them with shining eyes. So handsome, both.

Dressed in his ceremonial Guardian clothing, her father regarded her. His white turban shone like the glint of sun on river water. In a silk white kamis shirt and white trousers, he radiated quiet dignity. A white cloak swung from his shoulders, fastened by an ancient Egyptian gold amulet of their family crest, the Ieb twined with the Udat, the eye of Horus. His family crest was also embroidered in gold and emerald on the cloak, the edges of which were embroidered with gold.

Asad was a replica of his father. Fatima's heart wanted to burst.

Ramses crossed the room, draped an arm around his wife. She leaned against him and smiled.

"Well, Katherine, today is a memorable day for our daughter," he said, looking fondly at Fatima.

Pride and pain intermingled. Her mother wasn't allowed at the ceremony. No women were. The most important day of her life, and her beloved mother could not attend. It grieved her deeply.

Katherine hugged her. "I'm so proud of you. Remember, wherever destiny calls, always follow your heart." Then she whispered into Fatima's ear, "You are our voice, daughter. Speak well for us, the Khamsin women." And Katherine laid a finger over her lips.

She stood to lose everything or gain it. Fatima hugged her mother tightly, then she, Ramses and Asad left. From the entrance of the tent, Katherine waved good-bye.

Fatima mounted her horse and rode off, but she looked behind her until her mother became an indigo dot on the tawny sands.

Mountains and canyons kept silent watch, towering before her over their camp. The trio rode south through the plains, then came upon a short twist of rocky canyon. Fatima followed her father, her heart beating fast as a bird's.

Her father advised her what to expect: In the presence of other warriors, men removed their turbans. Bareheaded and bare chested, they fought. Her presence surely would upset the traditionalists, who regarded a woman as an unwelcome intrusion.

Yes, today she'd discover secrets only Khamsin warriors knew. Nervous excitement mingled with anticipation. Admitted into the tight male circle that women whispered of and warriors carefully guarded, she felt honored. And scared.

They arrived at the initiation grounds. To her dismay, the entire Majli had assembled before the largest tent. They resembled a row of dark vultures. Ibrahim stood beside his favorite grandson, Haydar. The warrior had stirred talk against her since she'd first ridden into battle. He'd pulled her aside, warning of dire consequences should she succeed.

"My grandfather will never allow a woman to become a warrior," he'd said, his small, dark features twisting with hate. "You'll fail, Fatima. By God, I'll see you fail."

She jumped to the ground now, mimicking her father's dismount. Ignoring the hostile stares cast in her direction, she unhitched her saddlebag. Ramses offered a reassuring smile.

"Pay them no mind," he whispered. "Those old she-camels have not spent this much time with a woman in years. If they drop dead from shock, simply step over them."

His words and conspiratorial wink served their purpose. Fatima stifled a laugh behind her hand. She arranged her face in the same expressionless mask as both her father and twin. That was, until she spotted Tarik.

Jabari and his son had stepped from beneath the shade of a thorn tree. Slack-jawed astonishment filled her as she stared at the man destined to be her responsibility. Tarik had settled his hands on lean hips, regally surveying his kingdom of dust and sienna sand. His uncovered hair glinted golden in the light of the harsh sun.

Bare chested, the father and son dressed in white linen kilts and leather sandals, resembling the proud pharaohs of old. Asad quietly explained the sheikh and

BONNIE VANAK

his heir always dressed thus at warrior initiations to honor the tribe's ancient Egyptian heritage. Black kohl lined the pair's eyes. Weskh collars, the wide necklaces worn by royals, draped their shoulders. Sunlight gilded these collars' gold design, decorated with carnelian and blue glass. Falcon heads, their own clan crest, adorned each end of the collars.

Fatima sucked in an awed breath. Tarik stood as proud and authoritative as any of his royal ancestors. One crook of his finger could command legions of men to scramble to obey. She realized again the heavy responsibility of guarding this man, her future ruler.

"Tima, you can pick your jaw up off the ground now," Asad remarked in an amused tone.

Marching forward, she did her best to ignore Tarik. But he advanced, followed by his father. At the smallest tent, he blocked her way. He gave a courteous greeting to her father and Asad. Fatima smiled in gratitude as the sheikh squeezed her palms.

Amusement danced across his face as Tarik greeted her. "Ready to train as a warrior, Tima? To go from boy to man?" He lay his long fingers on the crisp beard covering his chin. "Oh, wait. Not from boy to man. From girl to boy to man. No wonder the Majli look upset. They get easily confused."

Fatima dragged her gaze up to meet his—an effort, as he stood a foot taller. "They're not upset. They're constipated."

Choking laughter escaped her twin. Behind, she heard the sheikh also give an amused snort. Tarik didn't smile, but he dropped his condescending look.

Fatima pressed on. Winning his respect required playing at his level. That respect was equally important as the warrior training.

"I'm certain, though, when they witness my prowess

as a warrior, their discomfort will ease. Indeed, they'll be much relieved—in more ways than one."

"Old farts," Asad muttered defensively.

"Indeed," Tarik drawled.

Fatima burst into laughter. Tarik and Asad joined in. For a moment, time rolled back. She and the sheikh's son were not adversaries, but schoolmates, and with Asad and Muhammad, the foursome formed a protective core against the world.

But they weren't children any longer. Tarik gave her a long, speculative look. Fatima stared at his lower full lip, accented by the sandy beard. This was not a child but a man grown, with a man's sinewy, muscled body. A man's needs.

His words haunted her. *We will be lovers. Rest assured, you will be mine.*

Asad jostled her gently. "Tima, this is your tent. You get your own tent, separate from ours. Go and settle your things."

She ducked inside. Behind, Tarik's gaze burned through her thin cotton clothing. He would be watching her every move. She felt certain of it.

Khamsin warriors, the Majli and Fatima gathered in a circle. Though it was January and the weather mild, the burning yellow sun felt like a hot hammer beating on her tense body. The desert wind played with her vestlike jubbe. Her fascinated gaze riveted to Tarik, who was standing tall and majestic at the circle center, at his rightful place by his father's side. His broad shoulders rippled with muscle beneath sun-bronzed skin. Wind lifted his golden hair. He resembled Ra, seemed a sun god deigning to grace them with his presence.

Before they assembled, she'd watched Tarik command respectful attention with one quiet word, one piercing look. His manner was polite yet not familiar. He was the sheikh's heir, destined to rule. Though she'd grown up with him, Tarik's intimate circle excluded her. Fatima became painfully aware of their differences. His was a world of enormous authority and duty.

She stood erect as Jabari praised her courage in forging a new path.

"You sacrifice much, daughter of Ramses," Jabari said formally. "More than you'll ever know. God willing, you possess your father's strength to meet your destiny, wherever it leads."

She was given no time to ponder his words. She started training immediately. First came the test of physical prowess. She followed Tarik, his long-legged stride jogging through a twist of wadis. Bareheaded, dressed in shirt and trousers, he ran faster than a Khamsin wind.

"Tima, stop lagging!" he tossed over his shoulder.

As harsh breaths ripped from her lungs, Fatima vowed to keep up. Pain stabbed her side. Ignoring it, she picked up her pace. When Tarik finally stopped, a thin sheen of sweat glistened on his brow. Perspiration soaked her clothing.

Next was the riding test. She galloped over the plains on her mare. But when she pulled Indigo up in an expert show of control and jumped off, Tarik folded his arms over his chest.

"The real test of a warrior is not how long he remains on his horse, but how long he can stay mounted on a different saddle. After my riding test, I rode all night long. A most pleasant endeavor for both concerned. Or so her screams assured me."

All the men laughed. Fatima ignored them.

I'll show you. I will become a Khamsin warrior, jackass.

More training and tests followed. The first night she collapsed into bed, exhausted, only to be woken by the shrill Khamsin war cry. Warriors must be alert at all times and ready to charge into battle, Asad had warned her.

For two days she pushed herself, determined to meet each challenge. Only Muhammad went easy, dueling with her halfheartedly in sword training as if fearing to hurt her. Halfway through the exercise, he stepped back. Bemusement laced his deep voice, twisted his lean, handsome face.

"Fatima, why are you doing this to yourself? I don't understand. Why do you want to become a warrior?"

"Because I can," she told him, picking up her scimitar again. "Now let's do this. I can take it."

But the endurance test of silence the third day nearly broke her resolve. Strung upside down by her ankles—the position the Khamsin's enemies preferred to hang their captives—for two hours, she remained mute. Fatima hung, swaying in the hot sun, meditating as Ahmed had taught her. Beneath the shade of a sprawling acacia tree, Tarik and others ate a light lunch of cheese, flatbread and yogurt. Once or twice Tarik passed by, poked her in the waist and said in a speculative voice, "Hmmm, are you charbroiled yet, Tima?"

When they finally cut her down, permitting her to eat, her stomach recoiled from the food. Fatima forced herself to sip weak tea. Jabari regarded her somberly.

"Your father and I have business to discuss with your twin, Fatima. Asad will be unable to give you the unarmed combat test. When you finish your tea, Tarik will administer it."

Acid churned in her stomach. Tarik shot her a calm smile.

Of all the physical trials facing her, she feared this one the most. Though she was lithe and agile, she lacked a man's musculature. Fatima had hoped Asad would be lenient. She knew Tarik would not.

After her tea she followed him down into a rocky canyon's recesses, swallowing her trepidation. She shifted the rope over one shoulder. The unloaded Colt tucked into her belt loaned her confidence: If she failed at physical combat, the gun would suffice.

Tarik held up a hand, signaling her to stop. He pulled his shirt over his head. Bronzed flesh rippled across the smooth expanse of his back, and heat stroked Fatima's body. She swallowed hard, her mouth suddenly dry. She swung her gaze to the tawny rocks.

"Tie me up," Tarik ordered.

"What?"

Fists clenched together, Tarik lay on the pebbled ground. "Pretend I'm an enemy warrior you've captured. Use the rope and tie me so I can't escape."

Splendid idea. Do you want a gag as well?

Kneeling beside him, she wound the rope around his wrists, and down. Fatima ignored his sardonic expression as she tied a knot, securing the rope. Licking her lips, she sat back on her haunches.

"Now, Tima, I'll show you how ineffectual your knots are."

He twisted, working. In a few minutes, the ropes lay abandoned. Limber as a jungle cat, Tarik sprang up. Before she could applaud or shrug, he pounced, disarming her in a blur of motion. Pistol, scimitar and dagger were tossed aside. A surprised gasp fled her as Tarik forced her down. He sat on her stomach, pinning her wrists. Close to two hundred pounds of muscle and sinew held her trapped. Fatima writhed like a worm.

"Don't fight me, Tima. You can't win. Remember? We will be lovers." Tarik flashed a seductive smile rife with promise.

Scarlet heat flamed her cheeks. Words fled. All her brain cells turned to freshly-made yogurt. The firm, hot body holding her down posed a greater danger than its owner's steel scimitar.

Her gaze shot to his crotch, to the "sword" he wielded with equal skill, and equally as often. Fatima feared this weapon more. Tarik's scimitar could injure her body; his "sword" could wound her heart. Especially when he carelessly tossed her aside, as he had others.

"Surrender, infidel," he mocked, echoing words she'd used on him long ago.

"Never," she panted.

He brought his face close to hers. Warm breath feathered over her cheeks. His chiseled mouth looked moist, firm. What would it feel like to kiss him?

Increasing tension throbbed between her trembling legs. How would it feel if he spread her wide and kissed her there? Ran his tongue over her sensitive skin, as warriors did in the black tents, wringing soft cries from women's throats when night draped the desert sky?

"Surrender, Tima. You can't fight the inevitable," he said softly. "We're going to be lovers. I'll taste your honeyed delights soon, make you scream with pleasure until you beg for mercy. That's a promise."

Damn her emotions, for amusement shone in his velvet black eyes. He knew her thoughts, the dark, carnal thoughts making her violently ache.

"Promises can be broken," she shot back.

"I never break promises. You will be mine."

"Your *Guardian*."

"More," he murmured, and he lowered his head. His mouth—oh, his mouth settled on hers.

It was not the kiss of the stammering young men she'd danced with in England; Tarik's kiss was warm, authoritative, commanding all her senses. Her eyes fluttered closed as she drank in the sensation.

Sandwiched between the hard ground beneath her and the hard body above, Fatima felt the same odd quivering she had experienced outside the school-house. Her loins burned. The empty space between her legs tingled. Was this the desire whispered of by gossiping women? Was it the burning passion they experienced in the black tents when night fell with a sigh and women spilled open their thighs to the men pressed against them?

A tiny moan escaped her. Tarik gave no quarter. No mercy. His hand cradled her head, lifting it to meet his mouth. Resistance rose. If she caved in, he'd win.

Fatima pressed her lips together tightly. Tarik drew back, whispered, "Open your mouth for me, sweet Tima. Let me in."

He kissed her again, sucking on her lower lip, and her resolve melted like warm wax. Her limbs felt loose, pliant. Tarik thrust his tongue aggressively between her lips. She opened to him like a flower to the sun. He slipped his tongue inside, teasing, flicking.

Something hard poked at her stomach. Fatima moaned under Tarik's mouth's insistent pressure. Demanding. Claiming. Stroking her tongue, creating volcanic heat. She clutched his shoulders, fingernails digging into firm skin, pulling him closer. Her thighs opened and her hips thrust upward.

Panting, Tarik released her. Desire smoldered in his dark gaze, and he cupped her chin, squeezed gently. "That was a test, Tima. You failed."

Confused, drenched with dazed pleasure, she stared. "F-failed? Because I didn't tie you tight enough?"

"Failed because of your knots—and because you kissed me."

Pleasure faded, replaced by cold anger. She sat up, glaring. Passion and heat turned to dry dust. He'd used her. Used her feelings against her.

"You're a bastard, Tarik," she breathed.

Expression emotionless, he studied her. "I proved a

point, Tima. You're a woman and a natural target. Had the enemy caught you he'd rape you before killing you or selling you as a slave. You need to know this before you recklessly ride into another battle and get separated from us."

Fear squeezed her spine with sharp claws. Swallowing, she arranged her features in an indifferent mask.

"I wouldn't let them catch me," she asserted.

"I caught you. It could happen, Tima."

Softness edged his tone. No condemnation, only concern. Concern for her, a woman he saw needing protection.

I can protect myself.

She must demonstrate her aptitude. Winning suddenly meant more to her than simply becoming a warrior; it meant proving she could accomplish what men had. Surely she could best Tarik in some way. If not physically, then by her wits.

She gave him her coyest smile. "You're right, Tarik. I let myself get carried away," she purred in a sultry voice.

Doubt hardened his face. Fatima made a small expression of shame. "It was just . . . your kiss. I've never felt this way before. Ever. Oh, I wish . . ." She turned her head. A firm hand on her chin turned her back toward him.

"What, Tima?" he asked.

She slowly moistened her mouth with her tongue. Tarik's eyes were wide, dark.

"I wish you'd kiss me again, let me know that it was real."

Fatima ran a finger up the hard muscles of his stomach. Like granite. He shuddered. A bead of sweat rolled down his concave belly, trickled into the cavern of his navel. She rubbed in small circles, cooing as she did. No emotion showed on his face, but his audible intake of breath assured her Tarik fought for control.

"Kiss me," she whispered.

His mouth parted, Tarik leaned forward. Fatima pressed a finger against his lips, traced the curved line.

"Please, could you get off me first? The ground is so very hard, and it hurts my back."

Desire clouded his gaze. Tarik rose up, pulled her to a sitting position. He cupped the back of her head, brought her face close to his. Fatima steeled herself against her rising passion. *Think like a warrior, not a woman!*

Fisting her hands, she clubbed him squarely in the mouth. Tarik reeled. She kicked and rolled, grabbing her Colt; then Fatima sprang to her feet. When the sheikh's son rose, he found the gun muzzle pointed at his head. Sunlight glinted off the barrel.

"*This* is how, Tarik. I'd escape using my wits. Men have one weakness, you see. When there's the possibility of sex, they forget everything else."

Tarik dabbed at his reddened mouth. Studying the blood on the back of his hand, he gave a rueful smile. "You win this round, Tima. Very clever."

Flushed with victory, she nodded, and tucking the gun into her belt Fatima looked down. He attacked, spinning her around so that she was pressed helplessly against his body. A powerful arm hooked around her waist. His fingers splayed across her throat. Warm breath feathered over her cheek as he bent his head and spoke in a deep whisper.

"Never sheath your sword or lower your pistol. An enemy who baits his hook with sweet words of friendship can take advantage when you lower your guard. Remember that, Tima. Don't trust anyone—not even the warriors who protect your back. You might find a dagger sticking out of it."

He released her. Deeply shaken, she turned, expecting to see him gloating. Instead, he looked grave.

Sudden insight struck. "You're speaking more to yourself than me, Tarik. Who is your enemy?"

"No one," he muttered. "Come, let's return."

He strode off, but his earlier lithe grace was gone. Instead he walked like a man determined never to forget his danger.

Deeply troubled, Fatima scampered to catch up. Remembering how the Riders of the Jauzi wished him dead, she wondered if the attack wasn't truly an isolated incident. Was someone threatening Jabari's son? Who would dare? And why?

Chapter Eight

Four days into her initiation training, exhaustion claimed Fatima. Arriving late, she plopped down between her father and Jabari for the evening meal. She barely nibbled the delicious lamb, rice, flatbread and sauce as quiet conversation rippled around the scattered campfires. A fistful of stars glittered overhead in the dark velvet sky.

Bed called to her. Fatima stared at the large round platter arranged before the circle, but her head nodded, snapped back. Curling her toes, she fought her sleepiness by scooping up rice and lamb with the brown flatbread.

Sitting cross-legged on a blanket, Tarik dusted off his hands. "Tima, you eat like a gazelle. Perhaps that shall be the totem Ahmed visualizes for you."

The men laughed as she swallowed.

"I suppose your totem is equally suited to your personality, Tarik. Such as a laughing hyena."

His lips curled in imitation of that animal's laugh. "No, Tima, my totem is more feral."

"What then?" She glanced at the men, interested. Warriors' totems were sacred, revealed only to fellow warriors. "What are all your totems?"

Her father, Jabari, Asad and Tarik exchanged furtive glances. Tarik rubbed the back of his neck. "Totems are sacred, and women are not permitted to know them."

"She is becoming a warrior, and will receive her own totem. She should know ours," his father replied.

Jabari looked solemnly at her. He folded his hands on top of each other and then flicked open his palms. She realized it was a ritualistic gesture.

"The falcon," he said with quiet pride. "The symbol of progress, leadership and strength." He glanced next at his best friend.

Fatima's father made the same hand gesture, his spine straighter than a stone column. "Tiger. Power, adventure, courage—and strength in the face of adversity." Ramses looked to his son.

Asad took a deep breath, his chin lifting into the air as he repeated the hand gesture. "Snake. Wisdom of healing, change, and spiritual initiation." He nodded to Tarik.

The sheikh's son drew himself up, studied her with his dark gaze. He made the hand gesture, but with a certain slow grace—as if his palms opened only to her, and he cradled his totem as a cherished secret. His entire manner bristled with pride. "The lion," he said. "Leadership, a protector—strength and sensuality."

He uttered the last word in a deep drawl. Fatima's grip on her bread loosened. *Sensuality*. This fierce cat was graceful, full of power and sexual energy. Her gaze raked over the four men closest to her. They each harbored pride in stating their totems. So regal and dignified they were, each with their own individual powers.

Asad spoke up: "Tarik's totem represents the sun, the source of life. And the lion is very passionate, protective of his people—especially the females he selects for his pride," he joked.

Fatima met Tarik's fierce, penetrating gaze. A blush heated her face. She pretended absorption in eating her flatbread.

The men all joked amongst themselves about their totems now, an obvious bonding experience she could not yet share. Fatima felt alienated again, introduced to this new world.

"Oh, anointed one, please pass the rice," Tarik said, waving a hand at a wooden bowl.

She squinted as her father obliged. "Why do you call him that?"

Jabari laughed. "My son and heir chose to anoint your father when he was but a babe."

"Barely an hour old," offered Ramses.

"How is that?" Fatima drank her sweet tea.

"I pissed all over his face," Tarik said calmly.

Tea sprayed out and she choked. The assembled men roared with laughter. Fatima wiped her face, coughing.

"Happens all the time with boy babies. Tarik, you did me a favor, for I knew what to expect with Asad." Ramses chuckled.

"Don't worry, Tima. Even though all warriors usually do this as babes, we won't expect you to follow suit." Tarik grinned. More cacophonous male laughter followed.

"Why, Tarik," she replied, "if it's necessary to prove myself, I'd be happy to piss in your face."

Fatima clapped a hand over her mouth. Had she truly said that? Dead silence fell. Shock twisted her father's face.

A sudden raucous laugh split the air. The sheikh's son threw back his head, exposing his Adam's apple, and roared. Others slowly joined in. Across the fire, Asad nodded.

"My sister is capable of doing anything to fulfill her

destiny as a warrior, and as your Guardian, Tarik. Trust me. Tima is strong, determined to get what she wants."

"So am I," the prince murmured.

His intent gaze burned into her. Fatima focused on draining her tea. Anything to avoid that look, scorching as desert heat.

We will *be lovers, Fatima.*

Jerking her gaze away, Fatima stared at the ground. A sudden movement near Asad's feet caught her eye. The coiled object appeared to awaken. Her heart raced.

"Asad," she whispered faintly. "Don't move."

A deadly asp lay curled near her twin's foot. Pure fear energized her. Fatima groped for her dagger, sprang up and swiftly chopped the snake in half. It writhed then lay still. Shuddering, she wiped her blade with the silk sash at her waist, and sheathed it. Faces around the campfire stared, then the men began shouting at her. Jabari held up a hand for quiet.

"You killed my totem—how could you? The asp is sacred."

Her twin's look and censuring tone made Fatima reel back, wounded, as she once had in childhood. "Asad, it's deadly. Was I supposed to let it kill you?"

"Ahmed milked the venom from it. It's harmless." He took the dead snake and reverently set it aside.

"That asp, it was our warriors' totem of courage and good luck," Jabari observed dryly.

"Not anymore." Ramses sounded slightly censuring as well.

You didn't tell me. Again, the men had kept information from her. She had acted the fool.

"I hate snakes, even if they are sacred," she muttered.

A slow smile quirked Tarik's mouth. "Perhaps you have not met the right snake."

Fatima narrowed her eyes. "I doubt it. And if any more approach me, they'll die a slow death. Unlike the asp."

Sly chuckles sounded around the campfire. But Tarik did not laugh. His intent look merely intensified. "I wonder if they would, Tima. I truly wonder," he said softly.

A short time later, as they relaxed around the fire, Fatima fetched her father's darrabukka. In this alien, totally male landscape of secret totems, she longed for familiar comfort.

"Play it, Papa," she begged, holding out the drum.

Her father regarded the instrument ruefully. "Only if you grace us with a song."

Soon Ramses cradled the drum between his crossed legs, holding the goatskin head to the fire to stretch the skin. A wild rhythmic beat filled the air, and Fatima sang an ancient Bedouin love song to which she had belly danced many times. Her hands teased the air, snaking through it. She closed her eyes, letting the song's romance and the drum's frantic beat course through her.

When they were finished, her father smiled. "Absolutely lovely, Fatima. You always did enjoy singing and dancing. I think even your squeaky attempts at talk when you were little were song!"

Fatima laughed. She adored singing ancient Bedouin tunes. The music thrilled her senses.

"You dance as well as you sing, Tima," Asad added.

Her gaze shot over to Tarik, who had one knee bent, chin on fist. His expression remained unreadable.

"Yes, I heard Asad mention your skills in the belly dance. Why not demonstrate for us, Tima?" Tarik asked.

Disconcerted by his intense regard, she felt his gaze burn through her clothing. If she danced, even in this boyish grab, nothing would please him more. Well it would serve to remind them all that she was a woman.

She could not demonstrate her much beloved skill. Not now. Not here.

"It's late and I am much too tired for dancing," she said.

Excusing herself, she drifted toward her tent. But either the power of his will or his totem made her hips sway as she walked off.

When night had entirely shrouded the camp, Fatima slipped from her bedroll. Gathering her clothing, soap, shampoo and a towel, she silently left her tent.

Jabari had made provisions to accommodate her needs, separate from the men; however, the sheikh had failed to provide private bathing quarters. As was Khamsin custom, the men bathed daily. Two springs existed in this desert area; one small and cold, one larger and warm.

Gray moonlight speared the darkness as she walked the short distance to the warm spring. Senses alert, she kept watch for venomous night creatures. She heard only the hush of desert wind sweeping across the plain, and snores from the black tents.

Rock steps led down into the water. Steam misted the air. Fatima submerged herself, sinking up to her shoulders. Quickly she washed her hair, ducking beneath the water to rinse. As she ran the square soap cake up her long arm, she hummed a tune.

Wind rippled the silvery pool. Her reflection in the mirrored surface faded . . . transformed into Tarik.

Tarik, his hands sliding the soap across her body, into her secret places. Slowly he bent his lips to her neck, hands delving between her thighs, gently stroking. Her head fell back and she softly moaned.

"Surrender, Tima. Let go," his husky whisper commanded.

Desire, hot and fierce, pulsed through her like the

sun's burning caress. His mouth settled on her neck, nibbling as if she were succulent fruit. The sweet throbbing between her trembling thighs intensified with each teasing stroke. Cradling her with his hard body, Tarik caressed her aching flesh with expert flicks. Fatima panted, closing her eyes. Her fingers curled into white-knuckled tension as every muscle contracted. Burning pleasure built to a thundering crescendo . . .

We will *be lovers, Fatima.*

No! She slapped a fist against the water, spraying droplets and shattering the image. Breath rasped out from her straining lungs as she leaned back. A warrior shows no emotion.

Gradually control returned. No vision, this, only carnal thoughts brought on by moonlight, icy stars and her own wantonness. Warriors controlled their desires. So would she. *You will never have me, Tarik.*

Filled with resolve, she climbed from the pool. After drying off, she donned a long white nightdress. It floated about her ankles as she attached her sandals, wrapped a cloak about her shoulders and set back for camp.

Romance, moonlight—pah! She must think as a warrior preparing for battle. Banish carnal thoughts and sultry erotic longings. This was the power of the mind over flesh. Fatima marched through the canyon with hard resolve.

And then she heard it, floating on the wind, a steady, beckoning beat. Rapping out to her heart's rhythm, it called her to the dance. Gooseflesh broke out on her arms.

She loved to dance, to throw herself into the wildness of the beat. How much she'd missed bellydancing to her people's exotic music while in England. Yet now, trying to prove herself among the men, she didn't dare perform such a feminine dance. Fatima peered about. No one could see her. She could indulge herself.

Drawn by the exotic melody, Fatima dropped her bag, let her cloak slip off. She swayed like a river reed caught in the Nile's current, and beneath moonlight and stars, she began to dance.

He had called to her with his darrabukka, and she answered with each sinuous sway of rounded hips. Tarik's blood quickened. Hidden by shadows, he sat on a rock, the goatskin drum between his open thighs.

A sixth sense had awakened him earlier, alerted him to her departure. He'd followed, cursing his father's forgetfulness. Why hadn't he arranged for a private bathing facility for her? Tarik didn't trust the men—not when such a lovely, ripe pomegranate was dangling within reach.

Silent as mist he had trailed her, as noiselessly as he tracked enemies through the shifting sands. Tarik remained at the canyon mouth, guarding it as she bathed. He'd been tempted to gaze upon her nakedness, had steeled himself against it.

Content to wait until she bared her lovely body only for him, he'd granted her privacy.

Fatima had refused to dance before him earlier. Closing his eyes, he'd imagined it, her lovely body swaying, her hips undulating to the drum beat. His blood heated to a fever pitch, Tarik had run back to his tent, fetched his small drum. And now, here in this theater of rock and sand, he would see her dance for his exclusive pleasure.

His drum echoed through the canyon's rocky recesses as he played, softly, beckoning Fatima to dance.

I am calling to you, Tima. Hear my song. Dance for me, my little caracal. Dance. Banish your shyness. Release the wildness inside, the blazing passion you hide.

Beneath the full moon, Fatima spread her arms wide. She whirled, her long midnight hair flinging out as she

117

pivoted with perfect grace. Sinuously, she undulated to the drum's urgent pounding. Her hips rotated. Her diaphanous gown outlined her body, displaying each sensual curve.

Desire flamed through Tarik at the teasing sway of her rolling hips, shrouded by the gown's virginal white fabric. He imagined her naked beneath him, writhing in passion-drenched sweat. Her hips rose eagerly to meet his demanding strokes.

Caught in an eerie moonlit trance, his future Guardian performed a desert dance, arousing his deepest hunger. She moved as if in a dream—his dream, a Fatima mirage—a sensual being created from starlight and dark promises. Masses of wavy curls rode the wind as Fatima whipped her head around. Silver strands of moonlight gilt the silken mass. Fatima's head dropped back, exposing the long curve of her throat. A shapely turn of ankle flashed as her nightdress billowed out with each graceful pivot.

Tarik fully understood the wild desert call she answered, for his own heart thrilled to the beat. It roused to a full flame as much as it responded to the Khamsin's wild war call. They belonged here, the children of sand and dust and the sharp blue skies. Conceived in the heat of their parents' desire, raised in a barren land made fertile by the passion of its people.

Arid heat warmed their bodies by day and a blazing Egyptian moon burned in their blood by night. Small wonder he'd felt sluggish in cold, mist-shrouded England. His blood and bones demanded heat. Their plaintive cry begged for the tactile sensation of sun beating upon his skin, sucking sweat from his open pores.

Tarik surrendered to the ancient desert rhythms. He soared, his spirit joining Fatima's. His soul danced with hers to his drum's fierce pounding, the frenzied mating of his music to her movements. He stroked the drum's goatskin head, each rap a trembling caress across her naked flesh. Tarik drummed harder.

Sweat dripped down his temples, licked by the cool desert breeze. His muscles contracted, tension thrumming through his body and increasing with the drum's thrilling cadence. His member hardened to granite as his burning gaze swept over the exotic vision of Fatima dancing. She was dancing only for him, in the arena of towering canyons and ghostly moonlight. Ragged breaths tore from his lungs as he coaxed music from his spirit to rise and mesh with each sway of her lovely body.

Panting, Tarik stopped. He backhanded sweat from his brow, watching with hungry eyes as Fatima slowed, a dust devil whirling, then no more. Her fists clutched her soft white gown.

Abandoning the drum, Tarik stepped from the gray shadows into her vision. "Fatima. Come to me."

Desire laced the deep voice. Fatima cupped her breasts, frantically wishing for a shawl, a coat, a whole damn blanket to toss over herself. Moonlight silhouetted Tarik as he gracefully strode forward. Fatima lifted her chin and raked him with a cold, contemptuous gaze.

"Tarik. Out for a walk in the moonlight? Always take your drum with you, just in case you feel like a song? Or are you enticing the snakes to come out of their lairs?"

"One snake is already enticed to come out of its lair," he replied.

Moonlight displayed the prominent tenting of his trousers. A blush ignited her cheeks. Tarik did not smile; his expression remained hungry as if he'd spotted succulent fruit he desired.

119

She went to brush past. He whirled, catlike, capturing her wrist in a strong but gentle grip. "Fatima."

His voice was husky, deep, the sheer force of his masculinity overwhelming her. She swallowed hard, remembering her purpose. "Let go, Tarik. I'm not here for moonlight and games. I'm training as a warrior. Though I'm sure you enjoyed watching me dance. But that's all you're getting. Nothing more."

"Don't deny yourself, little caracal. You're a woman first. There are no warriors here, only a man and a woman answering the call that draws them together," he said softly.

His hands slid up her arms. Fatima trembled as his gaze burned into hers. Dark as the blackest night, penetrating as the jagged mountains all around.

"No," she protested. "I'm not like that."

"Yes. You are."

He kissed her ruthlessly, his mouth moving over hers as wildly as she had moved in her dance. His lips danced across hers, seeking and plundering, wild and free, nothing to leash him. A whirlwind stormed through her veins. He ran his tongue along her compressed lips, demanding entrance. Like a Khamsin wind; he invaded her soft places with hot swirls. There was no escape from the pounding force as he lowered her to the ground.

Mindless pleasure scoured Fatima. Down to her bones she felt his invading sensuality demanding surrender. Nothing stopped his dominating sexuality, a force of nature bent on taking what was his.

God, she tasted sweet—honey and spice. Tarik rolled her beneath him, plunging his tongue into her mouth, imitating the sexual possession of her body he'd later enjoy. His every muscle tightened with unbearable tension. He fought against the soaring urge to spread her legs wide and thrust into her, making her his at last.

No. Instead he summoned his warrior's control, kissing her ruthlessly, coaxing her desire. He ran a hand down her body, marveling at the soft, womanly curves. His tongue teased hers as it plundered her mouth. Lifting slightly off her, he skimmed her breast with one palm, thumbing a taut nipple beneath her flimsy night dress, delighting in her reaction as she surged upward into his palm.

Tarik shifted, tearing his mouth from hers. He kissed the long column of her slender throat. A soft female sound of excitement rippled from her, arousing his male instincts. He parted the lacy collar of her gown, expertly nimble fingers swiftly unbuttoning. She made a rough sound of distress and he quieted her with another kiss. His hand slipped into the gown, feeling silky, warm female skin.

Fatima writhed as he cupped her breast, his excitement flaring as he tested its heavy weight in his palm. His thumb expertly stroked the pearling nipple. Fatima moaned and he could wait no longer: He must taste her. Tarik drew aside the fabric and settled his mouth upon her nipple, suckling gently, accustoming her to his touch.

Fatima surged upward, crying out, hips bucking against him as his tongue swirled over the taut peak. Shock and wonder collided. Clearly she had never felt such sensations. This was passion, this torrid, out-of-control feeling, for her as much as him. He was intent on taking her, making her his own.

But as his mouth left her breast, replacing warmth with cold night air, as he pushed her gown past her trembling thighs and mounted her, pressing her into the hard sand, his manhood poking between her legs, she suddenly struggled, pushed at his hard chest.

"No," she whispered.

No, he agreed. Not here, taken on the cold, rocky ground. She deserved better, his Tima. A soft bed with satin sheets, candles, privacy. Whispered words of passion, a sweet wooing—not this frenzied coupling on the sand. Fatima in his arms all night; not a quick torrid coupling of flesh, but a melding of spirits as they had meshed here in drumbeats and dance.

His heart galloping in an erratic cadence, he felt every drop of blood surge through his veins. Tarik groaned and leashed his desire with tremendous effort. He rolled off, slamming a fist into his thigh. Springing to his feet, filled with frustrated sexual energy, he grabbed Fatima's hands, helping her up. Holding her at arm's length. Not daring to pull her closer.

"Return to your tent. And I warn you, Tima, the next time you bathe, bring your brother to guard the canyon. The next man that comes upon you may not be able to stop as I did."

Breathing hard, she stared at him with those wide, expressive eyes.

"Go!" he roared.

Fatima grabbed her things and ran, her long hair flowing behind her like a thick midnight cloak.

Chapter Nine

A sienna and copper sky greeted her as she stepped outside her tent two days later. Silently Fatima watched sunrise chase the darkness and drape the jagged mountains with muted light. Raising her arms, she greeted the Aten, god of the solar disk. Ancient rituals bred into her blood and bones beckoned: After morning ablutions, she sank onto the sands before her tent and meditated; cleansing her spirit, emptying it upon the thirsty sands, baring herself before her creator.

Honor ruled her heart. Nothing would stop her from becoming a Khamsin warrior. Not hot kisses, nor a warm velvet tongue slipping between her lips, plundering with ruthless passion.

The rustling of a tent flap, followed by a loud yawn, disrupted her tranquility. Fatima's eyes flew open to regard the velvet tongue's owner giving a catlike stretch. A contented smile spread over his face.

"Good morning, little caracal," he drawled.

She narrowed her eyes. "Don't call me that, Tarik."

"Fine. Little wildcat."

Mirth twinkled in his eyes. Gritting her teeth, she stared straight ahead at the mountains' rocky expanse. Consternation filled her as he sat cross-legged on the sand beside her. There would be no peace, no serenity here as Tarik settled his palms upon his bent knees. Fatima ground her teeth.

"Go away."

"Why? I wish to meditate. Warriors often greet the day by meditation when we camp together."

"Tarik, there's miles of sand and mountains. Can't you find a nice sharp rock to sit on and meditate there?"

"I like this spot. Offers a much better view."

"Of rocks and sand?"

"Of you."

His white teeth flashed. Fatima bit back an exasperated groan. She picked up her carpet and marched off toward a rock a few yards away.

The moment she sat, he ambled over with languid grace, lowering himself to the sand beside her.

"Stop shadowing me," she grated out.

Tarik cocked his head. "I'm merely teaching you again, Tima. A true warrior knows how to concentrate and shut out all distractions when he sinks into meditation."

If she trekked to the Sinai, he'd follow. Fatima watched as he closed his eyes. His long, dark lashes feathered his cheeks. His deep chest rose and fell as he breathed. Captivated by the mouth that had possessed hers the other night, she stared. Firm, chiseled and inviting, the full lower lip was accented by his golden beard. She remembered this mouth, warm against her trembling lips, plundering with arrogant confidence, an explorer charting new territory as his own.

Eyes still closed, Tarik spoke. "Tima, stop staring at me and meditate."

"How did you—"

"My father taught me long ago the art of 'keeping one eye open,' as he calls it—closing your eyes enough to fool those around you, while you are observing."

Amazed, Fatima leaned closer, examining his face. He appeared to keep his eyes closed. There was so much she needed to learn about men. Closer still . . .

His hand shot out, seized her wrist and tugged. Fatima toppled into his lap, face plunking solidly between his opened thighs. A wild flush claimed her body as she struggled to right herself. Tarik pressed a strong hand against her back, keeping her pinned. He uttered a dramatic sigh.

"Sweet sunrise, do not awaken me lest I open my eyes and my dreams vanish of a wild little caracal purring in my lap." Tarik opened his eyes, regarding her with an amused grin. "Ah! It is no dream!"

"Let go," she snarled.

"My fierce little wildcat bares her claws." Smiling, Tarik drew back as she broke free. Fatima narrowed her eyes.

"Concentration, Tima. Remember, a warrior never allows anyone to break his concentration. Ah, I see the others are finally awakening." Rising, he dusted off his indigo trousers.

The arrogant jackass! Even the towering rocks of the sheltering mountains couldn't crush his arrogance. Fatima sprang to her feet, silently fuming. True to his morning ritual, Tarik stopped before the mountain and performed intricate exercises. Fluid grace flowed through his athletic body as he stretched. Despite her anger, she couldn't help watching, his body and mind in perfect attunement. How she wished for such concentration!

But, Tarik could teach her while mocking her attempts and showing off his superior strength. A boulder would scarcely dent that insolent conceit.

A boulder?

Fatima halted. She gazed upward, seeing a dark shadow, a flicker of movement. The familiar feeling swept her into its vortex. Red flashed. *Danger.* Tarik was its target. Legs gathering speed, she rushed toward him, praying it wasn't too late.

Rising from a squat, Tarik relished the feeling of his muscles contracting and straining. Sun warmed his face as he stretched toward the Aten.

"Tarik!"

Fatima's warbling cry and an ominous thundering overhead split his concentration. Pivoting, he saw her rush forward, galloping at breakneck speed. Like solid rock she plowed into him. Instinctively he wrapped his arms around her, both falling to the tawny sands and rolling. Barely had the wind gushed from his lungs when a boulder struck amidst a shower of pebbles, crashing where he'd stood moments ago. Thick clouds of dust drifted skyward. Fatima lay atop him, arms about his waist. Her wide, terrified gaze met his. Emotion clogged his throat. He swallowed hard, willing himself to calm.

"I think you're in the wrong position, Tima," he joked hoarsely. "I'm supposed to be on top."

But his jest failed to erase the fear darkening her eyes. Loud, ragged breaths tore from her lungs. She slowly rolled off, flopping onto her back, staring at the wide blue sky. Yet again, she'd saved him.

Shouts alerted him that others approached. Tarik struggled to calm his galloping heartbeat. Wind blew away the dust cloud, revealing the mammoth rock that had nearly crushed him.

Standing, he offered Fatima a hand. She ignored it and struggled to her feet. Tarik grasped her shoulders, dismayed at their shaking. "Are you all right?" he asked quietly.

She gulped down a breath, nodded. Relieved, he allowed his emotions to surface.

"What the hell were you doing? You little fool, you could have been killed! Have you ever heard of shouting a warning? Such as, 'Run, Tarik?' Do you know how close you came to dying?"

Shouting now, he couldn't control his surfacing fear. Fatima flinched. She wrapped arms about herself, shivering. Instantly, he leashed his temper. Tarik gently cupped her chin, forcing her to meet his gaze.

"Tima, do you understand? I will not have you hurt trying to save my life. If destiny calls me to die, then so be it. But not you. I swear with every drop of blood that runs in my veins, if anything happens to you . . . I'll hunt down whoever did this and kill him, very, very slowly."

He released her, staring at her woebegone expression, his emotions in a lather. Fatima had no idea the risks she took, sticking so close by him. He couldn't allow this.

"I couldn't bear to see anything happen to you, Tarik. Part of me would die as well," she whispered.

Stunned, he watched two tears slip down her pale cheeks. Very gently, he brushed them away with his thumbs, his guts twisting at her anguish.

"You must understand, Tima. I'm a Khamsin warrior. My duty is to protect *you* from all harm. Not to place you in it. With every fiber of my being, I will keep you safe," he said hoarsely.

"And who's to keep you safe, Tarik? No one else can see the horrible premonitions I see. That rock nearly crushed you. I knew it would unless I threw myself at you. Your concentration is absolute. Shouting a warning would have been a minute too late."

He cupped her face, marveling at her skin's dewy softness. She was so much a woman, with a warrior's strong heart. "Thank you, Tima. But please, next time, try shouting."

I'd want to die if anything happened to you. He kept his thoughts silent and guarded.

Her gaze flew up the mountain. "I saw a shadow up there. This wasn't an accident, Tarik. This makes three times. Someone wants you dead."

Cold anger twined around his spine. Tarik glanced at the mountain. "Three?"

"The scorpion at the campfire. It didn't materialize out of nowhere. It was meant for you—the furthest from the fire until Jasmine left the circle. The battle with the Jauzi: I think someone gave them money to kill you, to make it look like an ordinary death in battle."

Huge, luminous eyes searched his, fright crystallizing those clear green irises. "You're not safe, Tarik. Until we find out who and why, you'll never be safe."

He gave her shoulders a comforting squeeze. "I'm more concerned about you. Let's get you settled in your tent with hot tea. You're trembling."

A faint smile curled her rosy mouth. "Tea sounds wonderful. I'm afraid I still lack a warrior's control. My Sight strips it from me, making me weak as a newborn. I hate it."

He skimmed her lower lip with his thumb, relishing the pliant softness he'd tasted the previous night. "Your Sight saved me yet again, Tima. I for one, am grateful for it."

Shouts interrupted them. Tarik squinted as a phalanx of warriors approached, flanking the chief elder. Beside him, marching in his prissy way, was Ibrahim's grandson, Haydar.

A shaky little laugh escaped Fatima. "I'm afraid tea

will have to wait. Ibrahim looks ready to roast me over an open fire."

The chief elder halted before them, his gaze locked on Tarik, not her. "Bring Fatima before us, Tarik, for the council has questions for her. We will meet immediately."

To Fatima's dismay, Tarik gave a brief nod. She watched the men march off and turned to the sheikh's son. "Tarik?"

"We must do as they say, Tima. Their influence is far greater than you realize. But I'll be with you."

Fuss, oh, so much fuss. Her temples throbbed. Fatima stood on shaky legs in the chief elder's tent, while he comfortably sat on the carpet. Please, don't let me collapse, she prayed. Don't let him find a reason to send me home.

Jabari's reaction had been swift and predictable. He, Fatima's father, Asad and ten other warriors climbed the mountain to analyze footprints. To find evidence of whoever tried slaying Tarik.

Upon their departure, Ibrahim had called her into his tent for questioning. Legs trembling, she faced the council of elders, a weak lamb set before salivating wolves. Not just roasted over an open fire, but speared and then roasted. Despite the council protests, Tarik insisted on coming.

Question after question they flung at her, battering her with relentless ruthlessness. Fatima curled her toes as she slowly answered their demanding questions. Dampness creased her palms. How had she known the boulder was falling? Why had she acted in such a manner? Why not cry out for help? Perhaps she'd placed the rock there herself, causing it to fall, meaning to act as Tarik's savior. The last speculation had come from Ibrahim.

Weary from her draining vision and the clawlike fear weakening her, Fatima frantically sought Tarik's gaze. Mouth flattened, he narrowed his eyes at the council.

"Enough!" The deep command in his voice shocked them all to silence. "I will not see her treated in this rude manner. Do you think she magically waved her hands and caused a bolder to roll down the hill? Again the daughter of Ramses has saved me. She deserves thanks, not interrogation."

He looked magnificent, hand upon his scimitar's hilt, eyes flashing. Shock twisted the elders' faces. Some sputtered protests. Tarik held up a hand, cutting them off.

"Any more questions, and I'll assume the asker is annoyed because his scheme was foiled."

Ibrahim's mouth worked violently. "Son of our honored sheikh, dare you accuse one of *us* of attempting to harm you?"

A muscle jumped in Tarik's jaw. "I see none here thanking her, deeply grateful as my father is. I can only judge what my eyes tell me."

Protesting murmurs rippled through the tent. Ibrahim seemed at a loss. Tarik puffed with authority.

"It's time for breaking our fast, and then more warrior's tests for Fatima. This matter is ended."

With a sharp wave of his hand, he dismissed them. Tarik whirled, his long blond hair fanning out. He held out a hand. "Come, Tima."

Her trembling palm met his as he led her from the coucil. He snaked through the rows of tents, guiding her to his sleeping quarters. She sat there on the jewel-toned carpeting. A soft breeze whistled through the open five. Over the glowing coals of a small brazier, he heated a pot of water. Fatima hugged her knees, uncertain of his motivations. If Tarik wanted her gone, he'd lost the perfect opportunity.

"Why did you step in? In a few minutes, they would

have had reason enough to send me away. Isn't that what you want, Tarik?"

His golden beard twitched as a muscle jumped in his jaw. "I detest that narrow-minded old goat. He won't win, Tima."

She sat up straighter, staring. "Is that it? I'm a pawn in your chess game? You want me to finish warrior initiation because you see it as a competition between you and Ibrahim?"

Tarik spooned tea into a small ceramic pot decorated with blue flowers. He added boiling water. "It's not, Tima. There are forces at work here you don't understand."

"Because I'm a woman and not a warrior? And am I not gifted with the almighty foreseeing wisdom?"

His calm gaze met her angry one. "Because you've been gone so long. Things have changed. The council isn't the governing body you knew. Ibrahim has grown in popularity and power. Each day he seeks to thwart my father however he can. He detests change, and wants a return to all the old traditions."

Tarik poured golden brown tea into two ceramic cups, handed one to her. The soothing scent of herbs drifted upward. Fatima slowly sipped as she absorbed the information.

Tarik sat on his haunches, hands braced on his knees. "My father is determined to honor our way of life while pushing into modern times. But Ibrahim and others have said my father scoffs at our heritage and wishes to abandon it."

Tea sloshed over Fatima's hand as her cup jerked. "That's ridiculous! How can anyone believe such lies?"

"Because they fear, and fear is an enormous motivator." Tarik gulped down his tea, wiped his mouth. "Ibrahim uses fear to control."

They sat in thoughtful silence for a few moments. The desert wind brushed across the tawny sands. Shadows suddenly draped them. Fatima glanced up to see her father, the sheikh and her twin. Tarik invited them to sit, offered tea.

Jabari's face twisted. "No coffee?"

"Tima likes tea," Tarik countered. "Father, would you honor us with *gahwa*, since you do it so well?"

Impatient, she started to ask what they'd found. But the sheikh's troubled look changed her mind. Clever Tarik gave him time to compose himself. They sat, watching in respectful silence as Jabari roasted green coffee beans over the brazier and set about performing the coffee ceremony he usually reserved for special occasions.

When the brew was ready, Fatima took a tiny sip of the sharp, cardamom flavor. The sheikh's dark gaze met his son's.

"We found nothing to substantiate Fatima's claim."

"No footprints, not even disturbed sand," Asad explained. "If someone did roll the boulder, he hid his tracks quite well."

A polite cough drew their attention upward. Ibrahim stood at the tent entrance. Jabari glanced up. Barely. At the chief elder's prodding, he explained what had happened.

"If someone is trying to kill my son, they are very clever," Jabari said evenly.

Ibrahim shrugged. "They will not succeed, I am certain—not with so many concerned for his welfare. In any case, it is good, daughter of Ramses, that you saved our sheikh's son. For this I thank you."

Stunned, she watched the old man. His face shifted to a sly look. "I understand you are to hunt. Since you are so skilled at protecting Tarik's life, I suggest he accompany you, along with his father, and of course, your own."

"But honored Ibrahim, our sheikh can't accompany Fatima. Tradition says it's his dinner she's to kill," Asad protested.

"True. But an exception can be made for a worried father to accompany his son. You may hunt for me, daughter of Ramses," Ibrahim offered. His sly smile widened. "I prefer gazelle. Herds often gather nearby, in the sacred wadi, to drink from the ancient spring."

He gave her a level look. "This movement you saw on the mountain, you saw it clearly?"

"It was but a shadow," she explained.

"Hmmm. Since nothing else was found, perhaps the shadow was cast by the sun," suggested the old man. Then she watched the elder nod politely and leave.

Her gaze shot over to Tarik, who looked unsurprised. "Yes, perhaps it was a shadow," he said. But he fingered his dagger, and the grim set of his jaw warned he didn't believe so.

Neither did she.

After breakfast, Tarik found Fatima training with her handgun as several sour-faced warriors watched. Rock chips flew as bullets pierced the heart of a gazelle painted on a boulder.

She lowered the pistol and noticed him, offering a welcoming smile. "I told them this gun must remain with me. I'll need it to protect you from whoever is trying to hurt you."

Smirks spread over the watching warriors. Acid pitched and rolled in Tarik's stomach at the subtle humiliation. He steeled his spine and gestured at the gun. "Where did you get it?"

"Grandpa gave it to me. It's a Colt 1911. Single action, semiautomatic." Fatima turned the pistol over, showing off the sleek blue barrel and walnut grip. "It has a kick when you fire, but I learned to handle it. It does jam if you fire rapidly, so I trained to make each shot count."

Fatima sounded like a grizzled combat veteran! Her

bright gaze sought his. "Want to try it? We could set up a contest."

Sweat beaded his brow. Competition? Like a feisty, diminutive caracal challenging a clawless, toothless lion, he'd go down faster than she could say, "Bang."

"It's beneath me to compete with a woman," he responded with an arrogant sniff. "I only compete with seasoned warriors."

Deep male laughter rang out from his men, so Tarik walked off—but not before catching the hurt flashing across Fatima's face.

Ah, little caracal, if you only knew I am no more seasoned with guns than a newborn babe, he thought in regret. *And never will I admit it to you and make myself look like an utter fool.*

A sheikh must be strong, not weak, before his men. *Khamsin warriors will never fight with guns. I will ensure this. Always.*

Fatima tried to gather her lost composure as evaluations began anew. Tarik's snub deeply wounded her, and left the other warriors laughing like hyenas. She stumbled through the long desert run, and the scimitar felt like a boulder as she dueled with her father. When long shadows spread over the sand, she tensed. Now she faced the hardest task. She must kill.

Armed with her mother's crossbow, Fatima set out for a nearby wadi in search of the chief elder's dinner. Like her twin, she loathed killing animals. Asad had passed this test and reconciled to killing prey to survive. She doubted she herself could.

Yet, displaying weakness now risked giving the others valid reasons to send her home. Tarik, Asad, Jabari and her father chaperoned her as she stalked prey in the width of the winding wadi. Sparse growths of acacia and tamarisk trees studded the grayish brown rocks and cliffs. A markh tree extended its bare brown branches outward like beckoning fingers. Fatima inhaled, smelling dry sand and the pungent odor of animal droppings. Pebbles crunched beneath her boots.

Sweat streamed down her back, pooling into the band of her trousers. Jabari stopped before a small tree bursting with crimson fruit. He picked some, tossing one to his son.

"Anab," Tarik murmured in satisfaction as he bit into the grape. "It will go well with the evening meal."

"Fatima's hunt is bringing us good luck," her father noted.

"This is your chance to escape cooking, as well as to impress Ibrahim, Tima. Rules are, whatever man brings down the prey doesn't have to cook it," Asad told her.

Tarik turned his head, sniffing the air. "Gazelle nearby."

Fatima turned, clutching her crossbow in sweaty palms. Hard enough to kill a small, innocent rabbit, but a swift, gentle deer? Her throat went dry as desert sand.

They rounded a bend in the wadi. Fatima's heart raced. A small gathering of gazelles cropped yellow and green grass. Ridged horns twisted upward from their pale beige heads. Hooves clicked over the pebbled earth as they followed the line of stubby growth.

Tarik's eyes widened with greedy excitement. He licked his lips. She could almost see him salivating as if tasting fresh meat.

Fatima looked at her twin, the sheikh and her father. All four men had the same hungry, predatory look, as if they had turned into their totems: snake, falcon, tiger, lion.

"There," Tarik whispered. "Now you have your target, Tima."

The men crouched, gesturing for to her to do the same. They lay in wait, watching. Then Tarik gestured for her to advance, indicating through the hand signals she had learned yesterday.

Nodding, she reluctantly crept forward. Sniffing the wind blowing her scent away from the deer, she wished fervently it would shift. But the small deer continued their peaceful grazing. Fatima lifted her crossbow, took aim at the closest deer. Her hands shook and she forced a steady calm . . . then fired.

One sounded an alarm through its nose, a sharp quaking cry, and the herd bounded away. Her target sank downward in a violent struggle. Fresh panic sank its talons into her. The arrow had not killed the animal.

The four men approached as she neared the twitching deer. "Not bad," commented the sheikh. "But you still have to kill it."

"Use the dagger," Tarik ordered. "Don't waste any more arrows." He squatted by the gazelle's head, pinned it down.

Fatima darted a glance at her silent father. He knew of her intense fear and dread of killing animals. Ramses's gaze was steady, his nod slow and reassuring. *You can do this.*

Swallowing again, she handed him the crossbow and withdrew her dagger. Dying sunlight glinted on the honed edge. Lying on its side, the gazelle struggled under Tarik's powerful grip; its soft expressive eyes seemed to plead for mercy.

Fatima's hands trembled. The animal's burning pain stung as if her own. It lay helplessly beneath Tarik's grasp, waiting for the killing blow. Begging with silent eyes.

"Do it, Tima. Quickly," the sheikh's son said quietly. "Can't you see she's suffering?"

Fatima's hand tightened around the knife handle. She stared at the creature, so lovely and elegant. Her mouth opened and closed, but no words formed. Instead, they echoed in her mind.

I cannot do this. I cannot kill.

"The mark of honor for a warrior is to be swift, and to

cause as little suffering as possible when dealing blows either to enemies or prey." Jabari squeezed her shoulder. "You must do this, Fatima."

Fatima kneeled next to Tarik. The dagger quaked violently in her hand as she brought the blade to the deer's long throat. But with a sob, she watched the dagger clatter to the ground.

Asad retrieved it and knelt. In a quick, efficient stroke it was over. The gazelle struggled no more. But one large, liquid eye stared sightlessly at her, almost accusing.

The four men fell silent. Fatima stared at the blood splattered over her shirt, eggshell white now streaked crimson. She scrambled to her feet, running blindly down the wadi. Bile rose in her throat. As she reached the bend, she halted. Doubling over, she heaved, emptying her stomach.

Blinking back hot tears, Fatima grasped a rock for support. Warriors killed. They did so with efficiency and detachment. They never cried.

But she couldn't help the sobs clogging her throat. For as Asad had removed the blade, the gazelle's face had shifted. It had become Tarik lying dead there, his blood slowly sinking into the thirsty sand.

Tarik stood in the chief elder's tent, listening to Ibrahim rail. His heart ached for Fatima, who had refused to accompany them back. Anguish had twisted her heart-shaped face as she sat on a rock, staring at the rocky expanses around them.

He didn't want her as his Guardian, but he didn't want this agonized look, as if the dagger had been sunk into her own heart.

And especially he didn't want her falling prey to Ibrahim's machinations, more helpless against that old goat's wiles than the gazelle had been under the knife.

Listening to the elder's rage, he knew she'd played

into Ibrahim's hands. Too preoccupied with the morning's near miss, he hadn't done a damn thing to stop it. Silently he cursed.

Ibrahim snorted with satisfaction. "I want her removed immediately. She did not kill the gazelle! How do you expect her to slay an enemy if she cannot even kill prey, honored sheikh? She lacks courage, and is too feeble to wield a knife!"

Tarik's fists clenched. Asad bristled. "My sister is a woman of honor and great courage. Don't you dare malign her, Ibrahim. Feeble? I dare say she'd outdo you in any task."

"Asad," his father warned.

"She didn't ask for this. It was put on her, to become a warrior. And I'd say she's doing a damn fine job, no thanks to you. I'd proudly take her with me into battle, at my right side, to defend me. Over any man!"

Tarik put a hand on his friend's shoulder, gave a warning squeeze. *Not now,* he signaled with his eyes. "Fatima is her father's daughter, with her father's courage. Killing a gazelle is hardly a test of being a warrior," he said mildly to the chief elder.

The chief elder snorted. "Rules are rules. Should we bend them to accommodate one weak girl? No!"

"You bent them to accommodate me." Tarik locked gazes with the elder, refusing to back down.

"A minor change, necessary for your protection. This is quite different. Send her into the desert on a mission and she will starve. I would not trust her to bring home my dinner."

With a whistle of desert wind, the tent flap jerked aside. Fatima entered, hair tousled, cheeks red. She jerked forward in a short bow and tossed a bundle at the chief elder's feet.

Tarik craned his neck. There were three desert hares, fully skinned.

"Here is your dinner, honored elder. I didn't want you to go hungry." Fierce pride radiated in her face. "I am my father's daughter, but my mother's as well. My mother hunts with the crossbow. If being a warrior means bringing home food, then consider me a warrior—and my mother as well! Even if I must eat desert hare and not feast on gazelle."

Fatima pivoted and stormed out, fire snapping in her cheeks. Tarik stepped forward, examined the hares.

"Ready for the pot. I'd say she passes the test, honored one. And since you are determined to follow every rule, it's your turn to cook."

Ibrahim sputtered. "I do not cook! I am not a woman."

"And Fatima is not a man," Asad countered.

The sheikh and Ramses smiled slowly. "Yes, honored elder. Rules apply to everyone—as you said," Jabari noted.

Scowling, the chief elder picked up the hares and stormed out of the tent.

"That is one meal I don't want to watch cooked or eaten," Asad commented.

"I don't know," Tarik drawled. "I think I'll enjoy watching him choke on every bite."

He rubbed the back of his aching neck. Fatima had once more undermined the chief elder's plans to thwart her. Stronger than he'd thought, she seemed determined to stay the course.

Which filled him with grave concern. How could he protect her from harm when she was determined to protect him? He'd taken action to guard his every step. Years of training and intuition guided him—training Fatima lacked. Sticking close by him endangered her. He closed his eyes, anguish stabbing him as he pictured the rock meant for him crushing her instead, her lovely heart-shaped face still in death.

Fatima will not die saving my life, he vowed grimly.

Resolve filled him. Days before, by the sacred spring he'd failed to take her. He would not fail again. Initiation ended soon. When Fatima officially became his Guardian, he'd find the opportunity. With her constantly shadowing him, their forced proximity would give them quiet, private time. That's when he'd remove her as his Guardian and give her the other position for which she was destined.

His lover.

Chapter Ten

I am not!

Staring in shocked disappointment at the tribal shaman, Fatima tried vainly to hide her disappointment. Ahmed had gathered the men together before the sacred spring, lifted his hands dramatically before the mountain. His booming voice had echoed through the rocky canyon. *Fatima's totem is a butterfly!*

Loud guffaws, not silenced respect, followed his words.

Tarik's sensual mouth quirked upward. She glared in frustration. Gone was the considerate man who'd brewed tea and confided in her about Ibrahim's ambitions. Replacing him was a man keeping her at arm's distance. One who seized opportunities to tease her, and to point out her shortcomings.

Tarik, Asad, her father and the sheikh all possessed powerful predator totems. And hers was a mousy, delicate butterfly? No wonder they laughed. Humiliated, she looked around at their amused faces. She had hoped so much for something strong to gain respect. Instead, Ahmed bestowed upon her a totem emphasizing her difference. Feminine. Not masculine and dominant.

She saw Tarik's mocking grin and cringed.

"A butterfly." Tarik tapped fingers upon his chin. "Pretty. So delicate and fragile." He stepped forward, lifting up her arm. "So, Tima, demonstrate for us your totem's powers. Can you fly?" More loud guffaws followed.

Mortified, Fatima lifted her chin, despite wanting to slink away. Or to fly. Her gaze shot to Ahmed. *How could you humiliate me?*

The shaman stepped forward in his quiet, commanding way. "Fatima's totem was chosen well. The butterfly represents courage to change, as well as grace. It is a deep courage that comes from within, from a strong soul, for the unknown pathway is hardest to tread." He rested a hand on her shoulder. "I chose this totem because you are all these things, daughter of the desert. Women have strength as well as honor. And this strength will serve you well in ways a man's strength never could. You are destined for great things. You must surrender to destiny, and in surrender, you will find your heart's desire."

Fatima nodded, overcome with gratitude. Challenge blazed in her eyes as she studied Tarik.

"Yes, Tima," the prince drawled. "You are destined for great things. Surrender to destiny and be complete." But his dark gaze burned into her and she knew what he meant: *You will be mine, Tima.*

Ignoring the heat flaring in her cheeks, Fatima bristled. "No woman is complete until she realizes her dream, Tarik. Mine is to hold a sword."

"When you're ready, Fatima, you may take up my sword. It will be glad to rest in your eager hands—if you can handle it."

What arrogance! Fatima turned to Ahmed. "May we walk? Alone?" He nodded.

When they were a distance away, she asked the question that had been burning in her for some time. "Ahmed, why did you recommend me as Tarik's Guardian? You knew other men would object, especially those who cling to ancient laws and traditions."

He gave a sly wink. "I wished to upset the council. It has been too long since those old goats have seen excitement!"

She laughed, but then asked again. Ahmed stopped, looked around the grayish, seemingly barren landscape. Wind fluttered the hem of his dresslike thobe.

"I have my reasons, Fatima. Destiny calls you in this direction. You can succeed. You *must*. It is hard, but never give up. Not even when it seems all is against you."

She scuffed her boot heel in the sand, disturbed by his lack of answers. "Right now the person most opposed to me is Tarik—and he is the one I am bound to protect!"

"Tarik is a brave, skilled warrior who would give his life for his men. This is the mark of a fine sheikh. He is also very proud. He swore a vow to protect our women, and you upset this. All his life he has believed that women should be protected and cherished, not thrown into an arena to be battered and tested. Do not be so quick to judge him, Fatima."

"I suppose it must be confusing," she admitted.

"Tarik is much like his totem, the lion," Ahmed mused. "If challenged, he reacts with fierce aggressiveness— especially if he senses another man desires to steal what he has marked for his own. He is a powerful leader, and a protective guardian of all those under his care. Relentless in hunting what he desires, he will be very possessive of his mate. I have never seen Tarik hesitate in pursuing what he wants."

He wants me. But not as his Guardian. A little shiver went through Fatima. "He can be brutally direct," she agreed.

"The lion also possesses enormous sexual energy. It breathes and hunts with passion, for passion rules all things in its heart."

A vivid flush burned her cheeks. "That part of his totem I believe," she muttered.

The shaman halted, turning to her. His gentle gaze seemed troubled. "We are facing a time of enormous change, daughter of the desert. You have your mother's heart, and you will help usher in these changes. Promise me this—no matter what happens, be true to your heart. Whatever comes your way, trust me. It is for the best, as painful as it might seem."

"I will," she promised.

Time for the test she dreaded most: battle with a warrior. And no ordinary battle, but a fight until her opponent wounded her. Honor was at stake. She must know the pain of injury she risked in defending her charge with her life, before swearing the Guardian oath.

On the wide, flat plain, she mentally prepared for the coming battle. Her razor-sharp scimitar reflected her eyes, round with apprehension, as she stared at it. Fatima flattened her mouth, trying to look tough. A familiar face appeared in the long, curved blade: She turned to regard her somber father.

"Tradition dictates a future Guardian must fight his charge. Your opponent is Tarik."

Jagged fear scraped her insides. Fight Tarik? A man who fought with the same ferocity as her father? She swallowed hard, watching the sheikh's son unsheath his scimitar. As he lifted the blade, its gleaming silver edge caught the sunlight.

Tarik brought the sword's flat edge nearly to his nose,

stared straight ahead. This was a warrior's stance, she realized, to focus all attention on the coming battle.

"Watch this," Jabari boasted with fatherly pride. "Tarik has tremendous concentration." He gave his son's back a powerful slap. Tarik continued staring straight ahead.

"Amazing," Ramses murmured respectfully. He glanced sideways at his daughter. Fatima offered a weak grin.

"Don't worry, Papa, you needn't slap me. I will tell you flat out that I have no such concentration."

His worried look said it all. He knew the test she would have against such a powerful opponent.

Standing beside his grandfather, Haydar watched with a cold smile. "Afraid of him, Fatima? He'll hurt you badly. Quit now and leave your fear for the wedding night, when a warrior will spill your blood on the marriage bed, as it should be."

She tilted her chin, looking him squarely in the eye. "I think you are the one who fears, Haydar. You fear I'll win."

A brief unguarded look, one of hatred and unease, flashed over him. Fatima turned away, concentrating on her opponent instead. Where would Tarik strike her? She raised her sword and prepared to defend herself.

Tarik reacted suddenly, with swift grace, swinging from the left. Fatima barely parried the blow. Parry, thrust—she fell back under his onslaught. Tarik swung again and again, a cold smile curling his lips. No mercy. He offered nothing but a flurry of blows she struggled to parry. And yet, she realized Tarik used only half his strength. Her confidence eroded. How could she defend him when she could not truly defend herself from him?

As if he heard her silent doubt, Tarik spoke. "Give up, Tima. Stop this nonsense. Women cannot be warriors. Should not be warriors. You can never compete as a man does. You lack a man's strength, a man's fierceness in battle."

She gave him a furious stare, though panting as he swung again and she feinted. "Never! I will never give up, Tarik. Never. Do what you must, but I will win this and become a warrior—and your Guardian."

New strength surged. Her spirit refused to capitulate. Even as her arm grew weary and her legs weak, she fought with new might infused by her honored ancestors; she felt them encouraging her.

In a swift, sudden move, Tarik struck. Fatima bit back a grimace as pain lanced her hand. Her scimitar went flying. Now was the time. Ignoring the blood dripping from her palm, Fatima swiftly withdrew the pistol hidden in her belt, sprang forward and laid the muzzle against his temple.

"Drop your sword. Now."

Tarik let his sword fall.

Fatima gave him a push. He fell gracefully forward to the sand. Had he anticipated this? She wasn't sure. Certainly he was giving in far too easily. No matter. She must demonstrate she had the upper hand. She jumped on his back, put the gun against the back of his head. Shocked gasps sounded. But she heard a smattering of applause. Fatima's glance told her it was Jabari.

"Guns, my honored sheikh, are the weapon of the future. Not swords. What good is a scimitar against a bullet?"

She rose, allowing Tarik to do the same. Some hidden emotion filled his dark eyes as he gazed upon her lacerated hand. And she could not tell who hurt more: her, with blood seeping from her first battle scar, or him with the streamlined anguish furrowing his brow.

He'd hurt her, this woman who'd caused his father to whip his backside years ago. *Honor women,* his father insisted when he'd first struck her. Never, ever hit or injure them. It is dishonorable. But now he had hurt her. It was not deep, but his sword had drawn her blood.

Her bright, luminous eyes locked with his. Bravely she fought the pain—with a man's resolve and a man's heart. Yet, still, Fatima was a woman.

His own vow mocked him: *I will hunt down and kill, very slowly, whoever hurts you, Tima.*

Sitting nearby, he watched her nibble the evening meal. Once or twice he caught her wincing. Now she sat alone near the fire, a thick cloak draping her shoulders as she studied the crackling flames. Acrid smoke burned his nostrils.

Tarik strode to the front of the nearby black tent where his father and Ramses played a game of chess. Ahmed watched with mild interest. Jabari looked up as his son approached.

"Tima is in pain," Tarik said bluntly.

Jabari stood, glancing over at Fatima, who sat with her back to him. Ramses followed suit, a worried frown creasing his brow.

"Your daughter hides it well, Ramses, but she will find little rest tonight unless we help." Jabari turned to Ahmed, who vanished into the tent interior. Tarik heard noises of the shaman mixing this and pouring that.

The other men resumed their seats. Ramses picked up his queen, rolled it back and forth on his thigh. "I am very proud of my daughter. But I worry what toll this takes on her." He looked at Tarik. "And on you. I know how difficult it was for you, Tarik. We warriors detest seeing a woman injured."

"It is the very reason I spared your mother's life when she unearthed the Almha," Jabari mused.

"No, that was so you could abduct her and make her your wife." Ramses winked at Tarik. "You should thank your father for his softness twenty-six years ago. Otherwise you wouldn't be here."

"Not everything was soft twenty-six years ago. Otherwise I truly would not be here," Tarik joked.

His father threw back his head and laughed, Ramses following suit. Tarik smiled ruefully.

The shaman reemerged, holding a golden goblet. Tarik sniffed the contents. "This won't give her bad dreams, will it?"

The shaman gave a wise smile. "Valerian root allows boys turning to men to obtain a good night's rest."

With a nod, Tarik carried the cup to Fatima. "Here Tima, take this." He placed the goblet in her startled hands.

"What is it?"

"Drink," he said firmly, then sat behind her. As she began to sip, he removed her cloak, pushed her long hair aside. He placed his hands on her slender shoulders and began to massage. She stiffened.

"You are too tense. You must learn to relax and warm your muscles before engaging in physical efforts or you can seriously hurt yourself," he scolded.

His fingers squeezed and released her rigid muscles. Her breathing quickened. Tarik tried to remain impartial, but her delicate jasmine scent teased his nostrils. Seeing her relaxed and defenseless, silenced, he was more vulnerable to her charms. A hank of glossy hair fell across his hand, caressing him like silk. He closed his eyes, saw Fatima lying upon his bed, midnight tresses spread out for his eyes alone.

A woman, not a man. Satin skin covered these wiry muscles. Desire flooded his loins as a contented sigh wrung from her throat. Night whispered around them, the soft call of desert creatures scrambling under rocks, the snapping and popping embers in the crackling fire. He reached over her shoulders, pressing his thumbs into the muscles below her collarbone. Fatima's head fell back, exposing her throat's slender column.

His hands slipped down, brushed her breasts.

Fatima gave a tiny gasp. Tarik froze. Time suspended itself. He imagined sliding his hands over those round slopes, cup their heavy weight. Paradise. Blood surged to his groin. His body tensed, heart thrumming madly as he'd done on the darrabukka.

Tarik summoned back control. Very slowly, he released her.

She turned. Flames were reflected in her darkened irises. A pulse beat wildly in her throat. Her mouth flattened in apparent disapproval, but her eyes reflected a desperate longing to equal his own.

"I'm going to bathe in the spring," Tarik announced loudly—casually, stretching as he stood.

Ramses glanced over and a twinkle lit his eye. "Ah, yes. Bathing in cold water at night. Very relaxing for a man."

Tarik shot him look icier than any river and went to gather his things.

Fatima couldn't think or breathe. Her body still tingled from his caress. And instead of slapping or upbraiding him, she'd sat, dumbstruck, rivulets of desire snaking through her.

Fatima gripped her knees with trembling hands as Tarik rose and announced in a bored voice he was going to bathe. Not daring to turn and expose her flushed face, she pretended to study the fire. Behind her, she heard him quietly leave. Soon after, the others announced they were retiring. When the tent flaps had all rustled shut and sighs announced they had settled in, Fatima stood.

Her eyes scanned the horizon and she pulled her wool cloak about her shoulders. Then, following in furtive silence, stepping as her twin had taught her to avoid detection, she set off.

Curiosity drove her. If she were giving up everything offered to a woman, shouldn't she at least glimpse what she sacrificed? A nagging voice warned of opening a door best remained firmly shut, Fatima ignored it. For once, she'd felt totally feminine and alive. Desire sang in her veins, and she wanted to explore these new feelings. Wanted to feel the same way other women felt: normal. Not different, not regarded with fear and apprehension by men when they learned of her Sight. Just for tonight, a woman, not a warrior.

The odd brew she'd sipped relaxed her, made her reckless. Fatima crept toward the sacred wadi. Hugging the canyon wall, she remained out of sight, following loud splashing sounds.

Rounding the bend, she halted. A pale yellow lantern cast a golden glow over Tarik, who was submerged in the spring. Doubts pushed through the hazy veil the drink had draped over her conscience. Spying on Tarik as he bathed? All her hard work to gain respect among the men could vanish with this foolish act.

Stricken by this attack of conscience, she started to creep away when moonlight gilded his blond head as it surfaced in the water. Tarik rose like an ancient Egyptian river god from the silvery depths.

Damn me for being a fool, she thought, creeping closer, hugging the shadows until she stood a few yards away.

Shocked astonishment filled her as he waded through the spring, carriage proud and majestic. As he emerged, water beaded on the thick hair of his chest. As he shook his head, droplets sailed in all directions, glistening in silvery moonlight.

Fatima froze. Her hungry gaze traveled up from his sturdy feet to the dark gold hair covering his long, muscular legs. She swept her gaze past his narrow hips—dragged it down again. A nest of sandy curls framed the object of her interest. She'd seen the same on her brothers when they were much, much younger and she'd changed their linens, but Tarik's was much, much larger. A furious blush claimed her cheeks.

Intending to flee, Fatima paused for one last glance. Which was when Tarik lifted his head and looked straight at her.

Immobilized, she stared back, her heart thundering. The cloak fell from her shoulders. Tarik's steady black gaze did not waver; it burned with living, throbbing heat.

She dropped her gaze, unable to meet his any longer.

"Come here, Tima, if you want a closer look," he drawled, folding his arms across his chest.

Once his words would have made her draw back and leave, but his tone taunted, dared her to call his bluff. Fatima threw back her shoulders and closed the distance between them. She advanced until her fingers could reach out and caress him. He resembled a lion, powerful if sopping wet. Leonine locks hung in curly strands about his face. Water clinging to his hard body glistened like wet diamonds.

She glanced up, locking her gaze with his. Deep black eyes drew her down into a vortex.

"What do you want, Tima?" Tarik asked in an oddly thick voice.

"I want . . . to touch you," she whispered.

Mesmerized, she caressed the hard angles and planes of his face. Tarik closed his eyes, and his spiky brown lashes feathered his cheeks. Her fingers drifted lower, tunneling through the springy hair on his chest, down, felt stomach muscles jump beneath her trailing fingertips. He shuddered as she explored, dipping with hesitation into the cavern of his navel, lower to the thick hair surrounding his sex. Intrigued, she dropped to her knees. There Fatima stroked hard thighs, felt the muscles tensing beneath the bronzed skin. Tarik released a harsh groan as her breath whispered against his belly.

Fatima bit her lip, stared at the very clear difference between their sexes. His shaft was thick and long, thrusting out from heavy testicles. She dared to touch. His sex bobbed, jerking upward as she ran her fingers up the long and increasingly steely length. Veins and ridges lay beneath the satin skin, and she tested the rounded head with a trailing finger. A tiny dewdrop of moisture glistered at the tip. Fatima swiped it gently with her fingertip and brought it to her mouth.

Salty. Tangy. Tarik groaned, fisting his hands in her hair as he watched her lick her lips.

"Tima, come with me," he rasped, pulling her up-right. "With you, heaven is but a heartbeat away."

Shyness made her draw back. Something deep inside warned that they would cross a threshold she'd regret. Through the haze of desire and languidness caused by the potion she'd drunk, a spark of protest flared. She wanted to be not lovers, not friends, but fellow warriors. She could not surrender the dream.

Tarik gathered her into his arms, pressing his lips against her head. Enveloping her. Internally, she struggled, knowing she must stand as a warrior. Fatima resisted as he lowered his mouth to hers . . . but melted as his lips sought hers in a gentle, seeking kiss. She felt his trembling passion. Fatima shifted against him eagerly, parting her lips as his tongue probed, sought entry.

He licked inside her mouth. Fire spread through her veins. She pressed closer, rubbing her breasts against him, needing to soothe their taut ache. His erection poked her in the belly. The sweet pain between her legs intensified: emptiness, needing to be filled, needing that masculine part of him sliding into her sensitized fe-male center. Needing them joined together intimately, stroked inside until her tension built and built and she cried out with desire to have him take her fully, make her a woman at last . . .

Tarik cupped her bottom, kneading the soft flesh. He deepened his kiss, was rougher now, urgent. She felt embroiled by a frightening force spinning her out of control. She lifted her gaze to his face and saw determined, hard desire. He was a warrior, accustomed to conquering. Tarik wouldn't stop until he took her at last.

Just like his other women. *We will be lovers, Tima.*

Never! She writhed. As he kissed her with ruthless intensity, crushing his mouth against her trembling one, she nipped him. Hard.

Tarik made an angry sound, broke off the kiss. Panting, he rubbed his mouth. "You've quite a bite, little caracal. But you should know you can only tease a man so much."

Breathing raggedly, he stared at her, his powerful body tense, his erection rising against his belly. Fatima backed off. She'd teased the lion, poked at it, and now he looked ready to devour her whole.

Tarik stood a foot taller than she, was muscled and heavy. He could easily overpower her. Indeed, he looked angry and aroused enough to try. Trembling she drew back, fearful he would. But a deep, secret part wanted him to take control, wanted to surrender to desire.

Shock filled her. Had she lost her wits? Fatima searched her muzzy brain and realized the source. The drink. The potion, damn it! He'd given it to her knowing it would loosen her inhibitions. Her ire rose.

"It's your fault, Tarik," she snapped, backing away. "You gave me that witch's brew to intoxicate me. I won't be your lover, not now, not ever! Did you think a simple drink would make me fall into your arms?"

His naked body gleamed like chiseled marble in the moonlight. "That drink was meant to give you simple surcease from pain, and from the wound I inflicted, nothing more. Trust me, Fatima. I need no potions to seduce women."

Deeply shaken, she stared. "Is . . . is that all it was?"

"Yes. Nothing more. Valerian root is given to boys becoming men who need a night's rest, as Ahmed explained."

Fatima buried her face in her hands. Her own lust led her here, not a potion. Stripped of all defenses, she shook, alarmed at how easily she'd capitulated to desire. To passion. To moonlight and soft words from Tarik.

I must be a warrior, not a weak woman!

With a soft cry, she turned and ran, fleeing into sheltering darkness. Behind her she heard a rumble in a prophetic, deep tone.

"No potions, Tima. You will come to me again, and it will be of your own free will, no excuse of drink or moonlight. It will be just you and me, a man and woman as it was meant to be."

Naked beneath his blanket, Tarik lay on his back. He could not sleep. Hours before, he'd returned knowing Fatima lay on her bedroll. Knowing she felt aghast at how close she'd come to becoming his lover.

Just feet away she was. He could slip into her tent, draw back the sheet, draw her into his arms. Cover her body with his and thrust into her sweet, womanly softness. Could claim what she'd denied him thus far.

He cursed having given her that potion, obliterating her shyness. No more potions. From now on there would be only Fatima, the girl-woman clamoring to be a man and denying the passion flaring between them.

Tarik closed his eyes, summoning sleep. Instead, he saw Fatima's dancing green eyes, her rosebud mouth parted as she encircled his cock with eager hands . . .

Finally, he slept. And dreamed. Fatima stood in the center of the sacred ceremonial circle, surrounded by the Majli, his father and Ramses and Asad. It was the Guardian initiation. Tarik watched as Fatima recited the oath. Ahmed took the ceremonial blade and held it up, saying the required prayers. But instead of tattooing Fatima with the traditional Guardian symbol, he handed the blade to Tarik instead.

"Take off your clothing," Tarik ordered Fatima.

She blinked with those expressive cat eyes and shimmied out of her clothing. Her body was smooth satin, honey gold skin over lush womanly curves. Her breasts were large, firm and tipped with coral buds. Tarik lifted the knife to her arm, but her right hand shot out and stayed the blade. She forced him to drop it. He looked down at her. "What do you want Fatima?"

"I do not want to be your Guardian, Tarik," she said in a smooth purr. "I want to be your lover." Then she snaked her arms around his neck and kissed him. He lowered her to the ground, fumbling with his trousers, growing hard as solid steel. She was so soft, so warm as he pressed against her, his excitement mounting. He parted her firm thighs, his cock plunging at last into her tight, wet warmth.

She was . . . Oh, the ecstasy.

Chapter Eleven

"The council is denying your admission, Fatima. They say you failed to adequately defend yourself against Tarik."

Her father's words were a blow. The yogurt she'd consumed for breakfast churned in her stomach, and Fatima squeezed her tea cup so hard it threatened to shatter. She set it down.

Today was the last day of initiation, when she petitioned the council for admission into the sacred circle of warriors. They'd denied her before even hearing one word.

"Adequately defend myself? All I need is my gun. I don't need strength to shoot!"

Lines etched Ramses' brow. He gathered her hands in his, and squeezed lightly. "Daughter, I know you can. Jabari himself suggested in the council meeting yesterday to change our laws to fight with rifles instead of scimitars. But Tarik opposed him for the very first time. He argued that men of honor fight with swords, fight, that so we can always see the eyes of our enemies."

156

Tarik was fighting against her becoming his Guardian with his every breath. Fatima leashed her rising temper. "And what of *women* of honor? Are they left defenseless merely because of archaic laws? I'll gladly look my enemy in the eyes as I shoot him!"

She stood, pacing the tent interior. "I've come this far. I won't back down. If they insist I'm weak and unable to defend myself, I'll show them. Tell them I demand another test."

His brows arched upward. "Demand?"

"Cajole. Threaten. Bribe. Whatever it takes."

He smiled. "Ah, Fatima, you are a warrior at heart. You refuse to surrender. There is no need. Jabari insisted on another test for you. You will demonstrate your shooting skills before the council instead. They finally did agree. Times are changing, my daughter. Your shooting test is tomorrow."

"With Ibrahim as the target?"

Ramses laughed. "We could only hope."

Assembled on the wide, flat plain, the men stood in a half circle, watching Fatima with great interest. The porcelain teacup set on a pile of rocks yards away looked ominously small.

The council had smugly granted Fatima's request for a new weapons test, then placed the target at a distance she'd surely miss. Tarik could barely see it, himself. Had he faced such a test, he knew it would end in shame; he could barely hit the broad side of an old mare standing a few feet away. Hell, a *dead* old mare.

His heart raced as he studied Fatima. Today this woman was trying to prove herself as a man. Not like the other night, when she was a woman only. Touching him. Tasting him. Making his body tighten with pleasure. To his amused dismay, he'd woken the next morning with wet stickiness on his belly. Dreaming of her, he'd spilled his seed in the night. He'd not done so since his youth.

Ah, little caracal, you drive me mad. You passed my test of resisting passion, showing a warrior's restraint. But will you pass this test and become a Khamsin warrior at last?

Standing proud and straight, Ramses' daughter raised her pistol, cupping her right hand with her left. Silence fell among the men. Wind lifted her long hair, which was secured behind her with a leather thong. She looked breathtakingly lovely in her boyish trousers, jubbe and shirt, an air of fierce concentration on her heart-shaped face. He saw her chest rise and fall once.

A gunshot split the air. Blue smoke drifted upward. Tarik watched as she lowered the pistol, tucked it into the holster.

"You are allowed another shot," Jabari noted.

"I don't need another shot," she replied.

Ibrahim scowled. The chief elder scurried toward the boulder. His loud exclamation shattered the silence.

"Allah, it cannot be!"

Tarik ran to see for himself. He jerked to a halt, nearly colliding with the elderly man, whose hands visibly shook. In his wrinkled palms were the remains of a broken teacup.

Ibrahim's mouth twisted. "Allah help us," he muttered softly. "This is a dark day for men of honor."

Tarik's own guts twisted. He plucked a shard from the man's hands, a symbol of his shattered future. How much longer would it be before his father insisted they fight with rifles, showcasing Fatima's skill and revealing Tarik's hidden failure? No, Ibrahim wasn't the only one fearing the changes to come of this.

"I put before the honored council of elders and our honored sheikh my formal petition to become a Khamsin warrior of the wind, and take up this scimitar to fight for my people."

Standing before the seated council, Fatima held her breath. Arms outstretched, she held in opened palms her grandfather's scimitar, symbolically representing her petition. If they denied the request, she'd be forced to hand the sword over.

The shattered teacup had become the center point of marveling discussions amongst the men. Several wanted to examine her Colt. Tarik turned away in apparent disapproval.

Fatima waited, watching Ibrahim. He smiled slowly.

"I do not approve of this woman becoming a Khamsin warrior. I have said all along that women belong in the black tents as wives and mothers, serving men and bearing them sons."

Fatima bit her lip so hard she tasted blood. All her work, the training, the struggles to endure the rigorous trials. Even her display of marksmanship had failed to sway him. No respect was gained, only the same closed-minded discrimination. Scanning the faces of the other Majli, she saw both doubt and curiosity.

Behind her, in silent chorus, generations of Khamsin women clamored to be heard. Her own mother's voice echoed. "You are our voice, daughter. Speak well for us."

I cannot let him keep me silent. This has gone beyond me. I have a duty to all Khamsin women. And as my father taught me so well, duty and honor above all else.

"Speak to us, daughter of Ramses. Tell us why we should give our approval for you to become a warrior."

The sheikh's words were formal, but warmth shone in his gaze. Jabari, husband to Elizabeth. Elizabeth had been the first portent of change, the white dove predicted to bring prosperity to her people. She'd changed her once-traditional husband. Jabari was the first sheikh to part with ancient rituals. They both had laid the foundation for this very day.

Yes, today things were to change further.

Losing her petition would not only silence the voices of all Khamsin women, but the sheikh himself. He had risked much to bring her here. *I will not disappoint you, sire.*

Bolstered by sudden resolve, she plunged ahead, each word enunciated to counter the stubborn deafness of her elderly male audience. Fatima lifted her sword in reverence, offered up her soul, a silent prayer to the Ancient Ones resonating through her.

Be with me, honored Rastau, my ancestor, first Guardian of the Ages. Grant me your courage, as in times of old.

"I'm more than the roles assigned to women in this tribe. Is that all I can hope to achieve—being a wife, a mother, fading into the background like the walls of our tents? I'd be shrouded in silence behind an indigo veil if Ibrahim had his way. My opinions count for nothing because I'm not a man?"

Pain stabbed her. It was a hollow ache, as if someone had stripped her insides out and left her empty. She must finish this. She had been silent far too long.

"I'm the best damn warrior candidate in the tribe. Not because I can swing a scimitar like my father. I can't. Not because I've killed many. I haven't killed anyone. But because I want it much more than any man. Giving up this sword would be the same as its piercing my heart. Yes, I'd want to be a wife and mother. But not unless I had something to pass on to my children, to tell them never to let anything stand in the way of following their hearts. We must all follow the path of the Khamsin warrior, strive to be noble and courageous and honorable, no matter what role we choose for ourselves in life. My children must. That's why I dream of being a warrior. Because I grew up with these ideals and need to embody them for myself."

Fatima gathered strength as if facing a Khamsin wind. Everything hung in the balance. Convincing these men to initiate her as a warrior was the hardest task she'd ever undertaken. It seemed as futile as melting granite. Yet she must try.

Her eyes met Ibrahim's. "The sheikh's son, as I am, is the harbinger of change for our people. Change is a good thing. Without it, a people can wither away. Where would our tribe have been if not for embracing a radical new religion more than three thousand years ago? Brave men risked all to become warriors to defend that new way of life. Now I stand before you as the portent of another change. Let me be a Khamsin warrior. Do not judge me for what I was born, but for who I will be—a warrior, a woman, a Seer and the best Guardian our honored sheikh's son can ever have. I vow to protect him with every last breath of my body and every last drop of my blood."

Silence rippled through the tent like mist. After a long moment which stretched into an eternity, a slow clapping began. It was Jabari, sitting in the middle, his face set in grim determination. He applauded alone at first, then others joined in. Fatima's heart soared.

Ibrahim did not applaud. But he gave a slight, grudging nod. "You have your answer, daughter of Ramses. You are hereby accepted into the sacred circle of men and warriors."

The elder's sullen glare tamped down her joy. His eyes narrowed, betraying his displeasure. "But know this. Falter and there is no grace, no mercy. You must uphold the code of honor of both a Khamsin warrior and a Khamsin maid. And what are these?"

Fatima lifted her chin. "A Khamsin warrior is loyal and brave in the face of death, a man of honor vowing to protect his tribe's women, his family, his honored sheikh and people with every bone in his body. A Khamsin maid is a virtuous woman who gives her family pride with her purity, which she surrenders only to her husband when they join together for life in sacred marriage."

Ibrahim smiled. "Words are merely words, Fatima. You must honor these codes with action. Your behavior must be above reproach. One mistake, and I will have your sword. Mark me well."

She nodded respectfully, lowering her sword. The warning was clear. She must tread carefully lest she lose everything she'd finally gained.

Fatima smiled, scanning the faces of the council, the beaming sheikh, her proud father and brother. And Tarik, who was assessing her with a long, thoughtful look. *We will be lovers, Tima. We will.* A tiny shudder raced through her, a premonition.

Chapter Twelve

They initiated her a day later on the wide sandy plain, her father watching with proud but anxious eyes as Fatima took the Khamsin oath. She received the Khamsin warrior uniform. Then, with Tarik nearby, she swore the Guardian of the Ages oath to safeguard him, even at the expense of her own life.

Ahmed inscribed the sacred falcon, Tarik's clan symbol, on her bare right arm with a knife. Biting back tears of pain, she stared ahead. Fatima refused to cry before the men. Especially before the man she'd vowed to guard with her very life.

When it was over, all the men released a loud Khamsin war call.

With great anticipation, Fatima awaited the feast. The sacred male ritual had once been forbidden to all female eyes. She would become the first to partake in the ceremony.

Her face streaked with drawings made from ash, Fatima sat on the sand that night. Crackling flames from an enormous bonfire sent black smoke arcing upward. The Khamsin warriors of the wind were each displaying a magnificent, deadly force. Bare chested, bareheaded men clad only in trousers swung scimitars in mock duels, and wild screams echoed as steel clashed against steel. Fatima's blood thrilled to the primitive grace, the raging fury, but only one warrior commanded her attention.

Tarik's blond hair flew about his head as he leapt forward with explosive precision. His sculpted muscles rippled as he clashed with his father. No, these were not son and father, but two powerful beasts tangling in a snarling rage. Tarik's chiseled profile silhouetted by the crackling bonfire, he fought like a powerful lion. Fascinated, Fatima watched shadows dance across the banded muscles of his back. This man was her charge, this powerful desert warrior who fought with ferocious strength. Her heart pounded at his virility, his ruthless determination.

The others ceased their swordplay to watch Tarik and the sheikh. Finally both men stepped back, panting, lowering their swords, an equal match. The men let out an ululating cheer, praising their prowess. Fatima cheered loudest of all.

Their swordplay over, the warriors sat in a circle, pounding rhythms on darrabukkas. Flames licked the still night air as ominous war chants arose. Side by side, Tarik and her father played their drums. Sweat slicked Tarik's wide shoulders, glistened in the fire's glow. Droplets on his dark gold chest hair sparkled like tears. Thick muscles in his arms bunched as he pounded on the goatskin.

His golden head tossed back, Tarik released a warbling war call. Ramses laughed with a flash of gleaming white teeth. Asad and the sheikh joined the dancing warriors. And with the end of each refrain, they lifted their swords and stabbed the night sky, raising their voices in one solid vocal sound, a chanted Khamsin war cry.

The dance ended. The warriors settled on the ground. Fatima praised their moves. No one responded. Ignoring her, they talked of battles and the sexual prowess they demonstrated in the black tents. Even Asad and her own father joined in, Asad enthusiastically describing a recent romp with a comely widow.

Fatima's chest felt hollow. They had forgotten her, the new initiate. She was as invisible now as she'd been in her indigo kuftan doing laundry. Alienated and alone in this bare-chested male world, Fatima hugged her knees.

Laughing at one man's description of how his wife recited the name of Egyptian gods as he pleasured her, Tarik glanced Fatima's way. His deep laugh faded. "Enough talk of sex," he ordered. "We're here to celebrate our new initiate, remember?" He thrust his sword upward. "To Fatima, Khamsin warrior of the wind."

Startled looks flashed as the men finally looked at her. A chorus of deep voices joined Tarik in the rightful acknowledgement of their newest warrior.

One man nudged Tarik slyly. "But, Tarik, you failed to tell us. What pleasures in the soft arms of a woman do *you* anticipate when we return?"

The sheikh's son glanced at Fatima. Intense heat flared, like a writhing tongue of fire as Tarik's smoldering gaze caressed her. The hollow between her legs pulsed. Fatima hugged her knees tighter, alarmed at the intensity of her feelings.

"I intend to delay my gratification," Tarik responded softly. "Some pleasures are worth waiting for."

Alarmed shouts rang through the camp the next morning, jerking Fatima awake. Her father stormed into her tent.

"Get ready immediately. A group out hunting spotted Jauzi Riders making their way toward our camp. We must ride."

Heart pounding, she obeyed, strapping on sword, dagger and tucking her Colt into her holster. This was it. Real. Barely a warrior and already her first battle loomed. She could only pray she was ready.

Rifles slung over their shoulders, the Khamsin rode hard and fast through the desert, veils draping their lower faces, eyes alert for the approaching Riders. Fatima rode close to Tarik, grateful he didn't try leading the pack. After a while dismay filled her, for he'd steered his mare ahead, blocking her advance. Instead of allowing her to protect him, he was protecting her. Grimly she vowed to change that when the battle began.

A few miles on, the enemy appeared, cutting off the west. Fatima maneuvered her mare out front, blocking Tarik as the two forces collided. Dust swirled upward as men and horses met, violent war cries shattering the desert silence. Fatima drove off one warrior aiming a sword at Tarik, slashing at him, and saw with horror the earlier situation repeating itself: The Jauzi all chose him as their target.

Screaming out a warning to the others cut off from the sheikh's son, Fatima went for her sidearm and hesitated. If she used her gun, it meant open fire for all, and in the chaos Tarik might get shot. She kicked her mare, headed toward Tarik.

"Can't you see they're all aiming for you?" she screamed back. "This is not battle, but assassination!"

Barely had the words been said when a Rider rushed forward, blade raised, screaming a war cry. She screamed a warning. Tarik swirled gracefully and cut the man down.

Another Rider raced forward. Horrified, Fatima saw him raise a rifle to his shoulder. The earlier vision of the gazelle flashed: Tarik, lying on the ground, his blood staining the sand.

No! She flung herself forward, pulling him down off his horse as a bullet sang through the air. Pain exploded in her shoulder.

"Fatima!" Tarik roared.

Must protect him. The thought surged wildly through her mind as she struggled to cover him. But he wrapped his arms about her and rolled away. More gunfire crackled. She saw her father and brother abandon their swords for their guns. Then, finally, victorious shouts from the Khamsin.

Her father's voice yelled as if across a great distance. Fatima squeezed her eyes shut. Tarik was safe. Nothing else mattered.

He rolled off her. "Tima, oh God, oh God," he rasped.

Fatima took tiny, gasping breaths. Warm, sticky fluid dripped down her arm and back. She squeezed her eyes shut.

Voices clamored, buzzed in her ears: her father's terrified cry as he called her name, the sheikh's shocked tones, her twin, a voice of calm amidst chaos. Someone ripped her clothing away from her shoulder; cool air washed over the burning flesh. Fatima bit her lip. A warrior did not cry, even when wounded.

Dimly she heard the words, "Stop the bleeding." Someone slid a leather strip between her parched lips. Tarik's deep, reassuring voice rumbled, "Bite down."

She felt him prop her up, lean her against his chest. There was more burning pain as something cool splashed over her wound. She bit down, willing herself not to faint.

His hand trembled as he stroked her hair. "Hang on, Tima. I'm here with you. I won't let go."

"Hold her," Asad instructed.

Tarik steadied her. Fatima squeezed his hand, bracing herself. Darkness rose up. Gratefully she sank into it, hearing Tarik's anguished voice whisper her name.

Blood. So much damn blood. Warm, sticky crimson was flowing from the ugly slash caused by the bullet that had grazed her; staining his hands, soaking his arm as he cradled her. A hollow ache settled in Tarik's chest. Oh God.

"Tima? Do you hear me? You stay with me. Stay with me!" he ordered harshly.

Methodically Asad bound the wound. Anguish paling his face, Ramses hovered nearby. Tarik laid his cheek upon Fatima's head, feeling her sun-warmed turban. He put a trembling hand on her forehead. It was clammy with sweat. He cradled her against his chest, ignoring the stares. The hell with them, he thought savagely. Let them think what they will. His only concern was for Fatima.

So damn cold, her skin was chilled as if doused with icy water. Fighting to keep his anxiety at bay, he crooned her, hoping to calm his fractured spirit and restore her physically.

"She could have died!"

"She is your Guardian now, my son. It was a deep wound, but it has stopped bleeding thanks to Asad's skill."

"Please, Tarik, calm down. This is upsetting for all of us," his mother added, her blue eyes deeply troubled.

His father and mother stood by the foot of Fatima's bed as Tarik paced. His new Guardian lay pale and unconscious, a large bandage covering one delicate shoulder. They had galloped back to camp, Tarik cradling her in his arms the whole time, refusing to allow anyone—even her father—to carry her.

GET UP TO 4 FREE BOOKS!

You can have the best romance delivered to your door for less than what you'd pay in a bookstore or online. Sign up for one of our book clubs today, and we'll send you **FREE* BOOKS** just for trying it out...**with no obligation to buy, ever!**

HISTORICAL ROMANCE BOOK CLUB

Travel from the Scottish Highlands to the American West, the decadent ballrooms of Regency England to Viking ships. Your shipments will include authors such as CONNIE MASON, CASSIE EDWARDS, LYNSAY SANDS, LEIGH GREENWOOD, and many, many more.

LOVE SPELL BOOK CLUB

Bring a little magic into your life with the romances of Love Spell—fun contemporaries, paranormals, time-travels, futuristics, and more. Your shipments will include authors such as KATIE MACALISTER, SUSAN GRANT, NINA BANGS, SANDRA HILL, and more.

As a book club member you also receive the following special benefits:

- **30% OFF** all orders through our website & telecenter! (Plus, you still get 1 book FREE for every 5 books you buy!)
- **Exclusive access to special discounts!**
- **Convenient home delivery and 10 days to return any books you don't want to keep.**

There is no minimum number of books to buy, and you may cancel membership at any time. See back to sign up!

*Please include $2.00 for shipping and handling.

YES!

Sign me up for the **Historical Romance Book Club** and send my TWO FREE BOOKS! If I choose to stay in the club, I will pay only $8.50* each month, a savings of $5.48!

YES!

Sign me up for the **Love Spell Book Club** and send my TWO FREE BOOKS! If I choose to stay in the club, I will pay only $8.50* each month, a savings of $5.48!

NAME: _____

ADDRESS: _____

_____

TELEPHONE: _____

E-MAIL: _____

☐ **I WANT TO PAY BY CREDIT CARD.**

☐ VISA   ☐ MasterCard   ☐ DISCOVER

ACCOUNT #: _____

EXPIRATION DATE: _____

SIGNATURE: _____

Send this card along with $2.00 shipping & handling for each club you wish to join, to:

**Romance Book Clubs
1 Mechanic Street
Norwalk, CT 06850-3431**

Or fax (must include credit card information!) to: 610.995.9274.
You can also sign up online at www.dorchesterpub.com.

*Plus $2.00 for shipping. Offer open to residents of the U.S. and Canada only. Canadian residents please call 1.800.481.9191 for pricing information.

If under 18, a parent or guardian must sign. Terms, prices and conditions subject to change. Subscription subject to acceptance. Dorchester Publishing reserves the right to reject any order or cancel any subscription.

JOIN NOW!

He drew in a deep breath as the tent flap jerked aside. A small group of men, Muhammad and Haydar, included, peered in.

"We came to check on Fatima. Is she all right?" Muhammad asked. Concern filled his gentle brown eyes.

"She will be fine," Jabari said.

Haydar gave a snort. "I warned you no good would come of having a woman as a warrior. Now look at her!"

"Leave. Now," Jabari told them in a cold voice.

The men scrambled to obey. Tarik fisted his hands. "I will not see Tima hurt! And, Father, you act as if it's nothing."

Anguish twisted Jabari's face. He gripped his son's shoulders, his fingers like steel. "I would rather have a bullet sink into my own heart, Tarik. She is like a daughter. But Fatima has sworn the Guardian oath. Her duty is to protect you with her life. I cannot change that."

Tarik narrowed his gaze. "Then I must change her duty."

He turned to her parents. Katherine wiped Fatima's forehead with a cloth. Asad sat beside his mother, clutching his twin's right hand, her father holding her left.

"I'm warning you. I'll do what I must to ensure she's safe and removed as my Guardian. Am I making myself clear?"

A sob caught in Katherine's throat. Emotion blazed in Asad's green eyes. Standing, Ramses locked steely gazes with him, turning from friend to fiercely protective father. "If you hurt my little girl, I will kill you myself," he replied thinly.

"Hurt her? I'd rather die myself," he replied evenly.

A low moan interrupted them. "Tarik," Fatima whispered.

Tarik knelt on the floor beside her. Gently he stroked her hair, wincing at the lines furrowing her chalk white brow. Two pain-glazed eyes stared up at him. With a trembling hand, she touched his cheek. He caught her fingers in his, rubbing the slender digits, wanting to graze his lips against them.

"Beware. The Riders. I saw . . . Someone paid them. Whoever did this . . . aims to take your life. The real enemy is among *us*. Trust no one . . . Only your family." Fatima's voice faded as her eyes closed.

Asad felt her brow. "Normal sleep. She needs rest," he assured them all.

Tarik stood as his father advanced on him looking deeply troubled. "Someone is trying to kill you, my son? I will have answers. One of us? A Khamsin warrior?"

Steeling himself, Tarik looked his father straight in the eye. "I already know the answer, Father. Yes, someone is trying to kill me. They have been for a while now."

Chapter Thirteen

A shocked gasp rose from his mother. His father, the great sheikh of the Khamsin warriors of the wind, turned a brilliant red. An interesting color. Like sunrise, Tarik thought calmly.

"You . . . you . . ." Jabari pressed two trembling hands to his temples—shaking with rage.

"Yes, I've known." Tarik nodded. "For some time. The first attempt was about four months ago. Someone cleverly cut the straps of my saddle before I exercised my mare."

"Tarik! How could you keep something like this from us?"

He steeled himself against the frantic worry in his mother's voice. "I had to, to avoid alerting my attacker. The two other attempts were less subtle. An asp in the latrine." His lips twisted in a wry grin. "That was a bit frightening. I nearly, well . . . had to use the latrine over that one." His little joke failed to elicit any amusement, and Tarik sighed. "I killed it with my dagger. The next time, someone shot at me as I went into the deep desert for meditation. Very few knew of my absence—"

"Shot at you?" the sheikh roared. "And you kept quiet?"

Tarik ignored his tirade. "The shot went wide, very wide. I saw a flash of indigo, gave chase, but Asad turned up."

"I sent him to guard you when I learned you sneaked off alone," Ramses said, exchanging troubled looks with his son.

Tarik had retrieved the bullet. It was a British .303, the type Khamsin warriors used for their Enfield rifles. He had intended to lure his attacker out with a shooting competition, risking his own humiliation, but Fatima's arrival delayed his action. Well, deep down he knew the truth: He did not want to display his poor marksmanship, his deepest weakness, before her. Especially not when she was such an excellent shot.

"It's known that the Jauzi are terrible shots, which is why they usually fight with swords. That Rider today didn't want to shoot me, only to distract from another attacker, who struck when Fatima threw herself on me." Tarik dragged in a deep breath.

Jabari stopped pacing, turned. His long fingers curled into white-knuckled fists. "You knew a murderer pursued you? I have given you credit for more brains than this! From this moment on, I will set ten warriors to guard you. You will not take a piss without them watching your every move." He glanced at his wife and Katherine. "My apologies for the vulgar language, but I am too furious to check my words."

Katherine's gaze remained steady. "I don't give a damn about your language. My daughter leaves to protect your son, returns wounded, and now your son tells us he's a killer's target, putting both himself and Fatima in danger? You men all talk of honor and bravery, are all words. Well, I'm her mother, and I have words, too."

She turned to Tarik, eyes blazing with with washed tears. "Do what you must to keep her safe. All I ever wanted for her was joy. Not this. And let everyone seeking to hurt my daughter beware: I have a crossbow and can hit anything—even particular male parts."

"On my honor as a Khamsin warrior, I'll protect her to the last drop of my blood," Tarik said.

Asad put up a hand. "All this excitement isn't good for my sister. She needs her sleep. Out, all of you."

Elizabeth gave Tarik such a look of censure, he blushed like a little boy caught robbing candy. "Tarik, you and I must have a long talk," she warned.

"Later, Mother. I'm not leaving Fatima now," he said quietly.

"We'll both discuss this with you, Tarik," Jabari said. "Ramses, when he leaves here, either you or Asad accompany him. No matter how much he protests." The sheikh looked furious.

"I'll stay with him." Asad nodded.

Tarik felt as young as he had when his father whipped him for hitting Fatima. If he could, he would do so again for daring to risk *my own life*, he thought ruefully. *He'll set a battalion of guards watching me. How am I to lure out my attacker now?*

A low moan from Fatima interrupted his thoughts. Asad handed him a goblet filled with liquid. "A sleeping potion."

Tarik settled on the bed beside her, propped her up. "Drink this," he insisted. "It will help you rest."

Fatima opened her eyes, her mouth a mutinous line. "I can handle the pain."

"Drink it. Now," he ordered sternly.

She compressed her lips. Tarik gritted his teeth. "Fine.

173

Be difficult." He pinched her nose shut. As she gasped for air, he poured the liquid into her mouth, closed it and stroked her throat. She swallowed, grimacing.

"That tastes worse than donkey dung!"

"It will help you sleep, and you'll drink it all."

Her parents exchanged odd looks. "Do you remember when you—," Ramses burst out.

"Isn't it just like when I—," Katherine interjected.

Suddenly Ramses grinned, and his wife blushed becomingly. Tarik glanced at both of them curiously as Fatima drank.

"We were reliving a moment, Tarik," Ramses explained. He studied his daughter thoughtfully, then glanced at his wife. "I think it best if we leave Fatima in Asad's care. Sometimes destiny calls to accept the path set before us. Even if, as parents, it means letting go."

Katherine nodded. They stood, linked hands like young lovers. They left the tent, smiling, leaving him wondering what was so damn funny.

Late in the afternoon he left Fatima's room to search out his parents. A warrior guarding their tent with a rifle said his mother was at the nearby warrior training ground. "Never have I seen such a thing!" the man exclaimed.

Tarik walked to the training ground, drawn by the crisp rattle of gunfire. Curiosity pricked him. Why was his mother at the sacred training grounds forbidden to women?

When he finally rounded a boulder and came to the site, he ground to an abrupt halt. Her face screwed up in determination, his mother shot a Webley pistol at a very large red bull's-eye painted on a boulder. Rock chips splintered another boulder far away. Standing beside her, Jabari looked resigned.

Now I know why I'm such a lousy shot, he thought, amused and astounded.

When Elizabeth stopped, struggling to reload, he called out, "*Pax.*" He said it jokingly, holding up his hands. "I know you're angry at me, Mum, but I am your only son."

She handed the pistol to his father, giving Tarik one of her famous looks that could make the fiercest warrior cringe. He braced himself. Worse than his father's rare but angry tirades was the stiff disappointment in his mother's voice.

"Someone is trying to kill you, and I'll be damned if I sit by helplessly. I asked your father to teach me to shoot."

Tarik sighed. Why were these women in his life so determined to protect him? "Mother, it's not necessary—"

"Yes, it is." Elizabeth stepped forward, anger snapping in her blue eyes. "For years I've concentrated on educating our men and women. It's about time I taught them something new. Women can handle weapons as effectively as men, and men won't always be there. And it's time you learned something as well, young man. You have responsibilities in this family. Did you ever think how your silence has endangered us all?"

His father prowled forward, looking equally disapproving. "You took enormous risks, for yourself and for all of us. What if the killer hurt your sisters trying to get to you?"

Remembering the scorpion that had nearly stung Jasmine, Tarik rocked back on his heels. "I . . . didn't think."

"I thought you had more sense," his mother went on.

"I'm sorry," he replied, feeling truly abashed. "I didn't want to scare you, or to risk anyone else's safety. I only wanted to flush out the assassin without alerting him."

Her face softened, and she touched his cheek. "If you had told your father, you both could have set a trap and caught the person without risk. You're a fine man,

Tarik, and will make a good sheikh. I just wish you'd stop insisting on doing everything yourself. You can be so stubborn."

"Stubborn? Sounds like someone else I know," his father jested. "Someone who insisted on breaking tradition yet again to haul me out here to teach her to shoot."

Elizabeth removed the Webley from his grip. "And I'll stay here until I can hit that bull's-eye. Or at least the rock it's on."

Thundering hoofbeats alerted Tarik to visitors. He whirled, regarding the intruders warily. It was Ibrahim, accompanied by his grandson. The chief elder dismounted and advanced. Flanking him, Haydar looked equally angry. Tarik held his tongue, secretly amused. He knew his mother in this kind of mood.

"It is true," Haydar breathed. "Grandfather, stop her!"

Ibrahim scowled. "Elizabeth, you have violated the sanctity of our sacred training grounds. You must leave at once!"

"Try to make me." She raised her pistol.

The elder grew pale as camel's milk. "Of course, honored wife of our sheikh, you are a mother, and mothers will do anything to ensure their children's safety. That is to be respected."

Elizabeth gave an unladylike snort and lowered the gun. "I'm a woman first and tired of these games you insist on playing. Honor and bravery, pah! What good are they when the values governing a people are discarded? Our tribal laws were intended to protect women. But you've turned them into shackles around our wrists. And you've dismissed the attacks against my son, unlike Fatima, who's done everything to save him. Listen to me, Ibrahim. No one, *no one*, harms my son. Do you understand?"

The chief elder gave a nervous glance at the pistol, then narrowed his gaze upon Tarik's father. "This is not the last of it, Jabari. I am warning you, you tread on dangerous ground."

The sheikh gave a slow, lethal smile. "You venture on dangerous ground. My wife is angry and does not yet have good aim. I would leave if I were you. Now."

The elder paled, whirled and left with his grandson. Tarik glanced at his mother, who looked ready to storm after them.

"Easy, my love," his father soothed.

"I'm tired of his games," Elizabeth snapped.

"I have better games in mind," the sheikh murmured. "Come, my love. Indulge me in a different target practice. We can resume your shooting lessons tomorrow."

She smiled. "You like it when I get my ire up."

Jabari bent down and kissed her. It was not their normal, tender kiss Tarik was accustomed to seeing, but smoldering, with deep intent. His father drew back, smiling. Elizabeth's eyes sparkled as she gazed at him.

Jabari glanced over at him. "Go back to Fatima, son. I know you are worried about her."

Tarik gave his parents a rueful smile. "I'm staying with her all night. Don't wait up for me."

"We don't plan on it," Elizabeth said softly, taking his father's hand.

A week later, Fatima was well along the road to recovery. The two families and their friends ate beneath a velvet sky dazzling with thousands of stars. Carrying a large platter of rice at to a low, rounded table, Fatima glanced over at her cousin's tent. Alhena was talking quietly with Tarik. Tarik's expression tightened. Starry-eyed, Alhena colored prettily. Finally Tarik detached himself and walked away.

Alhena spotted Fatima and drifted over with her usual lithe grace.

"What were you discussing?" Fatima asked.

Alhena gave an elegant shrug. "Tarik wants me to court his friend, but I told him I'd rather pick my own beaus." She hooked an arm through her cousin's. "Do you know Tarik's friend Abdul stutters every time he tells me hello?"

Fatima laughed. "You trip up their tongues," she said.

The two girls sat down to eat. Fatima, Tarik and Asad were leaving in the morning. Jabari had decided to send them to Fatima's cousin's house in Al-Minya, then to Cairo to see her brothers and investigate the rumors of recent attacks against Europeans. Kenneth and Graham, their former Khamsin brethren who were now in London, had planned a visit. The sheikh wanted to ensure their safety.

"After we visit Sayid, I'm spending a week at the schoolhouse to indulge in female companionship," Tarik stated.

Fatima's gaze roved everywhere, searching for reactions. Now anyone would know where to attack the sheikh's son. But no one looked surprised. Elizabeth looked stricken and Jabari scowled.

"Tarik," the sheikh began tightly.

Tarik looked as innocent as a newborn babe. "What, Father? The schoolhouse has enjoyable memories for me—as do the women inside."

"The mighty staff of Ra deigns to rise up and bless some poor villager's unsuspecting daughter," Asad joked.

"I'll have to guard your every move, in case that daughter's angry father charges you with a pitchfork. But don't worry, Tarik. I'm good at watching your back," Fatima said archly.

"You enjoy watching, don't you, Tima?" he replied. "Perhaps next time you will do more." Fire blazed in his dark eyes as he lifted them to her, scorching her with more heat than the campfire.

"If you're really going to have romantic adventures at the schoolhouse, then let Asad be your Guardian while you're there. I'll stay at Sayid's. You don't need my Sight to predict which woman you'll bed, Tarik," she snapped.

Jabari sighed and glanced at Asad, who nodded. "I'll do it, Tima. Tarik and I will stay at the schoolhouse for a week, then we'll get you on our way to Cairo," her twin offered.

An inner thrill infused her. The trap was laid, just as the sheikh and her father had planned last night. Knowing he'd be without his psychic Guardian for a full week, surely the killer would strike at Tarik in the schoolhouse.

Except, she actually would be secluded with Tarik at the schoolhouse, not Asad. The sheikh counted on her Sight to predict when the killer would strike.

Dinner ended, and Fatima excused herself. Tarik followed. Outside her tent, he caught her arm, his look intent.

"Tima, wait. I have something to ask you." Firelight from a nearby campfire cast shadows over his chiseled features. A hank of blond hair hung over his forehead. She felt a sudden urge to brush it back.

He lowered his voice. "Will you please consider giving up your position as my Guardian? I don't want to see you get hurt again. Ever. Let Asad remain with me in the schoolhouse. Stay here where you'll be safe. Don't act proud."

Dark purple smudges lined his eyes. He clearly hadn't slept well. His usual arrogance had faded. He cares, she realized with a start. This glimpse showed a more vulnerable man than he'd ever let through.

Fatima chose her words with care. "It's not a matter of pride, Tarik. If my Sight will predict the attacks upon you, how can I give this up? You're asking the impossible. I won't leave your side. Ever."

His mouth flattened to a tight slash. Slowly he released her. "You've made your decision, Tima. And I must make mine." He turned to leave but spoke over his shoulder. "Your Sight cannot predict everything, Fatima. Remember. Consider that a fair warning."

He vanished into the darkness, leaving her to ponder his words.

Al-Minya. Motor cars, donkeys and carriages bustled along the busy streets of the coastal city. Her cousin Sayid's opulent house, a short distance from the train station, commanded a lush view of the Nile's west bank. Verdant fields stretched beside the river's mirrored surface. The ochre house had three wings, with quiet, green gardens tended by an army of servants. The classic Islamic architecture featured towering domed minarets and mashrabiya latticework windows that allowed in the cool river breeze. Sayid boasted of having wired the house for electrical power and having his own generator, but Fatima knew it tended to sputter like an overworked mule gasping for breath.

"You know, they used to drown a female virgin in the Nile here to coax the annual flooding of the river," Fatima said as they slid off their mounts, handing the reins to a servant who appeared. "I hope they stopped that practice."

"Don't worry, Tima. I doubt there are any female virgins left from here to Cairo. I think Tarik saw to that." Asad winked.

"I saved some for you, my friend," Tarik replied dryly.

Ignoring them, Fatima sucked in a trembling breath. Cousin Sayid, who'd gained wealth from cotton exports, was known for his conservative views on women. From an early age Fatima was taught to not contradict him or insult him in his house. She felt like a gazelle wandering into a lion's den, unarmed, unable to defend herself. *Did my mother feel this way years ago, when the tiger cub flayed her cheek at this very place?*

Another male servant in an impeccable white thobe and red tarboosh led them inside. Luxurious Persian carpets covered the floor. Fatima craned her neck to study the soaring ceilings with their intricate blue mosaics. She tensed and felt the pull of healing muscles in her shoulder wound.

A loud, sonorous greeting echoed down the cavernous hallway. Dressed in white trousers and a white tunic, Sayid strode toward them. Round faced and short, he had a silver beard, a red sash about his thickening middle and gold sandals on his feet. He ground to an abrupt halt, his hearty hello cut off as he took in Fatima's clothing, turban and the lethal weapons strapped to her belt. She smiled weakly and murmured a greeting much more polite than her cousin's slack-jawed stare.

Asad stepped quickly forward, introduced Tarik and tried defusing the situation by explaining Fatima's new status. Sayid threw back his head, braying laughter like a donkey.

"I cannot believe it. I thought your mother gave birth to boy and girl twins, but I see I was wrong. Fatima, do you have an *ayir* like a man as well?"

When a furious blush flamed her cheeks, Tarik frowned. "Fatima has saved my life several times now. She deserves respect," he said, ice dripping from his voice.

Sayid's silk-covered shoulders lifted slightly. "Good,

that she saved your life, but I would prefer a man guarding me. Women are for pleasure and bearing children."

Of course Sayid, wealthy and opinionated, would never concede otherwise. Fatima forced a friendly smile as he clapped for a maid to escort her to her quarters, but she held up a protesting hand. Her cousin's harem, where she and her mother stayed on visits, was in another wing of the enormous house.

"I must sleep near Tarik, cousin Sayid. It is my duty to guard him. Might arrangements be made so I don't violate the honor of your household?"

Sayid spluttered. Asad regarded him with a steady look. "My sister is right. Or will you tell my father you denied her the right to do her duty?"

Confusion flashed over the older man's face. Finally he acquiesced. He escorted them to a lavish guest room with silk-paneled walls, an obscenely large bed covered with red and yellow pillows, and handsome cedarwood furniture. The room was connected to another equally lavish guest room by means of a large bath with pink marble fixtures and a claw-footed tub.

"Your quarters, Tarik and Asad," he boomed. "Only the best for my favorite cousin and the heir of the Khamsin sheikh."

Sayid smirked as he next took Fatima to a musty closet no bigger than a large sarcophagus.

"I will have my servants set up a bedroll for you, Fatima, so you may keep a close eye on Tarik. You may even watch as he indulges himself later with the entertainment I provide."

Smiling politely, she thanked him and ignored her churning stomach as she set down her rucksack on the carpet.

While Tarik and Asad explored the city, Fatima rested. She ignored Tarik's order to use the bed, instead curling up tight on a thin bedroll on the floor. A deep ache pulled at her shoulder, prohibiting sleep. She lay awake, ruminating over a possible list of men who wanted Tarik dead, until a servant summoned her to dinner. Sayid provided a lavish feast in their honor, including the area specialty: *kishk saidi*, wheat cakes fermented in buttermilk. Round platters of lamb and other treats adorned a long table made from Lebanese cedar wood.

Fatima sat with the women at the table's opposite end. She ignored the stares of her cousin's wives and daughters.

"Are you a man? Why are you dressed like that?" blurted one of Sayid's daughters.

"I'm a Khamsin warrior. All warriors dress like this."

Several murmured about her unusual profession, how odd she was. Fatima cleared her throat. "I'm the first female Khamsin warrior, sworn to guard our honored sheikh's son from harm."

"A woman cannot be a warrior," one protested.

"Women can be anything they want," she replied.

A derisive snort came from Sayid. "A woman desiring to be a man is a cursed thing. But you always have been odd, Fatima."

A bite of lamb clogged her throat. Fatima forced down some tea. She didn't want to insult Sayid, but his words lashed her like a whip.

Amber, Sayid's oldest daughter, sniffed. Beautiful, vain and spoiled, she'd long held disdain for Fatima. "I would not want to wear such a manly outfit. It's ugly. Perhaps you desire to become a man because you know nothing about being a woman."

Inside her manly boots, Fatima's toes curled. She gripped her teacup so tightly her fingers hurt. "I know how to be a woman. But duty calls me to wear this and carry arms to protect Tarik."

Asad loudly asked Sayid about the latest news from

Cairo. Much to Fatima's relief, the women fell silent. Rumors flourished of peasants attacking trains, targeting Europeans. Sayid snorted with derision as he mentioned women might join the protests.

"Ridiculous! England has been good for our economy. And, women? What is next, babes in diapers crawling in the street to protest?" Sayid slammed a fist on the table, making the china rattle.

Fatima lifted her head, her clear gaze meeting her cousin's down the table. *I will be silent no more.*

"I heartily support any woman who protests. Egypt is treated as England's stepchild, used for her resources and given no respect. Those who gain wealth from sucking at the teat of mother England naturally have no desire to become weaned. But I, for one, am tired of being treated as a second-class citizen simply because I am Egyptian."

Sayid looked taken aback, then scowled. But Tarik lifted his cup in a salute. "To freedom from England," he said softly.

Fatima and Asad joined his toast. Sayid did not.

Silent servants finally arrived to cart away the dishes. The women left as Sayid took Tarik, Asad and herself to a smaller room laden with jewel-toned Persian rugs and thick cushions. A trio of musicians waited on a raised dais. As she and the men sat Bedouin style, Sayid flashed a sly smile.

"In honor of your stay, Tarik and Asad, I hired Zuka and Noor to entertain you. Fatima, since you are so insistent on guarding your charge, you may watch."

Sayid leaned back against his mound of silk pillows and clapped. Two women appeared, dressed in diaphanous veils, their slender fingers bearing *sagats*, tiny brass cymbals. Heavily beaded shirts covered their arms, but fit snugly along their breasts, exposing the round upper halves. Coins jingled from their elaborate head-bands. Turquoise and purple skirts flowed with the sensuous sway of their rounded hips.

Sayid belched. "Like my payment? Look at their bellies."

Sparkling rubies winked in the women's bare navels. Fatima watched with unease as smiling musicians struck up a rapid polyrhythmic beat. The women swayed and undulated, waving their purple and turquoise veils, and the silks flowed to the floor as they were tossed away. Carmine-colored lips pouted teasingly, and the women rolled their hips and thrust out their ample bosoms. Fatima heard her brother's breathing quicken. His eyes dilated as he fixed on Zuka, the shorter, plumper dancer. Fatima felt an embarrassed flush coat her cheeks.

Noor, the taller, more graceful woman, danced toward Tarik. She thrust her hips out. Beads and spangles on her skirts jingled. Two hard nubs peaked through her shirt's thin silk. Noor's *sagats* clinked, a contrapuntal rhythm to every throbbing beat of the drum and every pluck of the rebaba, the horsehair bow.

Fatima remembered the night she'd danced in the moonlight, Tarik drumming madly on the darrabukka. In her white nightdress she'd danced—not to sexually arouse, but because her spirit answered the music's wild call. These dancers made the art seem vulgar. And Sayid called this total femininity, praising the women's hip-shaking, jerky movements.

"Watch closely, cousin," he advised her. "Perhaps you can learn something about how to act like a woman, since you are so obsessed with not being one."

Fatima pasted on a polite, tight smile until finally the music ended. Panting, Zuka reached out an elegant palm. Without a word, Asad took it, following as she led

185

him out of the room. A deep ache stabbed Fatima. She felt as alienated as in childhood, when he'd abandoned her for Tarik's friendship. Didn't he realize how humiliating this display was for her?

Noor's carmine lips formed a pouty smile. She crooked a slender finger at Tarik. "Your turn," she purred. "I am yours, my lord, for the entire night to do with whatever you wish."

Sayid slapped a thigh and laughed. "My gift to you, Tarik. Or perhaps you are my gift to her. I hear stories of Ra, the golden god whose formidable staff slays women with ecstasy." He gave Fatima a cursory glance. "Of course, if you are so inclined to guard him, you may stand by his bed as he indulges himself. However, you cannot protect him from dying of pleasure!"

Fatima willed herself to say with dignity, "The Khamsin code of honor clearly stipulates that my Guardian duties do not include standing watch over Tarik as he indulges himself, cousin." She forced a smile to soften her bitter tone. "But thank you for the entertainment, Sayid. It was most interesting. I now appreciate the real art of belly dancing." She stood with as much grace as she could muster, ready to excuse herself.

Tarik rose, grasping not Noor's hand, but hers. His palm was firm and calloused. "If you will excuse me, Sayid, I am weary. My Guardian and I bid you both good night."

Noor's pretty mouth dropped open nearly as far as Sayid's. "You do not wish my gift?" Fatima's cousin asked.

A flat smile stretched Tarik's mouth. "Thank you, Sayid. You are a generous host, but I am not interested tonight." He glanced at Fatima, who felt her heart beat fast as a tiny bird's. "Come, Tima." She swallowed her shock and accompanied him out of the room.

There was a small spring in her step as they entered

Tarik's luxurious room, but she whispered good night and headed for the closet. He arrived there first, taking her bag and placing it on the floor.

"Take my bed. You are still healing, and the ground is cold and hard. I will take the closet," he insisted quietly. She started to protest, but fell silent when he laid an index finger across her lips. Her mouth wobbled from the light pressure of his touch. "No, Tima. The bed is yours. There is no argument in this."

She looked up at him with widened eyes. "Tarik, why did you refuse Noor? She's so . . . beautiful. Asad did not refuse Zuka."

Tarik caressed her lower lip, very softly. "Don't begrudge Asad his pleasures, Tima. He is a man, and a pretty sway of the hips is most tempting for him. No longer for me. I desire more."

Afraid to ask what he meant, Fatima nodded, pulled away. "I'll take my bath first, if you don't mind. I need to. I feel . . . sticky."

"I'll stand guard against intruders," he teased.

She smiled. "Yes, please. Guard the door. Sayid will be spying on me to see if I truly do have an *ayir.*"

Mischief twinkled in his eyes. "And what of me, Tima? Aren't you afraid *I'll* spy on you bathing?"

"No," she countered solemnly. "You have too much honor, Tarik. You're not like other men. Good night." And she grabbed her bag to head for the bath, hiding a smile at the startled yet satisfied look flashing across his face.

Chapter Fourteen

The ruse started late the following day. Disguised as Asad, her lower face veiled in Khamsin indigo, Fatima prepared to leave with Tarik. The sheikh's son had shaved his beard and donned ordinary clothing. But as Fatima forced a polite thank-you and good-bye to Sayid in the front corridor, malice glittered in the eyes of the man's daughter.

"You are well suited for playing the part of a man, Fatima," Amber said. "You've never been attractive, and your poor mother fretted about you ever marrying. You're more successful as a man than a woman."

The insult was as effective as a sharp slap. But Tarik put a hand on Fatima's arm, steering her away before she could respond.

The ride back was long, and stars glittered overhead as they reached the schoolhouse. The gate unlocked, the horses bedded down with fresh straw, Fatima and Tarik went inside. Asad and the other warriors would be along shortly, according to the plan. Disguised as peasants, they would remain in a house next to the school-house and each night hide in the schoolhouse's barn, waiting for Tarik's signal before moving in.

Fatima hesitated at the row of bedrooms lining the corridor. "Which one . . . did you not use?" she half-jested.

Tarik gestured toward a door. "Sleep here."

"Oh, you didn't . . . ?"

"No. My mother slept there before my father married her. Of course, he tried seducing her in this very place." A wry smile curled his lips. "He didn't succeed, not until their wedding night. Which is why I'm a nine-months baby."

Fatima managed a weak smile. "Good for your mother. She resisted your father."

"*She* didn't resist," he said slowly. "Not really. He did. Now settle your things, wash up. There are some smoked hares in the larder. I'll make dinner after I bathe."

Amber's earlier insult rang in her ears. *You're not a woman.*

"I can cook," she asserted.

Tarik's dark gold brows rose, and he looked intrigued. "All right."

She tried to cook later, after she was bathed and refreshed.

Coughing as thick smoke billowed everywhere, she cursed gas ovens. Tarik peered over her shoulder at their charred meal.

"I do believe it's done," he said.

Fatima shooed him out. She mixed carrots and greens with oil and vinegar and brought all the food to the dining room. Beeswax candles flickered, casting a golden glow over the cedar table. Tarik stood as she entered, gallantly pulling out the chair opposite as she set the food down. He poured juice into two crystal goblets, handed her one as she sat.

189

His long, sun-kissed hair spilled past his shoulders. He wore loose black trousers, a black silk shirt and leather sandals. Open at the throat, the shirt offered a tantalizing peek at crisp dark gold chest hair. Tarik looked relaxed, yet the air of hidden strength clung to him. Dangerous, he was a lion at rest, utterly assured of his power and command.

A wry smile touched his sensual mouth as he glanced at the blackened meat. "The salad looks splendid," he offered.

They clinked glasses, sipped, talked about events in Cairo and Fatima's time in England.

"Know what I missed the most? Besides my family?" She drained her glass, feeling mellow yet sad.

"My wonderful sense of humor?" he asked.

"The desert—dryness swallowing you like a living thing. In England, roses are everywhere. People take them for granted. But in the desert, when you find a beautiful rose, it's so rare, you cherish every precious moment of its life because you know it won't last."

He smiled. "I felt the same in England. Everyone scurrying about like scarab beetles, pretending to be important. I missed the simplicity of our life, rides in the desert, listening to the stars at night because it's so quiet you can hear them sing."

Deeply touched, Fatima drank in his sensual mouth and the sculpted features once hidden by his golden beard. "You look so different now."

Tarik leaned back, resting an arm across the chair back. "More charming and handsome than ever? More like the scoundrel I am?"

"Hmmmm." She considered. "No, more like a little boy." She laughed at his crestfallen expression, speared a piece of burnt rabbit, chewed and made a face, then said, "I can't cook. And laundry—once I helped my mother and everything turned blue. Even my baby brother's diapers!"

A choking laugh escaped Tarik. "Indigo diapers—the best covering for a true Khamsin babe," he teased.

"I mean it, Tarik." Fatima sighed. The friendly cama-raderie they'd shared in childhood had returned, urged her to share confidences. For so long she'd held herself in check, knowing others regarded her as strange. Deep down she knew Tarik truly understood and appreciated the differences setting her apart from other women, even if he had issues with them. "What man would want me for a wife when I'm, well, seen as defective? I can't cook or clean. I have these odd visions that make me go into bizarre trances and scare everyone . . ."

Gazing at the intricate blue pattern on her plate she went on, "Do you know that in England, at my official debut into society, I went into a trance?"

"No," he said quietly, all laughter gone. "It must have been quite traumatic."

A bitter laugh escaped her. "For them, not me. I think I even—oh bloody hell, there I was, in a lacy white dress, my hair done like so." She twisted her long hair in one hand and demonstrated. "And this nobleman's son asked me to dance. I went into this trance, had this vision. It was hor-rid. I saw, I saw . . ." Fatima closed her eyes, shuddering.

"What, Tima? You can tell me," he coaxed.

Her eyes flew open, seeing the horrors revealed six years ago. "Men with guns, wearing these funny hats. Mud. Long pits and burnt skies. Gunfire, bones shatter-ing, blood. Screams—and this awful feeling of a global conflict that would not end."

He went still, his large dark eyes searching hers. "Oh God, my poor Tima. You saw the war a year before it happened." His hand took hers. Strong calloused fin-gers caressed her.

Closing her eyes, Fatima relished the comfort of simple human contact. Tarik never recoiled in horror, thought her odd, or manly. He respected her visions—always had.

I *can* be a woman, she thought, recalling Amber's remarks as if her cousin still taunted her. I can be as much of a woman as that whore hired to bed Tarik!

But no man wanted her for who she was; she was too different, too odd. Depression smothered her. A lump formed in her throat.

"Maybe Sayid is right. I'm really not a woman," she whispered, desperately hoping Tarik would keep touching her.

"You are very much a woman," he said softly.

His hand slipped away. Fatima suppressed a disappointed sigh as he leaned back, staring at the woven basket of fruit on the table. A mysterious smile curved his lips as he selected an oblong greenish brown piece and fished out his dagger.

"My father imports papaya from South Africa. It's quite juicy and sweet."

Fascination filled her as he sliced open the fruit. Shiny black seeds clustered in a hollow amidst bright orange flesh. Spooning out the seeds, Tarik studied her.

"My father gave it to my mother when she was trying to get pregnant. It's said to be good luck. The seeds represent fertility, and the shape is like a woman's, well . . ."

Realization slapped her. Her mouth collapsed into a wide O of shock. The oblong shape clearly resembled a womb.

"My father gave me the fruit for a different reason. When I became a warrior at thirteen, he used it to demonstrate how to make love to a woman with my mouth." With a wide smile, Tarik set down his dagger, picked up the fruit. " 'My son, know this for your wedding night. A woman takes longer to achieve her release than a man. Always give your bride her pleasure first,' " he mimicked in his father's strong voice.

Embarrassed heat flooded Fatima's face. "Er, Tarik, you don't need to tell me about this."

Mischief sparked in his onyx gaze. "Tima, you are a warrior now. Every Khamsin warrior is taught how to deliver the secret of hundred kisses to prepare his virgin bride for her deflowering."

"I don't need to know—"

"Oh, but you do, my little caracal," he teased softly. Clearing his throat, he again imitated his father's voice: " 'Your bride will be frightened and excited by what is about to happen. She will probably never have seen a man's erect member before, and the very sight may make her blush or fill her with fear about taking you inside her.' " The papaya shook in his hand, as if quivering in fear.

" 'Do not take your bride until she lies spent and trembling with passion. Then quickly mount her. Enter her slowly, easing your way. Push hard, for her passage will be very tight and resistant. Never, ever lose control. Think of less pleasant matters if you find yourself too excited, wanting to thrust hard.' "

Tarik slid his forefinger across the wet fruit's hollow, thrusting back and forth. A pulse beat wildly at the base of his throat. He threw back his head, moaned quietly as if he truly did push with determination inside a woman's silky body.

" 'You will feel a barrier, her maidenhead. Be firm and push hard and it will yield. She will cry out in pain. Quiet her cries with a reassuring kiss, then stop, letting her become accustomed to you. When she relaxes, thrust again and allow your release. But do none of this until she has pleasure first.' "

BONNIE VANAK

Halfway into the papaya's hollow, his finger suddenly shook. His dark eyes twinkled with mirth. A high-pitched squeaky laced his voice as if he were thirteen again, a boy turning into a man. "'But Father, how do I make her feel pleasure?' I asked."

"'I will tell you, my son. It is very important to bring your bride to climax first, to prepare her to take you. Her first time will be painful and she will bleed, but a Khamsin warrior is gentle and tender, always ensuring she is pleased beforehand.'"

Tarik assumed a stern look. "'Never take a maiden by force, Tarik. Your duty is to gentle her fears. Arouse her so that she will tremble with desire.'"

Fatima's breath hitched. She felt like a blushing virgin bride, fearful of the unknown yet trembling with desire.

"'First, undress your bride, praising her beauty, the firmness of her breasts, how womanly she is, the curve of her hips. Kiss her thoroughly on the mouth, her neck. Pay special attention to her breasts. Suckle her nipples. This gives her great pleasure, stimulating her instinct to spread her legs and allow you entrance. Then begins the secret of hundred kisses. Tiny kisses, like a bird's breath, across her naked skin. Follow these with small love bites, then slowly lick. Do this from the top of her body across her bare skin.'" Tarik's onyx gaze settled on her as he gave the fruit a slow lick. "Interested in the lesson, Tima?"

She steeled herself against his dark velvet voice, the sensual way his tongue plundered the fruit. "Is this how you seduce all your women, Tarik—using fruit? It's very inventive, but it won't work on me. I'm not some adoring, silly woman who'll melt at your feet like chocolate. I have a warrior's control."

"Oh?" he drawled. His slow smile warned he recognized and accepted the challenge in her words.

He tested the papaya with his finger. "Very gently,

194

Tima, you slide a finger into the secret hollow between her legs, testing her readiness. It will feel like this fruit—soft and yielding, but tight. If aroused, she'll be wet. The wetness is nature's way of preparing her passage for penetration. Your mouth will make her even wetter when you kiss her there."

His tongue darted out to slowly kiss the glistening edge of the succulent fruit, and Tarik's heated gaze met hers. He put a forefinger at the wet opening of the papaya. Dry mouthed, Fatima stared at him probing the soft orange flesh.

"See the wetness?" he asked softly. "Then, after you kiss her body, part her thighs with your hands. If she protests, praise her beauty. Be firm but gentle. Settle between her legs. A woman's secret hollow is like the petals of a beautiful flower. With your fingers, very gently part those petals. They will glisten with her arousal . . ."

With his thumbs, Tarik spread the papaya apart. Fatima desperately quashed a strangled moan. A steady throbbing had sprung up between her clenched thighs.

"Are you learning all this, Tima? Observe the tiny bud nestled at the center of the flower. This is a woman's pleasure center. When stimulated, she will writhe with each caress you deliver. Be careful, for it's delicate. Give it a tender kiss. Then settle your mouth upon it, taste its sweetness."

Tarik's mouth settled on the fruit. He kissed then suckled, the wet smacking sound thundering in her ears like her heart. This was the pleasure men gave to women, the source of the moans in the black tents. Her nipples tightened. She longed for the caress of that moist mouth. Sweat beaded her temples.

Tensing her body in a desperate fight against the erotic sensations he created, Fatima fisted her hands. The warrior inside her howled in outrage at this seduction. The woman inside her watched in aroused fascination.

"Love her with your mouth, lick and kiss her slowly. Make tiny circles with your tongue, flicking, moving faster if she moans. Give her pleasure until she screams, her body quivering with release, her honeyed juices flooding your mouth . . ." Laving his tongue upon the fruit's wet flesh, he demonstrated. Faster he stroked the fruit. "Mmmm, so delicious, so succulent and juicy," he whispered. "Sweet. So sweet."

Hands gripping her chair's edges, Fatima squirmed. Their gazes caught, met as Tarik suckled. He tore his mouth away from the papaya, passion darkening his gaze.

"Like this, Tima. Licking, sucking, making her hot and moist—so hot she writhes and twists beneath you, her hips jerking in preparation to meet your thrusts when you enter her, slide into her tight, wet channel like a sword entering its sheath. She will feel your member, the hard knob slowly entering her, and she will welcome it because at last your bodies are joined and that aching emptiness between her legs is filled . . ."

Blood thundered in her veins as he resumed licking the fruit, his mouth curving over the edge, sucking, flicking his tongue. Fatima gripped the chair in white-knuckled despair. Frustration had sharp teeth. She wanted Tarik's head between her legs, his mouth upon her flesh. A whimper rose as she fought the urge to plunge her hands between her legs, to give herself relief from the throbbing ache.

Making loud suckling sounds, Tarik flicked his tongue faster, faster, delivering heat to her, stoking her fire until she would burst into an inferno of quivering, naked flesh. "Oooohhhhh, yes!" he shrieked in a woman's high-pitched voice.

A harsh cry was wrung from Fatima's own lips. But she was denied fulfillment, and she fell back, trembling. The papaya fell from Tarik's loosened fingers onto the

196

table with a soft thud. He ran a tongue over his wet mouth.

"Mmmmmm. Delicious," he purred. A lazy, seductive smile curled his lips as he retrieved the other section of papaya, offered it. "Care for a bite?"

Fatima gulped, struggling to regain her lost composure. She had to deflect the sexual tension he'd created. "I-I . . . I don't want fruit. Er, is there something else to eat?"

Tarik went to a large wooden cupboard and retrieved a small box. He offered it on opened palms. Mirth twinkled in his dark gaze. "Chocolate. It . . . melts. But it should be savored slowly."

Chocolate. It would melt on her tongue as women melted from his seduction. Clever Tarik knew. But, her mouth watering, Fatima stared at the rich, dark confection.

He sat beside her, selected a small square. "Sweet, succulent chocolate, Tima." He leaned closer, holding it near her lips. The rich, tempting fragrance teased her nostrils. He withdrew the square, licked it slowly, his dark gaze holding hers hostage.

A tiny, anticipatory shiver snaked down her spine. He grazed her mouth with chocolate, smudged her. Her tongue darted out, tasting the rich sweetness. Tarik lowered his head, running his tongue across her lips. His tantalizing masculine scent of sandalwood, musk and clean skin flooded her nostrils. Fatima dragged in a startled breath as he sucked on her lower lip. Then the sheikh's son withdrew, held the square out.

"Come, Tima—indulge," he coaxed.

Her lips parted slightly in acceptance. Tarik ran the chocolate about her mouth, teasingly withdrawing it. The square tasted sweet and rich, decadent as he traced her lips. Her mouth opened wider. He popped the chocolate inside, his gaze igniting with fiery intensity as she savored the morsel.

The sinfully rich scent flooded her nostrils, the taste lingered in her mouth. A deep moan welled up in her chest, the agonized cry of a woman torn between resisting temptation and surrendering to pleasure. But if she submitted, he'd claim more than her mouth.

"It's good, isn't it?" Tarik caressed her lips with his thumb, then leaned forward. "I'm going to taste *you* now," he whispered.

His mouth settled on hers, firm and warm, his tongue leisurely licking chocolate off her trembling lips. Fatima closed her eyes, yearning.

I am a warrior! She recoiled, gave him a light push.

"I'm going for a walk." Fatima pushed up and away—from him and from the sensual web he wove over her. She must clear her mind and her heart, because he had the power to break it, to shatter it into a million tiny pieces, to leave her behind to pick up the shards of her broken dreams.

Yet, her cousin's hollowed taunts followed her as Fatima escaped to the garden. *You make a better man,* Amber whispered.

Fatima plopped unladylike down on a rock. Moonlight spilled into this lush garden, splashing plants and flowers with silver. With an angry tug, she yanked off her indigo turban, combing her long hair out with trembling fingers.

I can be a woman, I can! For once, just for once, she longed to know what it felt like; to experience passion as a woman did and capitulate to the intense feelings she had for Tarik. To feel his powerful body join with hers as they became one, to finally surrender to the passion she'd tried to keep at bay. To be a woman in Tarik's arms.

Even at the risk of losing her heart. . . .

* * *

He went into the garden, studying the night-blooming jasmine, the quiet palms and the small trickling fountain his father had installed as a gift to his mother. He examined a tall, twisting bush with a fat, contorted trunk. Carmine blooms with pale yellow centers stretched out as if beckoning him to choose.

The wild desert rose. Tarik admired its beauty and ability to thrive in the desert's barren landscape. He picked one blossom, studying the delicate petals.

The flower reminded him of Tima. His father had affectionately nicknamed his mother his "desert rose," but the name suited Fatima as well. Like the plant, she had settled in rough, inhospitable terrain. The challenges she faced as a warrior and Guardian were enormous. Yet she never once complained. Fatima valiantly struggled to bloom wherever she was planted. Time and again she met obstacles with determination. Like the desert rose she blossomed, bestowing her grace as a rare gift. He had never seen a woman more beautiful, for he saw the entire woman, her sacrifice, her struggles, her honor.

He harvested the blossom and searched for his Guardian. She was sitting cross-legged on a flat gray rock, looking forlorn and lost. Moonlight filtered through the sprawling branches of a tree, dappling her glossy black hair. Without a word he sat down beside her. She stiffened.

"Leave me alone, Tarik," she said in a wooden voice.

He brushed the soft petals of the rose against her silky cheek.

"I brought you this. *Adenium obesum*." He offered it to her.

"You know the Latin?" Fatima said, the pique leaving her voice. She took the flower, inhaled deeply.

"Oxford. My father didn't waste his money after all."
He gave her a playful wink.

Her large, green eyes were too introspective. Tarik
longed to see them sparkle with her usual effervescence. They regarded him with such solemn intensity
that it made him ache.

"Why did you bring me this, Tarik? For a Latin lesson?"

"I brought you a flower as a man brings any woman
flowers."

"Do you see me as a woman, Tarik?" she whispered. "I
am a woman, but some say I'm not. What am I?"

"You are every bit a woman—and more," he replied.

How dare that bitch Amber suggest she was anything
but? Caressing Fatima's cheek, he marveled at the soft
texture. No amount of man's clothing could cloak the
sweet silkiness of her skin, the pouty mouth ripe for
kisses, the graceful curve of hips and breasts. Legs
toned with muscle had a delicate turn of the ankle. His
hands longed to span her slim waist. She had a sensitive
heart, so tender he wanted to shield it from ever witnessing life's ugly side.

Yes, a woman at her deepest core, Fatima possessed
also a warrior's fierce resolve and courage. And a
unique beauty. Like the desert rose, she was rare,
comely, and he wanted to breathe in and savor every
precious moment they were together.

He longed to see her tossing her hair from side to side
as she rode him, her ruby lips parted in passion as he
cupped her breasts, teasing the nipples to hard nubs. He
wanted to hear her breathing ragged and fierce, nails digging into his shoulders as she climaxed.

Tarik could wait no longer. Leaning forward, he took
her mouth. At first she recoiled, but as he persisted her
mouth grew pliant beneath the insistent pressure. He
settled a hand over the back of her head, holding her
steady as his tongue leisurely traced her lips then thrust

inside. She tasted like deep, rich chocolate, and desire. A deep growl rose in his chest. God, he wanted her. His breathing grew ragged; his heart raced.

Desire flooded his loins. Tarik groaned and tore his mouth away. He sought her eyes, sparkling with passion in the moon's luminous glow.

"I want you, Tima. Tonight. Now. Will you be my woman?"

A tiny jerk of her head was all the answer he got. It was enough. Tarik swept her into his arms, cradling her against his chest as he swept into the schoolhouse, heading for her bedroom.

She was his at last.

For so long she'd denied herself, but no longer. Her cousin's haunting taunts echoed in Fatima's head: *You are not a woman, but a man.* Pushed past caring, resenting the femininity of those women who easily awed men, she was determined to become a woman in Tarik's arms.

Absorbing his kisses, Fatima fisted her hands in his shirt as he gently lowered her onto her mattress. Her mouth opened, and shyly she met the bold thrusts of his tongue. Wetness from her arousal streaked down her thighs. Her nipples tingled, chafing unbearably against her rough linen shirt, her warrior's attire contrasting with the damp gush stirring from her womanly center. No longer did she want to restrain passion, but to welcome every uncontrollable feeling.

With a harsh rasp of breath, he tore at the fastenings of her binish and shirt. Drawing them off, he bared her breasts. Fatima trembled, her nipples hardening beneath his admiring gaze. Tarik bent his head and kissed one pearling peak with reverence. Taking it fully into his mouth, he sucked, flicking it with his tongue.

Fatima arched and cradled his head to her breast. His tongue swirled over the tautness. Panting, Tarik removed his mouth, his entire body tense as if fighting for control.

Drawing back, he impatiently removed her trousers. Tarik kicked off his sandals, yanked his shirt over his head and tossed it aside. Fatima inched backward, licking her lips as she took in his bulging biceps, the smooth play of shoulder muscles bunching as he tossed the garment aside. Candlelight flickered over his taut golden skin. *Hers. All hers.*

His. All his.

Naked at last, she was baring her body only for him. Her honey gold skin glowed like a dewy peach half. Fatima's breasts were shapely and plump, tipped with taut red nipples. Desire darkened her green cat eyes. He kissed her, wrapping his arms around her slim waist, hot aching need roaring through his veins. Tarik ran his hands over her lush curves. So soft, like the most delicate silk. So womanly, hidden beneath the rough cotton of her garb. He had uncloaked a rare treasure.

The edges of his control began to slip. He pulsed painfully, needing to plunge into her wet warmth.

Ah, Fatima, Fatima. Little wildcat. I'll take care of you, he silently promised. Shifting his weight, he ran a finger down her breasts and belly. His hand tunneled through the sweet, silky curls, delved between her feminine folds. He slid a finger across that silken flesh. Wetness drenched his fingers.

A soft cry wrung from her lips. Filled with masculine satisfaction, Tarik raised his head. He wanted her more than his next breath. His balls felt tight and heavy. Against his loose trousers, his cock throbbed.

"I need you," he breathed. "Tima, ah God, Tima!"

Fatima opened to his probing tongue as he kissed her, tasted him exploring her mouth. His flesh was firm and hard beneath her fingers as she stroked his back. He dragged his mouth away and she felt keen disappointment until he draped hot kisses along her neck, feathering her skin down to her breasts. He was so masculine, so muscled, so different from her own body. And beneath his urgent kisses existed something deep and primitive, roaring for freedom.

Tarik drew back, impatiently shoving down his trousers, releasing his throbbing sex. It jutted out like a stone column. The round head was reddened. A drop of clear fluid glistened at the tip.

As he wrapped her hand around his jutting erection, Fatima drew in a trembling breath. Her fingers did not meet. He was huge! How could she ever take that swollen thickness inside her? The thought excited her even as apprehension grew. What would his male sex feel like pressed between her legs?

A Khamsin woman remains a maid until marriage.

Tarik was challenging the one thing that stood between her and her maiden state. She'd always felt in control this way. No longer. He towered over her, a powerful body molded of hard muscle and sinew. Golden leonine locks flowed down past wide shoulders. His fathomless onyx eyes glittered with dangerous intent.

Her arousal shifted to fear. Dry mouthed, Fatima scrambled back. He advanced, and nervousness deadened her limbs.

He mounted her, kissing her deeply. Her palms pressed against his bronze chest, tangled in the crisp, dark gold hair there. Fear joined with primitive instinct. Her hands caressed his smooth muscles, felt ridges of rippling strength. Beneath him, she writhed, legs parting, needing him to fill her emptiness.

"Tima," he said, a hot breath against her cheek, "you drive me wild, my little caracal." Fisting his hand in her hair, he kissed her relentlessly, then tore his mouth away. His masculine power made her tremble.

"Was it ever like this with Michael?" he panted, trailing fiery kisses over her throat. "Perhaps it's best you're not a virgin. You know how to handle a man."

"No, no," she cried out. Oh God, she'd forgotten her lie at the schoolhouse about losing her virginity. A low moan tore from her as Tarik drew back, taking his erection in hand. He intended to take her now. This had gone beyond control.

How could she tell him? Her mouth opened on a protest, but dry panic seized her as he spread her thighs, exposing her vulnerable feminine center. Aching need twined with terror. He cupped her bottom, pulling her to the bed's edge and leaned between her legs. She lay motionless beneath him as he pressed his arousal against her, circling her tiny bud, teasing it with long strokes. She arched, pressing against him, growing desperate for something she didn't fully understand.

An ages-old instinct urged her to accept. She longed for him to make her fully a woman. *So be it.* Fatima momentarily closed her eyes, silently surrendering all. No one need know she'd no longer be a virgin. What did it matter to one who could never wed?

So excited that he could not contain himself anymore, he felt like a wild, raging beast. Tarik ran a trembling hand down Fatima's belly. He stared with incredulous wonder at her carved cheekbones, their delicate pink color; her mouth swollen from his fervent kisses. Never had any other women had been like this. Exotic Fatima was soft as satin, luscious and womanly. All other women paled beside her, sips of sweet juice temporarily sating his thirst. Not Tima. She was a rare wine, rewarding his palate with her tangy, spicy taste. He would drink from her yet never quench his thirst.

Great, shuddering breaths tore from his lungs. His cock throbbed painfully. Needing to join his flesh to hers, he positioned himself. The deep, primal instinct was surfacing, and he answered its demanding call.

"Look at me, Tima," he commanded.

Her large, green eyes widened as he rose above her. He pushed inside, pressing past the resistance of her inner muscles. As he thrust into that sweetness, she enfolded him, hugged him tightly. He groaned, gripping her rounded hips, steadying her as he penetrated.

So tight. So deliciously tight. Ah God, it had been so long for her. Tarik pushed forward, answering the call to possess and claim. To make her his, so that she'd never remember another lover.

Fatima arched her body, erotic bliss fading to shock. His hard thickness slowly penetrated. Tarik's arousal felt like a thick iron bar pressing between her legs, though he murmured soothingly as he pushed. Fatima gulped down a breath. Insistent pressure became real pain as he rocked back and forth, determined to gain entrance. His fierce, dark gaze burned into hers. He thrust deep, sheathing himself to the root.

Torn asunder, Fatima bit back a cry as she gripped his arms. Pinned beneath his heavy weight, impaled and stretched beyond compare, she writhed helplessly. Slick inner tissues slowly adjusted to the demanding male intruder.

Tarik's sluggish brain registered the stubborn barrier rent under his determined thrust. He froze with shock. A virgin? She had lied! Michael hadn't been the first. He was. And he'd rudely taken her without any gentleness. Now he realized her moans were not desire, but fear. She writhed like trapped prey.

Tarik softened his voice. "Tima, lie still. Quiet. Hush. Hush, sweetheart." He spoke to her in a low, hypnotic voice. He brushed a kiss against her trembling lips. "That's it. Hush . . . quiet now. It's all right. Lie still."

Her rosy mouth wobbled as she tightened her fingers around his shoulders. Huge, pain-glazed eyes stared at him helplessly.

"It is done, Tima. There's no going back now," he told her gently.

He groaned, desire and need battling against coherent thought. Panting, he braced himself on his palms and started to slide off her. She laced her hands around his neck.

"No, Tarik. Don't stop. Please. I need this. I need you," she whispered. She wrapped her legs about his hips.

He withdrew slowly, thrusting forward gently, trying to leash his passion. But she raised her hips to meet his thrusts, and her inner muscles squeezed him like a wet satin fist. A deep groan ripped from his chest. Tarik plunged into her, his heart hammering as her silky sheath clenched him. Ah God, she was hot, sweet wetness. No one else but Fatima, always Fatima. Fatima haunting his dreams, Fatima's rosy mouth teasing, her soft body pressed under him.

Mine, he thought savagely as the tension built. No one else's. No other man would claim her now. He gave one final thrust. Throwing back his head, he climaxed hard and fast. Bucking and shuddering, he gripped her hips, a feral growl tearing from his throat. Fatima lay quiet as his hot seed spurted deep inside her.

Gently as he could, he pulled away. She cried out as he slid against her delicate tissues. Tarik bent down, chased a tear with a kiss. He licked the wet salt dripping from her eyes. It was soft but cold.

Regret speared him as he remembered how she had cried out in pain. Going to the bath chamber, he ran water into a small basin. He hunted through a cabinet for herbs, added them to the water, then rejoined her, carrying the basin, a white washcloth and a soft towel.

Fatima lay still as a limestone carving of an ancient pharaoh's bride. Crystal droplets clung to her smoky lashes. At last she turned her head away.

"Tima," Tarik said in his gentlest voice. "Open your legs. I need to do this, it will lessen the pain."

Her legs clamped together, but with a deep sigh he eased them open. He wet the cloth and bathed her, wincing at the blood. Then he rinsed and placed a clean cloth between her legs.

"Leave it there for a while, and let the herbs do their healing. That should help," he said softly. He slid next to her, draping her with a protective arm. "Sweetheart, why did you lie about your virginity?"

Her luminous green eyes, beautiful as the green grass on the banks of the Nile, clouded with emotion. "You were so teasing, so superior. Acting as though I knew nothing. I resented you."

Tarik rubbed the heel of his palm against his brow. How could he not have recognized her defiant tone, that stubborn jut of her lip? He could blame no one but himself.

She drew the sheet to her breasts, her lovely face coloring. "I told you Michael was my lover. We kissed. But I didn't feel anything more than friendship for him and I said that, so he stopped. Nothing else happened."

Savage male possessiveness filled him. She was his after all. Michael had never known the pleasures of Fatima's soft body, her silky skin. He was her first and only lover. "I was your first, Tima. Had I known . . ."

"You would have stopped, apologized and told me to have a nice day?" Bitterness laced her voice.

Ah, his Tima—sharp as a scimitar. With his thumb, he wiped away a tear rolling down her cheek. "I was beyond stopping. But I would have been much gentler, little caracal. I would have given you release so that you would forget the pain of our joining amidst the pleasure. No real man desires to inflict pain upon a woman, even the necessary pain of her first time."

Tarik pressed a soft kiss to her tear-streaked face. "The first time always hurts for a woman."

Her lovely cat eyes narrowed and a derisive sniff sounded as she yanked the cloth from between her legs. Padding to the bathroom, she vanished inside. Each muscle tensed on her lithe body as she returned. Fatima slid between the sheets.

"So now I know what it is to be a woman. But I'm also a warrior," she asserted. "I can handle pain, certainly from becoming a woman."

Tarik jammed a frustrated hand through his hair. He must show her the exquisite pleasure of being a woman or risk losing her forever to the warrior's way.

"It will not hurt next time. There will be only pleasure, I promise."

"There will be no next time, Tarik. I doubt I can experience pleasure from this."

"You will," he insisted. "You're much too sore now, but tomorrow I'll show you. I'm going to love you until you sob and beg for release."

He cradled her to his chest, filled with fierce protectiveness. She was his. He had sealed her to him in the bond of the flesh, her sheath had been invaded by his sword. No longer a combative warrior, she was fully woman. And tomorrow, she'd discover the ecstasy found in total and complete surrender in his arms.

Chapter Fifteen

Fatima awoke to an aching soreness between her legs, and a deep regret: Tarik's arrogant prediction had come true. *We will be lovers, Tima.*

Shafts of dusty sunlight gilded his sleeping face. Tarik lay on his side, at rest like a contented lion. Dark gold locks covered the snowy pillow. Her gaze caressed his nude body, the dark hair on his chest, the strong clean lines of hard muscle and long bone. He was devastating. If she capitulated fully to passion in his arms, how much power would he then wield over her?

Those penetrating eyes opened sleepily, blinked. A lazy smile touched his mouth. Tarik stretched and purred with contentment and, snapping awake, he rolled over and captured her in his arms. He planted a tiny kiss on her brow. Fatima jerked away, pushing against his chest.

Tarik heaved a deep sigh, rolled out of bed. Despite her bitterness, she couldn't help sneaking a glance. His taut, rounded buttocks flexed as he prowled across the room. He stood, stretching, legs spread slightly apart.

His sex swung gently between his legs. In its state of rest, it looked much less threatening. Muscles rippled beneath the golden skin of his back as he walked to the door.

Damn, he was striking, that body filled with godlike grace. And he was dangerous to her. As he walked to the door, with a regretful sigh she sank back into the sheets, pretending to sleep.

He wisely left her alone until luncheon. She ate the rabbit he cooked, reading at the table and avoiding his attempts at conversation, only mumbling "no" when he asked if she'd had a vision concerning trouble ahead. After lunch, he left her to read on an overstuffed chair in the library.

Absorbed in the tales of ancient Arabian nights, Fatima shifted her weight, trying to ease her stiff muscles. A deep male voice startled her out of the book.

"A hot bath will help ease your soreness," he observed. "Use the bathtub in the master bathroom."

A good idea. Stretching, she walked to the room. Tarik had renovated this schoolhouse to include modern amenities such as running water, but Fatima jerked to an abrupt halt. Joy and dismay filled her. Steam rising from a sunken marble tub misted the air. The decadent rose-scented expanse was practically a Roman bath.

Anticipating her needs, Tarik had drawn her this bath. Or did he have other plans? Regardless, Fatima pinned up her hair, stripped and eased herself into the water with a contented sigh. She closed her eyes.

"Better?"

Her eyes flew open. Naked, Tarik stood nearby. Dry mouthed, she watched him join her.

"I can bathe alone," she said.

"You need someone to wash your back," he murmured. Fatima jumped when his hairy thighs brushed hers as he settled behind her.

He grabbed a nearby basin, dipped it into the water, cascaded water down her breasts and belly. A jolt of pleasure rocked her. A square cake of sandalwood soap sat in the silver dish, and he picked it up, foamed his hands. Bubbles frothed. With gentle hands, he began washing her.

The soap slid over her rounded shoulders, brushed the hollow of her throat, caressed her aching breasts. Fatima threw her head back, shuddered. "I'm already clean," was her whispered protest.

"Relax, little caracal," he murmured into her ear. "I'm going to take very good care of you."

Pulling her back against his opened legs, Tarik cupped her breasts. His soapy hands kneaded her flesh. Fatima threw back her head. Soap-slicked fingers pulled hard at her nipples until they lengthened, their color a deep rose; his thumbs expertly flicked the cresting peaks. Fatima felt a gush of wetness between her legs. She ached for him to touch her there. Just a little. One small touch. Her inner passage clenched, thinking of his fingers sliding into her wet cleft, wanting him there. This wasn't being vulnerable, but satisfying an excruciating need.

It's giving him control over you, another voice mocked.

All coherent thought fled as Tarik skimmed the soap over Fatima's soft trembling belly. Tension mounted as he neared the one place she most craved him to touch. The tiny bud he'd mentioned as a woman's pleasure center throbbed, seemed to engorge as he teased the soap across her belly, sliding it lower and lower.

Stomach muscles jumped as his fingers swirled over her navel. The mingled scent of sandalwood and rosewater filled her nostrils. Curling one arm around her, an anchor in an ocean of sensual pleasure, Tarik rested his cheek against her hair. The soap descended farther.

Fatima dragged her gaze down to watch in trembling fascination as bubbles lathered the black curls covering her womanhood.

Anticipation curled her toes. She flinched as he slid the soap between her legs. It felt warm and slippery.

"Easy," he soothed. His touch was absolutely gentle. Pleasure began filling her as he stroked. It sharpened, building into pure feeling.

"Are you still in pain?" Tender concern laced his voice.

Words failed as he teased the soap between her feminine folds. Fatima gripped the tub edge, breath whistling through her lips. The delicious motion halted.

"I'm hurting you," he stated quietly.

No. But her edginess was as demanding and intense as pain.

Fatima drew in a lungful of air. "I'm . . . okay," she managed.

His thumb flicked over the tiny swollen bud nestled in her center. "Are you certain?"

Closing her eyes, she curled her toes. "Oh. Um. Yes."

"Good. Because it's time you learned something, little caracal. Something very special, that has nothing to do with being a warrior, and everything to do with being a woman." A tiny voice inside warned that she was in trouble now.

Tarik stood from the bath. Silvery droplets clung to the golden hair covering his chest. His thick penis jutted out from its nest of crisp dark hair. She quickly toweled off and grabbed a soft white robe, muttering excuses as she left. Excuses he ignored as he tugged the robe off, exposing her nudity. He swept her into his arms and carted her into the adjacent bedroom.

Sunlight streaked through the latticework windows, spearing the thick Persian carpet. The enormous four-poster hinted at what normally transpired here. Soft white sheets caressed her naked back as he settled her on the bed.

Fatima's heart raced with anticipation. Tarik hunted in a carved wood chest, withdrew four red silk cords. Now she knew exactly what the bed was used for. She eyed him warily.

"No." She scrambled to the bed's center.

"You're so determined to be a man, you fear what it's like to fully become a woman. You'll do anything to resist it because it means losing control. And you will not lose control," he said softly, advancing.

The cords swished back and forth in his hands. Dry mouthed, Fatima stared.

"You don't need to demonstrate the rope test." She offered a weak smile. "I'm certain you're an expert at tying knots."

"You *want* this," he asserted, his bold gaze frankly studying her. "Deep down, you crave what I can give you. But you're afraid of letting go. If I give you pleasure, will you run away from me as you've been doing today? Be honest, Tima. You weren't honest when I took your virginity. If you say no, I'll stop. Right now." His deep voice dropped. "Or do you want to lose control?"

Honesty, she thought, the internal throbbing building between her legs. He deserved it. A trembling breath hissed from her mouth. "I want to," she whispered.

"Trust me," his silky voice murmured. "I'll never hurt you, Tima. I'll only bring your deepest, darkest desires to light."

But that is what I fear most, she thought desperately.

"Tarik," she whispered, filled with apprehension.

"I'm going to take good care of you, Tima," he said again. "Very good care of my precious caracal."

Alarm raced through her as his hands slipped up her

213

naked thighs, stroking, creating a flare of heat. He was going to do it to her again. Her insides clenched in an agony of anticipation, a memory of past pain mingled with new pleasure.

"You know so much about being a warrior," he murmured, stroking her hair. "Let me teach you about being female. You're afraid to surrender, Tima. Afraid of letting yourself feel. Because you're so worried about being as tough as a man, you're afraid to embrace the woman inside. You think it's the same as your Sight when you lose control. It's not. Trust me." He slid one rope around her ankle, knotted it efficiently and tied it to the bedpost.

"Tarik." She swallowed hard.

He leaned over the bed, his burning gaze locked with hers. "Don't you want to know what it's like, Tima, for once to lose control without fear? Without worrying about what the next moment will bring? Surrender to passion. I promise you, I would never, ever do anything to hurt or humiliate you." Gently he rubbed her ankle, his thumb caressing her chilled skin.

He stretched out her arms and legs, quickly tying them to the bedposts. Next he stripped off his robe. Laying on the bed, Tarik took her mouth in a sweeping kiss. His tongue probed past her lips, licked the inside of her mouth. His hands slid down her body. A deep moan rose as she responded. She felt herself softening beneath his caress.

Tearing his mouth away, he studied her, unsmiling. Then his lips sought other territory, grazing her chin, sweeping her neck. He kissed and nipped, and chased each tiny bite with his warm tongue.

Awareness dawned. The secret of hundred kisses! Her body roused. Tarik's mouth felt like warm honey drizzling slowly over her sensitive skin. He feathered tiny kisses everywhere. Warmth infused her all over. He settled his mouth upon one breast, kissing it tenderly then taking her pearling nipple into his mouth: slow, swirling flicks of his tongue. Dampness gushed between her legs. Fatima dug her behind into the mattress.

Tarik rained tender kisses across her belly. Very gently he pressed her legs open farther, staring at her rosy, wet flesh. Embarrassed, she tried pulling them closed. The silken ropes creaked in protest.

"Don't shy away from me, sweet Tima. You're so beautiful, lovely as a desert rose," his husky murmur assured her.

He soon lay between her legs, pressing warm lips against the inside of her trembling thigh. He buried his head there. The burnished gold of his hair contrasted sharply with the damp black curls of her feminine mound. His mouth settled upon that moist flesh. He gave a long, slow lick. Fatima arched, gasping. More. She needed more. Very gently, he slid his tongue over her pulsing slit.

"What a beautiful flower you are, my lovely Tima," he crooned.

Nothing had prepared her for the intense jolt of arousal as Tarik slowly licked her swollen bud. Her body jerked violently. The clenching of her muscles was so powerful that she feared losing control. But the ropes held her fast, as he'd predicted; there was no escape from the hot pleasure of his mouth feasting upon her.

She strained against her bonds as he suckled her. His slurping, lips and tongue slowly stroking. Tension blossomed, expanded, until a great heat filled her loins from his skilled kisses. Each nerve ending sizzled until her whole body pulsed and throbbed with pleasure. The sweet pressure intensified, concentrated on her engorged and beseiged bud.

Her legs fell apart wider, willing to admit his thick, hard length once more. Warmth infused her whole body. Something wild and so explosive she couldn't contain it coiled in her loins. She couldn't control herself, couldn't leash herself. Thrashing on the bed, she

BONNIE VANAK

felt herself arch upward, her back bowing, her hips pumping in nameless, pleading need.

"Let go," Tarik commanded softly. "Don't hold back, Tima. I want to hear every lovely cry from your lips. Let me hear you, sweetheart. Let it come. It's all right."

The scorching tension exploded as his tongue slid over her once more. Fatima arched. She screamed at the intensity, fists clenched. Great ragged breaths tore from her throat. Tarik remained with her, his tongue gently licking, lapping at the moisture seeping from her. He continued his tender ministrations until her flesh ceased quivering.

Her heart thudded erratically as she gulped deep breaths. Perspiration soaked her body as if she'd dueled relentlessly with her scimitar. Then cool air washed over her leaden limbs. Dazed lassitude drugged her.

She felt the bed shift, opened her eyes with effort to see him carefully untying her. "That, my beautiful wildcat, is what it is to be a woman," he whispered, dropping a kiss on her perspiring brow. "And you are every inch a woman."

He slid back into bed and captured her in his arms. "You're mine now, Fatima. Mine. Forever," he said, kissing her lips.

She blinked, a distant memory tugging. "Yours, Tarik?"

Gently he stroked her hair. "A girl never forgets her first lover, the man who made her a woman," he said. He curled her body next to his. "Sleep," he urged.

His thick, hard sex prodded her belly. Awareness came over her. He'd not yet satisfied himself. "What about . . . you?"

Tarik pressed a finger against her lips. "This was only for you, sweet Tima. Later, when I'm certain you're not sore."

I'm not feeling too terribly sore right now, her muzzy brain replied, but she drifted into a contented sleep.

Chapter Sixteen

Fatima stammered through her lessons. Their third day together, Tarik was teaching her to speak ancient Egyptian. One knee bent, he sat on a thick cushion in the brick courtyard, in front of a sandalwood table under a shady fig tree. Dates, pomegranates and cheese lined the table. Tall glasses of fruit juice sat before them.

"Khamsin warriors are taught the ancient tongue from the time we can crawl. You should learn as well," he'd advised.

Just before dawn, she'd seen Asad and the other warriors slip out of the stables on the building's opposite side to mingle with the peasants in the village. She and Tarik had had no contact with their silent protectors, who would not move in until the signal. Fatima had felt a faint sting of guilt, wondering if her twin suspected her lovemaking.

She stumbled through reading a yellowed text then stopped. "What is this? A spell to cast on the unwary?"

Tarik leaned forward. "A love poem. From a lovesick priest of the Aten, to a woman he adores. We discovered it buried in the ancient city. He kept his poetry a secret."

"How sad that he never shared that part of himself with her."

These past days seemed enchanted, as if the verdant gardens cast a mystical net over them. Their idyllic paradise wouldn't last, but Fatima relished each precious moment.

Tarik slid her a glance. "Tima, I have a secret . . . and unlike that priest, I want to share it with you. It means much to me."

Curious, she watched as he vanished inside, then reappeared carrying rolled up papers. He sank to his knees beside her, then hesitated. "This is another reason I frequent this schoolhouse. I come here to escape . . . in my art."

Slowly he unfurled the papers. She gasped in awe at the lifelike drawings. Khamsin life. Horses. And herself. Fatima marveled at his skill.

"These are wonderful, Tarik! Why are you keeping this a secret from everyone?"

His expression grew rueful. "Art is not a manly profession, and to become sheikh, I must have the council's respect."

Fatima didn't agree. She studied one drawing of intricate ancient art. "What's this?"

"A rock tomb we discovered—your brother, Muhammad and I. I've been copying the art on the walls. One day, perhaps, I will share it with my mother so she can teach the tribe's children to draw."

"Perhaps one day you should teach them yourself." Fatima set aside the drawings, loving the smile she'd coaxed from him.

His smile fled as he gave her an intense look. He hadn't touched her since yesterday, when he'd made love to her with his mouth. A delicious edginess filled her. Her hungry gaze caressed his long limbs, the muscles beneath the black silk trousers.

"It's growing warm out here," he murmured.

He pulled his loose shirt over his head. Each bulging muscle seemed sculpted from an artisan's chisel. Fatima studied his firm, sensual mouth. Desire pulsed as she remembered his tongue delivering slow licks to her feminine center. She needed more. Wanted more. She craved him like food. Like . . . chocolate. A tiny sigh escaped her.

"You look tense. You must learn to relax." He dropped his voice to a seductive murmur. "Are you still hurting?"

Every one of her muscles tensed. "No," she managed. *Just when I look at you.*

Tarik stood and stretched out a hand. "Come, Tima." He led her inside to the big bed. Fatima eyed it dubiously.

"Get undressed and lie on your stomach. Close your eyes."

Wondering what he planned, she nevertheless obeyed. She heard him rummaging about. Anticipation seared her. Soon he returned, carrying a small bowl filled with scented oil. After setting it down on the bedside table, he flung her long hair over one shoulder. Then Tarik covered his hands with oil and rubbed them. The scent of tangy cinnamon and wild honey filled her nostrils.

"Close your eyes and relax," he murmured. "Let me take care of you. You're too tense."

He stroked warm oil over her bare back, kneading her knotted muscles. Pressure from his fingers sliding over her back created a delicious friction. He circled her skin, digging gently with his thumbs, then stroked along the small of her back. His oiled hands dipped between her legs. Fatima shrieked as he slid a finger along her sex.

"Turn over and lie on your back against the headboard," he said. She did so, moaning as he cupped her breasts. Sliding his oiled hands over the tight nipples, he kneaded them—delicious friction caused by his strokes proved painfully arousing.

His mouth settled upon a taut nipple. He laved it with a hot breath as she strained against him, then Tarik released it with a pop, licking his lips. "Mmmm, I love tasting you."

Sitting back on his haunches, he parted her legs with his hands. Fatima swallowed, watching a pulse jump in his neck. His arousal jutted out: He was not immune to this, either.

A jolt shot through her as his oiled fingers began massaging between her legs. One finger slid between her wet folds, then up to encircle the tiny swollen bud. Her body went taut. Fatima dragged in a breath, whimpering.

"In some sheikh's harems, the woman is prepared for him by sensual massage and the oiling of her sheath. The oil makes even the tightest passage slippery, ready to receive a man's cock, no matter how large it is," he whispered.

A furious blush filled her cheeks. She squirmed as he slid an oiled finger inside her, the delicate tissues clenching around him. "One finger," he murmured. "You're very tight."

Her face flushed. Tarik stroked her very gently, pleasure pulsing everywhere as he slid slowly along her inner walls. Watching her reaction, his dark gaze burned into her.

"W-what are you doing, Tarik?" she wailed.

"A woman's sheath is very sensitive. Every woman has

certain points that, when stroked, intensify her pleasure," he whispered. "I'm seeking yours, Tima. And
when I find it, you will welcome my cock when I take
you again."

His finger felt enormous inside her. Fatima arched
her head back. Moisture from her intensifying arousal
aided his efforts, and the pleasure built higher and
higher as she gasped for air, gripped fistfuls of sheet. A
loud sob wrenched from her throat as he found a spot
and stroked. Fatima screamed.

"Ah. *There*," he murmured with satisfaction.

Hot pleasure exploded in her loins. Tears dripped
down her cheeks. She squeezed down on his finger in
contractions so intense, wetness spurted from her.

"Excellent," he crooned. Her head fell back and she
sagged bonelessly against the pillows. He let her rest,
then began building her pleasure all over again, his
ragged breathing warning her how much control he exerted. She watched, eyes heavy lidded as he shifted between her legs.

"You're more relaxed now, sweet. Let's try two fingers." Tarik inserted another long finger inside her.
"Two, excellent. You're wet, so very wet. That's good."

His fingers stretched her. Fatima began angling her
hips, thrusting as Tarik slid his fingers back and forth. "I
think you're ready for my cock now. Do you think
you're ready, little caracal? Can you take all of me?"

Wordlessly, she gulped air. Tension coiled inside her
until she felt like screaming, begging, anything.

"How bad do you want my cock, Tima?" he breathed.

"Please," she begged, her hips pumping. Her legs
spilled open. Desire became a relentless master, driving
her to wild excess, willing to do anything to release the
hot torment.

"I smell your desire, little caracal. It drives me wild,
wanting to lick you all over again. Are you ready to

come?" Fatima squirmed as his fingers thrust harder. Frustration bit her with sharp teeth.

"Tell me. Do you want to come?" he commanded.

"Yes," she sobbed. "Please, Tarik."

He watched, his gaze capturing hers as she bit back a cry. "Don't hold back. I want to see you come, hear you cry out. Say my name, Tima," he said thickly.

Her body grew taut as a bowstring, and Fatima gripped his arm, waiting. Tarik flicked a thumb over her swollen bud. She screamed his name on a rising sob and ecstasy burst inside her. Breathing heavily, her dazed eyes saw the purely male smile of satisfaction touch his mouth. Moisture seeped from between her legs onto the bed. Her heart thudded and she panted.

He let her lie quietly for a moment, then, Tarik turned her toward him, his gaze intent. "Give me your mouth," he commanded.

She obeyed, parted her lips for his kiss, tasted her musky arousal on his mouth, cinnamon and honey. He cupped the back of her head, holding her steady for his possession as his tongue thrust inside, flicking, penetrating, conquering.

Blood drained from her head. Moaning, she gripped his shoulders for support as Tarik rained kisses gentle as baby's breath across her body, kissing her collarbone, spanning her rib cage with his hands. Cupping her breasts, he kneaded them, flicking the hardened nipples with his thumbs. Molten fire streaked through her. She wanted this. Needed it. He bent down and encased one taut nipple in his mouth, suckling heavily. His tongue laved the peak, tugged it. Releasing with a loud pop, he licked his lips.

Finally he mounted her, his heavy weight pressing her into the mattress. Lacing his fingers through hers, he stretched her arms above her head. Fatima lay motionless, trembling as his body slid over hers. The crisp hair on his chest rubbed her hardened nipples. He kneed her thighs wide apart and settled his hips between them. Panic seized her as the hard round knob of his penis pushed into her. *Too big*. She fought back a whimper, uncertain if she could take him.

"No pain, sweet Tima. This time, only pleasure," he whispered tenderly. "You can take all of me. Relax, little caracal. Relax and let me love you."

His thick erection began filling her as he pressed forward ever so gently. Tensing, waiting for the pain, she laced her fingers tightly around his. Tarik rose above her. But as his hard length sank slowly into her, the pain never came. Wondering, she loosened her grip. His intent gaze locked with hers, jaw clenching.

A pulse throbbing wildly at the base of his neck illustrated how much control he exerted. Tenderness replaced her anxiety. Fatima reached out, slid her hands tentatively about his neck. His eyes darkened to black pools.

"Tima, you are so beautiful. When I look at you, it is like witnessing the dawn racing across the sky," he said in a husky whisper. "Are you all right, my sweet?"

Pleasure began building again. Fatima rolled her hips, eager to have more of him inside her. "Tarik . . . it . . . it does not hurt this time," she said on a gasp.

"I only want to give you pleasure, my sweet love."

"More. I want more." She barely recognized the sultry purr of her voice.

Irresistible pleasure burst through her, her body accepting this time, welcoming the male intruder. His thick length filled her as he penetrated to the hilt, sheathing himself fully. She flinched then relaxed, letting the joy ripple through her. The sensation of being filled was fantastic. Tarik rested his forehead against hers. His big body trembled.

"Fatima, oh my little Fatima, I've dreamed of this moment. You are the rain refreshing my parched soul. I drown in your essence. You and I are children of the desert, our spirits melding together as one as they were created in heat and passion. Feel me coming into you, filling you as you were meant to be filled, my body and spirit joining yours. Do you feel the wild desert rhythms driving through your blood as they do mine? Listen to my heart, little caracal. It pounds as wildly as my darrabukka. Come and dance with me," he whispered.

Fatima closed her eyes, hearing in the thrumming of her heart an echo of his darrabukka's wild call. Her hips undulated, beginning the dance. Tarik groaned and began thrusting in long, slow strokes.

Blood roared in Fatima's ears, rushed to her loins. Her limbs quaked wildly as he reached up, adjusted her legs about his hips, withdrew then surged into her, each glide as delicious as dark chocolate upon her tongue. Hot pleasure pooled between her legs. Her feminine center clenched him greedily.

The air grew thin and Fatima gasped for breath. Her heart pounded so loudly it sounded like the thrilling cadence of Tarik's darrabukka. Scorching heat like her beloved sunshine spread throughout her body.

Pulling back, he spread her knees wide with his hands and thrust into her, his gaze fiercely intent. It held hers. His hips hammered into her, hard male flesh smacking against her soft yielding femaleness. Fatima arched, her nails digging into the hard muscles of his back. Her hips bucked as he rode her hard and fast. A scream rose from her throat.

"Come for me, Fatima. I need to watch you," he urged hoarsely. "Let go, little caracal, let go."

Tension built, pooled in her loins. Pleasure so intense she couldn't bear it built to a shattering crescendo. It burst, thrumming from her loins through her body like liquid fire. A scream tone from her throat as her hips jerked convulsively, Tarik rode her throughout, his shaft hammering into her as he gripped her hips. Tossing back his head, he groaned, his big body bucking and shuddering as he released his seed.

Collapsing atop her, he pillowed his head beside hers, his breath coming harsh and heavy into her ear. They lay locked together. She welcomed his heavy weight pinning her down.

Slowly, he pulled out, sliding wetly from her. He rolled onto his back, cradling her. For a minute they lay there, their ragged breaths easing, the thundering cadence of their hearts resuming normal rhythms.

Fascinated, Fatima ran her hands over his smooth, taut buttocks, up the muscles bulging beneath warm golden skin. She caressed his hardness, marveling at the differences in their bodies. Hers was pliant, yielding. His was chiseled marble, not a spare ounce of softness. Until she gazed into his eyes. Those were soft with emotion. But was it love? Or was she just another woman he'd seduced?

Fatima stroked the hard ridges on his abdomen. "How am I . . . ?" her voice trailed off. "How was it with your other lovers?"

Silence fell between them for a moment. Tarik appeared to wrestle with a decision. Finally he spoke, his voice thick with emotion. "I've had lovers, Tima, but I've never been in love with anyone but you. The woman at the schoolhouse? I made love to her because she reminded me of you. When you returned, I broke it off. Because I want only you."

Peace and joy twined together as she gazed at his solemn expression. "And I want only you," she whispered. "I just didn't like admitting it. I love you, Tarik."

A crooked grin touched his mouth. He kissed her temple. "And now we both have admitted our feelings. We're equal."

Curling against him, she let contented bliss fill her. Whatever the future brought, she only wanted to cherish this moment of lying safe and secure in his arms.

"Tima? Come love, time for dinner. I'll teach you to cook today. And then, after we eat, I'll teach you something else."

His voice teasing, Tarik searched for his Guardian. They had spent the morning making love in long, leisurely bouts. He felt insatiable, craving her as a man in the desert yearned for water. He loved to watch her climax, seeing the rapt wonder on her face, the green of her eyes darkening to emerald, her mouth parting in trembling awe. Each sweet cry wrung from her filled him with tenderness.

He went into the library. She stood by the bookshelves. A volume fell from her opened fingers. He started for her, but froze, stricken by her unmistakable expression.

Apprehension and deep sorrow filled him. This paradise they'd created vanished as if whisked away by a sandstorm.

"Someone wants you dead. I see shadows in the darkness. Tonight, when the moon climbs high into the sky. If you sleep tonight, you will never awaken," she murmured dreamily.

Cold dread seized him, and Tarik gently jostled her. Fatima jerked forward, her wide, green eyes staring as she realized her words. A violent trembling seized her as she stuffed a fist into her mouth. Tarik drew her into his arms, resting his cheek against the top of her head. He let her absorb the warmth of his body, let the horrifying vision fade with the comfort he provided, then reluctantly set her away.

"I'll go warn Asad and the others that tonight is the

night. As for you, you're sleeping alone tonight," he insisted.

"No!" Fatima wrenched away. "If your killer insists on attacking tonight, I must be there, Tarik. I'm your—"

"Guardian. But you're also my lover." He caressed her trembling cheek. "My life. I won't let anything happen to you, Tima."

"It won't!"

"How do you know?"

A distant look came over her. "Because. I saw it happen."

Later, Tarik made love to her fiercely. She clung to him, as if fearing to let go. Relentlessly he brought her to one shattering orgasm after another, relishing her sweet cries as she arched up into him. He sought solace in her soft body, wanting to die inside her. When he finally climaxed, gasping for air, he collapsed atop her, shaking from dazed passion and renewed fears. Whatever happened, she must stay safe.

Resisting the urge to draw her close, to fall asleep with her in his arms, he firmly marched her off to her room. Against her vehement protests he laid a finger across her lips, kissed her cheek, pulled on trousers and went to bed. There he dozed, dreaming of blood and betrayal.

Something stirred the air.

Tarik was instantly awake, drawing the straight dagger from beneath his pillow. He stilled, sniffing. He caught the musky scent of sex—Fatima's unique fragrance of woman and roses—and something else filled his nostrils. Pungent. Heavy. Another man. He saw a shadow.

It could be anyone. Asad even. But Tarik's gut said no. Whoever this was, he had a target. *Me.*

Tarik gripped his dagger, tensed for action. The

shadow moved noiselessly forward. Tarik sprang out of bed, wielding his blade, and kicked at the shadow's legs. There came a loud grunt, but the man didn't fall. Instead his arm swung around and burning pain lanced Tarik's skin. He gritted his teeth, danced away, his senses kicked into full alert.

Better deal with this before he cuts something much more precious, he thought grimly. But he drew back, waiting. He heard heavy breathing, saw the blade come for him again. And a sound tightened his chest like wet leather: the bedroom door opening. Fatima.

"Get back," he grated out, rushing forward. But it was too late.

Fatima released a cry of pain. Tarik's blood chilled. He fought to control his fury. This insolent bastard had dared attack her? No emotions. His eyes, now accustomed to the darkness made out his assailant's shorter bulk. Tarik dropped, rolled and sprang up behind the man, immediately pinched the space between the shoulder and neck. A loud groan sounded, and the man's dagger dropped, clattering to the floor. The would-be assassin collapsed. Not taking chances, Tarik pressed his knife to the man's stomach.

"Tima, light the lamp!"

There came shuffling noises, the acrid scent of struck matches. Light flooded the room. Tarik's worried gaze raked over Fatima's binish, settled on a long tear in the sleeve. Crimson dripped from the slash. Then his lover gasped, hand flying up to cover her mouth.

Tarik's blood went cold with her next words.

"Oh, God! Muhammad!"

Chapter Seventeen

They tied his cousin with the same silk bindings Tarik had used in love-play with Fatima. To his relief, her wound was slight. He bandaged it, then studied the awakening Muhammad. His shock turned to fury, then despair as he stood over his friend.

"Why? *Why?*"

Cold hate twisted Muhammad's expression. He spat at Tarik. "You selfish bastard, you have no honor! Debaucher! You seduce women and leave them. You don't deserve to lead our people."

Tarik narrowed his gaze. "You tried to kill me because I'm a womanizer? No cousin, speak the truth. You have nothing to lose now. You know your destiny. You know our laws."

Muhammad blanched, his sneer vanishing. Tarik's heart sank. His cousin, his own flesh and blood. His friend. They had played together as children, fought together as warriors, broken bread at meals. Never had he shown any ill will before Tarik gripped his shoulders, shook him so hard the man's teeth chattered.

"Why?" he blurted out. "Why! Tell me, damn it!"

Muhammad stared at Fatima, his jaw clenched beneath his black beard. Finally he looked at Tarik, with a look of pure malice deadlier than a knife wound. "Your mother, that . . . bitch. Your father grew weak marrying her. She polluted our people with her ideas, brought chaos with her Western ways. She's stirred up the women, making them think, like Fatima here, that they're equals to men. She deserved to die, but it was far easier to kill you, cousin."

Recoiling, Tarik stared, shaken by his cousin's vitriol. He scarcely registered Fatima's hand squeezing his arm, her reassuring whispers.

"Our friendship in childhood, your loyalty? It wasn't a lie, cousin. Admit it. It wasn't."

Emotion clouded Muhammad's gaze. "I was a child then, and then I grew to see the truth when *she* pointed it out to me. My woman, the one who should have been mine. But you seduced and abandoned her like you do to all women. You're an abomination, the White Falcon who should never have been born."

"Who Muhammad? What woman?" Fatima whispered.

Contempt filled his gaze. "I promised silence. It matters not. He's seduced legions of women. Bastard."

You're an abomination, the White Falcon who should never have been born.

Tarik jerked out of Fatima's embrace, pulled her by the hand outside. His throat worked in a loud, warbling war call. Sorrow mingled in the haunting cry. Eleven Khamsin warriors spilled out of the barn where they'd been hiding, including Asad, who ran up to Tarik, scimitar in hand. His sharp gaze raked them.

"It's Muhammad," Tarik said dully. "I've tied him up inside."

Asad muttered an oath, motioned for the others to

follow him inside. Tarik collapsed on a nearby stone bench, shaking.

His cousin. His friend. He'd trusted him. He'd loved him like a brother, and all these years, he'd been hated. Everything was a lie. Could he trust anyone? No. His guts squeezed. Tarik felt himself pull into a tight, safe shell. Trust no one.

There came a gentle pressure on his arm. "Tarik, don't turn from me," a soft voice insisted. "Look."

He jerked away, needing to retreat into a cave where thick walls shielded his emotions, hid his true self from the outside world. *Trust no one.* But the gentle voice kept insisting. Tarik finally turned.

"Tima," he choked out.

She said nothing, but enfolded him in her arms. Tarik drew back. Fatima refused to let go. Finally he capitulated. God, he needed her. He clung to her, shaking.

"He was like my brother—my only brother," he whispered. "Oh God, Tima. It hurts so much. Don't let go."

"I won't," she promised fiercely. "Ever. I'm here, my love. It's just you and me. I'll never let go."

Moonlight spilled from overhead, a wash of silvery light making the tears on her cheeks glitter like pale stars. But she kept her promise and held on to Tarik all through that night.

Two days after the attack, Fatima sat with Tarik in the ceremonial tent. Anxiety gnawed her stomach. Her lover had become a distant, silent wraith, refusing to eat, talking little. More was at stake now, for the council discussed Muhammad's fate. Tarik's cousin would die.

Looking equally pale as his son, Jabari faced the stricken council members. An air of hushed expectancy hovered. Taking the life of a fellow warrior was a mark against the executioner. Even in a case such as this, one of justice, the tribe would whisper of the dead warrior's blood forever staining his executioner's boots. Shame would dog the one who delivered the killing blow. There would be no honor, no stories told by the crackling campfires of the man who took a life without a fair fight.

"Muhammad attempted to assassinate my son, whose Guardian of the Ages vowed to protect his life with body and soul. By law, Tarik's Guardian is our appointed executioner."

Cold horror snaked up Fatima's spine. She stared at the sheikh. She, who had never yet taken a human life, must now take one? And not as a warrior. Her palms were clammy as she thought of taking her scimitar and delivering a killing blow. But she had asked for the honor of this position; she would fulfill her duty.

"Sire." She struggled to keep her voice even. "I respect and understand the law. If this is my duty, I will perform it to the best of my ability."

Tarik jumped to his feet. "No, Father. Fatima saved my life yet again. Her vision saw Muhammad attempting to kill me. Now we punish her by forcing her to take a life, not in honor as a warrior, but as an executioner? And Fatima lacks a man's strength. What if her first blow is not merciful?"

Fatima's stomach churned. She swallowed hard, envisioning the gruesome scene. Her gaze shot to Tarik.

Jabari centered his palms on his knees. "Tarik, it is my duty as sheikh to uphold the laws of our people as laid down thousands of years ago."

Ibrahim challenged: "You worry so about a woman taking a life, Tarik, but should you not have considered the possibility when you agreed for her to become your Guardian?"

Sudden insight struck Fatima. The sheikh could not excuse her; his hands were tied by the council. If he made an exception for her, he'd be seen as weak, ineffectual, as having made the wrong decision to choose her as a Guardian. A cloying tension hung in the stale air. Muhammad's punishment was a political play, Tarik's cousin a pawn. And she was the captured queen the council was using to checkmate the sheikh.

Furtively she reached out, touched Tarik's calf, tapping it once. He glanced at her, worry furrowing his brow. But he resumed his seat beside his father.

Summoning every last ounce of her strength, Fatima lifted her chin. "Honored sheikh of the Khamsin warriors of the wind, members of this esteemed council, I will do my duty as Tarik's appointed Guardian. I will not shame the name of my honored father or the Guardians who went before him."

Tarik's lips thinned to a slash. Fury flashed in his eyes as he scanned the council. He said, "My Guardian is a warrior, and a woman of great honor. Remember that, my elders. When she performs this duty, no blood will be upon her boots. Let it be upon mine. I will carry the shame of executing a fellow warrior. Fatima's sword may deliver the killing blow, but it shall be my hand."

Oh God. He couldn't mean it.

Ibrahim flashed a grim smile. "It is not allowed, son of Jabari. The law clearly states that a Guardian must act as executioner. Muhammad's execution, as our laws state, will take place tomorrow at dawn."

Fatima closed her eyes, swallowing hard.

"*I* will be the executioner."

Her eyes flew open to regard her father. His face had blanched, but his stance remained proud as he stood. "I am a Guardian of the Ages. You state only a Guardian may take such a life."

The chief elder's eyes' widened. "This is not an option, Ramses. You cannot."

"I will," he replied calmly. "I am Guardian of the Ages

to our honored sheikh, and therefore, to all his progeny. It is my right to perform this duty—as it is the right of any Guardian."

Jabari leaned forward, locking his gaze with the chief elder's. "My Guardian has stated his wish. I grant him permission to do this duty and act as a substitute for his daughter. Our laws were laid down to grant a quick, painless death to the condemned. A Guardian possessing the ability to wield a sword with such strength is Ramses. Enough of this matter; it is ended. Gather all the warriors at dawn. Muhammad must pay for attempting to kill my son."

The sheikh stood. Fatima and Tarik also jumped to their feet, as the elderly council struggled to stand. Respectful nods followed Jabari as he left the tent.

Fatima's knees wobbled precariously. She had won. But at what price? As Fatima glanced at her father's bloodless face, she knew the price would be dear, indeed.

Much later, she returned to her tent. Ramses sat in the main quarters, sharpening his sword. Granite rasped over metal, the noise giving her gooseflesh. His features were set in stone, and he did not look up as she sank down beside him.

"Papa, please. I can't let you do this."

"It is too late. What father would allow his beloved daughter to endure such shame?"

"But Papa, it's not *your* duty!"

He set down the scimitar and looked at her. "I must. For Muhammad's sake and yours. He will die quickly, painlessly, and—"

"His blood will stain your boots. You're a warrior of tremendous honor. The others . . . they will not look upon you the same after. They'll talk of nonsense, of his ghost haunting your spirit. Isn't there another way?"

"There is not," Ramses said quietly. "The only alternative is an option the council knows Jabari would never exercise—to order Jabari's brother-in-law to execute his own son, to prove his loyalty."

Fatima sank back onto her trembling haunches. There was no hope then. Her father would suffer this shame, and also suffer the haunting knowledge he had killed a man he had fought beside, had broken bread with, had danced the warrior's dance before the ceremonial bonfires. Muhammad's blood would not only stain his boots but his very spirit.

Tears burned her eyes. She picked up her father's hands—strong, calloused and loyal—and kissed them. A single tear dripped onto his skin.

A rustling noise drew her attention. Her mother stood at the entrance, her long, dark hair damp as if she had just come from bathing. Her skin glowed, and the delicate aroma of flowers scented her. She held out a hand to her husband.

"Ramses, Elizabeth told me what happened. Let me banish your ghosts," she said softly.

He stood and she went into his arms. Ramses released an anguished groan as he kissed her deeply.

Katherine broke away and touched his cheek. Oblivious to their daughter, the two stared at each other intently. Wordlessly they walked, hand in hand, into the bedroom.

This was the true love shared between a husband and wife, Fatima mused. It was the true joy: When the darkest times struck, you had someone at your side to endure with you, to provide comfort.

Silently she slipped from the tent as the sounds of lovemaking began.

At dawn, all warriors gathered at the training grounds. Fatima was the only woman present. Rose and lavender streaked the sky as sunlight broke the horizon.

Fatima had never seen an execution. She stood next to Tarik at the circle center. Clad in white trousers and white kamis shirt, and barefoot, Muhammad was bent over, hands tied behind his back.

Her father approached, his dark-bearded face absolutely expressionless. A lump clogged her throat, thinking of how ashamed he was, how absolutely difficult this task to complete. Her heart ached: for Tarik, who'd lost a friend and relative, for Muhammad, who harbored only hate and now must die. She tried to stiffen her spine. Her legs felt weak as newly churned butter.

Jabari faced the assembled crowd, read the death edict. The words buzzed in Fatima's ears. Sickening fear seized her spine, and she struggled to remain upright: Knowing what her father faced, she must not disgrace him.

Tarik glanced down at her. He looked at her father, who was slowly raising his sword. Fatima's hands began shaking wildly. She closed her eyes and then realized that would demonstrate her cowardice. Opening them, she uttered a tiny sob. Then Tarik seized her against his hard chest, cradling her head gently in his large hands. She inhaled his scent—sandalwood, cloves and masculinity—wanting to crawl inside his binish for comfort.

"Do not look, Tima," he ordered in a hoarse whisper.

A violent shudder wracked her as she heard a blade snick through the air. Was it done? Fatima quivered. She knew she must turn around.

Still pressing her face against his chest and shielding her sight, Tarik turned. She heard his deep voice rumble, "Is this Fatima's reward for once more saving my life—being forced to watch this? I will not stay any longer, and neither will she." Aggression laced his voice.

"Yes, my son, take her away," she heard Jabari say.

Fatima choked back an anguished sob at the low agony in the Sheikh's voice. Tarik herded her off; his arms still securely about her. She stared at the men's boots as she passed.

The surrounding wadi was deep, winding. A ways on, Tarik collapsed upon a flat boulder. Silently he held out his arms. Fatima resisted until she saw his stricken look. Then she embraced him and wept. Tarik rested his cheek atop her head, trembling as he held her.

"Muhammad and I used to train together. Father pitted us against each other because I needed to work on my timing and he was fast on his feet. He was my friend. His father and my father were more like brothers than in-laws. Tima, why—why did Muhammad turn against me? Who could have turned him against me? The only woman it could have been was Salome, the widow. She had been my mistress, but she married a few months ago. Did Muhammad become obsessed with power, thinking he might be next to rule? What madness is in men that they lust so for control and risk everything? He has shamed his father's name forever."

"I don't know, Tarik. How could he? How could he break the code of honor? He swore an oath of loyalty to our sheikh." She squeezed her eyes shut, willing her tears away and the twisting agony to ease. But they did not.

"Tima, hold me. Just hold me," he choked.

They clung to each other, Tarik's arms like steel bands around her.

"W-what will . . . w-where will they bury him?" she whispered.

"They won't. The law orders his body to be dumped into the Nile, his spirit lost forever," the muffled answer came.

Fatima uttered a tiny moan, burying her face in

Tarik's shoulder. Air rasped into her lungs and a deep chill sank into her bones as she envisioned Muhammad's body sinking into the cold, dark Nile—drifting down, buffeted by an uncaring current, forever lost and condemned to darkness.

"Cold. So cold." Her teeth chattered with uncontrollable spasms.

"Lean against me, Tima. I'll warm you."

He tugged off her turban. His large palm stroked her tangled hair. His soothing touch comforted her. It was a man's touch, caressing her tenderly. It made her feel womanly. She was tired of being brave, of toughing it out as a man. The earthy, spicy scent of his binish filled her nose. Strange, how she hated the Sight's crippling vulnerability yet trusted Tarik who also rendered her weak as a newborn colt. Patterns forged in childhood emerged now: Tarik had never mocked her visions or pulled away in revulsion when she succumbed to their power. Always he'd comforted, provided necessary support.

Fatima lifted her tear-streaked face to his. "I don't understand. If I can predict the future, why wasn't I shown the darkness in his heart to prevent Muhammad from even trying? Maybe someone could have done something, talked to him. What's the point of being an oddity if I can't prevent bad things from happening?" she said.

Tarik cupped her face in his hands, his thumbs gently wiping away tears. "There's nothing you could have done to save Muhammad. He brought this on himself, Tima. Your Sight did save me. You have a gift—a beautiful, rare gift. I know how frightening it must be for you, but it is good. And you're not an oddity."

"Not to you."

"Never," he agreed softly. "Ever."

She only wanted to ease the terrible aching in her chest. "Kiss me, Tarik. I'm so cold. I need you to make me forget death, and to feel life again," she whispered.

He leaned forward, angling his mouth toward hers. Warm breath feathered her chilled cheeks. Close, closer, oh. His lips settled over hers in a gentle kiss, light as butterfly wings. Fatima's eyes fluttered shut.

This was a kiss of dreams, of magic, starshine and the whisper of desert nights. Blood sang in her veins as she pressed close, feeling his warmth wrapping about her like a wool cloak. He chased away the icy cold with heat, filled the hollow inside her with his solid strength. His taste filled her mouth while his unique, spicy scent filled her nose. Softly, his coaxing mouth moved over hers until she moaned. Tarik became more aggressive then, sliding a hand to the back of her head and holding her steady.

His tongue slipped past her parted lips. Nothing else existed but this, his mouth coupled to hers. Dawn whispered around them in a hush of desert wind, and he drew away, cupping her face. The intense wildness in his eyes scared her a little.

"I won't let anything happen to you, Tima. Never. You're my life. You're the only one I can trust. I'll never let you go, ever. I can't let you slip away from me."

Picking up his hand, she kissed his long fingers. "And I'm not leaving your side, Tarik. I won't."

"I ask you again, Tima. Will you consider stepping aside as my Guardian? The danger to my life is past."

Wrestling with her emotions, she studied his gaze. Something warned her of an underlying threat behind Tarik's question, but she dismissed her concerns. How could he threaten her when they'd shared so much?

"No," she said fervently. "You still need looking after, and I'm the one to do it."

A shield dropped over his face. "I'll do anything to ensure we're together and you're safe. Remember that."

He stood, gripping her hand. Instinct warned her to pay attention to the despairing note in his deep voice, to his words of warning, but she knew she was being silly. These were words from a distressed man who'd just witnessed a painful execution. Surely they didn't mean anything.

Tarik rode off to the deep desert that day, taking Asad with him. He insisted on Fatima remaining behind to comfort her father. "I need to meditate, Tima," he said, turmoil shadowing his dark eyes.

Her father didn't need her; he spent the entire day secluded with her mother. Fatima remained inside, struggling with an ancient Egyptian text. Finally she set the papyrus down and she stepped outside.

Sunlight warmed her face, but people turned and stared. Women, sloshing milk in goatskin bags to make cheese, whispered. Men sharpening their scimitars or oiling rifles gave her cool, disdainful looks. Words floated everywhere. "Fatima—her fault . . . Ramses is an honorable warrior . . . If not for her, Muhammad wouldn't have tried killing Tarik."

So, her fears that the execution would shame her father were unfounded. Instead, the tribe blamed her. The angry looks cast her way reddened her cheeks. Her steps faltered slightly. Still, Fatima tilted her chin up, refusing to look down in shame.

Sand swirled in little eddies about her as she headed for the women's bathing facility. There she showered, toweled off and brushed her hair. The mirror reflected her deeply troubled expression, so she forced a smile as the door opened. Nadia entered, her once assured step now hesitant and faltering.

"I'm . . . sorry, Fatima. So sorry." The young woman

twisted her hands. "And thank you for saving Tarik's life."

Surprised, Fatima set down her brush on the polished counter.

Sorrow covered Nadia's face. "Muhammad was like his brother. My uncle is devastated, as is my whole family. Why must men hate so? My father treated him like a son." Gone was the self-absorbed, haughty sheikh's daughter. The recent tragedy had given her a sad maturity. A tug of deep sympathy pulled at Fatima.

"Power, perhaps. Or maybe Muhammad felt he was in Tarik's shadow all the time. Some men feel inferior in that way."

Nadia's curious gaze traveled over Fatima's binish, over the sharp dagger at her belt. "And we women are accustomed to feeling inferior, is it not so? Except you."

Inferior? The sheikh's pampered daughter, whose mother had garnered the admiration of Khamsin women for her intelligence, gentle compassion and determination to educate them?

Nadia's voice dropped. "The women say you don't need a warrior to defend you. You can do it yourself with your gun. I . . ."

Another surprise. Fatima decided to breach the distance between them. "Would you like to learn about defending yourself?" At the girl's eager nod, she gestured to a stone bench. "Let's sit. I'll tell you all about weapons. And then I'll tell you why women have just as much right to do the things men can do. . . ."

Late that evening, Tarik and Asad returned to camp. Fatima watched as they ate silently the meal Elizabeth prepared then sat about the fire, talking. Flames leapt into the clear sky, sending swirling showers of orange sparks like luminescent insects.

When Asad murmured good night, Fatima and Tarik

remained by the fire's comforting warmth. He squeezed her hand.

"Stay with me tonight, Tima," he urged in a low voice.

"In your tent? Tarik, I can't," she protested.

"No one is there," he insisted. "My family is staying with Uncle Ali. They need to heal from this terrible experience, and Uncle Ali needs to assure my father he didn't share his oldest son's hatred. Our family tent is empty."

She hesitated, staring at his hand, then dragged her gaze to meet his troubled eyes. No one will know, she told herself. He wanted her. Needed her.

Fatima stood, taking his hand. First she stopped by her own family tent, calling softly to her twin, "Tarik and I are going to walk. Tell Papa and Mamma not to wait up for me," she explained, not meeting Asad's eyes. She had never lied to him before.

Asad nodded and vanished back inside, so she turned. A hush of night stars swept over her like weeping diamonds, and the desert wind stirred the sands. Tarik led her back to his room. They undressed and fell onto his soft bed. No regrets. Tonight, he needed her. And she'd be there for him.

Hungry for her gentle touch to restore his broken spirit, Tarik closed his eyes. He surrendered to her soothing caresses, her soft lips that feathered gentle kisses over his tired body. His desire sharpened. Tarik steeled himself against it as he rolled over, taking her with him. Very gently he kissed her, loving her slowly. Rapt wonder filled her face as she clung to him.

"Love me, Tima," he whispered. "I'm weary and so empty. Fill me, and make me forget."

Her palm cupped his cheek. "Let me love you, Tarik."

Satin thighs slid against his aching muscles as she wrapped her legs about his waist. Tarik moved over her soft body, wanting to hide his body and soul inside her. He savored each succulent taste of her lips, her silky skin against his naked flesh. Desire darkened her eyes. No more pain for his little warrior; only cries of pleasure would wring from her mouth.

Scorching heat thrummed in his loins as her wet feminine flesh yielded to his hard cock. Slowly he sank into her tight sheath. Leashing his passion, he thrust with long, deep strokes to make her pleasure last. Seeking relief from the sorrow rending his heart, he made sweet love to her, chased the aching loneliness away by joining his flesh to hers. So much lost. Muhammad—friend, fellow warrior, cousin. Trust no one. But Fatima. Oh, Fatima. Muhammad had hurt her while trying to kill him. Never again, Tarik silently vowed as he watched her passion-dazed features. You will not risk yourself for me again.

If he lost her, he'd die. He would not lose her. He'd bind her to him, tie her down if he must. He'd do anything. His Guardian. They belonged together, body and soul.

Beneath him she tensed, a sign of her approaching climax. Tarik shifted his position, angling his thrusts. Bucking against him, she damped her cry against his shoulder. He let his passion forth, and wrapped himself around her as he came.

For a full minute he lay atop her, reluctant to leave her warmth. Finally he slid off, panting. He uttered a small, satisfied sigh. His heart and soul. His Tima.

Boneless with pleasure, Fatima curled her body beside Tarik's. The wild tension gripping him had seemed at last to ease. She dozed, when suddenly gooseflesh pricked her arms. Something was terribly wrong.

The tent flap jerked aside. Cool air washed over her. A deep, male voice rang out.

"Yes. She's here, sire," her twin said flatly.

Oh God. Immobilized by panic, Fatima could only stare. The sheet had slipped down to bare her breasts and Tarik immediately yanked it up to shield her face. But, too late. The sheikh's booming voice clouted her ears like a roaring wind.

"Fatima!"

Chapter Eighteen

A warrior must always be prepared to face the unexpected. As silence sharp as a scimitar descended, Tarik rolled out of bed and jerked on his trousers. The sweat of lovemaking glossed his body and that of his lover. Defiantly Fatima sat up, clutching the sheet. Pride and concern for her twined in him like mating snakes. No coward, his Tima.

"Sire, please listen to me," she said.

"Shhh, Tima," Tarik warned, his jaw clenching.

"You've dishonored her! You've used her for your pleasure." Jabari's furious gaze was riveted to him.

"I love her," he replied. "This isn't your business."

"It is now. Do you think I can turn my back on this? You know what must happen now, Tarik. You know the consequences."

He did, and he welcomed the inevitable, though his heart twisted at the pain he'd cause Fatima. How ironic: He, who had sworn to do anything to remove Tima as his Guardian, had been caught in a trap not of his own making. Tarik drew himself up as she left the bed, wrapping the sheet about herself. Shielding her with his body, he confronted his father.

His nostrils flaring, the sheikh's mouth thinned to a tight slash. "I am gravely disappointed in you, Fatima. But more so in my son. I know his reputation among women, how he marks each conquest like a battle victory."

Tarik struggled to leash his temper. "A reputation I no longer merit, Father. Have you kept watch on my every move? I have seduced no one lately."

"Except Fatima." Fury burned in his father's gaze. "Your protector. I should have guessed what your plans were, Tarik, when you vowed to remove her as your Guardian."

Fatima glanced over with wide, uncertain eyes. "Tarik? What is he talking about?"

Asad smiled slowly. "I'll tell you, Tima. When you were wounded and unconscious, Tarik swore he'd do anything to remove you as his Guardian. And now he has."

Fury boiled inside him. Her twin. He should have known.

Her wide, hurt eyes searched Tarik's. She asked. "Is this true?"

Steeling himself, he folded his arms across his chest. "It was, Tima. I would have done anything not to see you hurt. But I didn't mean for it to happen like this." He gave Asad a hard look. "Unlike your brother, who had other plans in mind."

"I needed to force your hand, Tarik, since it was obvious you were taking advantage of my sister. And now you must do the honorable thing," Asad shot back.

Betrayed. Fatima's hands shook uncontrollably as she ducked out to an exterior room, dressing quickly. She reemerged, to find her lover and twin. The sheikh had left, the damage done. Unsmiling, Tarik stood, arms folded across his chest. Asad stood by him, studying her.

"I told the sheikh you were with Tarik, Fatima. I followed you both back here," he said unapologetically.

The full impact of the situation hit her, the shocked pain hurting worse than a thousand knives sinking into her back. "Why did you do this?" She gaped at him.

Asad gave her a cool look. "I did it for your own good. Tarik vowed never to see you hurt again. After you were shot, we couldn't bear the uncertainly. As his Guardian, you would get hurt—or even killed—unless we did something. Thus, I informed the sheikh you were in his tent."

"My own brother," she whispered. Her chest tightened like wet leather as she faced the prince. "And *you*—you knew what would happen."

Her lover watched through hooded eyes. "I will not lie, Tima. I intended to do this sooner, but I changed my mind, for I didn't want you to get hurt like this. But now that your brother has taken the decision from my hands, I can't say I'm sorry we were found out. I'll never let you go. Ever."

How could she have not paid attention, forgotten his determination? Ruthless in pursuing what he wanted, he'd hunted her like prey. And like a stupid rabbit she'd fallen before him, surrendering to his unstoppable force. Fatima slapped her head. Stupid, stupid! She had gained everything only to lose it with a foolish act of lust, her own desire betraying her.

"Bastard," she whispered, struggling against the tears burning her throat. "You manipulative bastard." She rushed him, but Tarik easily caught her hands and deflected her pummeling blows.

"It is done, Tima. There's no going back now." The deep authority in his voice was a painful echo of their first time together.

Asad's mouth worked, as if he struggled for words. Fatima jerked herself out of Tarik's grip. She passed both men, whirled and faced them, limbs shaking as if stricken with unbearable cold.

"This isn't over. I won't be your pawn any longer, Tarik—and as for you, my brother . . ." A hollow feeling filled her bones, leaving her as chilled as a stone tomb. "Oh! If not for Mama and Papa, I wish I had never left England!" Fatima stormed outside.

A soft desert breeze caressed her icy cheeks. Fatima lifted her head to the blurred outline of stars glittering in the dark velvet sky. Why? she whispered. Why had she achieved the dream, only now to watch it spill from her fingers like tiny grains of sand?

It was her fault. Because she'd given in to pleasure and passion. Because she'd wanted to know for once what it felt like to become a woman. And now she knew.

But she'd lost everything.

The following morning Fatima splashed water on her face. A small gilt mirror over her washbasin reflected her reddened and swollen eyes. Grief and shame weighed her down. How could she bear to look upon her father now? She would have gone from being his biggest joy to his biggest disappointment.

Ducking out of the tent before her parents could question her, she walked toward the camp edge. The wadi where she'd played as a child offered slim refuge now; she felt lifeless, without substance, as gray and phantasmal as the mists that stole over her grandfather's house on the moors, curled around the windows, seeping through them.

Sheltering limestone rock flanked her as she vanished into the wadi's deep recesses, found a boulder and sat. She lifted her face to the burning yellow sun's caress, but it failed to lift the deep chill permeating her bones.

* * *

Courage, man. Tarik steeled his spine and went to Ramses' tent to ask formal permission to marry his daughter.

Ramses sat before his tent, sharpening his scimitar. Seeing Tarik, he set down his sword, jerked his head inside The two men went in, and Katherine rolled down the flaps then left, fury filling her eyes.

Dread filled Tarik. He'd insulted Fatima's parents. Badly.

Ramses folded his powerful arms across his chest. He did not invite Tarik to sit. "You hurt my little girl," he said, anger threading his deep voice. "You seduced my only daughter."

"I know," Tarik said softly. "I came here to formally request your permission to marry her, sir."

"You have it, of course." Ramses fell silent.

The flat disapproval on the man's face cut Tarik like a knife, and it hurt even more when Ramses turned away. "What I did hurt all of you. I'm sorry for that. But I'm not sorry this happened. If it makes you feel better, hit me."

Ramses whirled back with lethal grace, astonishment touching his mouth. "What?"

"Hit me, sir. I know you want to. She's your daughter."

"I am a Khamsin Guardian, sworn to protect my sheikh and you, his heir. That would violate my duty," he said with dignity.

Tarik sighed, rubbing the back of his neck.

After a moment, Ramses narrowed his eyes in thought. "It is best you marry Fatima. She lacks honor, and is no better than Cairo's rutting whores."

Red fury filled Tarik's vision. Fatima, a whore? "How dare you say that?" Tarik roared. He drew back a fist . . .

A powerful blow to his jaw made him stagger backward. Ramses smiled grimly. "That is for hurting my little girl. Hitting you in self-defense does not violate my honor."

Tarik ruefully touched his mouth, examined his bloodied fingers. "I deserved that."

"And more," Ramses stated thinly. He narrowed his eyes again. "I have one question, Tarik. Do you love Fatima?"

"More than my life," he answered quietly.

Fatima's father clapped a forgiving hand on his shoulder. "I knew it. You are worthy of my daughter, but you must always strive to remain so. Having taken her honor, you must now fight to protect it."

Wordlessly, he nodded. A flat smile touched Ramses's mouth.

"Oh, and Tarik? I would not go hunting with Katherine anytime soon. She is still very angry—and an excellent shot with the crossbow."

Tarik swallowed, resisting the urge to clap a protective hand over his groin. "Thank you, sir. I'll remember that."

"Good. Now let us get your father and my son, and go find your bride-to-be."

The moment he both dreaded and anticipated had come. Joining her father, his and Asad, he stalked toward his mare, placing his right hand upon his scimitar. The hilt felt reassuring. Tarik thought of relinquishing it, never again to be a warrior. Intense grief speared him. How could he ask Tima to do the same? *I must. I will not see her endanger herself like a man. Never again.*

They rode toward the mountains in somber silence. Tarik steeled his spine, anticipating her despondency over the sheikh's decree. He could only hope the soothing balm he offered would ease her pain.

Tucked into his binish were two items he'd present to

his Guardian. Cradled next to his heart, the carmine desert rose reminded him of his lover's rosy cheeks, her petal-soft skin. The small gold circle he bore would fit her slim finger perfectly.

They rode deep into the twists and turns of a wadi, finally spotting the indigo-draped Fatima sitting in morose dejection on a flat boulder. He'd sensed where to come.

"I knew I would find you here. It was your favorite hiding place as a child," he called out as they approached.

"Go away, Tarik," she said dully.

He gently unfurled her clenched fingers to place the rose on her opened palm. "For you. I know you love them."

Hope seized him as Fatima inhaled the flower's delicate fragrance. A slight smile curled her lips. Then it faded. She looked at him with an air of guarded expectation. Judging from the rapid intake of her breath, she expected the worst. And his father, their sheikh, was about to deliver it.

Anxiety clenched Fatima's stomach. Something horrible was happening; the four men regarded her as grimly as executioners. Pain speared her palm as her fingers clenched the rose's thorny stem. She set the flower down with trembling fingers.

The sheikh rubbed his bearded chin where gray feathered the luxurious black. His lips were set in a thin slash.

"Fatima bint Ramses Sharif, I am removing you as my son's Guardian of the Ages."

Sharp pain arrowed through her. "Sire, I . . . I . . ." *Get hold of yourself.* She drew in a calming breath. "Sire, I understand your anger. But I've done nothing to compromise my ability to guard your son, our future sheikh. My ability to protect him—"

"Nothing? You are his lover, Fatima. How effective a

Guardian of the Ages can you be as his lover? Will your eye be sharp, your sword swift if your thoughts are soft and sighing with passion? My son needs a Guardian to do what a Guardian must—risk his life to protect him. Tarik's intent will be to guard you now, to defend you. By simply being his lover, you endanger him."

Tarik held out his hand. "I'm sorry, Tima. I must have your dagger and your scimitar."

The muscles in her throat constricted as she swallowed. Fatima looked away, her jaw growing rigid. "Am I required to grovel before all the warriors, to apologize for not being worthy of their company any longer?"

"No," he replied quietly, watching her. "You will relinquish your weapons to me, Tima. The law requires you to surrender them to me because you are no longer my Guardian."

Dull resignation filled her. Fatima unsheathed her dagger and handed it to him. Slowly, she withdrew her sword from its protective silver sheath. It slid free in a rasp of metal that grated on her aching heart. With one finger she stroked the intricate design on the flat of the blade.

"My grandfather gave me this sword. It was my maternal great-grandfather's. It has been in my family for generations."

Sunlight glinted on the blade's razor sharp edge. The longer she held it, the harder it would be to let go.

"Tima, I must have it," Tarik said in a soft tone.

With a violent hiss she threw the sword and sheath down. They thudded into the sand. Tarik picked both up with reverence, wiped grains of sand from the sheath. He handed the sword to Asad, something guarded in their glances.

"Tima, give me your right hand," Tarik ordered.

Biting her lip, she did so. His fingers felt warm,

strong, and he very gently clasped her hand. A chilled metal circle fashioned from twin bands of gold felt restrictive, binding as Tarik slid it onto her finger. A round emerald winked in the brilliant sun.

Fatima stared at the ring as if Tarik had placed prison chains upon her. But as he lightly stroked her fingers, sensual heat fused with her deep anger and fierce anguish.

No. Never again. Desire had trapped her in this cage. She would not capitulate again.

"The ring is from our tribe's gold in the sacred tomb. I had it fashioned with an emerald in Cairo—a melding of the old and new. I thought of adding a diamond, but this emerald was the only jewel that did you justice. The jeweler thought me odd when I took it outside to see if the color snapped and sparkled in the sunlight like the fire in your eyes."

"How poetic," she snapped. "Ah, yes, my 'eyes are like jewels, my lips like rosy pomegranates . . .' "

"No. Your eyes are the color of river grass, green like when sunlight touches it as it sways and bends with the Nile current."

Fatima stared at the ring. Suspicion filled her.

Tarik fell to both knees, gently clasped her right hand. Nearby her father, his, and Asad watched.

"Fatima, I have something to ask you formally, before my father and yours. Will you marry me?" he asked solemnly, his expression softening. "Will you do me the extreme honor of becoming my bride?"

His wife, not his Guardian. A ring, not a sword.

"No!" She snatched her hand away, struggled to free her finger from the circle. She tossed it down.

Tarik picked it up. No emotion showed on his face, but a muscle in his jaw jumped violently. Those broad shoulders lifted ever so slightly as he stood, palming the ring.

Fatima jumped to her feet, heart pounding so fast she could scarcely catch her breath. "That ring, Tarik. You bought it on that trip to Cairo right after the council voted to approve me as your Guardian." She whirled, regarding everyone with fury. "Were you all in on this? Was this your plan? Train me as Tarik's Guardian, throw us together, and wait so you could trick me into being his wife, what you really wanted!"

"No, Tima. My father and yours had nothing to do with this. I bought the ring in Cairo because it was my intention, eventually, to ask you to become my bride." Tarik's expression tightened. "But not like this."

"I won't marry you, Tarik," she snapped, fisting her hands. "You can't force me. Your plans have failed."

"You will marry Tarik, Fatima." Her beloved father's look of censure stabbed her to the bone. "It is not an option."

"Fatima, you dishonored your father's name and our people. You will marry my son. Our laws state it clearly. If you do not, you face banishment from our people."

Sinking back onto a boulder, Fatima stared at the sheikh in astonishment. "Sire, you cannot—"

"I can," he returned, his jaw tensing. "And I will."

"You can't do this," she cried. "It's not fair."

"Life is not fair, my beloved Fatima," the sheikh said quietly. "We must accept what is with grace."

Not her. Ever. She whirled, narrowing her gaze. Her lower lip wobbled. "I . . . I . . ." Words failed.

Fatima gathered her tattered dignity together and looked at her father. With all her strength she forced the words out. "I'm sorry, Papa, for failing you. I'm sorry." Her voice broke.

"I am gravely disappointed in you, daughter. It is best that you marry Tarik. He will be a good husband." His stern expression softened. "I love you, Fatima, and only want what is right for you."

Tears burned the back of her throat, threatening to gush out in sobs. Warriors did not weep. But she was no longer a warrior.

Tarik squeezed the ring so hard it dented his palm. *Fatima, Fatima.* She had gotten under his skin, dug in deep like sand sinking between his toes. He hadn't expected her to warble joyously when he proposed, but neither had he anticipated this outright refusal with tearful fury.

Grief lanced his heart as he watched her slender shoulders droop. Fatima's jaw locked as lines formed in her elegant brow. Watching her fight to control her emotions, Tarik thought of the exquisite desert rose he'd presented the night they'd first made love. He felt as if he had marched toward a blazing fire to throw the flower into the inferno.

"Tima," he said in his softest voice, steeling himself for her reaction. "I have no desire to see you banished. I only wish you would do me the honor of becoming my bride."

Distress etched her face. "But you *would* banish me from my family, from those I love. For not marrying you."

Tarik gathered her hands in his. "It is our law. I seduced you, a Khamsin maiden, so now we must marry."

"But what if I were not a maid?" she challenged.

"We know that isn't true," he replied, glancing at her silent father and his. "There was proof of your virginity."

The flush raced across her cheeks until her entire face burned bright red. Tarik resisted her attempts to yank her hands free. "I love you, Tima. I want you to be my wife. We can have a good life together. Will you have me?"

"I suppose that choice is removed." She narrowed her eyes at his father, who sighed.

"The law must be upheld, Fatima. But I swear as

sheikh of the Khamsin warriors of the wind, if you marry my son, no one else will know the circumstances."

Bitter laughter spilled from her lips. "No one will know how I was betrayed. How utterly noble of all of you to preserve my . . . dignity. So no one knows I'm a fool."

"Fatima, that isn't so," Ramses said, looking stricken.

"Don't deny it, Papa. You raised a foolish daughter who believed she could trust the man she guarded with her life." Fatima yanked her hands away. "I have no choice, Tarik. I was separated from my family for eight years and now you threaten to take them away from me again. So I will marry you. But I warn you; Don't expect me to meekly obey your every command."

"I wouldn't want that," he said gently.

"And what will you tell our people as the reason for my marrying you and surrendering my position as your Guardian?"

Tarik studied the moisture glittering in her eyes. "I will tell them the truth. I asked you to do me the honor of becoming my bride, and you accepted."

"The wedding will take place upon the next full moon," Jabari said, glancing at Ramses.

Both fathers and Asad murmured flat congratulations and walked off. Tarik stood, looking down at Fatima. She seemed fragile as faience, hands shaking as she picked up the rose he'd brought. He knew when the onslaught came, it would pour out in a hideous flood of grief, sorrow she'd share with no one but the silent desert.

She bent her head, seemingly absorbed in the rose. Her chest heaved from the violence of her breathing. Helpless anguish gripped Tarik. Had his reasons justified his actions? It was too late now. He'd rather die himself than see her take another blade for him, or a bullet.

And what of the dagger piercing her heart, his conscience taunted. *You wounded her worse than any blade.*

He wanted to gather her into his arms, to let her sob out everything she held inside. He placed the tips of his fingers on her shaking shoulders. Fatima jerked away.

"Good-bye, Tima," Tarik said quietly. "We will expect you for dinner, but . . . take your time."

As he began to turn, he saw the desert rose slip from her trembling fingers, spill onto the sand. It lay there in the sun, wilting under the blistering rays. He walked quickly away, not wanting to witness its demise.

Chapter Nineteen

They married the first night of the full moon. Beneath a glittering carpet of stars, Tarik stood dressed in white, moonlight gilding his golden hair. Regal as a proud, ancient pharaoh, he took her hand and solemnly vowed to love and cherish her forever, and to protect her with his very life. Forcing a smile, Fatima stated her own vows, but her heart was sundered in two. Painful reminders of her warrior initiation filled each word.

When he bent his head for the customary kiss, she compressed her lips and pulled subtlely away. Tarik did not force her. He offered a wide smile for the watching crowd.

The wedding feast held no joy. Proffered congratulations were accepted with a smile. Fatima ignored the sly remarks that her lack of appetite meant she feared her approaching deflowering. Across the fire, her cousin Alhena flirted outrageously with several men. Once Fatima caught her looking over with a sullen glare. As the cousin least expected to marry, Fatima suspected her union had caused Alhena jealous bewilderment.

When the time finally came to retire to their new

home, she walked straight and tall beside Tarik. Ribald remarks about their wedding night were met with a confident smile. No one would know her hand was forced. Her parents hugged her good-bye, but when Asad stepped forward to do the same, Fatima turned away. Her twin's betrayal still hurt like a sword cut.

Sorrow filled Asad's green eyes. A lump welled in Fatima's throat. She'd never hurt her twin before. For a moment she wanted to offer forgiveness, but bitter anger mingled with her sorrow. She ignored her twin, following Tarik out and to their tent.

Thick, jewel-toned Persian rugs adorned the spacious interior. Tarik sat against mounds of silk pillows in the main room. Fatima tore off her heavy gold coin headdress, letting it fall. It tinkled as coins hit the carpet. She sat, ignoring Tarik. They waited for Ahmed, the shaman, to deliver the wedding night blessing customary for all sheikhs and their heirs.

When Ahmed did enter, Fatima didn't bow her head for the prayer to bless their marriage and her chance of delivering healthy sons. Downgraded from a warrior and Guardian to an expected broodmare, she resented the shaman's words. And when he handed her the golden goblet of Syrian Rue—the drink all brides consumed to ease their wedding night fears, and all grooms sipped to ensure their performance—she pushed it away.

Tarik took a customary sip, graciously thanking the shaman as Ahmed stood. The elderly man squeezed Fatima's shoulder.

"Remember what I told you before, daughter of the desert. Surrender to destiny, and your heart's desires will come true."

She gave a humorless laugh.

The married couple sat in silence after he left. Then Tarik stood, held out his hand. "Come, Tima," he ordered softly.

"I'm not consummating this marriage," she hissed. "Not tonight or any night. You'll have to force me."

"I'd never force you." His dark eyes glittered with intent. "But you must accept that we are married now, and there is no turning back. And I do not intend to remain celibate."

"You should have considered that before you seduced me."

"I didn't exactly seduce you that night, if you recall. You most willingly came to my bed."

Stung, she sprang at him, wanting to hurt him as she herself hurt. Tarik grasped her wrists and pulled her to him. She expected him to kiss her, to toss her on the bed, to bend her to his will. But he merely gathered her close, stroking her hair and murmuring as if she were a child needing comfort.

This gentle consideration threatened to unleash the deep sorrow dammed inside her. No! No more tears. She'd not break down and cry before him. She'd rather fight.

Fatima allowed herself to go limp against his chest. His arms loosened. When they did, she broke free—pushed at him, hard. Caught off balance, Tarik stumbled, his arms pinwheeling for purchase. She hooked her foot around his ankle, watched him tumble gracefully to the carpet.

"How the mighty do fall," she mocked. "I still know that move. You forget I'm a warrior, Tarik, no matter what people call me. Not a meek wife."

Tarik panted, his dark eyes growing hard as steel. He stood. "So that's what you want, little caracal? I can play."

A finger of fear stroked her spine as he advanced. His look intent, he radiated such masculine force that she doubted she could stop him. She forced herself to stand her ground. Fatima hunched over, prepared to struggle.

At last he pounced, a graceful leap like that of a lion. He tumbled downward, taking her with him, rolling to prevent her from injury. But instead of pinning her down, he tickled her ribs. Writhing, Fatima screamed in protest.

Suddenly, voices outside roared with laughter. Tarik stopped and Fatima froze. The ritual—they'd forgotten! Only their immediate families knew she wasn't a virgin. Men were standing outside their tent, listening to Tarik prove his prowess with his bride.

A shadow dropped over her new husband's face. She saw him as he'd been so long ago, back in the schoolroom, a mutinous mask cloaking his boyish feelings as children mocked him for his golden curls. Her anger faded. Whatever feelings she held about this marriage, she would not shame herself and Tarik. The masquerade must continue.

Fatima cleared her throat and moaned as if suddenly caught in passion's throes. "Oh, oh, oh, oh, Tarik! Oh yes, yes, yes! Right there! Oh God, I cannot believe it! It's so big, it will never fit! Your mighty sword is huge! Oh, please don't hurt me!"

He shot her a bemused look. She jerked her head at the tent wall, gestured to her ear. He nodded, then played along.

"Don't be afraid, my little butterfly, I will show you pleasures you have never dreamed of," he boomed in a stilted voice.

Fatima rolled her eyes. A warrior he was, but no actor.

"Yes, my little butterfly, my manly sword is a weapon of enormous power. No one else can give you the ecstasy I can deliver with my manly weapon. See how it quivers with passion for you? My manly weapon. Your tender flower opens to its mighty power. I will be gentle with you, my shy little virgin—"

"Oh, for God's sake just put it in already and stop talking," she yelled.

She gurgled with laughter at his surprise. Tarik clapped a hand over her mouth, the palm warm and caressing as he, too, heaved with silent laughter. Bawdy exclamations came from outside, followed by shuffling feet. They were leaving. Good.

Tarik craned his head, listening. Catching him off guard, Fatima rolled, pinning him beneath her. He looked up, desire darkening his eyes, a wry smile on his lips.

"Trying to best me, Tima?"

"You know I can."

"Three out of five wins," he suggested softly. With a graceful twist, he flipped her beneath him. "Got you. I win one, you win one. Winner takes the loser to bed."

"Not fair," she protested. "What if I win?"

"You get to be on top." He flashed her a wicked grin.

"No tickling allowed. Promise."

"Promise," he agreed, and freed her.

Wasting no time, Fatima hooted a war call and spun, slamming him to the carpet. One hand effectively cupped the most vulnerable part of him, and she straddled him and smiled. Alarm sprang into his eyes as she very gently squeezed. Against her arm, his erection hardened.

"Tima," he rasped.

"Yes, dear?" she said sweetly. "Does this make it two?"

A jerky nod, and she released him.

Breath wheezed out of his lungs in harsh bellows. Tension coiled in his thick muscles. His powerful body seemed poised to strike, like a prowling lion, but then Tarik stripped. Fatima's eyes widened. From its nest of dark gold curls, his steely erection jutted nearly to his navel. A shudder of desire seized her. She felt herself weakening in resolve.

"I'm not fighting you naked!" she protested.

"Yes, you are," he countered, fingering her gown.

He swiftly undid the fastenings, stripping the eggshell white garment from her body, baring her to his hungry gaze. Muscles rippled beneath his bronzed skin as he flexed his biceps, staring at her. Demonstrating his strength, his ability to claim her.

It was strength she also possessed. Fatima allowed herself to smile. As he advanced, she darted out of reach, laughing. "Not that easy, Tarik. It won't be that easy."

Challenge flared on his lean face. "I wouldn't have it any other way, wife. It will make victory all the sweeter."

She raced toward the bedroom, feeling his hot breath on her back. Fatima ground to an abrupt halt, whirled and dove for the carpet, hooking out a foot. But he anticipated her move, and fell gracefully, reaching for her.

In a minute he'd mounted her; faster than she could react, he'd pinned her beneath him as she struggled wildly. Fatima writhed, trying to toss him off. She gasped as he put a knee between her thighs, spread them and settled between them. That hard, thick length of his sex probed at her soft entrance. He halted, drew back. His fingers tunneled down through her curls and over her slick, female folds.

"You're wet for me, my love. You can't hide your desire, Tima. Surrender," he said with satisfaction.

"Never," she breathed, but he cut off her words with his mouth, kissing her deeply.

"Three out of five," she protested feebly.

"I lied," he murmured, quieting her with his lips. He plundered, licked, claimed.

Rolling her beneath him, he pinned her wrists to the carpet, feathered kisses over the hollow of her throat, the slender slope of her shoulders. Fatima hooked her legs about his hips, drawing him closer. He rose above her, face stamped with savage male triumph, positioned himself at her wet entrance and thrust. She recoiled slightly at the insistent pressure, gasping. His crisp chest hairs created a delicious friction against her aching, tender breasts, and he held her gaze fiercely as he hammered into her. Then Tarik drew back, clasped her knees wide and began thrusting harder, penetrating deeper than before. Her inner muscles went wild.

"Mine, Tima," he whispered thickly. "You're mine and no one else's. Mine to have and to hold. I'm going to ride you hard and fast, sweetheart, to make you remember. Only I will possess your sweet body. None other."

"Please. Oh, please." Her voice became a pleading sob.

"Say it, Tima. Say my name," he commanded.

The tension built, riding low and hard in her loins. Fatima reached for it, clenched her body as erotic pleasure tore her in half. No mercy, no pity—his thick length slammed into her, his fingers like steel as he gripped her hips. Wildly she clawed at him, the need for release consuming her. Tarik laughed softly at her scratching his back, shifted his position. Slowing, he teased her, rubbed against her intimate core.

A sudden sharp pleasure speared her, and Fatima screamed, bucking her hips, desperately poised on the edge of climax. "Tarik!" she sobbed, nails digging into his chiseled shoulder muscles.

"Yes, my little caracal," his deep, husky voice murmured. "Oh yes. Let go. Let it go. Come for me, my love."

A sudden, sharp twist of his hips sent her spiraling over the edge. Fatima convulsed, shrieking as she clutched him, her body arching off the floor. While she still shook from the powerful climax gripping her, his fingers dug into her tender hips as he threw back his head, released a harsh groan and shuddered. She felt his hot seed spurt deep inside her.

Still trembling, she lay back, dazed and awash with pleasure. Her husband collapsed atop her, his heavy weight pressing her into the ground. Harsh breaths bellowed in out of his lungs. Her own heart hammered frantically, finally slowing to a regular cadence. Making no sound, Fatima caressed he thick muscles of his back, felt his cock twitch inside her.

Passion claimed her once more. But though she was capitulating to his heated kisses and skilled lovemaking, she silently vowed never to become a meek wife, eager to serve his needs, a woman approved by Ibrahim or others of his narrow-minded ilk.

Slowly Tarik raised his head, his long golden mane curtaining his face. Sweat beaded his temples, dampened the hair at his brow. He pressed a singularly sweet kiss to her forehead and his dark gaze grew frighteningly intent.

"You win, Tima."

She pushed back a lock of his hair. "I don't want to win, Tarik. Never did. All I wanted was respect and acknowledgement as an equal, not to be considered a weak, inferior woman."

"Inferior? My Tima? Never," he murmured, carefully sliding from her, leaving her strangely bereft and empty. She felt his seed trickle out of her secret hollow.

Tarik uncoiled his body, sweat glistening on the hard curves of his muscles as he held out a hand. Fatima grasped it as he pulled her upright, then swung her easily into his arms, cradling her against his chest. Very carefully, he laid her down on the bed. Curling up beside her, he molded her into the curve of his body. He draped an arm about her, holding her close.

Her eyes fluttered shut as he soothingly stroked her hair. Murmured endearments shifted to heated whispers, dark promises of erotic pleasure. Lifting the dark masses of her hair, his lips tenderly grazed the nape of her neck.

Fatima bit back an excited whimper. Tarik was insatiable, and ruthless! He rolled her onto her back, mounting her and kneeing her thighs open. Moisture created by their earlier joining eased his way as he thrust. Lacing his fingers through hers, he pushed so deep she cried out, the pressure so intense she wasn't sure she could take him all.

He stilled, gazing down at her, his broad shoulders looming over her in the flickering light. He braced himself on his hands, his body joined intimately to hers. "Come with me, Tima. Come with me to paradise, my beautiful little caracal, my warrior, my wife. Take my life from me, for I am yours forever. My spirit is joined to yours, my body melded to yours. I love you, Tima."

"Tarik," she whispered, afraid to say the words, afraid of granting him any more power over her.

He loved her slowly then, kissing her, whispering how delicious she felt as he moved inside her, how tight and warm, how she pleased him. Each skillful thrust was angled to send sharp pleasure spearing through her, until her hips met his in eager response. The blossom of erotic excitement flowered and burst. Fatima clutched him, sobbing out his name. Satisfaction shone in his fierce dark gaze. His powerful body stiffened as he threw back his head, giving a loud warbling shout. The Khamsin war cry.

Ecstasy died. Fatima stared over her husband's muscled shoulder at the tent ceiling as he collapsed heavily upon her, his weight pressing her into the mattress.

This was the war cry she'd never again hear or respond to. No longer was she a warrior, but a wife.

Bracing himself on his palms, Tarik raised himself up. Sweat glistened on his curved muscles, beaded the hair on his chest. He pressed a soft kiss to her forehead and gently slid out of her. She winced at the soreness in her muscles. Her body ached, but not as much as her spirit.

He rolled over, removed a jeweled wedding dagger from the bedside table, unsheathed it. Tarik made a small cut inside his thigh. With his fingers, he smeared blood on the sheet.

"What are you doing?"

His intense gaze met hers. "The sheet is customarily presented to my father and the council as proof of the bride's purity, and ensuring my heirs are sired by me."

A hot blush crept up her throat. As Tarik set down the dagger and drew her into his arms, exhausted by the tumultuous sex and the strain of the day's emotions, she drifted to sleep.

She dreamed: a shifting mosaic of images, angry faces, a sword and a sheath. Blood, staining the sands. A face drifted, a ghost fading into the mist. Leaving terrifying knowledge.

Fatima shrieked, bolting upright, struggling out of Tarik's warm arms. "He's not the one!"

Tarik came instantly awake. "Tima, sweetheart, hush now. You're dreaming. What happened?"

His alertness chased away the wispy nightmare images. Fatima clung to him, burying her head in his shoulder.

"He's not the one, Tarik. I don't know what that means. I don't know! But it terrified me," she whispered.

"You're safe," he soothed. "I won't let anyone hurt you."

But as he kissed her tenderly and she snuggled

against him, Fatima had a dreadful feeling she could not banish. Something dark and evil, with razor-sharp claws, stalked his family. And it lurked much closer than they realized.

Chapter Twenty

The days following their wedding proved as dull as the as the consummation of their marriage had been tumultuous. Jabari delayed the customary seven-day honeymoon. Urgent matters consumed his 'and Tarik's attention, among them the growing unrest throughout Egypt. Peasants held demonstrations and rumors flew about like sand flies. Graham—their friend and the Duke of Caldwell—had sent messages, telling he'd arrived safely in Egypt and would soon visit.

Worried about revolution, the Majli and the Jabari convened from dawn to long past dusk. Tarik, summoned to those meetings with Asad, again his Guardian, didn't return home until the sun dipped well below the tawny mountains. Sometimes when he returned home, Fatima wasn't there.

Since their wedding night, she had turned her back on her husband. Her dream had disturbed her so deeply that she'd insisted on accompanying him to the council meetings, fearing the worst. When he'd gently refused, giving her a light good-bye kiss before sauntering off, her heart hardened.

Her duty performed, the marriage consummated, she stiffened each time he drew her into his arms. After the first two nights of her refusal, Tarik had taken to bed with a sigh, the stark coldness of his bare back presented to her gaze. Fatima tensed against her quivering urge to touch the hard muscles of his bronze skin. But few days later, her monthly courses arrived, giving her a valid excuse to sleep apart.

Yes, the council meetings often stretched into the night. Lonely and resentful, Fatima had sneaked back into her parents' tent and slept in her old room. When Tarik voiced his angry disapproval, she'd replied that he didn't bother sleeping in their bed, so why should she?

Now Fatima stood in their bedroom, folding laundry—the one wifely task she'd mastered and that made her mind drift into dull oblivion. She paused upon seeing Tarik's indigo binish. Grief welled up as she caressed the garment. Once this uniform of a proud warrior had covered her own slender body. She'd sat in the hallowed male sanctuary of council meetings next to her arrogant charge. No longer.

Dropping the binish, she stole to her husband's trunk. Out came her great-grandfather's scimitar. Tarik had taken good care of it, polishing the sheath, honing the blade. She stroked the silver sheath with deep regret.

"You know, when I handled your father's scimitar, he was outraged because I was going to chop vegetables with it."

Dropping the sword with a clatter, Fatima turned and faced her amused mother.

"But you, daughter, would never use a weapon like that. You used it in battle. Do you know how proud I am of you?"

"Proud? How? I've done nothing but fail as a warrior."

Katherine touched Fatima's cheek. "You've carved a pathway for women in our tribe. You risked all, and achieved your dream. You're still a warrior. No one can take that away from you."

Fatima fiddled with folding laundry again. "What are you doing here, Mother? Bringing over dinner again?"

"No. I'm here to teach you to cook."

"And so am I."

Elizabeth appeared in the doorway, a soft smile touching her mouth. "Nadia and several other women agreed to give you their favorite recipes and teach you how to make them. Only my lessons come with a price you must pay."

Fatima's shoulders lifted slightly. "I have nothing to give."

"Yes, you do," the sheikh's wife insisted. "Lessons in how to fire a gun. Jabari thought it an excellent idea. If he continued to teach me, he'd face more trouble with the Majli."

Convulsive shock raced through her. The sheikh, who had sternly ordered Fatima to marry his son, wanted his women armed and educated?

"But a woman teaching another woman to shoot . . ." Her mother winked at her. "Jabari already succeeded in striking down the law decreeing it is illegal for women to carry daggers."

"But not to shoot guns," Fatima protested.

"If caught, we'll just say one discharged. We are weak, helpless and silly women. What do we know?" Elizabeth countered.

Fatima laughed. "Mother, do you want to learn as well?"

"Elizabeth and I both agreed it's more important that she learns first. She's the sheikh's wife, and she will set the example."

Katherine's knowing gaze met Elizabeth's. Fatima understood, and her respect for Jabari's wife grew. If caught, Elizabeth faced a severe penalty, but she was willing to risk it to pave the way for other Khamsin women.

As they set about lighting a small fire in the home's clay oven, Elizabeth spoke softly. "There is more to life for women than cooking and having babies, Fatima. Don't give up your dream or lose your voice. I know marriage is difficult, challenging at first. But trust me, my son doesn't want to see you silenced."

"He married me out of necessity," she blurted.

"Tarik doesn't do anything he doesn't want. If he had no desire to marry you, he wouldn't have." Elizabeth gently squeezed her hand. "When he sees what he wants, he pursues it with all his heart. He wanted you as a wife. Suppressing yourself to become a *meek* wife, that's what Ibrahim wishes. Not Tarik."

The glowing kindling of the clay stove caught and ignited the wood. Fatima stared inside, remembering shared passion. Her innocent faith in Tarik shattered, she couldn't turn back time and give him her trust. Tarik had hunted her as ruthlessly as stalking a caracal. She'd surrendered to his heated kisses and tender intimacy, and now the cold gold ring shackling her to him forever bit into her finger. Fatima stirred the water in a pot, watching it bubble and froth.

She glanced up at the hopeful faces of his mother and her own. No more meek silence. Suppressing her views only let those narrow-minded council members win. The women needed her.

Fatima set down her spoon. "Douse this fire and let's start another. Elizabeth, I'm teaching you to shoot. Any man trying to stop us better be a lot better shot than me."

Her mother beamed. "I doubt it's possible, Fatima. The men adore playing with their swords too much to become expert marksmen."

"Especially in the bedroom," Elizabeth put in, giggling. They all laughed.

"Indeed," Fatima mused.

"Fatima, what are you doing?"

Tarik felt his jaw drop in incredulous shock. First his father had been teaching his mother to shoot, and now his wife was? Weary from endless hours of bickering meetings, sexually frustrated from his wife's refusals, he rubbed his chin. Stubble shadowed his tense jawline and his eyes felt scratchy from sleeplessness. When an outraged Haydar had informed him Fatima was holding shooting lessons for Elizabeth, he'd thought it a bad dream.

His mother turned, lowering the weapon. Tarik's bleary eyes registered an incredible fact. A small hollow pockmarked the inner ring of the red bull's-eye on the rock. Damn, his own mother shot better than he did!

Her back to him, Fatima shoved a magazine clip into her Colt. "I'm showing your mother what it's like to load a pistol. That isn't against our laws. Does anyone else wish to learn?"

Haydar and the other warriors who trailed behind Tarik stared. Hostile murmurs indicated they resented this display of skill. Especially since a woman demonstrated it.

"Tarik, are you allowing this?"

Tarik glanced at Haydar, who bristled with indignant fury. But he kept his voice mild. Never allow emotions to rule, his father had taught him. "Why? Do you need lessons?"

"The law doesn't allow women to fire weapons!"

"The gun discharged accidentally," Fatima put in, her saucy chin uplifted, her green eyes sparking with challenge.

Haydar snorted. The men looked expectantly at

Tarik. They waited to see him officially teach his wife her place.

Tarik's calm gaze met Fatima's furious one. God, she was beautiful, her silken curls beneath the indigo scarf billowing in the wind, the color snapping in her high cheekbones. Silent, he watched her caress the gun's grip, her slender, fine-boned fingers holding it with assured skill. Tarik thought of those silky hands pressed against his flesh. His body tightened with hard need. After two weeks without sex, he burned for his lovely, passionate wife.

Resting a firm hand on his sword hilt, Tarik leveled a meaningful look at Haydar. He made a decision: "The gun misfired. My wife told you what happened. Anyone daring to accuse her otherwise will suffer my anger and the consequences."

Fatima's heart galloped madly. She watched her husband, filled with natural authority, quiet Haydar's squealing protests with a few words. The men murmured sullen apologies and stole furtive glances at her and Elizabeth.

She'd expected a scathing lecture. Her anger faded, replaced by curiosity and doubt. Why had he defended her, knowing she lied? There were so many layers to this man, and she had a feeling she'd barely peeled one back.

Tarik watched the men leave, then turned, his mouth a tight slash. Fatima licked lips that suddenly went dry.

"Mother, leave us." His voice was a flat command, and he never took his steely gaze off her.

Elizabeth left, flashing Fatima a reassuring smile. Tarik folded his arms across his chest. "Fatima, give me the gun."

Swallowing hard, she emptied the chamber and

handed it over. Tarik tucked it into his belt. She steeled herself for a condemning lecture.

"The next time you wish to teach anyone how to shoot, come get me. If I am around, no one will dare squawk about it."

"Is that an order, sir?" she taunted.

"It's just good advice. You came close to outright rebellion today. The men are tense, ready to fight and have no real enemy yet. You make an easy target for their anger."

She had never considered that. Fatima drew in a shaky breath. "All right."

"Another thing, Fatima." His eyes took on a dangerously intent look, a hungry lion spying succulent prey. "Tonight you will be in my bed. No more of this sleeping apart. You're my wife, and you will sleep with me."

"I can't sleep with you in the same bed."

"I don't plan on either of us getting much sleep," he growled softly, his eyes dark with desire. His masculine will overwhelmed her. Fatima drew back, alarmed. He wanted her, and she'd put him off. And he meant to have her. Tonight.

A shout rose on the horizon. Tarik shaded his eyes. Fatima stood on tiptoe as she strained to see.

"They're here," her husband said flatly.

The English visitors had arrived? That meant among them was her very dear friend, Michael.

Sweat dappled his temples as Tarik wound a long length of hemp rope about his waist. Today he would break in an Arabian stallion the Duke of Caldwell had purchased. Named Osiris, after the god of the underworld, the temperamental horse could kill a careless man. Already the beast had kicked one unwary warrior who'd turned his back, sending him home with a broken ankle.

With Egyptians rioting in Cairo against the British, the arrival of these English friends presented new problems. Maybe Graham and Kenneth considered their heritage as Khamsin warriors a fitting defense against possible attack, but they did not look Egyptian anymores Michael especially looked English—Kenneth's oldest son and Graham's heir, who would inherit the duchy.

Ahead of Tarik, Fatima ran to greet the group. Her shout of delight rang through the camp. "Michael. Over here!"

The young man turned and waved, then laughed as she rushed into his arms. Jealousy pricked Tarik like a sharp dagger. This was Michael, Fatima's "good friend." With eyes as blue as a clear Egyptian sky and hair dark as Fatima's. He was Graham's nephew, handsome, wealthy and someone who could offer Fatima much he could not.

All I have is a kingdom of sand, dust and heat.

Tarik hid his emotions as Michael enveloped Fatima in a crushing hug. Laughing, he released her. "So good to see you, Fatima!" His deep voice radiated warmth and affection.

A hollow ache settled on Tarik's chest as he studied the pair, who now walked toward him. Fatima appeared easy and friendly with Michael. Mine, he thought savagely, fisting his hands. Yet he didn't own her. No one did.

Her fine bone structure, her long flowing hair—all of her echoed the nobility of the ancient queens. She was an Egyptian royal gracing them with her presence, and that made her husband even more protective.

With a deep breath, Tarik tried to calm the rapid beating of his heart. He strode confidently toward Michael and smiled. The younger man spotted him and returned the grin.

"Tarik! Father told us of your wedding. Congratulations!" The youth gave his dry palm a hearty pump.

Clad in a khaki suit and a broad-brimmed white hat, Michael looked urbane. Tarik felt like an indigo-draped barbarian, and new emotions bubbled to the surface with volcanic fury. *You wanted my wife. You nearly deflowered her, claiming what I claimed.*

A roaring need to crush and pound filled him. Disgusted, Tarik ruthlessly leashed his temper. He drew a calming breath, alarmed at the intense feelings inside him. Fatima, always Fatima was whipping his emotions into a whirling sandstorm.

"How was your journey? We've heard rumors of riots in Cairo. Where are your sisters, Badra and Jillian?" Fatima asked.

Michael's mouth pulled downward. "They're in England. Father, Uncle Graham and I came alone, dressed as Egyptians. We spoke Arabic the whole trip. It was risky for us to come, even disguised."

"Why *did* you come, then?" she asked, eyes round.

Tarik kept silent, knowing the reason. The younger man's gaze swept over the sand. "Uncle Graham brought . . . gifts, at the sheikh's request. Rifles and ammunition, enough to finally outfit every warrior. Father hid them in mummy cases."

"Actually, it was my request," Tarik put in mildly.

Wind played with the light blue scarf covering Fatima's raven hair. So beautiful, and she was such an excellent shot. Tarik put a hand on his sword hilt. The handle felt reassuringly familiar. Now he was left with no choice but shame in demonstrating his woefully poor aim.

"You said as much, Tima. What use is a sword against a bullet? We need guns if the riots spread. My first concern is protecting our people. Swords are no longer enough."

He studied Michael. "What's happening in Cairo?"

Lines furrowed the young man's brow. He removed his hat, sweeping back a thick shock of black hair. "Demonstrators, mostly students, are causing disruption. Rioters broke into shops and Muski Street was filled with people throwing rocks until the military arrived—including Jamal, Fatima. He was arrested."

Fatima released a horrified gasp. Tarik slid a comforting arm around her waist.

"Uncle Graham's influence managed to free him, on the condition he leave Cairo," Michael said. "He and Kareem came with us. We left them at Al-Minya to visit friends. They'll be here shortly."

"Egypt is on the verge of revolution," Tarik put in quietly. "If necessary, the Khamsin will fight, but for now, I'm glad your brothers are away, Tima."

"It's despicable. They're burning railway stations, attacking police stations. Dozens of British officers and soldiers are dead!" Michael snorted. He replaced his hat, his expression grave. "The violence has spread far beyond Cairo, and is affecting local provinces. There'll be more violence. Authorities arrested Saad Zaghlul and his mates, banishing them to Malta. Jamal says Huda Sah'rawi plans to organize a women's march to protest her husband's arrest. The very idea! Don't Egyptians understand they cannot fight England's might? Are they mad?"

Fatima pulled away from Tarik, her hands fisted and shaking. "It's about time we Egyptians demonstrated our anger. No wonder my people are rioting and rebelling! When the war ended, we were denied autonomy. I would join those women and show the British exactly what I think of their domineering attitudes."

"You wouldn't. I would prohibit it, Tima," Tarik countered.

"Why? Because it's a women's march?" she challenged.

"It's too dangerous." He studied her carefully, as he'd scrutinize a horse ready to bolt. "You forget our guest. Let's show him the horse his uncle bought, shall we? I've had enough talk of politics these past days."

Her nostrils flared, like those of a filly ready to rear. Fatima thrust out her saucy little chin, her rosy mouth trembling with apparent anger. Mute defiance shone in those blazing green eyes. Her passion for Egypt, equaling his own, sent a jolt of desire arrowing through him. Hunger seized him as he remembered cupping the heavy weight of her soft breasts, her honeyed limbs hugging his hips as he sank into her wet heat. His cock twitched violently. Tarik felt dimly grateful for the binish's loose folds concealing his reaction.

Michael's interested gaze flicked back and forth between them. Tarik ignored him, sauntered to the corral as they followed. They came to a makeshift pen fashioned from acadia wood. A gleaming black stallion reared and kicked.

"Graham's purchase. I'm breaking him," Tarik explained.

Michael's thick black eyebrows lifted. "Rather a challenge, eh? He seems quite untamed."

Tarik's meaningful gaze met Fatima's. "He will need a strong master. The trick to taming a wild spirit is patience, understanding, love and respect—as well as a firm hand."

Those green eyes narrowed in indignant fury. "Are you so certain you can restrain a free spirit, Tarik?"

"Not restrain," he corrected with a small smile. "Gentle. I accustom them to my touch and they willingly submit."

Roses of anger blossomed on Fatima's lovely cheeks. Tarik enjoyed watching her color. Perhaps she'd demonstrate the same passion tonight in their bed.

"Why are you breaking Osiris, Tarik? Don't you have important meetings?" Fatima turned to Michael. "My husband is much occupied lately. I'm so glad you're here. We can go riding together—like we always did in Hyde Park."

Suppressing a possessive growl, Tarik tightened his fingers about the rope. Not a chance in hell would she ride with Michael. You'll ride *me* tonight, my sweet, he silently vowed.

Michael gave Tarik a cheeky grin. "Really, old chap, if it's too much trouble for you to break him, meetings and all . . . Besides, can you really handle him? He looks too wild."

Tarik's jaw tightened. "I can tame anything—unlike the English, who are used to soft mounts and easy rides."

Michael's lips went white. "Are you suggesting I'd fail?"

"Would you like to try?"

"I'd do more than try."

Fatima bit her lip, appalled by her husband's simmering hostility. Her emotions were boiling at the heartwrenching news of Jamal's arrest, and she'd lashed out in helpless anger. Those words intended to annoy Tarik had provoked him into attack, like a sharp stick jabbing an angry lion.

"Stop it, both of you. Michael, Osiris is too dangerous for you. Tarik is accustomed to breaking horses," she pleaded.

His sullen glare indicated his hurt pride. Fatima suppressed an exasperated sigh. "I can't allow you to get hurt. Not after all you've done to help my brother."

Michael nodded, then scowled at Tarik. Her husband returned the look with a dark stare and swung over the corral railing.

Seeing the intruder, the black stallion reared. Anxiety

churned inside Fatima as Tarik daringly dropped his rope and approached Osiris without anything to restrain him. If her husband had forsaken caution to upstage Michael . . . She aimed a beseeching look at him to be careful.

The magnificent beast's black coat gleamed in the yellow sunlight as he paced and snorted. In a soothing voice, Tarik spoke Arabic. Enthralled, Fatima watched. Her husband had a magic touch with animals, knew how to speak to them, when to approach and when to back off. The snorting Osiris lowered his head, allowing Tarik to stroke his glossy mane.

Tarik conversed with the horse as one would a beloved companion. His large, powerful hand gently caressed the beast's neck. Then he grasped the mane and, in one graceful motion, swung up onto its back. Osiris squealed in angry protest and bucked. Tarik held on. Fatima's fist flew to her mouth. Finally Osiris tossed his head and slowed. Spent, the stallion allowed Tarik to guide him in a gentle canter about the corral.

"Well, I'll be damned," Michael said softly. "Well done."

Pride burst inside her as Tarik shot then a confident grin. This was her land, her people—the people of the horse whose deep voices, loving touches and love for animals could always turn a wild beast into a friend. She could rove far from home, but the desert would always be within her. No fancy riding park in London, nor the most glittering fetes could equal the burst of joyous pride she felt now. This was her home. Her husband. And she'd be damned if the British marched all over them, repressing them like parents disciplining rebellious children.

A new goal rose like a distant star. She would march with Huda Sah'rawi and join her fellow Egyptians in rebelling against England's imperialist grip. She'd recruit

Tarik's mother to join her. The violence in Cairo would not stop a Khamsin warrior of the wind. Her mother was right: Even stripped of scimitar and gun, she was still a warrior.

Tarik's dark gaze met hers across the corral. In it she recognized defiance and challenge. She lifted her chin, meeting his look with equal intensity. Her husband smiled slowly, even white teeth gleaming in his sun-darkened face. *Tonight I'll ride you,* he silently mouthed.

A tiny shiver of sensual excitement raced through her.

Chapter Twenty-one

They feasted beneath a sparkling canopy of stars glittering like diamond teardrops. Michael, seated next to Alhena, conversed easily with her. Fatima's pretty cousin dimpled under his rapt attention, and the campfire sent showers of orange sparks dancing upward.

Fatima sat beside Tarik. He rested his palm on her knee in a fierce display of male possession. Asad, sitting nearby, quietly bade Fatima hello. In mute protest, she turned her head. Tarik's heavy sigh of disapproval tore at her heart, but still she could not forgive her twin's duplicity.

Graham and Kenneth soberly described the riots in Egypt. When they mentioned the planned women's march in Cairo, Elizabeth gave an approving nod.

"The world would see the British military as bullies if they attacked a peaceful march by veiled women. I'm thinking of joining them to show support. It's time."

Several heads snapped over to stare in rude shock at the sheikh's wife. Jabari studied the fire, rubbing his chin. The news didn't surprise Fatima, since she had put the idea into Elizabeth's head while they were preparing dinner.

"Mother, the council is heavily divided on us championing liberation from England. Father's influence is shaky. If you march, it will shear them further apart," Tarik said quietly.

Jabari gave a troubled smile. "Your mother knows I fear for her personal safety more than any influence I will lose with the Majli."

"I wish *I* could go, Mother," Nadia chimed in. "A woman can equal a man's determination. We women should stand up for ourselves. My friends also agree with what you told us, Fatima."

Salah made no comment. But he raised his head briefly. Fatima recoiled at the hardness in his eye. Then it faded, replaced by his usual look of ambivalence.

Tarik rested a hand on one upturned knee. He offered a cool, slightly self-mocking smile. "Once I held influence over the young Khamsin women. Now they listen to my wife instead of hounding my heels, following me with adoring eyes. Ah, me."

"Fatima is the best thing that ever happened to you, my friend, and you know it. She's more than enough woman for you. Your perfect match in every way," Asad spoke up.

"I do know it," Tarik agreed, mischief dancing in his dark eyes. "Thank you for your compliments to my lovely wife. But I think she should also thank you herself. Will you not, Tima?"

Silence filled the air. Fatima struggled with her emotions, met her husband's encouraging nod. She had not spoken to her twin since the wedding. God, she missed him.

"Thank you, Asad," Fatima whispered.

Relief smoothed the worry lines from her brother's

face. He left his place and settled beside her; Tarik moved over.

Asad took Fatima's palm, squeezed it tightly. "The people need you, Tima, your strength and courage in risking all to follow your dreams. You have the ability to change us, if we are willing to accept those changes and grow."

"Yes, Fatima, you certainly have affected change," Alhena said, her smile not quite reaching her eyes. "The warriors are now reluctant to court us women, fearing we carry daggers."

Salah chuckled, unsheathed his dagger and gave it to Nadia. "For you, my little dove. If you turn into a falcon in the middle of the night, feel free to pierce my breast with it. I trust you, because you don't know which end to use."

Crimson flushed Nadia's face. She pushed his hand away, while Fatima bristled. Time spent in cooking lessons with Nadia had revealed her insecurities. Determined to help, Fatima had bolstered her sister-in-law's self-confidence with lessons of her own.

"Your wife is courageous and intelligent, and learns quickly, contrary to what you believe, Salah," Fatima snapped.

Salah looked genuinely taken aback, and he sheathed the blade. He affectionately kissed Nadia's temple. "I'm sorry, my love. I meant no insult, I was merely teasing. If you want to learn about weapons, go ahead. We need more warriors. Perhaps Fatima will lead you onto the battlefield against the British."

"I will do whatever I must to protect my people and show those insisting on repressing us that we will be silenced no longer," Fatima countered.

Salah looked interested. "Tarik, what do you say?"

"I say Fatima can match a man on the battlefield and elsewhere," he drawled in response.

"And I say your wife and Elizabeth have doomed us as a people, Tarik. They should be silenced, not applauded." The harsh, condemning voice caused ripples of shock. Fatima turned, unsurprised to see a scowling Haydar looming before them, his dark eyes filled with contempt. "I came to hear the duke's assessment of what transpired in Cairo. My grandfather does not like being uninformed."

"No one invited you here, Haydar." A muscle ticked in Tarik's jaw. "Return to your family, and any news Kenneth and Graham have will be shared tomorrow."

"I warn you, Tarik, and you, my sheikh," Haydar continued, ugly anger shadowing his face. "Your wives will bring us all to absolute ruin!"

Silence reigned. Then Fatima gestured morosely to the tray of sweet dates rolled in almonds. "I agree. These dates we women made will ruin the men, making them as chubby as sheep. I got the recipe from your mother, Haydar."

Her pointed look found the warrior's thick waist. Tarik laughed. With a dramatic flourish, Haydar stomped away.

Graham watched him go with mild interest. "Unpleasant fellow. Was he upset we failed to invite him for dessert?"

More laughter broke out. Tarik picked up a date and rolled it between his fingers. "My wife has become a most excellent cook. Sweet, succulent and very tempting," he murmured.

With deliberate slowness, he slid the date between his parted lips, sucking it as his heated gaze met hers. A shy blush covered her. Tarik watched her through hooded eyes like a lion lying in wait, tail twitching in hungry anticipation. Finally he rose.

"Please excuse us, honored guests, but I'm a newly married man who has neglected his lovely bride due to

286

pressing council business. I bid you a peaceful good night. Fatima." He held out an authoritative palm.

Swallowing hard, she placed her hand in his, smiled good night. He'd all but told everyone what would soon transpire! Her palm trembled in his steady, assured grip.

When they went into their black tent, he pulled her roughly into his arms. His mouth moved over hers, demanding and ruthless, claiming and coaxing. Fatima sagged in his strong embrace, her lips automatically parting. His tongue thrust into her mouth, making little flames lick along her skin. Scorching intensity seared her, flaring up from between her legs.

She ached. She wanted. A tiny whimper fled her lips.

Tarik pulled back, his gaze fierce. "Know this, Tima. Warriors will sing praises of Fatima, the woman warrior who could best men with her caustic wit and enormous courage. But there is one place you will never best me. That's here, in our bedroom. Here, I am your master."

Wordlessly, she stared, caught in the helpless grip of hot desire. Tarik stripped. Her hungry gaze roved his body, the smooth bronzed skin rippling with muscle. He reminded her of a powerful cat, and nude he stood before her, his erection proudly towering to his navel.

"Get undressed," he said.

She lifted her chin. "Is that an order, sir?"

"Do it or I'll tear your clothes off," he grated out.

His eyes warned he'd do so. Fatima shrugged out of her clothes, feeling her control slip. She wanted him, badly. Judging from the tautness of his body, the ragged sharpness of his breath, he wanted her as much.

Tarik pounced, capturing her in his arms, his mouth crushing hers. Everyone outside, including Michael, would hear her screams of pleasure. And Tarik darkly intended it, she realized as his mouth moved lower, his tongue swirling across her heated flesh. His hands cupped her breasts, kneaded. He rolled the nipples between his fingers, pinching lightly until her legs splayed open and she rubbed herself against him. A rough growl rose in his throat.

Tarik tipped her backward onto the bed, pinning her wrists to the mattress. Driving a knee between her legs, he settled between them. Then his thick cock plunged into her shuddering female flesh. He penetrated in a single, hard thrust. Fatima arched, her body shuddering in feminine shock as he impaled her. Her nails dug into his chiseled arms. Fatima wrapped her slender legs about his, forcing him closer.

He rode her hard and fast. It was wild, explosive sex, searing as a hot Khamsin wind, forceful as the burning yellow sun. She hissed and marked him with her fingernails on his back. He groaned and gave a possessive nip to her neck, marking her so that all would see she was his. They tangled together, two wildcats, clawing and hissing, as their naked bodies writhed and ground against each other in the heated fury of mating.

Breath fled Fatima with each fierce stroke. She dug her nails into the thick muscles of his arms as the tension burst inside her. "Do it," he commanded roughly. "Cry out my name."

Unable to hold back, she screamed his name. Her body convulsed in shuddering spasms as her sheath squeezed him tightly. Tarik joined her cry, his deeper voicing of her name echoing through the tent. Then they lay tangled together, sweat slicking their bodies. Gradually their breathing resumed to normal. Tarik slowly withdrew from her.

After a few minutes, he rolled over, propping his head upon his hand. He was a large, contented cat, purring with pleasure. One muscled thigh rested over hers, its dusting of dark gold hair gleaming in the lamplight.

A daring thrill seized her. Her master in the bedroom? She'd show him. . . .

Absorbed in the rosy flush of passion tinting his wife's honeyed skin, Tarik traced a finger lightly over her body. He sat up, took a slender foot in one hand. The delicate appendages were so feminine. The arch curved; her toes were elegant and small. He marveled at how such dainty feet could support such a strong, athletic woman. His woman. Tarik ran his fingers in a loving caress over the top of her foot. Wriggling her toes, she gave him an amused look.

"Inspecting my toes?" she teased.

"Enchanted," he replied, his fingers drifting upward, rubbing small circles as he explored. He gently stroked her thighs and parted them, studying her rosy flesh. Tarik felt himself harden again, but concentrated instead on arousing her.

A soft moan rippled from her throat as he caressed her. She pulled away, turning, her eyes darkened. "I'm hungry."

Tarik strode over to the cedarwood table and the basket of fruit. A loud rumble rose from her belly. Grinning at her charming blush, he peeled an orange and offered her a slice. With great eagerness, she bit into it. Fatima suckled, slurping juice. Her rosy mouth encased the slice.

Tarik's body tightened. He hungered to be that orange, to feel her warm lips caressing him, her tongue eagerly lapping. A rivulet of juice trickled from her mouth. He leaned forward, licked it off, tasting its sweetness and her. Dropping the fruit, she pursed her lips and sucked on his tongue.

She drew back with a naughty smile. "You taste good, Tarik," she purred. "I want to taste more of you."

Swallowing hard, he watched her drop to her knees. His penis bobbed heavily. A sultry look entered her eyes. She picked up the orange and squeezed. Juice dripped onto his throbbing cock, each droplet creating exquisite pleasure as it slid down his overly sensitized skin. A sweet smile touched her mouth as she encased his penis in both hands. His beautiful little caracal lowered her head.

I'm going to die, he thought in a hazy agony of torment.

Just like his wildest fantasy. She imitated her action with the fruit, encircling the head of his penis with her mouth. Tugging, her tongue swirling eagerly over him, sucking deeply.

Fisting his hands in her hair, he arched back. Ah Tima, sweet erotic ecstasy. Tarik watched her closed eyes, her lovely lips moving over his shaft.

Tension built, stretching him taut. Tarik fisted his hands in the masses of her soft hair. He tried pulling her off. "Sweet Tima, stop, I'm going to . . ."

Not shifting her position, she continued suckling him. Shuddering, he bucked as the orgasm seized him, his hot seed spurting into her working mouth. Lungs bellowed as his heart thundered loudly. At last the spasms ceased. Fatima drew away, planted a tiny, tender kiss on his spasming cock.

He stared. Fatima wiped her mouth with the back of her hand. "You showed me a Khamsin warrior's secret of hundred kisses. That, my dear Tarik, is a Khamsin woman's secret of one kiss."

Uncertain if his legs could carry him, he found his way to the bed and collapsed. Following him down, she curled her body around his, stroking his damp chest hair. They dozed for a while. Tarik blinked as she stroked him awake.

"Can't best you in the bedroom, Tarik?" she challenged, her touch light and teasing. His cock gave an interested twitch.

A lazy smile drifted over his lips. "Well, equal me, perhaps. Just perhaps."

Giving a mock scowl, she rolled over, tickled his ribs. He caught her slim wrists easily in one hand, then bent his mouth to her breast, licking a nipple. She gasped and arched, squealing in protest as his tongue swirled over the tip. "Not fair!"

"All's fair in battle and the bedroom, my little caracal."

"Fair? I'll show you fair," she said sweetly. Fatima's mouth swept over his damp, salty-sweet skin. She kissed and then nipped him. Tarik growled and mounted her.

Fatima raked her nails over his muscled back, hissing. He panted, his eyes darkening. "All right," he breathed. "You little wildcat."

Rising up, he gave back her freedom, but before she could attack, he pounced. Fatima squeaked as he rolled her onto her stomach. His weight pressed against her bottom. Air hit her drenched folds as he spread her thighs wide apart. She felt exposed, vulnerable and rawly excited. He bent over her, positioned himself and thrust. Deep. Fatima cried out with the shock. Tarik gripped her hips as he rode her.

"Like this, Tima? Fierce as a desert windstorm flooding your veins? Do you feel it in your blood?" he breathed.

Harsh breaths ripped from his lungs. He ground his hips against her yielding softness. His engorged cock slammed into her, harder, faster. It was raw, animal sex, wild and unceasing. Lost in its throes, gripped by passion, they joined their bodies. When her release came, Fatima screamed out a high-pitched Khamsin war call, not caring who heard. Tarik's hoarse, ululating voice joined hers. They were two warriors, finding sexual completion in each other.

Afterward his wife lay in quiet repose, her eyes fluttering shut. Tarik watched her protectively, guarding her sleep. Thoughts swirled inside him like a boiling sandstorm.

"I love you so much, my little caracal. If anything happened to you, I'd die inside," he whispered, stroking her hair.

Her assertive personality, spirit and never ending energy for life drew him like a cool oasis did a weary traveler. Tired of fawning men currying favor for their own purposes, Tarik needed Fatima. Her energy, her dreams and hopes.

He molded his body to her curves, cupped her soft, full breasts in his palms, marveling at their heavy weight, their yielding softness. She stirred and moaned a little. For a long time he lay awake, staring into the darkness, his troubled spirit soothed by the young, slender body he held close. Drowsiness claimed him. Tarik drifted off to sleep.

A soft rustling startled him fully awake. Senses sprang to full alert. Carefully he eased his arms from Fatima, scanned the bedchamber, listening for danger.

He sat up and lit the lamp. Cursing beneath his breath, Tarik slipped from bed, his gaze riveted to the gruesome object lying on the plush Persian carpet. Behind him, Fatima stirred. He heard her utter a shocked gasp.

"What is it?"

Fatima recoiled, distress darkening her green eyes. The beautiful white dove he cradled lay still, crimson flowing where a dagger pierced its snowy breast. Held in place by the dagger was a papyrus. Silent rage filled Tarik as he plucked the dagger free and unfurled the paper, scanning the hieroglyphics.

"Tarik, what does it say? Please, tell me!"

He raised his furious gaze to his wife's troubled one. "Anubis, god of the dead, crushes beneath his feet Horus, the falcon god—my clan's symbol of power. The cobra is delivering a death blow to Horus. Whoever sent this is warning me that someone in my family will soon die."

Chapter Twenty-two

Gone was the playful, sensual Tarik, replaced by a ruthless, authoritative warrior. His mouth set in a tight slash, he set out for his father's tent after breakfast. Fatima insisted on accompanying him. Dread filled her. The secret she'd harbored all these years festered like an old wound.

After Tarik broke the news to his shocked parents, Fatima addressed Jabari. "I wish to confess my crime, sire."

Jabari's grim expression eased into a puzzled frown. "What could you possibly have done, my dear Fatima?"

"The crime of withholding information many years ago. It's my fault your wife lost so many babies."

Elizabeth's eyes widened to the size of ripe plums.

"Continue, Fatima," Jabari ordered.

She laced her fingers together. "I knew what was causing Elizabeth's miscarriages. And I withheld the information."

Absolute incredulity twisted the sheikh's face. "Fatima, you were only five when Elizabeth had the last loss."

"I knew," Fatima leveled her gaze at him. "It was the tea. It was poisoned—enough to cause her to lose the babies. I saw this in a vision when I was five years old."

Three shocked gazes studied her. Elizabeth adored English tea. She drank it constantly, even during her pregnancy.

"That is why you told me to never drink tea again," Elizabeth whispered. "And I didn't, and then six months later I was pregnant again with Nadia."

Anguish filled the sheikh's dark eyes as he squeezed his wife's trembling hand. "Fatima, you are not to blame."

"I didn't tell you. I didn't understand the vision. And part of me liked how you treated me as an adored daughter. Maybe I was afraid of losing that."

"You will always have a special place in the heart of my family," Jabari said softly. "Thank you for telling us."

Elizabeth managed to smile at her through her tears. "If you had not told me not to drink tea, Fatima, I wouldn't have birthed Nadia. Stop blaming yourself. You were only a little girl, shouldering a very large burden."

Now for the very hard part. Fatima steeled her spine. "You realize that Muhammad didn't poison the tea. Whoever did it wanted to ensure you never had children, Elizabeth. The assassin has wanted you dead since the moment you married Jabari—you, the white dove whom legend said would deliver peace and prosperity to the people. He sees you as a usurper who brought havoc."

Elizabeth blanched.

"You know what the dead dove really means," Fatima whispered. "I knew the moment I saw it, though I did not want to." She shuddered, and Tarik slid a comforting arm about her waist. His touch felt reassuring, strong.

Jabari's jaw clenched. "Yes, I do. Somewhere out there, someone wants my wife to die."

"No! It's too dangerous!" Tarik thundered. He slammed a fist on the low sandalwood table. China cups holding breakfast tea rattled. Fatima flinched but held her ground.

She'd just informed him about joining Huda Sah'rawi's march against British tyranny. Tarik hadn't taken well to the news.

Questioning Haydar about the dead dove had proven fruitless. Tarik and Jabari relentlessly probed him, but the man vehemently denied any involvement. Life had gone back to normal.

"It's perfectly safe, Tarik. We are marching veiled, and without weapons. The British won't dare to attack unarmed women. Kareem is chaperoning me in Cairo. We'll stay at his friend's mother's house. Very respectable, and safe."

"Fatima, I forbid you to march."

Fatima lifted her chin. She must not capitulate, for this march meant more than asserting her desire for freedom from England. It showed she could equal any man's determination. For Tarik's mother, now silenced with a warning of violence, she must assert herself for the good of Khamsin women. Elizabeth was right. It was time.

"Try to restrain me. The only way you will stop me from joining Huda in the march is to tie me down."

"That's a possibility," he said in a low, dangerous tone.

Fatima drew a calming breath. Somehow he must understand that her actions were more than mere willfulness.

"This is my chance to show support in Egypt's struggle for freedom. It shows the British we women are willing to risk all as our men do—to stand behind them, as I would stand behind you. You and I are the Khamsin's future, Tarik. We should promote change and demonstrate a willingness to move forward without fear. Would you stop such progress, husband, and all you've desired to accomplish?"

Her cajoling captured his attention. Tarik halted, seemingly struggling with his emotions. His hand reached out, cupped her cheek, stroking her with a bemused expression on his face.

Then, with an anguished roar, he turned and marched outside.

He would seek familiar comfort. His world spun on its axis and tossed him about in a violent sandstorm of upheaval. And the name of the sandstorm was Fatima, his beloved wife. He could not control her, yet for the sake of his future leadership, he must. Yet it felt like roping a Khamsin wind.

Tarik strode through the camp, his tormented gaze seeking the horses at the camp edge. As he neared his father's tent, Jabari called out, "Son, we must talk. Now."

Troubled, he followed his father into the tent, alarmed when Jabari rolled the flaps down for privacy. Tarik sat before the low sandalwood table piled with papers, watching him with a guarded look. These past few days had taxed his father.

"I am worried about your mother, Tarik. The dead dove is a warning. I need to spend more time with her."

His stomach knotted as he studied his sire.

"My hands are tied with the council. One half agrees with my policies, the other is set on blocking my every move. They respect your suggestions more than mine." Jabari raised his gaze. Startled, Tarik saw for the first time the weariness there, the utter exhaustion.

"It is time, Tarik. I am ready, and you are as well. I have tendered my resignation to the council. Effective in two days."

Convulsive shock slammed him. "You can't mean it."

"I do," his father said calmly. "You are the new sheikh of the Khamsin warriors of the wind."

Chapter Twenty-three

I'm not ready to assume command. I can't do it.

Tarik grappled for his lost composure. He scanned his father's face, the grooves bracketing the mouth, the purple smudges shadowing the eyes. The weariness. Jabari was tired of the political battles, of the constant pressure from the council.

He kept his thoughts guarded. True, he would be installed as sheikh in a formal ceremony in two days, but no power would come truly until an official council vote four weeks later. This ensured a smooth transition of power, gave the new ruler time to demonstrate his command, to display his qualities as a leader.

"Why, Father? Why now?"

His father gave him a level look. "It is time, Tarik, for you to assume power and responsibility. You have the education and the training." His gaze grew solemn. "And it is best you assume command while I still can provide guidance if you need it, for I remember my own struggles as sheikh after my father died. You can do it, my son. I have full confidence in you."

You do, but will those old she-goats? Tarik raced over the possible voting split. Ibrahim, of course, would rally votes against him; he wanted the Hassid clan out, permanently.

But the others had always listened to Tarik with grave respect. A contradiction arose. If they voted Tarik and his clan out because they viewed him as a radical breaking with tradition, then they themselves broke a tradition spanning centuries.

The next in line would be, of course, the chief elder's closest relative. Haydar.

"Haydar cannot even milk a camel without tipping the bowl, let alone rule," Jabari said.

How easily his father read his thoughts.

Tarik offered a rueful smile. "Still, the odds are not in my favor."

An impish twinkle gleamed in his father's dark eyes. "My resignation gains me a seat on the council. And since the council will be thirteen members by my joining them, the Majli will appoint another elder to even the number to fourteen. Your uncle Ali, my brother-in-law, is next in line. I advise you to maintain a low, modest profile until the vote next month."

A low profile? Tarik's heart raced. "Yes, of course. And what of my very modest, shy wife? What do you advise for her?"

Shocked, he watched his regal father throw back his head and laugh. "Ah, Fatima," he said fondly. "Such an irrepressible spirit. She is your best asset, my son. Trust me."

"Tima is planning to march with Huda Sha'rawi in Cairo, Father." He picked up a fountain pen, rolled it between his fingers. "I told her no."

"You may try to stop her, but her spirit is like the wind, Tarik. She will go where she will."

"And you approve, at such a crucial time?"

"I told you, times are changing. And she is a portent

of change—as you are. Rein her in, and you risk losing more than the council's vote. You could lose your wife," he warned. Jabari regarded him with a thoughtful look. "Tarik, do you remember what I told you about your namesake, my father, and your grandmother? How she went to Cairo because life here restricted her? How his men ridiculed him for letting her go?"

"He rode into battle recklessly without his Guardian, and was killed. He wanted to prove his valor as a leader. He lost his life," Tarik recalled. "Which is why I must stop Fatima."

"Which is why you must *not* stop her. My father privately agreed with my mother's radical ideas, but didn't support her because he feared losing others' respect if he listened to a woman." Jabari's gaze grew distant. "It was a mistake I vowed never to make. I can only hope the same for you."

Doubt filled him. He could not make himself vulnerable to Fatima. A sheikh must be strong. Not weak.

A crystal decanter of dark red liquid sat on the sandalwood table. Jabari uncorked it, poured some into two goblets. A half smile curved Tarik's lips.

"Ibrahim had better not see you drinking wine or he'll banish you from the Majli," Tarik observed.

The sheikh lifted a black eyebrow mockingly. "I will merely set your mother upon him. Since her shooting lessons, he greatly fears her. She is my greatest weapon."

They laughed and clinked glasses. "To my father, the youngest elder on the council. May you impart wisdom to the old she-goats," he said.

"Guard your tongue, lest I cut it out for you, son—I am not old," Jabari countered, offering a mock scowl.

Tarik drank, but as he did, doubt filled him. How could he ever live up to his famous, beloved father? More importantly, how could he win the Majli's respect if Fatima violated his wishes and marched in Cairo?

* * *

Two days after being named sheikh, Tarik left the council tent, grateful for the reprieve of lunch. Inwardly he clung to his strength. How had his father accomplished so much? He barely could get the she-goats to agree on buying ammunition for the new rifles Graham had smuggled in for them.

Then again, his father didn't have a revolution boiling outside his door, and constant meetings with the Majli. Tarik ran a hand over his jaw. Mixed in with worries about holding leadership with the quarreling Majli was his underlying concern about Fatima. She itched to bolt, like a wild horse.

He stormed into their tent, fury filling him as he discovered Fatima stuffing clothing into a large rucksack.

"Kareem and I are leaving for Cairo," she said. "I'll be staying with the Al-Azziz family, his friend's mother. I'm marching with Huda. You're sheikh now, and our men look to you as an example. The women do the same with me. I must do this."

Tarik slammed his hand upon her rucksack. "If you leave, Fatima, I'll send men to drag you back. This is a crucial time for me, for our people. You will remain in our tent."

Her calm green gaze met his. "It's a crucial time for women and all Egyptians, Tarik. Do you believe in what the women are doing—what we are *all* doing in protesting British tyranny?"

Dumbstruck, he struggled for an answer. Finally he jerked his head in acquiescence.

"I knew it," she said softly. "And that eases my decision. In your heart, you want this for me. And for yourself as well."

Burying his head in his hands, he thought of the tenuous grip he held as sheikh. Artwork buried in an ancient tomb he dared not show, fearing his men think him weak. Feelings buried deep in his heart, shielding himself from vulnerability.

"I love you, Tarik. But I can't stay here and do nothing." Her soft, melodious whisper brushed against his ear.

Barely feeling the soft lips on his chilled cheek, he didn't raise his head. When he finally did, she was gone.

Tarik sank to the floor, worn down by anger and fear. Finally he struggled to his weary feet and left. Sunshine stabbed his eyes. Running a hand over his chin, he leashed his emotions as the scowling chief elder approached.

"I came to call you back to the meeting, Tarik, and I saw your wife. I hear she is leaving for Cairo," Ibrahim said, contempt filling his voice.

"You hear correctly," Tarik replied, tensing.

"Haydar told me she's boasted of her plans to all the women. Marching in that ridiculous women's protest. Go and fetch your rebellious wife," Ibrahim advised darkly. "If you do not, I will inform the tribe you are a weak leader. A man who cannot control his headstrong bride cannot lead men. And we *men* will remove you as sheikh when we vote."

At dawn he stole off, leaving his father in charge. Tarik rode the train north, sinking into his thoughts. At the Cairo station he took the tram, the vehicle containing only a few tight-lipped British soldiers. They looked with suspicion at his scimitar and dagger. Tarik turned a shoulder and leaned an elbow on his rucksack, staring out the window. Most Egyptians rode horse-driven vehicles, shunning the British-operated trams.

At the address of Kareem's friend, he assessed his surroundings. The narrow alleyway looked deserted, even in midday. Sagging balconies with rusty iron grates stretched overhead as he prowled down the alley. Paint chipped off the white exteriors. In a doorway a white cat sat licking one paw, he knocked forcefully.

I want my wife.

A middle-aged woman opened the door. When he asked about Kareem, she introduced herself as Zeinab Al-Azziz. Kareem and her son were visiting Alexandria. Brusquely Tarik revealed his identity. Her tremulous smile faded. With profuse apologies, she seated him on a red divan in a shabby living area while she scurried upstairs, calling Fatima's name in great agitation.

"Tarik?"

Clad in a black abbaya, Fatima stood at the foot of the stairs. Uncertainty shone in her luminous green eyes. One hand gripped the stair banister with white-knuckled tension.

"You will come home with me, now," he ordered.

"I will not, Tarik. I'm going to the march."

Springing to his feet, he roared with all the fury of hurt male pride and simmering frustration. "Damn it Tima! You are my wife, and you will do as I say!"

His thundering voice made her flinch, and Fatima's slender throat worked as she struggled with her emotions.

"Tima—ah, God." He heaved a deep sigh of regret and he crossed the distance between them. Moisture glistened in her eyes. Troubled, he gently wiped away a crystalline tear trickling down her cheek. Couldn't she see how much this endangered him at a crucial juncture? He'd lose respect.

Just as your grandfather did, his father's solemn voice echoed in his mind.

Swallowing his pride, he gripped her hands in his. "Tima, listen to me. I can't risk losing any status with the council. I've just gained leadership. Return with me, be at my side, support me. There will be other marches."

"Do you believe in what the women are doing?"

"Yes," he stated firmly. "You know that. But that's not the point."

"It is. Don't you see? You support women marching to protest the British, but you're hiding it from the Majli. If you give in to them now, Tarik, what's to stop you from doing so again? Sometimes the greatest strength a person can have is to stand on the courage of his convictions, no matter how much opposition or hate he faces. No matter what others call him."

A strong leader admitted his weakness. He embraced it, and used it to rule with compassion, not by sheer force of will. That's what she was saying.

"Do you believe in me, Tarik? Do you believe in the cause we're marching for?" she whispered.

His heart wrenched. Tarik closed his eyes, seeing his expectations of rulership slip through his fingers like sand, blown by uncaring winds. A hollow ache settled in his chest. He'd lose power, but what was the greatest loss?

If you lose yourself.

Far too long he'd hidden part of himself away, buried like the ancient pharaohs deep in the sand. No longer. As sheikh, he must embrace himself, even his flaws.

Resolve filled him. Tarik opened his eyes. "There's only one way you'll march today, Tima."

Her mouth wobbled precariously as she stared at him.

"If I come with you."

Fatima's smile of gratitude lifted his spirits. "But only veiled women are marching, husband. You must dress as one."

Tarik recoiled. "Dress as a woman? Never!"

"But I was made to dress as a man, as a warrior, to become your Guardian. Why will you not do the same for this once? If you do believe as I do, and will be at my side."

305

He felt part of his old stubbornness melt away as she gently squeezed his palm. Tarik picked up his wife's hand and kissed it. "Very well. I will. And all the demons of hell, the Majli or England won't stand in my way."

Chapter Twenty-four

Tarik made a splendid sheikh and a powerful warrior. He made a splendid man. With his chiseled muscles and broad shoulders, he made a lousy woman.

Clad in the same modest black abbaya as Fatima, thick fabric veiling his lower face, her husband resembled a giant. Fatima bit her lip, hoping he'd blend in.

Reaching up, she tucked a stray hank of blond hair back into his head covering. "I think this will work," she assured him.

"If you can fit in as a warrior, I can do the same as a woman," his deep, husky voice asserted.

The soft jangle of the telephone interrupted. Fatima turned to see her hostess pick up the receiver. A few short words, and she hung up. "They're ready, Fatima."

Swallowing hard, Fatima slipped her clammy palm into Tarik's strong, assured one. Tiny lines fanned from the corners of his eyes as he smiled. "Remember, don't leave my side, no matter what. Even the most peaceful protest can turn ugly."

They left the house, her heart beating fast. Sunlight

streamed down upon them, filtering through the colorful strands of wet, dyed wool drying overhead. In the alley's shadows, a dog slunk hopefully toward a small pile of refuse.

Wending their way to the main street, they walked to Garden City park. Dozens of carriages waited there, with scores of black-draped women. Some carried placards in French and Arabic, protesting the British as oppressors and tyrants. Resolutely, Fatima and Tarik joined them, marching in a tidy column. Shouting out slogans, they moved as one force, one mass voicing their rage.

Tarik's palm clasped hers reassuringly. Her heart soared with joy at his daring, his willingness to show support for the cause they both embraced. And at much risk. He won't get caught, she thought in desperate reassurance. No one will know Egypt's greatest sheikh is disguised as a woman!

Students observing the force of women shouted encouragement and joined them. But suddenly, at Qasr-Al-Aini Street, the column shifted. Fatima's heart lurched with dread. The women had planned to parade past the Italian and French legations, but this route took them toward trouble—toward the house of deposed leader and exiled revolutionary Saad Zaghlul, whom British troops guarded with zealous force.

Groups of boisterous students formed long columns on either side of the women, shouting as they walked. In minutes the house of Zaghlul loomed before them. In front were columns of grim-faced British soldiers and Egyptian police bearing rifles. Fatima's veil fluttered with her gasp. Tarik's hand gripped hers tighter.

"Such dear things. Let them rot here in the heat, mates," one soldier chuckled. "They won't get far."

Fatima bristled. Tarik's hand firmly nestled in hers,

she pushed her way forward to the column's front until she came face to face with a cluster of British.

"Let me pass," she snapped in perfect English.

Surprise, then tight-lipped anger flashed over their faces. The men lowered their rifles. "Stay back," one advised.

"Don't provoke them! They will kill you," a woman screamed.

A British soldier jabbed a finger in Fatima's face. "Go home, you stupid illiterate peasant."

Anger boiled inside her. "I *am* home. Live free Egypt, break from the great bullying brute named England!" she shouted.

With a strangled grunt, the man slapped her face, hard. Fatima cried out in shock more than pain. Tarik bellowed in fury and slugged the soldier. Chaos ensued. Two soldiers grabbed Tarik as he fought and kicked. Roaring with rage, he twisted free, fury spitting from his dark eyes.

They had mistaken Tarik for a weak, helpless woman. Now they faced the full-fledged wrath of a Khamsin warrior.

Horror speared Fatima. Her husband was in danger, and it was her fault. Two more men fell under the punishing blows of his furious fists. Fatima tried to pull Tarik back. "Tarik, stop," she screamed. "They'll arrest you!"

A loud *thwack* sounded as a soldier struck Tarik in the temple with his rifle butt. He reeled back, grabbing his head. Crimson seeped between his fingers, but he held his ground, fists raised. Fatima's heart went still with panic. She must get him out of here, and knew only one way.

"Tarik, please, help me—get me out of here before they hurt me." She tugged on his sleeve, appealing to the protectiveness she knew he felt for her.

He went still, his dark eyes searching hers.

"Help us, please," Fatima turned and begged the other women in Arabic. "Distract the soldiers so we can escape."

Word rippled through the crowd. Students began chanting, distracting the military. The two soldiers holding Tarik at rifle-point turned, realizing they faced an angry mob. Tarik broke free and grabbed Fatima's hand, tugging her off into the sheltering forest of black abbayas. They fled.

It occurred to her as they ran that, if they caught him, the British would arrest Tarik. Hot shame poured through her. The new Khamsin sheikh, jailed for protesting as a woman? That would destroy him.

Together they raced down the street, pausing in a shadowed doorway to tear off their abbayas. At Tarik's suggestion, beneath they'd donned western clothing. Blood matted the long blond hair spilling down his back. He grabbed her hand and they walked at a brisk pace until they reached the safety of Zeinab's house.

Seeing them, the woman clucked with distress. Immediately she went to fetch water and towels. Fatima made Tarik sit down at the table. Blood dripped down his temple from the rising lump. Tarik touched his cheek, staring at his red fingers.

"A new war wound," he mused. "Interesting."

It was her fault. Fatima dabbed his head with a wet cloth. Her hand shook like a flag caught in a blustery wind.

Tarik grabbed her hand. "Are you all right, little caracal?"

Her composure fractured into tiny shards. If she'd lost Tarik today, either through gunfire or arrest, the Khamsin would have lost their leader. Her stubbornness had nearly sacrificed him.

"You could have been arrested, Tarik. I'm sorry."

His onyx eyes solemnly met hers. "It wouldn't have

been a bad thing, to be arrested for fighting those bullies. There are far worse things, little caracal—such as hiding yourself away."

But his assurance didn't sway her realization. After Fatima bound his head with clean linens, she gathered his strong hands in hers, kissed the purplish bruises on his swollen knuckles.

"I didn't intend to endanger you. All I wanted was a chance to speak out, to voice my protest against England. I'll stop speaking out for women's rights if it will hurt your chance at being sheikh. I'll apologize to the council for my actions, beg their forgiveness. I won't have you lose your ambitions," she whispered.

A rueful smile tugged at his mouth. "Quieting you would be like silencing the wind. And you speak for others. I must reconcile *all* our people. Our women's rightful place is not behind the men, as Ibrahim says, but at our sides. I now understand what my father wanted all these years. And being a true leader means having the strength to stand up for what is right—just as you have. You are far more important to me than the Majli."

Fatima fell silent with joy, made speechless by his immense faith and belief in her. Her heart pounded with love for him.

"When we return, I am informing the council of the tomb drawings, and I'm taking time to teach art in the classroom to our tribe's children. I'm no longer ashamed of anything." He gave her a pensive look. "And, Tima, I have something to ask you." His strong throat muscles worked as he swallowed. "If you agree, I'll appoint you as weapons instructor to our warriors. I want you to teach the men how to shoot. We cannot fight with swords if others fight with bullets, and many of our warriors can't hit the broad side of a mountain."

His mouth flattened and he added, "Including me.

That's why I've argued against using rifles in battle for so long. It's not just a matter of honor, but one of aim. Mine is, uh, rather poor." A muscle jumped violently in his jaw.

Marveling at Tarik admitting his shortcoming, she kissed his palms. "It would be an honor. All it takes is practice, my love. And time. I had plenty of both in England."

A rueful smile touched his mouth. "I thought you spent your spare moments attending tea parties and flirting with counts."

"I felt more at ease behind a gun—away from those haughty aristocrats who only coveted my grandfather's money."

Tarik tipped up her chin, forcing her to meet his tender gaze. "I'm glad you did. I'd have to mete out severe punishment to any man who dared show interest." He reconsidered. "Except for Michael. He's forgiven, because he's family, after all."

"Kissing cousins?" she dared to tease.

A low growl rumbled from his chest, and Tarik grabbed her hand to herd her upstairs. In her room, he crooked a finger. "Come here, my fierce warrior," he ordered with a teasing smile.

"I'm a woman now, remember? A wife. And what about your head?"

He kissed her. "A most amazing wife. And *my* woman. My head is fine. It's not what hurts."

Stepping back, he peeled off his shirt. Hunger filled Fatima as she stared at his rock-hard body. Her palms slid up his muscled stomach, pressed against his rib cage. Warm flesh rippled over bronzed skin as he tensed beneath her exploration. A crooked smile touched his mouth.

"Keep touching me like that and we'll never make it to the bed. The floor is looking very appealing," he drawled.

She stared at him, this arrogant warrior who'd had the courage to open his heart. They had forged a new bond in their marriage. Confidence filled her. It was time for the next step.

Fatima brushed a hank of blond hair back over his brow. "Tarik, I'd like to start trying for a baby. I want to have children."

Surprise touched his expression. "Are you sure? I thought you didn't want to be a mother."

"Not until I'd proven myself. I wanted to have something to pass on to my children. I do. I can teach them to have the courage to follow their dreams, no matter how difficult the road. You've proven it's worth it."

She watched hunger darken his gaze. He drew her close, cradling her against his narrow hips. His warm breath feathered over her ear as he bent his head and gave her lobe a delicate lick. "Yes. Let's make a baby, Tima."

Tarik shed his clothing and she did the same. She sank to the bed on her back, holding out her arms. "I've heard this is the best position to conceive," she whispered. "You can go deeper inside me."

Muscles in his shoulders flexed as he leaned over her—all that rippling, tightly-leashed power. She slid her hands over his lean hips, curled around to his taut buttocks, pressed him close to her.

Her husband feathered light kisses over her neck, nibbling at the hollow then sliding lower to capture a taut nipple in his mouth. His tongue flicked over the hardening bud and fire blossomed in her lower belly. Fatima writhed as his teeth gently nipped, then his warm tongue soothed the biting sting. He suckled her deeply.

He rubbed his body against hers, and his muscled legs settled between her outstretched ones. Uttering a deep growl he claimed her mouth, stroking his tongue deep inside. Twin bands of muscles on his back flexed beneath her caressing fingers.

Tarik pulled back, a rough wildness in his eyes, the lion uncaged. Fatima purred, relishing the thrill of having his powerful body joined to hers. Arousal heightened as she thought of the baby they'd conceive today, created in hot passion and tender love.

His penis jutted out, thicker and longer than she'd ever seen it. Tarik took his hand and stroked, watching as she stared and licked her lips.

Desire throbbed in her loins. Her wet core clenched, hot with need. She needed him inside her, now.

"I'm going to love you deeper than you've ever felt, Tima," he said. "So deep you'll feel like I'm forever a part of you. I'm going to plant my seed deep inside and fill you with my baby, Tima. Our baby." A growl rumbled from his chest as he spread her legs and draped them over his shoulders.

Leaning forward, he locked his eyes with hers. True to his word, his thick length filled her, pushed deep, drawing out her startled gasp of pleasure. Hands fisted in the sheets, she whimpered at the electrifying sensations of him nestled tight against her womb. He withdrew, pushed slowly back into her wet, yielding flesh, then he leaned over her, his gaze fierce.

He began thrusting in earnest, angling his shaft in long, hard strokes. Their flesh smacked together as her hips eagerly met his rhythm, her body squeezing him tight. A throaty cry wrung from her as he penetrated deeper still. Sweat slicked the muscles roping his broad shoulders. The musky scent of maleness and arousal filled her nostrils. Her inner muscles tightened unbearably, the pleasure so intense she couldn't bear it, had to find release.

"Ah, God, I'm going to come—come with me,

Tima—come on sweetheart," he grated out, cupping her buttocks and lifting her against him. Against her buttocks, she felt his testicles draw tight, ready. The thought hurled her into a shattering completion. Fatima bit back a scream.

His teeth grinding, Tarik threw back his head; muscles and sinew tensed as he crushed his spurting cock against her womb. Again and again, he pumped his seed deep inside. Fatima squeezed down, eagerly milking every drop.

He fell atop her, his head pillowed beside hers, hot breaths gasping into her ear as she tenderly stroked circles on his back, feeling his heart thudding violently against hers. Tangled together, sweat slicking their bodies, they lay in each other's arms. At last he separated their bodies.

He splayed a palm over her trembling belly as if protecting the new life they'd created. "We just made a baby, Tima. I'm certain of it," he said. He drew her against the hard curve of his shoulder. "How well we fit together. You're the sheath I've hungered for my whole life."

"A vessel for a sword?" she asked archly. "Is that what I am to you?"

Sincerity filled in his dark eyes. "How little you know, my little caracal, of a sheath's importance. Have you ever seen a sword left out of its sheath? It grows dull and useless if left unprotected. Yes, be my sheath. Shelter me when I am weary from fighting, let me nestle inside your softness, caress me with your love. Protect me from the outside world. Let's join our bodies together, tucked away in our own private sanctuary. Hold me close, Tima. I'm weary. Unsheathed, a sword is expected to always be ready to fight. Only nestled inside its sheath can a sword find peace."

Her annoyance faded, replaced by tender understanding. Fatima saw Tarik's life as if stretched out like the sandy plains of Amarna. He was always struggling to live up to others' expectations, guarding his thoughts and actions, just as she'd fought against those expectations.

She touched his cheek. "Without the sword, the sheath is unfulfilled. She longs for the blade to fill her, to fit snugly inside her and come home. To wrap herself around him and let him find rest. Come Tarik, nestle inside me and I will protect you from the world."

Something deep and unfathomable flickered in his eyes. "I need you so much, my little caracal," he whispered. "I didn't need a Guardian to protect my body; I needed you to protect my heart, to hew my dreams and to listen to yours. For us to be together—not as a Guardian and the sheikh's son, but as a man and woman loving each other. When you became my Guardian, I was flattered that you'd sacrifice your life to save mine. And yet, that wasn't the part of me that needed saving the most."

"I'm still your Guardian, Tarik. I'll always be there to shield you from those who would harm you."

A wry smile touched his mouth. "Well, I don't think I need a Guardian, but I need you, my heart's mate. I want you to share yourself with me, Tima, as I will share myself with you."

A shadow darkened his expression. "I have little to offer compared to some. My kingdom is one of sand and heat. I have no English titles, like Michael. No riches. I can't offer you a home filled with treasure or jewels. You deserve those, Tima."

She shook her head, amused. "Your kingdom is more precious to me than any gold, Tarik. The desert is my home, my life. It flows in my blood as it does in yours. What need have I for priceless jewels when I have the shining sun? Or a palatial English mansion when I have the splendor of the black tents and the richness of family?"

Tenderly he nuzzled her cheek, gave her a warm kiss. "Ah, Tima, we were destined for each other—the sword and the sheath."

A sudden gleam lit his eyes. Fatima moistened her mouth slowly, watching as his breathing grew ragged. She hooked her hands around his neck. Her hot whisper in his ear promised all the sensual delights she could offer. And more.

"Fill me, husband. Fill me with your sword, and I'll keep you safe, always."

He obliged her. And as they loved each other slowly and thoroughly once more, Fatima banished all thoughts of their return. There was time later to learn if the Majli would reject Tarik as the new Khamsin sheikh.

Chapter Twenty-five

Upon their return, Tarik kept a low profile. When others asked what had happened, he refused to answer. He advised Fatima to do the same.

A week later, the council met at dawn to vote. Sour fear curdled Fatima's stomach, and when Tarik told her to dress for an appearance before the Majli, she steeled her spine.

Her head throbbing, she walked with her husband into the ceremonial tent. Dust motes danced in beams of sunlight. The couple stood and bowed before the elders; who sat in a horseshoe shape. She spotted Uncle Ali, looking dignified and proud, sitting next to Tarik's father. Jabari, looking like a young boy amid a sea of gray-beards, tossed her a reassuring wink.

Tarik's deep, commanding voice rang throughout the tent. "Honored elders, before you officially cast your votes approving or disapproving me as your sheikh, you must know something. It may influence your decision."

Tarik's look of pride made Fatima's heart soar. "I present to you my wife, my greatest love and my greatest asset. She is also my advisor. Know this: Elect me as your sheikh, and you must accept her at all council meetings. I will ask her questions, solicit her opinions and advice. My first act as your new sheikh would be to appoint her as firearms instructor to our warriors."

An arrogant half smile curled his lips. "'Men of honor fight with blades,' my father said. But men of honor who desire to protect our families and way of life will fight with bullets. We must cherish our past while pushing ahead to greater heights. Recently I discovered art in the cliff tombs. I have a gift for drawing, and have been sketching the art and will soon share my drawings in the classroom so that our children can learn our rich history. Warriors, too, can teach in the classroom much as the women do. It is but one change I propose. We are a people shrouded like mummies by outdated traditions that are desiccating us until we become like bones bleached by the sun. The Khamsin will not remain mired in outdated tradition. We will embrace fully this century and all it has to offer us, our children, and future generations."

Dead silence fell. Tarik's warm, dry palm clasped Fatima's as he challenged the elders with a fierce look. Tremendous love filled her. He amazed her, this proud leader, her husband who stood willing to risk all for her, and for the good of his people.

Ibrahim slowly stood on bandied, trembling legs. Ashen faced, he looked ready to sail Osiris's boat into the underworld. But instead of voicing a protest, he heaved a deep sigh.

"It is a sad day for the Khamsin . . . ," he began ponderously.

An amused snort came from Jabari. "Tell them, Ibrahim. Tell them what you, I and every council member knows."

Ibrahim's hands shook as he smoothed his indigo binish. "My wife . . . she . . . ah . . ." He paused, looking helpless. "I could not fight her on this. I am too weak."

Mirth twinkled in Jabari's eyes. "Because she, like all Khamsin women, staged their own protest here. Until the Majli votes you in as sheikh, my son, they will not cook, clean or . . . uh, perform any wifely duties. Tarik, your uncle Ali and I are the only contented warriors. *Very* content."

As if staging its own protest, Ibrahim's stomach grumbled loudly. The chief elder's hollow cheeks puffed as he blew out a loud breath. "Shall we get this over with? I am hungry."

A chorus of loud voices agreed. They stabbed their daggers quickly into the carpet, voting Tarik their new sheikh.

Eyes shining with joy, Tarik hugged her. "I see, my dear little caracal, that protest is a good thing."

Tarik called for an enormous celebration to take place the next day. Joy rippled through the camp. Grumbling warriors sighed with relief as meals—and other more discreet activities—promised a return to normal. The next morning, Tarik, Jabari, Asad and both of Fatima's parents went hunting. Sitting in their tent, Fatima brushed her hair. A delighted smile touched her mouth. She set down the brush, pressing her hands to her abdomen. Weeks after their extensive lovemaking, she felt certain.

"A new sheikh for the Khamsin, and a new baby for the new sheikh," she said softly. "Wait until I tell him."

A sudden chill snaked down her spine. Every instinct cried out a warning. Fatima turned, stricken with a cold sense of foreboding. Elizabeth was in danger. She knew it.

Wind rushed into the tent as the flap jerked aside. Alhena ran inside, worry lines riddling her brow.

"Fatima! Thank God you're here. I saw Elizabeth leave with her art students for the Amarna tombs. Haydar went after them—something about having found

320

Tarik's recreations of tomb art. After this business with the dove, she shouldn't be with him! You know Haydar hates our family ever since he lost Nadia to Salah. I'm sure he's seeking revenge."

Tiny hairs rose at the nape of Fatima's neck. "Did you tell Tarik?" she asked.

"I sent my father to find him. If I raise a fuss and send men after her, Ibrahim will make trouble. But if you and I go . . . You could dress as a warrior. He wouldn't notice anything."

Fatima retrieved her warrior's clothing. In minutes she was dressed and armed, her Colt at her waist. "Let's go."

They galloped for two hours. The whole way, Fatima prayed they'd make it in time to save Elizabeth from any potential danger.

The towering limestone shimmered in the midday sun. Not bothering to wait for Alhena to dismount, Fatima leapt off her more, squinting at the tombs nestled deep in the lee of the Amarna cliffs. Elizabeth's mare and other horses waited patiently.

Withdrawing her gun, Fatima climbed the stone steps. At the tomb entrance, she wended her way through the columned antechamber, calling Elizabeth's name. No answer.

As she stepped into the shadowy gloom of the main chamber, Fatima called, "Elizabeth? Is everything all right? Are you in trouble?"

"No. Our people are. But that will change once the sheikh's meddlesome wife is out of the way and Tarik finally becomes the leader his father never was."

The familiar voice caused her to whirl. Something hard struck her head. Darkness descended.

Chapter Twenty-six

Fatima awoke with a throbbing head, suffocating darkness enshrouding her. Panic seized her in its icy fist as her hand slid along the smooth sides encasing her up to the lid of what seemed to be a coffin.

A scraping noise overhead drew a sob of relief. Light flooded the narrow sarcophagus. Fatima blinked furiously. Something sharp pricked her neck. A sword tip?

"What a fitting end for you—left here to rot, your voice finally silenced, no longer stirring up women."

The face peering down at her caused no great surprise. She had ignored her instincts. What irony. So attuned to the danger surrounding others, she'd failed to see it for herself.

Fatima fought to conceal her fear. "Ah, Salah. You are the jackal in our midst, feasting on the carrion of the tribe's deepest fears. But we are stronger than you think. The Khamsin women don't cower before men who bully them. And I never will. In a fair fight, you would be my slave."

"You bitch," he breathed. "You could never best me in a battle to the death. Dare to try?"

"You wouldn't give me the chance," she rejoined. "Cowards like you prefer to kill the helpless. But know this. When you kill me, my spirit will rise in all women. When you silence me, ten thousand new women will cry out to be heard. Their voices will ring in your ears until you have no choice but to listen."

Salah appeared to struggle with a decision. He glowered at her. "I won't kill you. Not yet. Sit up."

His sword tip remained at her neck. Calculating her options, she slowly sat up. Dread filled her at the sight of ten hostile warriors surrounding the coffin.

"Poor, misguided Tarik, thinking only Muhammad wanted him dead. We all took turns." Salah laughed.

"Traitors. You'll suffer the same fate as Muhammad, your names banished to darkness, your ancestors shamed," Fatima warned.

The warriors flinched and muttered uneasily. Salah pressed his sword into her neck. "Shut up, bitch, and look."

Torches set on the sandy floor flooded the chamber with light. The sarcophagus was near the stone steps leading down to the unfinished burial chamber below.

Numb horror immobilized her as two men bore the limp form of her mother-in-law. They bound her with ropes, leaving a length trailing from her wrists and ankles. Then they hooked either end to iron sconces on each opposite wall. Elizabeth's body was now suspended lengthwise over the steps. The men lit two candles and stuck them into the sconces, leaning them against the ropes.

"She's not dead. Not yet," Salah said softly. He barked an order. Flickering light revealed what lay below, and Fatima bit back a terrified cry. Sharp daggers jutted up through wooden boards, rising from the steps like iron teeth.

"When the candles burn through the ropes, Elizabeth will be impaled—a painful, fitting death for the Khamsin's greatest enemy. Our ancestors punished their enemies by impalement."

"Let her go, Salah. Your quarrel is with me."

"She is the harbinger of chaos. My father cursed the day Jabari married her. But he lacked the courage to do anything. After Tarik was born, Father poisoned her tea so she'd miscarry. When he died, I vowed to finish his work. I organized men who espoused my beliefs, and married Nadia to gain Jabari's trust."

The warriors stared uneasily at Elizabeth. Their thoughts were clear. They disliked killing Jabari's defenseless wife, for deep inside still existed their code to protect all Khamsin women.

Fatima lifted her arms. "You men who dare to kill the sacred white dove are doomed! Her death screams will haunt you until you die in shame, your heirs disgraced for all eternity. I am the Seer, the truthsayer, who sees and knows the future."

Fear clouded the eyes of Salah's warriors.

"Salah! Are you done yet? Just get it over with," a melodious voice demanded from the entrance to the tomb.

Fatima now knew every drop of the anguish Tarik had felt over Muhammad's betrayal. Alhena drifted over, her hips swaying.

Her throat dry, her mouth cracked, Fatima asked the same question Tarik had: "Why?"

A low moan interrupted. Elizabeth twisted on the ropes suspending her. Alhena's smug smile faded. She turned to Salah.

"You said nothing about Elizabeth! You said only Fatima—that you'd make it look natural and that Tarik would marry me at last. I was the best lover he ever had!" she cried.

"Mind your place, woman," Salah said.

Oh God. Fatima riveted her gaze to Alhena. "It was you," she whispered hoarsely. "The woman at the schoolhouse that he was making love to when I returned—Tarik's mistress!" Jealousy stabbed her, until Fatima remembered Tarik's confession. *I've had lovers, Tima, but I've never been in love with anyone but you.*

Ugly anger brutalized her cousin's face. "I could have convinced him to marry me, but when you returned, he didn't want me anymore. You upset everything, pretending you could equal a man. I could have had power, position as Tarik's wife!"

"Power and position, Alhena. But not love. You don't love him. Not like I do," she said softly, suddenly pitying her cousin.

Contempt flashed on Alhena's face. "Who needs love? Muhammad loved me, but he was nothing compared to Tarik!"

Salah's gaze found Alhena. "Who could blame him for falling prey to your charms—even if you are used goods? And now you can comfort poor Tarik in his grief over losing his wife and mother."

"I never wanted Elizabeth to die! Cut her down!" Real fear clouded Alhena's gaze. Shadows cast by the flickering candlelight danced over her face.

"Shut up, you little bitch. I don't take orders from a woman," he roared. He backhanded her and Alhena cried out.

The sword point at Fatima's neck eased. She twisted and leapt up, only to be struck by a powerful fist. Moaning, she fell, her eye blackened by the man towering over her. Scampering footsteps alerted her to Alhena's escape.

"Get her before she rides back to camp!" Salah bellowed.

Go, Alhena, Fatima silently prayed. A slim hope filled her.

It faded as another warrior unwound a long greenish brown coil and placed it atop her feet. Paralyzed with fear, Fatima stared at the sleeping asp. Willing herself to remain still, she tried centering her breathing. Anything to quiet the terror echoing through her head.

Salah laughed. "You have a chance to show your bravery as a warrior. I learned how to hypnotize asps. Lie still and it will not bite. Try to save Elizabeth and you will awaken it." He gave her a steady stare. "If you survive, come outside and fight a real warrior. If you win, you'll save both your lives."

His hand, cold as a reptile's tongue, stroked her cheek. Fatima fought a shudder. "Warriors are willing to sacrifice themselves. Will you? I think not. You will prove yourself a weak woman . . . and die like one."

His low laugh echoed through the chamber as he left. Fatima and Elizabeth were alone in the cave. Elizabeth moaned, twisted. Terror flashed across her face as she opened her eyes and saw what lay below.

"Don't move, Elizabeth! Stay still," Fatima called out.

Her mother-in-law's frantic gaze met hers. "Are you all right?"

"Slightly. I have company. A cobra."

Fatima lay still, eyes trained on the candles. They were burning low, licking the musty air inside the tomb.

"Don't move, Fatima," Elizabeth called out faintly. "The cobra won't bite if you remain still. Tarik will come. I've had a good life. I can handle dying . . . if I know you'll live."

The asp around her feet shifted. Fear curled up Fatima's spine. With luck, she could survive one snake bite. But asps attacked until they felt safe and no longer cornered.

"Promise me only one thing," Elizabeth continued, her voice breaking. "That you'll have babies with my son. I think Jabari . . . will bear this more if he has grandchildren to comfort him."

Fatima slid a protective hand over her belly, aware of the tiny life she carried. No one will die today but traitors, she vowed.

A cold tongue licked her ankle as the asp awakened. She had to act now, before the snake became too alert. Salah had jeered at her fear. He'd forgotten the power of her resolve.

Very slowly, Fatima drew her feet up. A hiss sounded as the cobra awakened. *Now.*

With every ounce of strength she twisted her feet, flinging them upward. The asp sailed up and over the coffin edge. Fatima sat upright. Awake and free, the asp hissed in fright. Then it wended its silent way toward the beckoning sunlight.

Fatima vaulted out of the coffin. Her frantic gaze searched the tomb. Rope lay nearby. She threaded her way down the steps through the daggers, threw the rope over Elizabeth's waist and tied it. Next she returned to the heavy stone coffin and wound the rope around to act as a pulley.

"When I say 'Now,' swing your weight toward me," she ordered.

A creaking moan warned the ropes suspending Elizabeth were giving way. Fatima pulled with all her might, swinging the woman toward her. As the rope snapped, Elizabeth released a terrified scream but Fatima yanked so hard that she cleared the steps and landed on the sand, inches from the daggers.

Fatima untied Elizabeth. "Listen carefully," she said

in a low, urgent tone. "Salah's outside. He wants to kill me in battle to prove that a man can fight better than a woman. Scream as if you're dying, then hide. His men are cowards and won't look upon a woman in pain. They're already afraid."

"Never," Elizabeth breathed. "Two women are better than one. I will fight with you, or die with you."

Fatima seized her mother-in-law's hands. "We'll be two dead women. I have a slim chance of surviving a battle with Salah. Not without my Colt."

"No!" Tarik's mother argued. "I'm coming."

Left with little choice, Fatima made a decision. Faking the sound of a dying woman, she released a deep, agonized scream and used the technique her twin taught her, pressing her fingers hard against Elizabeth's carotid artery. She caught the woman, who slumped into unconsciousness. "I'm sorry," she whispered, then dragged Elizabeth to a corner and left.

Blinding sunlight stung her eyes. A low chuckle chilled Fatima's blood as she cleared the stone steps.

"Fatima! You *are* brave—but too late to save poor Elizabeth, I see. Are you a true warrior? Will you fight?" A loud clatter rang in her ears, and sunlight glinted off the polished surface of a scimitar Salah tossed at her feet. He gave a derisive snort and beckoned. "Will you die like a man?"

Barely had she retrieved the weapon when Salah attacked. Fatima staunchly defended herself. Warriors did not surrender. Neither would she. Today if she died, she would die a warrior's death.

Urging his lathered mare into a gallop, Tarik bent over the horse's neck. His pulse thundered in his ears. Salah was missing. So were his mother and Fatima. Several had seen Salah riding off toward Amarna.

He'd returned from the hunt early, wanting to surprise Fatima with a quick bout of lovemaking. Instead, Nadia was in his tent, an ugly purple bruise on her cheek.

Between hysterical sobs, she'd told him what happened. Yesterday she'd followed Salah to the tombs, suspecting him of having an affair. She'd caught him leaving with Alhena, murmuring about making someone pay. Salah had hit her, threatened to kill her if she told. Summoning all her courage, Nadia had spied on her husband and his ten warriors this morning. Having failed to kill Tarik, the son of the white dove they hated, the men had sworn a blood oath to kill Elizabeth and Fatima, the radicals upsetting their world, or to fall upon their scimitars.

Nadia had turned to Haydar, the only man outside her family she trusted, and sent him to look for the hunting party to find Tarik and their father. She hadn't dared trust any other warrior. Then she'd come back to Tarik's tent to wait.

Utter desolation seized Tarik. *If Salah kills my wife or my mother, he will die slowly.* He saw his life stretched before him, Fatima suddenly a ghost shadowing his vision. Pain settled on his chest like a boulder.

As the cliffs opened up onto the flat desert plain of Amarna, a slim figure darted from behind the rocks. Tarik pulled his mare to a halt, narrowly missing Alhena.

"Help them," she screamed, shaking. "Tarik, Salah's going to kill Fatima and your mother!"

His stomach clenched violently. Tarik gestured toward the rocks. "Stay hidden and wait for help!"

He galloped away. Horror pulsed through him as he spotted Salah and Fatima fighting, surrounded by nine motionless Khamsin warriors. His wife could barely parry Salah's blows. She had too little strength.

Tarik pulled up short, swore and leapt off his mare, unsheathing his scimitar as he ran. A red haze of fury clouded his vision. Releasing a bellow of Khamsin fury, he rushed forward, brandishing his sword.

"Salah! You are mine!" he swore.

Ten against one. Ten fanatics, all willing to die for their beliefs. Willing to die to restore what they saw as order in the tribe. Fanatics, they would not stop. They wanted Fatima dead. But if they were offered him instead, the white falcon they despised more . . .

Salah grazed Fatima's hand. She cried out, her scimitar clattering to the ground. He shoved her, hard, and she tumbled onto her back. Placing a boot on her chest, Salah grinned and raised his scimitar for the killing blow. Tarik ran faster, legs pumping frantically. Too far away to attack. He had no choice.

His bellowing shout halted the sword's descent. "Salah! Stop! Kill me instead! My life for hers!"

Sobbing with relief, Fatima saw the blade stop a whisper from her throat. Tarik appeared in her line of sight.

"My life for hers, Salah. You've wanted me dead all along. Kill me, spare my wife. What is she but a weak, useless woman anyway?" Tarik said, panting.

No, Tarik, she silently pleaded, raising her gaze to regard her husband. Sword held in a defensive stance, he towered above her, an indigo giant amidst the tawny sands. He was sacrificing himself for her. Oh God, she needed her gun—any damn weapon!

"Kill me, Salah. It's what you want." Tarik lowered his sword, his face flushed, labored breaths ripping out of his lungs. The cords of his strong neck stood out in stark relief.

Fatima felt grief well up inside her, a visceral ache. She dared not move or speak lest Salah kill them both.

Salah released a harsh laugh as his men warily

watched Tarik. He could take them all, her husband. She believed that.

"Swear you will spare Tima. If you have any honor left as a Khamsin warrior, you will let her live. Swear it before your men—a blood oath upon your father's honor—and I will do the same, giving myself up without a fight," Tarik said quietly.

Several gasps sounded. A Khamsin ancestral blood oath, the most sacred oath, could not be broken without deeply shaming the deceased. Fatima choked down a sob. *No, please, no.*

Uncertainty crossed Salah's face. He spared a glance to his men, who studied him with ruthless intensity. Tarik had tipped the scale. No one wanted to kill a defenseless woman. And if either man dared to violate the oath, he'd blacken his father's name.

Her brother-in-law unsheathed his dagger, raised it to his palm. "I swear a blood oath upon my father's honor that Fatima will go free and unharmed if you take her place, Tarik."

Tarik cut his own palm, swearing his oath.

Pain wrenched Fatima's arms as Salah jerked her upright. Freed, she rushed into Tarik's embrace.

"Hide her in Haggi Quantill," Salah ordered. "Do not touch her. When I bring you the head of Tarik, she will go free," he added.

"No, no, don't do this," Fatima wept, clinging to her husband.

"I must. Because I love you more than life itself," he whispered hoarsely. "I gladly give my life for you, little caracal. To the last drop of my blood." His warm lips frantically sought her mouth for one last kiss. Then he tore away, despair shadowing his eyes. "I love you more than my own life. Now go!"

Men seized Tarik, holding him back as others hauled

away the sobbing Fatima. He watched in desperate relief as they mounted and rode off. Fatima's tear-stricken eyes looked at him; her hysterical protests rang over the sand until she became an indigo dot in the distance.

It was done. If Salah dared to hurt her now, his own men would turn on him for violating a blood oath. But it was too late for Tarik. A deep ache filled him as he faced his assassin. Please, let it be quick, he silently prayed.

The cruel smile touching Salah's mouth warned it would not. Tarik's brother-in-law sheathed his scimitar, picked up his riding crop. He struck his thigh in slow, precise strokes.

One of Salah's men glanced uncertainly at the others. "Should we allow him to die without fighting? Where is the honor in killing an unarmed man?"

"It is his choice. And this jackal has no honor." Salah pointed the crop at Tarik. "Tarik bin Jabari Hassid, I sentence you to death for destroying the morals of the Khamsin and invoking chaos with your radical ideas concerning our women."

The warriors stripped Tarik to the waist, forced him to kneel. In methodical, savage fury, Salah beat him. The blows of the crop stung like fiery needles. Tarik bit back a scream. He would not give this jackal the satisfaction. His back arched in agony, his flesh shuddered. But he did not cry out.

Finally, Salah ceased. Warmth dribbled down Tarik's back. Someone yanked his hair. A dagger glinted in the sun. A scratching noise sounded as Salah sawed off the golden locks they all hated. A rough boot on Tarik's bleeding back forced him to bend over. He sucked in a pained and whistling breath through his teeth, praying that Fatima would go on. If he believed in miracles, he'd believe that Fatima was pregnant, that part of him would continue on as his baby grew in her belly.

I love you Tima, he repeated silently, staring at the sand. My love for you will never die. The warriors jerked on his arms, forcing his head down for the swift blow of Salah's scimitar. *I always will love you. Never forget, my little caracal.*

The sour stench of his terror swam in his nostrils. Summoning a warrior's strength, he fought back a shudder. Silence fell, broken by Salah's satisfied grunt as he raised his sword. Squeezing his eyes shut, Tarik prayed for courage.

Gunfire suddenly splintered the air. Blood splattered Tarik's bare torso and screams echoed everywhere. Tarik's eyes flew open.

Salah tumbled backward, still clutching his sword. Crimson flowed in a sluggish stream from his chest. Around him lay the five remaining warriors, each moaning in pain.

Alive. I'm still alive. Oh God, I'm alive!

Tarik weakly struggled to his feet, tears of relief stinging his eyes. His rescuer ran forward in an indigo blur.

"You bastards," a wobbly female voice cracked.

His rescuer emptied spent ammunition, fumbled for more, jamming it into the pistol. Then, standing over the moaning men and Salah, she emptied the gun again. The men all fell silent.

Tarik blinked. His astounded gaze sharpened on his sister. The smoking pistol was cupped in her hands and anguished grief twisted Nadia's face. "Salah, you bastard. You'll never hurt me again. You thought I could never learn to handle weapons? You were wrong. Fatima taught me. She taught me well."

His father, Ramses and hundreds of loyal Khamsin warriors, including Haydar, arrived minutes after. Nadia

333

and Elizabeth, who had just awakened, tended to Tarik's wounds. Tarik blearily looked up into his father's anguished face.

"Oh, God," Jabari choked out. "My son, what did they do to you? What the hell did that jackal do to you?"

Tarik could not reply. Elizabeth quietly explained. Anguish tightened his expression as Jabari hugged his family.

Suppressing a grimace, Tarik shrugged into his shirt and binish. A dark look entered the eyes of his father, who watched. "Go, son," he said quietly. "Go get your wife. I'll remain here with your mother and Nadia."

Ramses, Tarik and several warriors rode off to the sleepy village. Discreetly, they made inquiries. An elderly widow had seen Fatima taken to a house a few doors away.

Soon Tarik and Ramses crouched on either side of the building's front door. Listened. Ramses signaled. Tarik kicked it open.

"Fatima!" he bellowed.

The beloved, familiar voice surely existed only in her dreams. Numb with grief, Fatima sat in a chair, eyes trained on the door, waiting for a sneering Salah to present Tarik's head as a gruesome trophy. Her energy drained, she had lost all hope.

Then the door had banged open. His cropped blond locks wildly mussed, Tarik bolted inside. "Fatima," he cried again.

"Tarik," she whispered, her lips cracked and dry.

He spotted her, relief flashing in his eyes. Dimly she heard her father bellow in rage, saw him brandish his sword and rush toward her captors. Tarik too whirled and slashed, furiously attaching one of Salah's men. The man fell. Hope loaned her strength. Fatima struggled out of restraining hands and she ran into Tarik's arms, burying her head against his chest. If this were a dream, she prayed never to waken.

A flood of other Khamsin warriors rushed inside and battled Salah's men. Tarik pressed Fatima's face against his chest as justice was served. In minutes, it was over. Ramses hugged Fatima, kissed her temple and nodded for Tarik to take her outside, away from the carnage.

"Tarik," she sobbed. "I thought I'd lost you."

He clung to her, closing his eyes. "Tima," he choked out. Wordlessly he buried his face in her sweet-scented hair. Having come so close to death and losing Fatima, he only wanted to hold her and never let go.

The next morning broke with sunbeams spearing the tent floor. Fatima awoke and studied her sleeping husband. His close-cropped blond hair revealed every angle and plane of his high cheekbones, but the haunted look clinging to him had finally vanished.

Giving the excuse that his son and Fatima had never known a honeymoon, Jabari had wisely ordered them sequestered for a full week. "He needs your love now more than ever," Jabari had quietly told her. "My son is like the walking dead, hovering between one world and the next."

It was true: Tarik's physical injuries were healing faster than his emotional wounds. He'd spoken little, ate less. Distant shadows haunted his eyes.

Outraged at Salah's duplicity, Ibrahim had ordered every tribal member to sign a blood oath of loyalty to their new sheikh, but even when presented with the hundreds of pages of bloody thumbprints, Tarik did not react. Salah's betrayal had sucked out his spirit.

Thus, Fatima had spent the past week nurturing him,

coaxing him back to life. Her news of the baby was what succeeded. Tarik's old protective streak arose. His blank shock had fled, and he'd ceased shuffling about like a condemned man.

Today was a big day. Asad would leave with Graham and Kenneth for England, to attend medical school. Their father had broken a long-honored tradition. Their new sheikh no longer needed a Guardian, he'd solemnly stated. Tarik had a wife who was not only part of his heart, but his right arm.

Shown mercy because she tried to save Elizabeth and Fatima, Alhena was banished. Her furious father had arranged a match with a peasant farmer, a distant cousin in Luxor. Alhena, who'd coveted power and prominence, would fail to achieve either.

Yesterday, Nadia visited. The once pampered princess was now quiet and sad. Though praised for saving their sheikh, people cast uneasy glances at her. They whispered of "the black widow" who'd killed her husband. Even Haydar had lost his ardor for her.

Nadia apologized for concealing Salah's dark side. "Maybe it would have prevented all this," she confessed.

"But you saved my life, thanks to Fatima's teaching you to shoot. Don't berate yourself, Nadia," Tarik had gently admonished her. "You weren't strong enough them, but now you are. Sometimes the darkest times bring out our greatest strengths."

Slowly, the story was pieced together. Tarik had capitulated to Alhena's seduction. She'd acted amicable to his breaking off the affair, hiding her true feelings.

Muhammad, secretly in love with Alhena, knew he couldn't win her hand unless he gained power. With Tarik gone, his chances of becoming sheikh increased. Muhammad agreed to take full blame if caught, leaving Salah free to kill Tarik. But Salah's plans had changed after Tarik married Fatima.

"Salah thought you had too much power over me. With you dead, Alhena would coax me into marriage and Salah would influence me through her," Tarik told Fatima. "Yet in the end, the temptation to kill me—the golden-haired abomination—proved more tempting than eliminating you, Tima."

Intense love now filled her as Fatima stroked her husband's shortened hair. His eyes fluttered open. The torment swirling these had finally vanished.

"How do you feel?" she asked in a throaty whisper.

"Like I'm all new again. And given a second chance." Tarik sat up, framing her face in his large, strong palms. "I never thanked you for having the courage to save my mother. If not for you . . . ," he choked out.

Fatima slid her fingers over his. "A warrior does what a warrior must. It was necessary, even with . . ."

Seeing the distress that must have etched her brow, Tarik asked, "What, Tima?"

"I'm worried about the baby." She bit back her concern and offered a wobbly smile. "With everything that has happened . . ."

Tarik kissed her temple, laid a possessive palm over her belly. "Our child will be fine," he stated firmly. "Cobras are the protectors of kings. The one you spared will safeguard our child, who will be the next ruler of the Khamsin."

"And what if the baby is a girl?"

Fatima watched his expression grow pensive, as if he wrestled with a weighty decision. Tarik bent over, kissed her belly. "I promise, no matter if you are a boy or a girl, little one, you will be my heir. The next Khamsin sheikh."

Fatima's eyes widened. "You mean . . . But what of the council?"

Mirth twinkled in Tarik's dark gaze. "You taught me

how delightful it is to break tradition. Why not break another?"

"You're very naughty," she sighed as he drew her close. "Want to be naughty some more?"

"Don't tempt me," he murmured, but his lips met hers.

Epilogue

Tarik paced back and forth, agonizing over each dragging minute. Anxiety gripped him. This infernal waiting!

Nearby, equally restless, Ibrahim wore a pattern in the dusky sands. Now and then he raised his head, looking stricken and moaning as loudly as the screams originating from inside the tent.

"Why did you vow your firstborn would be sheikh, no matter what the gender?" the chief elder wailed.

"Why is it taking so long?" Tarik demanded, scrubbing a hand over the day-old bristles shadowing his jaw.

"It takes far less time to make a baby than to birth one," Ramses grunted, winking at Jabari. "Trust me in this."

A loud, shrill shriek warbled through the air. Blood drained from Tarik's face. His father and Fatima's winced.

"I'm going in there," Tarik announced, scowling. "Tima needs me. This time they're not barring my way."

"Another tradition broken," Ramses mused cheerfully. "Your son is matching my daughter in this, Jabari."

Ignoring his remarks, Tarik stormed into the tent. An

elderly woman posted at the entrance squawked. He ignored her protests, marched to his wife. Perched on two large birthing bricks and nude, Fatima strained to deliver their child. Her long, raven curls spilled over her breasts. Movement rippled across her large belly. Katherine squatted below her, massaging her and murmuring encouragement as Elizabeth and Nadia supported her weight on either side.

Tarik went to Nadia, motioned for her to leave. A crooked grin touched his sister's mouth. "What took you so long?" she challenged, winking at Katherine.

He gripped Fatima's waist, supporting her weight with one broad shoulder beneath her arm. Fatima's eyes rolled wildly back as she panted wildly, then she glared at him.

"You did this to me!" she screamed.

"Don't listen to her, Tarik. I called your father worse when I birthed you. I think it was 'an insufferable randy goat with the consideration of an old mule,'" Elizabeth advised.

Tarik brushed a gentle kiss against Fatima's soft temple. "Call me anything you want, little caracal, if it takes away the pain, love," he whispered tenderly. "Let's deliver our child."

She screamed as another contraction rippled across her belly. Tarik murmured soothing assurances and encouragement, and glanced down as Katherine ordered Fatima to push.

"Look," he said softly, his fascinated gaze riveted to the small dark head appearing between her legs. "Tima, our baby's being born."

With a loud grunt and a cry, she bore down, her face contorted with fierce concentration. Tarik clutched her, bearing her weight, crooning soft assurances. Their baby slid into the world and into Katherine's capable hands.

Wetness touched Tarik's cheeks as he stared at the bloody, reddened infant now squalling and kicking. Fatima sagged against him, crying as well. "Oh Tarik, we made a baby."

"The most beautiful baby in the world," he whispered, absolutely, incredibly in love all over again.

A short while later, cradling his swaddled child against his chest, Tarik left the birthing tent. The newborn felt light as air in his big, clumsy hands. He gently arranged the blanket to shield the baby's eyes against the glaring sunlight.

Three pairs of anxious eyes swung wildly over to him. Tarik went to his father and Ramses. "Look," he said proudly, showing them the tiny bundle. "Come meet your first grandchild, and the future sheikh of the Khamsin warriors of the wind."

Proud awe flickered over their faces. Jabari cuddled the baby with expert ease, and Ramses peeled back the blanket gently to study the baby's tiny, wrinkled features.

Ibrahim stopped his frenetic pacing. He darted over to the grandparents. Relief smoothed his craggy face. "A boy? Praise God, you did it, Tarik! You sired a son."

Tarik's wicked gaze met his father's amused one. "No, Ibrahim. I sired a beautiful little *girl*. We're calling her Rose, because she's as lovely as a desert rose."

A loud thud followed those words. Jabari sighed with reluctance and handed Rose to a clucking Ramses, who was anxious to hold his granddaughter. "Shall we go inside and see how your beautiful wife is faring?"

Tarik gave a disparaging glance at the prone figure of the chief elder. "What of him?"

"He will wake," Ramses said, cooing at the child. "And then faint again when he realizes Rose will become Khamsin sheikh one day."

The three men entered the tent, approaching the

large bed where Fatima lay propped against a mound of silk pillows, looking tired but elated. Elizabeth and Katherine, tidying a pile of clean diapers, glanced up and smiled.

Fatima held her arms out eagerly for her baby. Ramses very gently handed Rose over. Fatima kissed her downy forehead. Emotion welled in Tarik's throat as he sat beside his wife, sliding an arm around her and his child.

"Here's to a new beginning," Jabari said, smiling proudly.

"A good one," Ramses added. "Our future is just starting."

It *was* a good beginning, for all of them and the Khamsin. Tarik knew his destiny had come full circle. He no longer needed Fatima to predict the future, for it was right here: He could face whatever happened, for he had her by his side.

The Panther & the Pyramid

BONNIE VANAK

Graham Tristan has been tormented too long. He is physically strong: during his childhood exile, he rode with the Khamsin—Egyptian Warriors of the Wind. He has learned their code, is called The Panther. Now he has returned to his rightful place as the Duke of Caldwell. And there is a new face—that of a woman—that haunts his dreams.

Hair the color of blood. Eyes the color of emeralds. The memory threatens to consume him. In his dreams, this woman threatens all he seeks to protect, all he thinks to hide. She is more perilous even than the ancient treasure that draws him back to Egypt. This woman will uncover his heart.